Beyond the Mulga Line

S. E. Jenkins

To Rick,

With my very best wishes
and my thanks,

love, Sue

Dec 2017

Also by S. E. Jenkins

THE OUTBACK NOVELS:

The Kookaburra Bird
A Place Like Jarrahlong

Beyond the Mulga Line

Published by FeedARead.com Publishing – Arts Council funded.

A CIP catalogue record for this title is available from the British
Library.

This book is a work of fiction. Names, characters, businesses, or-
ganisations, places and events are either the product of the author's
imagination or are used fictitiously. Any resemblance to actual
persons, living or dead, events or locales is entirely coincidental.

Quotation from *"High Flight"* a sonnet written in 1941 by John
Gillespie Magee Jr. (1922-1941)

For my daughter, Georgia, and my brother, Sam;
also in memory of my father, George,
and my sister, Kate.

.

Author's Notes

In recent years there has been an increase in the amount of information available in books and on the internet about child migrants who were sent overseas to Canada, South Africa, Zimbabwe [formerly Rhodesia], New Zealand and Australia in the twentieth century. The last children sent to Australia on the Child Migrant Programme arrived in 1970, and all of those sent to Australia will now be retired or approaching retirement. Unfortunately, some may have been unable to contact family members in the United Kingdom from whom they were separated in their youth, and there will be some child migrants who still bear the physical and emotional scars resulting from their experiences of living on the farm schools and in the orphanages to which they were sent.

The Mulga-Eucalypt line lies across a junction of the major land forms, ecosystems and climates of Western Australia. It is where the south-west meets the desert and the two ecosystems intermingle. On the ground one can see the change from dense shrubland in the south to the more arid region of the north.

Australia's involvement in the Vietnam War lasted from July 1962 – January 1973 during which almost 60,000 Australian Army, Airforce and Navy personnel served in Vietnam. Throughout the course of the war 521 Australians died and over 3,000 were wounded. The main aim of Australia's involvement was to support South Vietnam in order to stem the spread of Communism, but by 1969 anti-war protests were gathering momentum against the policy and the deployment of service personnel to fight in Vietnam, this resulted in Australia withdrawing troops in the lead-up to January 1973. After January 1973 the only combat troops left in the country were those guarding the Australian embassy in Saigon and they were withdrawn in June 1973.

Rainfall: Measurements used.   100 points = 25.4 millimetres
                                 1 inch = 25.4 millimetres
The references to drought and cyclones in the storyline reflect what does occur regularly in central Western Australia although not necessarily in the years in which the story is set.

PART I

[January 1968 – July 1969]

CHAPTER 1

Jon Cadwallader picked up the wire strainers he'd been using to repair the fencing and threw them into the back of the truck. It was the third time in as many months that he and George had had to mend the wire between Jindalee and Reef Hill Station, and he was sick of it. Kit Kennilworth was always quick to complain, accusing him of deliberately letting Jindalee stock water on Reef Hill land.

He wiped his grimy hands on his strides and considered the situation. Three months back he'd blamed the wild camels which occasionally careered through fencing, dragging out whole sections in the process, flattening it to the ground, but now he was convinced Kit and his sons were the ones responsible for the damage that allowed his cattle to stray, and he knew it wouldn't do to leave their poddies unbranded for much longer. Jeb Samuels, who'd owned the station before him, had had similar problems and had intimated he should watch his back when it came to the likes of Kit and his boys.

Jon rolled up the spare barbed wire, collected the unused fence posts, placed them in the back of the truck, and then glanced across to George. 'I wonder what's triggered this spate of unneighbourly behaviour,' he said, wiping sweat from his brow.

George shrugged. 'You know Mister Kennilworth, he's like a dog with a bone when his mind's set. Y'ready for a brew?'

'Aye, my throat is pretty parched.'

While George lit a fire, Jon collected the knapsack from the cab and pulled out the sandwiches the station cook had made for them. He squatted on a fallen tree trunk with his dog, Blue, by his side.

'I don't see what Mister Kennilworth's got to gain,' said George, putting the billy on to boil.

'Jeb reckons it's Kit's acquisitive nature, when my cattle stray

1

onto his land for water he's able to snaffle a few of my cleanskins,' said Jon, handing over George's sandwiches. Soon, the only sound to be heard was the crackle of dry wood flaring while they ate and watched the billy boil.

'That lad of his, the young 'un,' said George between mouthfuls.

'Todd?'

'That's 'im; he's a nasty piece of work. He'll end up in Fremantle jail if he's not careful.'

Jon smiled. George Pinjupi wasn't one to keep his thoughts to himself, and his wife, May, was the same, she'd talk to you about anything and everything. And their youngsters, Tom and Daisy, were cut from the same cloth: open and chatty, the pair of them.

'And Todd ain't above rapin' a black girl when he fancies one,' added George.

'Todd isn't likely to end up in jail for that though, is he? Not while Constable Nickson's still running the show.' Jon bit into his sandwich. That was the trouble with the outback, he thought, there were too many whites who didn't rate Aborigines, saw them as second-class citizens, there to be used or abused as the mood took them. But things were changing, Aborigines were demanding fairer treatment which had led to the new government legislation on pay, and then there was the land rights issue that everyone was arguing about; it all added to the current tension between whites and blacks.

While Jon pondered the complexity of it all Blue's hackles rose and he growled, his attention drawn to the bush. George tilted his head, listening. Jon, too, stopped eating and listened – horses! Without a word, he got to his feet and waited as the riders approached.

Kit Kennilworth and his youngest! What were they doing on his land? – and then Jon saw the girl lashed to Todd Kennilworth's horse by a length of rope that secured her by the wrists.

'G'day to you, Mr Cadwallader,' said Kennilworth, raising his hat in greeting.

A first, Jon noted – Kit wasn't usually so polite. 'What're you doing on Jindalee land, Mr Kennilworth?'

'Rounding up a runaway.'

Jon glanced at the girl and saw the fear in her eyes.

'She helps out the missus at the homestead, one of them gals from the orphanage. I see you've already repaired the fence.'

'That's right,' said Jon. 'Someone keeps cutting the wire.'

'Abos,' said Kit. 'You know what the bastards are like. You going to let us through, or do we have to take the long road?' He indicated over his shoulder at the girl. 'She's not exactly up to it in this heat.'

Jon was inclined to agree. The girl, who looked about fifteen, was covered in sweat and dust, her dress was torn and she'd lost one of her shoes.

'She could ride pillion, if you had a mind,' said Jon mildly.

'Couldn't risk it. No telling what the little bitch'd do. You know what these Pommy kids are like, scummy little bastards the lot of them, thieves too, if you give 'em half a chance.' He looked pointedly at Jon as he spoke, and smirked.

Jon clenched his fists but kept his face bland. Everyone knew where he was from, from Karundah, the orphanage for boys out in the bush, the other side of Merredin. He'd been one of the *"scummy little bastards"* the British Government had shipped to Australia that Kit was referring to. He looked at the girl again and saw the lurid bruising on her temple, the split lip, and the terror as she struggled to free herself from the rope.

'Looks like she's taken a beating,' commented Jon.

Kit glanced in the girl's direction. 'Not yet, but she'll get a flogging just as soon as I get her home: half a day it's taken to track her down.'

'Stop that!' snarled Todd, giving a sharp tug on the rope, yanking the girl off her feet.

She staggered but managed to keep her footing.

Todd laughed.

'You going to cut the fence for us then?' asked Kit.

Jon put down his pannikin and walked over to the back of the truck.

'Nice of you to be so neighbourly,' said Kit.

Jon leaned over the tailgate, picked up his rifle, shoved a cartridge into the breech, rammed it home, and then turned back to Kit, the rifle pointing at the ground, the implication clear. 'You tell your lad to undo the rope and then maybe we can talk.'

Kit's face darkened as blood suffused his already ruddy complexion. 'What the hell do you think you're about?'

'I said, let her go, Mr Kennilworth, or I'll blow your ruddy head off.'

'You wouldn't dare,' growled Kit.

'Try me.' Jon's eyes never left Kit's, conscious that the others

3

were watching the stand-off.

'Let her go,' ordered Kit.

'He can't make us, Pa,' said Todd.

'You heard me,' snarled Kit.

Todd slowly dismounted, fury etched on his face. He yanked on the rope, making the girl stumble again, and roughly untied the rope.

Jon caught the girl's eye. 'Get into the truck.'

She hesitated, terrified of all of them, and for a moment he thought she was going to try and escape back into the bush. 'It's midsummer,' he called to her, 'you won't last long out here, not in these temperatures.'

She sidled round the back of the horses, crossed over to the truck, opened the door and leaned against the passenger seat.

'You won't get away with this, y'bastard,' yelled Kit, 'I'll have Nickson on you.'

'The gate is that way.' Jon nodded in a south-westerly direction.

They watched as Kit and his son rode off. Jon turned to the girl. 'I'm going to drive us to Jindalee, and then I'll take you back to the orphanage, all right?' He saw her weighing him up, unsure of him and, as he waited, he recognised in her his own desperation at that age. 'What's your name?' he asked after a moment or two.

She stared at him, her grey eyes wary. 'Shirley, Shirley Jones.'

'Are you happy to come with us, Shirley?'

She chewed her lip, scrutinizing him from behind a curtain of long brown hair, then nodded and got into the truck.

Jon shut the passenger door after her, and then he tossed the knapsack, billy and pannikins into the back of the truck while George kicked sand onto the remains of the fire. He whistled for his dog and then turned to George and handed over his rifle. 'Do you mind riding in the back with Blue?'

'No, boss, she too strung up. She won't want no blackfella next to her jus' now.'

'Aye, reckon you're right,' said Jon.

CHAPTER 2

Jon sat on the verandah at Jindalee staring sightlessly out into the bush, Blue curled up at his feet. He'd been an idiot to get involved with Kit and the girl, it was just asking for trouble. So now what did he do? He didn't know much about the girls' orphanage at Goolong except that girls were placed with families once their time there was over. Some went to work as maids in towns or the city, others ended up on stations like Reef Hill working as house girls. He'd always taken a couple of lads from Karundah, replacing them as they moved on to other work or when they returned home to England. The two he'd got at the moment, Graham Eastman and Bertie Grey, were decent enough, but taking on lads meant he'd never considered offering placements to girls. He didn't want the responsibility; it was difficult enough to bring the lads around after their experiences at Karundah without having to keep an eye out for shenanigans between youngsters, especially when hormones were rampaging through their veins. He heard a door bang, muted conversation, a bath being run, and soon after came Val's measured footsteps.

She sat down on the chair next to him. 'She's been raped,' she said baldly, 'viciously too, and beaten.'

Jon wasn't surprised; there'd been talk about the younger Kennilworth lad, Todd. 'I don't suppose she said who did it?'

'Not yet. She's still in shock. She needs to see a doctor.'

'That bad!'

'Yeah, that bad.'

They both lapsed into silence, lost in their own thoughts for a while. Jon gazed out across the bush at the sun sinking in the west, as he often did, watching the orange orb seemingly growing bigger

5

as it neared the horizon, an illusion that had never ceased to fascinate him. He turned away from the setting sun, blocking his worries about Shirley and the trouble his actions would bring and looked at Val for a moment or two. 'You ever regret leaving Liverpool, Val?'

'What on earth has made you ask that?'

'I just wondered, it's just so different living out here than to living in Liverpool.'

'For God's sake, we've lived here all our adult lives, longer for you. Why? Have you regrets, Jon?'

'No.'

'There you go then...anyway there wasn't anythin' for me there. And what sort of a future would I have had with my family background? Any decent bloke would've run a mile.'

'Thanks for that, Val!'

'You know what I mean; besides, you'd seen more of life than most and you were never one to judge a book by its cover.'

'I did once.'

'Yeah, well, you were a touch infatuated, weren't you, and Merle was...is...stunnin'.' She smiled at him. 'But at least you were intelligent enough to come to your senses in time. And don't forget, we were still kids then, hon.'

Val was right. He'd fallen for Merle McGhee at seventeen and it had taken him a while to realise she wasn't the right one for him. Were women always more perceptive than men? he asked himself.

'When did you know, Val?'

'Know what?'

'That I was the one for you.'

'When I first saw you.'

'Sefton Park?'

'Yeah, Sefton Park, when you were watchin' the football, you with your blond hair and your tanned good looks—'

'Steady on, you'll make me blush.'

'What, after all this time!'

'It's only twenty years or so.'

'Is that all?' She giggled. 'You weren't exactly taken with me when you first saw me, you thought I was brash.'

'And your breath stank of tobacco.'

'You never said.'

'That was only because when you turned up at Alice's place you'd stopped. I might have done if you'd still smoked.'

6

'Alice smokes.'

'Well, that's different. Alice Macarthur wouldn't be Alice without a cheroot and she's not about to stop smoking, not at her age.'

Jon heard footsteps. He glanced over his shoulder and saw Shirley standing in the doorway dressed in one of Val's frocks, an anxious look on her face. He stood and pushed his chair towards her and fetched another one for himself. Then he grabbed the cord dangling down from a rafter and gave it a yank setting the bell indoors jangling.

'Thank you,' Shirley murmured, moving the chair closer to Val.

'You want?' asked Yang-dhow. Their cook hovered, awaiting instruction.

Jon turned to the girl. 'Do you like tea?'

'Yes,' she whispered.

'Milk? Sugar?'

She nodded.

'Tea, please, Yang. Do you want another one, Val?'

She shook her head.

'Right away, Misser Jon,' said Yang.

'And some of those biscuits you made, Yang,' Jon called after him, then he turned his attention back to the girl. 'Are you feeling a bit better?' he asked, noting the tense expression on her face.

She nodded again, her eyes fixed on the ground.

'We think that you should see a doctor. Are you all right staying here for the night and then we'll take you to the clinic in Pilkington?'

Shirley looked at him with frightened eyes.

'You'll be safe here,' reassured Jon, but he could see she didn't believe him. He frowned. 'There's a spare bed in our daughter's room. You can sleep there, but if you're not happy then we'll drive you back to the orphanage now.' He glanced at his watch. Even as he spoke he knew it wasn't an option. It would be hours before they'd reach Goolong and he didn't fancy a long drive in the dark and then the wait for the orphanage gates to open in the morning. 'You want to stay or go back to the orphanage?'

'Stay,' she muttered, avoiding his eyes.

Jon stood up. 'I'd better go and help George unload the truck.' He whistled his dog. 'Come on, Blue, old mate.' He picked up his hat and slapped it on. 'I'll be in for tea, Val. Where are Ruby and the boys?'

'Out with Alistair, Alice, Daisy and Tom, paintin'.'

7

Jon grinned. 'I can't see Jamie being keen, or David for that matter.'

'Jamie wasn't.' Val chuckled. 'He went under protest. Can't say Ruby was that keen either; she doesn't like it when she's not top dog, David was all right though: easy goin', that's David, happy to go along with the crowd. But no worries, Alice will keep them in line. She's got her knittin' with her and her rattan chair, and you know Alice, she won't take any backchat from naughty kids.'

'How long are Alice and Alistair staying?'

'They're plannin' to go back in the mornin'.'

'It'd be helpful if they stayed an extra couple of days. God knows what is going to blow up after my run-in with Kit. We might have to make a trip to Goolong.'

'I'm sure they'll be happy to help us out, hon; it's not as if Alice needs to be at Jarrahlong all the time, Jim Sandy's been overseein' the place for years.'

After the evening meal, while Val was putting their boys to bed, Jon, Alice and Alistair retired to the sitting room with their coffee and a snifter on the side: bourbon whiskey for Alice and brandy for the rest of them.

Jon settled back into his favourite easy chair and looked over at Alistair. 'Alice says you've been in Perth for a few days.'

'That's right,' said Alistair. 'I've been selling my paintings.' He swirled his brandy and took a sip. 'Graham Sutton takes as many landscapes as I can paint. He has galleries in Sydney and Melbourne and apparently they're selling well there too.'

'He's opening one in Adelaide in the autumn and we've been invited,' said Alice.

'Yes, it seems people want scenes of the outback these days: cattle musters, sheep grazing under eucalypts, billabongs, you know the sort of thing. Have you seen Tom's work recently? He has a real talent.'

'In what way?' asked Jon.

'Well, he has a wonderful eye for colour and composition, quite distinctive too, probably his Aboriginal perspective on the landscape. Graham Sutton has taken a couple of his canvases.'

'Not sure George will be happy about that. I think he rather sees Tom following in his footsteps. George encourages him to be out with us whenever he can, and, like his dad, Tom does have a way with the cattle.'

'The lad is bright enough,' said Alistair. 'In my experience, able youngsters can pick and choose when it comes to a career; they're often talented in more than one field.'

'What about the others?'

'Your boys and Daisy aren't that interested, and Ruby, well, Ruby is Ruby. She can't sit still long enough to finish anything; she'd rather be out riding and rounding up the cattle than wielding a paintbrush.'

'I've never seen anyone who loves the bush as much as she does,' said Alice. 'When she's over at Jarrahlong she spends all her time with Adie, picking his brains.'

'She won't have much luck there,' commented Jon. 'They don't come more close-mouthed than Adie.' He pictured the old Aborigine who'd been with Alice since the early days, back in 1908 when Alice and Jack had first taken the pastoral lease on Jarrahlong. Taciturn he might be, but it had been Adie who'd taught him all he knew about sheep and cattle when he'd first turned up at Alice's place after escaping from Karundah.

'Don't you believe it,' said Alice. 'Adie likes having her around and he likes teaching her about the land and how to manage my sheep. His eyes light up when he sees her and, more to the point, she likes him, she jabbers away at him in his own language as if she were a native.'

'Ruby speaks Aboriginal?'

'Yes. Didn't you know?'

'No, I didn't.'

'Maybe that's where her talent lies, in languages. Maybe she has the ear, whereas Tom has the eye,' said Alistair.

'What ear and eye?' asked Val, joining them.

'Did you know Ruby can speak Adie's Aboriginal dialect?' asked Jon.

'Of course, I do, hon.'

'How long have you known?'

'Since she told me Adie was teachin' her. Didn't you know that's one of the reasons she's always over at Jarrahlong?'

Alice chuckled. 'You're going to have your hands full with that one!'

'We always have had,' said Val dryly. 'I don't know where she gets it from.'

'A lamb never strays far from the ewe,' said Alice.

Val glanced at Alice. 'And what's that s'posed to mean?'

'That she's her mother's daughter,' said Alistair.

'Talking of youngsters, how has Shirley settled?' asked Jon as he handed Val coffee and a brandy.

'She's sleepin' in Ruby's room, but she's terrified. She doesn't trust anyone, even me. She keeps her eyes on me as if she's afraid to turn her back. Tonight, when I caught her eyein' up the bedroom window, I told her it couldn't be opened from the outside, only from the inside. I also reminded her she'll be safe here, that no one will hurt her, although I'm not sure she believes me.'

'What're you going to do about her?' asked Alice.

'Get her to a doctor first,' said Jon. 'Would you and Alistair stay on for another day or so and mind the boys for us? I think it's best if I drive Val and Shirley to the clinic.'

'No worries,' said Alice. 'Alistair can continue with his painting class. I'm sure they'll be enthralled at the prospect.'

'Less of the sarcasm,' said Alistair, a smile on his face.

'Then what's the plan?' asked Alice.

'That depends.'

'On what?'

'On what Kit Kennilworth does.'

'What do you think he'll do?' asked Val.

'Knowing Kit he'll have spoken to Nickson; I think we can expect a visit from the constable first thing, which is why I want to leave for Pilkington early. If Shirley has been raped we'll have stronger grounds for keeping her away from the Kennilworths.'

'She can go back to the orphanage, can't she?' said Alice.

'If she does they'll only send her to another station.'

Alistair helped himself to more brandy. 'Why don't you offer her a placement?'

Jon frowned, 'I've already got two lads from Karundah; it'd be asking for trouble.'

'And what if she were your daughter?'

'Well, she isn't.'

'But you take my point?' said Alistair. 'Anyway, you already have the set-up here and Boswell is a good tutor.'

'True,' admitted Jon.

'And he's already teaching the two lads from Karundah and the Aboriginal children; one more isn't going to make much difference, in any case Noel won't have as many pupils in his class now that David and Jamie will be away at boarding school as of next week. Are they looking forward to it?'

'Jamie is, David's not so keen, but as Val says, they have to go otherwise they'll miss out on their secondary education.'

'Yes, and it will give them a chance to get to know lads their age from off the stations in the area,' said Alistair.

While the others chatted together Jon considered Alistair Farlane's suggestion. He was right; Noel Boswell was a first-rate tutor. When he and Val decided they needed a teacher for their boys they'd found Noel the same way Alice had found Alistair – when she'd wanted a tutor for Bindi Henderson – through an advert in a British paper.

'How long has Noel been with you now?' asked Alistair.

'Getting on for eighteen months, I'd say, since we last flew to England to interview him and a couple of others.'

'What made him stand out?'

'Cambridge,' said Val, interrupting. 'He went to Cambridge, same as you, Alistair.'

'You know everyone was shocked when you brought him back to Jindalee. No one thought he'd stick it,' said Alice. 'They had bets on it in The Grand; they gave him three months.'

'No, we didn't know that,' said Val, surprised.

Alice made light of Val's reaction. 'Yeah, well, with burns like his, he stands out, and everyone said he'd never cope with the Australian sun after having all those skin grafts.'

'Does he ever talk about it?' asked Alistair.

'Not often,' admitted Jon.

'How did it happen?' asked Alice. 'I've never liked to ask.'

'Not like you to be backward in coming forward, Alice,' said Jon, a wide smile on his face.

'Less of the cheek, Jon Just, I didn't give you the third degree when you turned up at Jarrahlong, did I?'

'True, but you were dying to ask.'

'That's as maybe; so, how did it happen?'

'He was a Hurricane pilot,' said Val, 'he bailed out of his burnin' plane not far from the Kent coast. You know what aviation fuel's like when it catches fire. There were a lorra young fellas like him, maimed, or worse.'

Alistair shook his head. 'Mine was a pretty uneventful war compared to fighter pilots like Noel. You don't exactly see that much action in the Pay Office. There and again, I was an old fellow, not deemed suitable for active service, hence the desk job.'

'Noel spent the rest of the war in hospital, one of those guinea pigs who underwent reconstruction and pioneerin' skin grafts, didn't he, hon.'

'What did the kids make of him?' asked Alice.

'Didn't bat an eyelid,' said Val. 'Jamie asked him straight out what had happened and Noel told him and after that Noel couldn't put a foot wrong with any of 'em. They regarded his burns as a badge of honour; in any case it's amazin' how quickly you stop noticin' his scars.'

Jon refilled his coffee cup and offered the others a top up. 'Maybe that suggestion of yours isn't such a bad one, Alistair. What do you think, Val?'

'What's that, hon?'

'Alistair's suggestion that we employ Shirley at Jindalee.'

'I didn't think you were keen on offerin' jobs to girls. More trouble than they're worth, you said.'

'Yeah, well, that was until today.'

'Will you be able to persuade the authorities?'

'Yes, if we make a big enough donation, it'll swing it,' said Jon cynically. Paying for a new dormitory wing at Karundah had smoothed the path there when they'd first offered placements for boys; he didn't see it would be any different at the girls' orphanage. And Nickson would be no problem, of that he was certain, even if Kit Kennilworth cut up rough. He'd got enough on Constable Nickson to hang him, and Nickson knew it. Catching Nickson out in the bush with a young Aboriginal girl had shocked him. The girl, barely twelve or thirteen, hadn't said a word when he'd chanced upon them; she'd gathered up her things and had run off back to her camp and Jon had wondered then what sort of hold Nickson had had over her.

Barely a word had been exchanged at the time, but Nickson knew the relationship between them had changed forever.

CHAPTER 3

When Jon, Val and Shirley arrived back from the clinic in Pilkington they found the constable's ute in the yard parked next to Kit
Kennilworth's. Jon swore under his breath as he stepped out of the
cab and saw the pair of them waiting for him on the verandah,
mugs of tea in their hands. Trust Yang-dhow to offer them the
usual hospitality, he thought as he strolled over to them. Val followed behind holding the girl's hand. She nodded a greeting to
Nickson and Kennilworth and led Shirley into the kitchen.

Nickson got to his feet and hitched up his trousers. 'Mr Kennilworth here says you've abducted his house girl.' He indicated the
kitchen where Val had taken Shirley.

'Is that what he told you?'

'Aye, he did, said the girl had run away and he and his lad had
tracked her onto your land, that he was making his way home with
her when you threatened him with a gun and took her. Is that
right?'

'It bloody well is,' muttered Kit in his distinctive gravelly voice.
'The bastard had his rifle, told her to get into his truck; me and the
lad had no option but to let her go.'

Jon glanced at Kennilworth and held his gaze. 'And did you tell
the constable here why she ran away?'

Kit's face flushed under his tan. 'You know what those orphanage kids are like, Ben, lying Pommy bastards, the lot of 'em, you
can't trust anything they tell ya.'

Jon clenched his fists but managed to keep his voice calm. 'Todd
raped her. Did Kit tell you that?'

'Nah, he didn't,' snapped Kit. 'The bitch was asking for it. You
know what they're like, Ben, cats on heat, the lot of them.'

'Seems to me you stepped right out of line, Jon. She's Mr Kennilworth's responsibility; you need to do the right thing and hand

13

the girl back. Can't have you setting a bad example; other lasses like her will take it into their heads to scarper when something doesn't suit.'

'Maybe you should read what the doctor says.' Jon pulled an envelope out of his pocket and handed it to Nickson. He waited while the constable opened it, put on his reading glasses and took out the single page. No one spoke as the constable finished reading and handed it to Kit. Kit took his time and then folded the sheet of paper, his ruddy face even redder under his tan.

'There'll be a pretty big stink about that,' commented Jon.

Kit glared at him. 'I told you, Ben, it was just a bit of rough and tumble; you know what these gals are like.'

Nickson didn't answer; he glanced at Jon and then at Kit.

'I'll take this all the way to the top if I have to,' said Jon, looking Nickson straight in the eye. 'And God knows what'll come out in the wash; there're a few people hereabouts who won't want their dirty linen aired in public.'

'What about the lass?' asked Nickson.

'She stays here for now, then, when she's up to it, we'll take her back to the orphanage if that's what she wants.'

'You bloody well won't; the gal is coming back with me,' snarled Kit.

Nickson chewed his lip, his cheeks flushed. 'Maybe the lass'd be best here for a while, Kit. You know, a woman's touch.'

'Nancy can look after her,' said Kit. 'She's plenty of experience with these gals, knows not to take any nonsense off of 'em.'

Nickson picked up his hat and turned to Jon. 'We'll be goin' then, you'll let us know what happens?'

'I'm not having this,' yelled Kit. 'She comes with me, or else—'

'Or else nothing,' growled Nickson, his tone hardening. 'And if you've got any sense you'll drop it.' He turned on his heels and headed out to his ute.

Kit watched Nickson walk over to the vehicle, his face an ugly shade of red, his eyes wild with uncontrolled fury as he listened to the constable starting the engine. He turned to Jon. 'You've not heard the end of this; I'll get ya and no mistake, y'bastard.' His piggy eyes glared at Jon with pure hatred. 'You'd better watch your back when you're out tending your stock; it's all too easy for a fella to have a nasty accident out in the bush. You get my drift?'

Jon didn't grace Kit's threat with an answer; he turned his back on the man and went indoors.

14

* * *

A fortnight later, after the evening meal, Jon strolled over to Noel Boswell's place and knocked on the door.

He'd liked Noel from the first; he was an interesting fella, but initially he'd had doubts about employing him. He'd worried about the effects of the fierce Australian sun on his rebuilt face and on the skin grafts. But it had been Noel who'd convinced him. Look at me, he'd said, I'm a mess, my fingers are stumps and everywhere I go I'm stared at. There are fewer people in the bush; they'll get used to me and I've still got a first-class brain – that, at least, wasn't damaged.

Val had persuaded him to take a risk and employ Noel. We can always book him a berth on the next boat home if it doesn't work out, she'd said, and as usual she'd been proved right; Noel had settled in in no time and seemed to like outback living as much as they did.

'Come in,' came Noel's familiar accent. 'It's not locked.'

Jon stepped into the kitchen and grinned. 'Since when did you take to locking the door?'

'Figure of speech, I never locked the door back home in England either. What can I do for you?'

'I've a new pupil for you.'

'That young girl you've taken in?'

'Yeah, Shirley, but she's not going to be easy to reach; she's been with us for a couple of weeks now and she's still withdrawn, won't say a word to me or to Val.'

'What about Ruby?'

'Ruby has no patience; you know Ruby, and Shirley picks up on it. Anyway her education is about as lacking as the two lads from Karunda, but she's bright enough.'

'Have you squared things with the orphanage?'

'Yeah, we went over to Goolong last week; she's officially in our care now.'

'Any difficulties?'

'Nothing a hefty cheque couldn't sort out.'

'While you're here, I've been thinking about the Aboriginal children.'

'What about them? Is there a problem?'

'No, not at all. I'm just concerned that what I'm doing with them is a bit biased.'

15

'Biased? What do you mean, biased?'

'Well everything in the classroom is English based.'

'Well, that's what I want.'

'But how about some Aboriginal material…for balance?'

Jon frowned.

'I think the orphanage lads should be taught about Aboriginal culture; it'd benefit them in the long run…you know Ruby's learnt the local Aboriginal language, don't you?'

'Yeah, according to Val, Adie, the stockman over at Jarrahlong, has been teaching her. Is that what you're getting at? – because I'm not sure teaching them Aboriginal is going to help much, especially if they end up working in another state; there're several different languages, not to mention the various dialects.'

'No, I wasn't thinking of languages, more the cultural side, basic knowledge about the Dreaming, maybe showing them some Aboriginal art, teaching them basic survival skills that Aborigines learn from their parents: bush tucker, bush medicine, that sort of thing, it'd do them good to learn an appreciation of another culture.'

'What's brought this on?'

Noel glanced down at his feet, the colour rising in his scarred cheeks. He bit his lip and then looked at Jon. 'It's Bertie, I heard him calling the Aboriginal children abusive names,' he hesitated, '…and I didn't like his tone either.'

'Did he now!'

'It's not his fault; there are plenty who think like that.'

'Yeah, don't I know it! – but we don't tolerate such attitudes, or language, at Jindalee.'

'Exactly, and all the more reason for them to learn something about Aboriginal culture, it's one of the world's most ancient and, according to my reading, it's a rich one.'

'You're not wrong there, mate,' muttered Jon thinking back to his all too brief time with Curly, his first Aboriginal friend who had taught him a lot about Aboriginal beliefs and skills for living in the bush before his untimely death.

'Is that a yes?'

'I suppose so.'

'How about your boys, did you get them settled in their new school?'

'Yeah, at least they're still there,' joked Jon, 'and we haven't had a message from the headmaster asking us to collect them!'

CHAPTER 4

Jon squinted through the red dust churned up by Val's utility as she drove through a particularly bad patch of bulldust. He felt the towing rope give and then the jolt as she took up the slack and her ute hauled his out of a hole. He swore aloud, he could have done without a broken camshaft, especially when they'd run out of spares. There was too much to do back at the station to spend time on a trip to town. He glanced at his watch, ten o'clock; sometimes the drive into Charlestown seemed interminable, usually it didn't bother him, but there and again he wasn't eating dust as he was today. Normally the journey into town was relaxing, it gave him time to think things through, chew over problems that had arisen, like the Kennilworth issue. The tow rope slackened again and then tightened as he bounced over the corrugated track. The damned road hadn't seen a grader in months; he'd mention it while he was in town – driving in the outback was bad enough without being jolted to kingdom come, all because some lazy bastard couldn't get his finger out and keep the roads smooth.

Two hours later they drew into Charlestown. It was still a back-of-beyond sort of place but a town on the up since one or two prospectors working for mining companies had moved in looking for potential sites, for nickel and other increasingly valuable ores. Four of the derelict buildings had been renovated and now Charlestown had a barber, a hairdresser, a hardware store specialising in prospecting gear, and a grocery store, but the bitumen still stopped at the edge of town and the rest of the buildings still looked faded and not that different to how they would have looked at the turn of the

17

century. Jon smiled as Val pulled up outside Wes Chapman's double-fronted garage with the two battered red and cream fuel pumps.

It was twenty-two years since the first time he'd been taken to Wes's garage, that time by Ed Scally towing Alice's old utility truck, with him at the wheel. He'd been rising sixteen at the time, Ruby's age, and he didn't know how to drive; it had been Wes who'd taught him the very next day. And, looking back, it was almost as if time had stood still. The exterior of Wes's garage had hardly changed, except perhaps there was rather more rust on the corrugated iron fronting the building, and the white paint stating the owner's name was even more illegible than it had been back then. There were even some of the original posters advertising oil and a dance in Merredin, now very faded and partially concealed by newer ones that had been added in a haphazard, higgledy-piggledy fashion that revealed the history of the town's social life for those who cared to study the detail of them. He didn't even bother to glance at the area behind the forecourt and garage, knowing full well that it would contain Wes's sprawling collection of cannibalised trucks, utes and trailers which he used for spares. Jon pulled on the handbrake and stepped out of the cab as Val greeted Wes with a peck on the cheek.

'I'll leave you two to talk business while I catch up with Rachel,' she said. 'See you, Wes.' And she was off, strolling down the broad street without a care in the world, heading for Rachel and Ty Henderson's new place down along from Ed Scally's where they'd lived with Rachel's father until their own home had been built.

'She'll be gone ages,' commented Wes. 'Rachel's on her own this week. Ty's taken Joe dogging over at Cavanagh's Creek Station, seems they've got a problem with dingo and feral dogs attacking the sheep, and Scal's gone to Perth for a few days.'

'Amy still at secretarial school?'

'Yeah, she finishes shortly though, plans to get a job in a solicitor's office or so Scal says. How about your two, they settled in all right?'

'Yeah, Val went over to Perth the other weekend to check up on them, she says Jamie's fine and David's happier now he's palled up with a lad from off a station out Geraldton way.'

'That's good, I reckon it's always a wrench seeing kids off to boarding school. Now then, what can I do for you today, Jon? Take it you've got a problem with the ute.'

'Yeah, it's got a broken camshaft; we carry spares for most

things as you know, but we're clean out of camshafts at the moment, besides, it's probably done some damage. Will you have a look at it?'

'No worries, mate, let's shove her on the ramp.'

Jon unhitched the towing rope and together they manoeuvred the ute into position.

'Ya got time for a cuppa?'

Jon grinned; he reckoned Wes had shares in a tea plantation the amount he drank. 'You betcha, mate.' He settled himself on the nearest bench seat while Wes filled two quart pots and added enough condensed milk to turn the tea a khaki hue.

'What's the latest gossip? Anything I should know about?' asked Jon, idly watching the comings and goings on the main street.

'I suppose you mean Kennilworth?'

'No, not particularly, I haven't seen the fella for a couple of months. So what's he been shouting his mouth off about this time?'

'That house girl of his that he sez you stole off of him. He's been bending everyone's ears by all accounts, wants the gal back.'

Jon bristled. 'He doesn't own the girl, and she's not a bloody slave, besides, that happened ages ago, two months gone.'

'Well, he's still riled about it; says he's the one with responsibility for her and that you only got to keep her because you bribed the nuns over at Goolong.'

Jon sipped his tea. Truth to tell, Kennilworth wasn't far wrong but it had been the right thing to do. In the weeks since Shirley had been living with them she'd said very little except that both her parent and younger brother had died in a car accident and, soon after, she'd been shipped out to Australia, as he had, at the age of eight. She'd had a tough time of it and then latterly Todd raping her had been the last straw, no wonder she'd run away from Reef Hill. But at least she wasn't pregnant and he was sure that with time and patience she'd come to trust them as he had learnt to trust Alice. He pulled his thoughts back to the present. 'What about Nickson?'

'You know Nickson, anything for the easy life. Nickson won't give you much strife and without his backing there isn't much Kennilworth can do and, as you say, it's old business, Nickson won't do anything about it now.'

Wes had just about summed up the situation; the constable was a lazy so-and-so and, in any case, Jon knew he had too much on

Nickson for him to get awkward.

'Changing the subject, do you think Alex Bartokas will sell the pastoral lease on Wanndarah?'

'What makes you ask that, Wes?'

'Word is Alex has had enough of the struggle, that the drought in the first half of the decade crippled him. Les Harper says Wanndarah has been running on empty for some time and that Alex is in debt to him and to the bank. You think he's right?'

Jon considered the question. 'Wanndarah isn't as well placed for water as Jindalee, it always was a dry station, at least that's what Alice told me once. I suppose Alex hasn't had the spare cash to sink new wells and bores as we've done on Jindalee.'

'Aye,' agreed Wes, 'that's what others have said.' He put his empty mug on the side, stood and hitched up his britches. 'Alex was in town the other day, brought in his ute to have a busted spring fixed. While he was here he told me a Pommy mining company has bought the mineral rights to a section close to your boundary, west of Lake Desolation.'

'Which company is that?'

'Glenshea Holdings I think he said. I'm hoping there'll be a bit of business in it for me, they're likely to want to hire a grader to push some tracks through the bush in the lead up to drilling.'

'I wouldn't bank on it. These companies often take out rights to stop others, especially if they think there might be something worth drilling for in the future.'

'You mean like hedging their bets?'

'Aye, something like that. Did Alex mention putting Wanndarah on the market?'

'No, but he did say he didn't know how much longer they could keep going, things being as they are.'

'I can't see anyone rushing to put in an offer to buy Wanndarah if he does put it up for sale, not if a mining company starts trampling over sections of it.'

Wes pulled a couple of mints out of his pocket and tossed one to Jon.

'Thanks,' said Jon unwrapping the sweet. 'I feel sorry for Bartokas; he's a nice bloke and a grafter.'

'Isn't always enough though, is it?'

'No, you're right, Wes, it isn't.'

'Talking of stations for sale – do you think Alice will ever sell up and move into town? She isn't exactly a spring chicken any more.'

'Alice will never sell Jarrahlong and I can't see her shuffling off this mortal coil anytime soon, can you?' said Jon, sucking on the mint.

Wes grinned. 'She'll outlive the lot of us, she will, but what about after? I suppose that mongrel, Greg Morton, will inherit the place.'

Jon shook his head. 'No, I don't think so, she says she's going to leave Jarrahlong to me.'

'Thank God for that! I never did take to that great-nephew of hers. Still, one day you'll have your hands full running two stations.'

'It won't be a problem, when the time comes, Ruby'll manage Jarrahlong, she's a natural and she's got an old head on her.'

'And what about David and Jamie? I suppose they'll share the running of Jindalee one day.'

Jon bit his lip. 'The lads aren't that interested, but they're young, maybe they'll change as they get older and if they do then we'll just have to come up with a plan that will accommodate the both of them.'

'And if they don't?'

'Then maybe we'll end up signing the pastoral lease back to the original owners one day; that'd really upset the Kennilworths.'

'Back to the Jacksons, you mean?'

Jon grinned. 'No, the Aborigines.'

Wes sighed. 'If I were you I wouldn't joke about that, you know what people are like around here when it comes to blacks.'

'Yeah, I know. I was just being flippant, seems to me people are getting too het up about all this land rights talk.'

'That's as maybe. All I'm saying is that if the locals think you're planning on signing over Jindalee to Aborigines your life won't be worth living. Kit Kennilworth for one would be out for blood on more than one count, and there are plenty of others who'll be backing him. Some don't like you favouring black stockmen as it is.'

'Alice employs blacks.'

'Alice is different. She's been here longer than you, and she's a woman; white stockmen weren't keen on working for the fairer sex in the old days so she didn't have a lot of choice.'

Jon didn't comment, he knew Wes was right. Talk of Aboriginal land rights was a big issue, even in the city, and out in the bush it was even more controversial. 'The thing is people around here don't seem to accept that the country in these parts was occupied long before it was taken over by the Crown and the pastoral leases sold off in the 1800s.'

'Maybe because they weren't around then; anyway, that's all in the past. It's not exactly relevant to the argument now, is it?'

'You're wrong, Wes. Ever since Val and I have owned Jindalee, regular as clockwork, mobs come in from the desert and camp around Red Rocks over on our southern boundary, between us and Jarrahlong. Adie told me once there's a pretty powerful spirit associated with the place and that white fellas'd be wise to give that patch of land wide berth, so we always have.'

'Jindalee hasn't belonged to Aborigines for over a hundred years. Jackson owned it first, then the Samuels—'

'A hundred years is nothing. Aborigines have been around for forty thousand years, perhaps longer, living off the land, long before white fellas came along.'

'Gerraway with ya!' said Wes.

'It's true; at least that's what Alistair says. And it's not just on Jindalee that there are sacred places, there's Stan's place too, at Yaringa Creek; once a year Aborigines turn up there and add a bit of fresh paint to the rock face and then melt away again back into the desert.'

'Yeah, but they don't live there, do they?'

'Not anymore, but that's not to say they didn't once. The fact is, like it or not, black fellas regard the land as theirs and lived on it long before white fellas arrived.' Jon remembered the blocked-up cave near Kangaroo Soak that he'd found a couple of weeks back, with a pile of Aboriginal bones and broken artefacts. Had they been members of a tribe who had once lived on the land he now called his?

'Still don't see there's a problem. You're happy for them to carry out their rituals. It's not as if you don't allow 'em on your land, is it?'

'It isn't that simple though, the ones that come in from the desert for the corroborees aren't Jindalee or Jarrahlong stockmen. I don't know where they come from. I know some of them work for the Kentons over on Harrison Station, but I'm not sure about the others.'

Wes hitched up his pants and sat down. 'Les Harper hasn't any time for them, says they get a bit of booze in them and they're fighting drunk. There's been more than one or two killings between blackfellas over the years.'

22

'That's partly because in the past we've forced tribal enemies to live together on missions and the like so is it any wonder there's trouble? Add the booze and agitation from these fellas banging on about equal pay and land rights and you've got a poisonous mix that doesn't do anyone any good.'

Wes leaned back against his work bench. 'I've never looked at it like that.'

'No, and think on, I've been living here for over twenty years and I'm still trying to get to grips with Aboriginal sensibilities. I think I understand them and then something happens out of the blue and I realise I know nothing, except that underneath it all it's a bloody mess.'

'I can't see how you can put it right, not after all this time,' said Wes.

'I don't think there is any way of putting it right, and even if you try someone's going to lose.'

Wes stretched out his legs and studied his boots for a moment or two, thinking. 'Changing the subject, have you met a fella called McDonald, Gus McDonald?'

'No,' said Jon. 'Why?'

'There's something about him. He's been around for a few weeks now, but is keeping a tight lip. Connie says he's just a lone prospector out doing a bit of fossicking here and there over on Wanndarah and other places, looking for that elusive gold reef, like Stan Colley in the old days. Seems the fella's got a map of the area showing where all the mineral leases are, including yours over at Yaringa Creek. So you haven't had a visit yet?'

Jon shook his head. 'Is he staying at The Grand?'

'Connie says not; no one seems to know where he's staying. If you ask me he's probably dossing down in the back of the old Holden he runs about in.'

Jon pictured Wes and Connie speculating about the stranger over a quiet beer or two. That was one thing about Connie Andersen, the landlady of The Grand, there wasn't much she missed and being behind the bar she heard more than most.

Wes frowned. 'You reckon he's working for Glenshea Holdings? Word is that they're looking for more than gold these days. Les Harper says it's nickel they're after, seems there's a demand for it in America – the Vietnam War and all that. By all accounts they can't get enough to satisfy their needs.'

'Well, I haven't heard anything, but if I do I'll let you know.'

Wes chuckled. 'You never know you might be sitting on a small fortune over at Yaringa Creek, look well if it's rich in nickel and Stan spent his life looking for the wrong stuff.'

Jon grinned. 'Don't think so. In any case, I don't suppose there was much of a market for nickel that far back. Anyway, I better go and pick up Val. How long before the ute is ready?'

'I'd give it a week, should have it fixed by then. You're not in a hurry for it, are ya?'

'Nah,' said Jon, 'I'll drive me Rolls-Royce instead.'

'Aye, they're pretty fine cars, them Rollers.'

'Can you imagine me driving a car like that? I'd never hear the end of it.'

'Well, you wouldn't be the first station owner to buy one. Did I ever tell you the tale about an old pastoralist who had a thing about Rollers?'

Jon shook his head and Wes chuckled to himself.

'Can't swear to the truth of it, mind, maybe it's one of them myths, but apparently the fella bought himself a new 'un every ten years or so; he'd order the latest model and have it shipped over.'

'From England?' asked Jon.

'Aye, from the Derby works. When the new 'un arrived the fella wasn't happy, sent the damn thing back on the next boat, said it wasn't fit for purpose. Anyway, Rolls-Royce was that concerned when the car arrived back in Derby they sent out their top man to make enquiries. And you'll never guess what the problem was.'

Jon grinned. 'He didn't like the colour.'

'Nah, it was the running boards.'

'Running boards?'

'Aye, the latest model didn't have any. The old fella said the new version was neither use nor ornament as it was, seems he couldn't carry as many sheep with the new one. The sales executive nearly had an apoplexy.'

'I'm not with you.'

'The old fella used his Rolls-Royce like a ute; he'd stick his sick sheep in the boot, or on the back seat and lash 'em to the running boards when he needed to get them back to the homestead.'

Jon chuckled. 'That's a good one. So, what did they do?'

'They customised the new model, added running boards and the old fella was rapt.'

'Get away with you! You're having me on.'

'I dunno. The fella who told me swore it was true. Fact is some of these old pastoralists are daft enough to do such a thing.'

Jon thought of Alice and nodded. 'You're not wrong there, Wes, you're not wrong there.'

Jon left Wes and set off in Val's utility truck for Rachel and Ty's new home to see Rachel and pick up Val and, as he drove, he reflected on his conversation with Wes and the latest developments over on Wanndarah. He didn't fancy prospectors and mining corporations tramping over Jindalee if the mood took them, searching for nickel, not that he could do much about it if they'd bought the mineral rights. Maybe he should look into it and peg and register likely spots, but at least Yaringa Creek was safe from them.

Jon smiled to himself; there'd be hell on if the locals discovered that Stan had found the gold reef he'd spent thirty years searching for just weeks before his death. He recalled his shock when he learned Stan had left him his mineral rights and the horror when he'd found Stan's letter in a trunk asking him to carve the old fella's name and dates in the lightning-strike chamber, deep underground. Months it had taken him to get around to doing it, months of disturbed nights when Stan turned up in dreams nagging him about fulfilling the dying request and it was then he'd found the gold that had made him wealthy beyond his dreams. It was Stan's gold that had bought Jindalee, but the wealth came at a price: Yaringa Creek had had to be worked so the licence didn't lapse. It wouldn't have done for another prospector to claim the lapsed lease and chance upon the rest of the reef that was still buried in the rock. A big find like the one at Yaringa would mean the valley would become an open pit like the one at Kalgoorlie and then the Aboriginal Dreaming would be destroyed and Stan's grave desecrated. Having a couple of his men pan for gold along the creek at Yaringa was well worth it if it saved Stan's grave and the Dreaming from a mining company.

CHAPTER 5

Four months after Shirley came to live with them, Jon and Val sat finishing their breakfast one Sunday morning. It was a lovely late autumn day and the sun was streaming into the kitchen.

'You fancy a change of scenery, Val?'

Val looked up from the ledger she was about to scrutinise. 'You goin' to whisk me off to Kal for a spot of lunch, hon?'

'No, better than that, I'll get Yang to make us a pack-up; we can ride over to Kangaroo Soak for a picnic, maybe even camp out for the night.'

She smiled. 'Remember the time you took me to the green pool over on Jarrahlong?'

Jon grinned. 'I couldn't easily forget that, you really made me sweat it out, didn't you? I thought you'd never listen, let alone say yes.'

Now and again she mentioned the day she'd agreed to marry him, the time he feared he'd lost her for good. That had been a similar sort of day, but in summer, not late autumn.

'You made me scramble up that rocky outcrop, and there was me thinking you just wanted to show me the view.'

'Well, I did…sort of, it's a pretty place.' It was one of his favourites, and he'd hoped the beautiful scenery and his honesty about his feelings for her would make her change her mind about leaving the outback for the city.

'And you ruined your watch.'

'True.' He'd been that strung up he'd completely forgotten to take off his wristwatch before swimming in the ice-cold water. The soaking hadn't done it any good; it never worked after that.

Val held up her hand to the light, admiring her diamond engagement ring, the sun catching the facets that bounced splinters of colour off the walls. 'I've often wondered where Stan bought it from,' she murmured.

Jon glanced across at the ring Stan had given him for her. 'Probably a jeweller in Kalgoorlie, or maybe Perth, Stan never said.'

'Do you think Alice ever regretted turnin' him down?'

Jon recalled the day Stan died, the day he and Val were there, in Stan's shack by Yaringa Creek. 'No, I don't think she did. She was very fond of him but not fond enough to marry him. She considered him a friend, nothing more, nothing less. I think it took her a long time to get over Jack's suicide.'

Val tilted her hand again, letting the stones catch the light. 'If you do ever come to terms with it, imagine the guilt, the feelin's of despair...'

While Val cleared away the breakfast things, and washed up, Jon reflected on Val's words. Alice would have experienced it all, the guilt, the *what ifs*, and *if onlys*. The drought in the thirties that had driven Jack to kill himself had been protracted. According to Alice, Jack wasn't the only one who couldn't take any more, others had shot themselves too. It was all a question of degree, he guessed, and family support. The dry spell they'd experienced in the year he'd escaped from Karundah had been bad enough; Alice's sheep had been dying then, dozens of them, daily. He remembered the first time he'd gone out with Adie to the billabong to check on the flock. It was the stench he always recalled first, the sweet, sickly smell of decaying flesh, and then seeing the sheep belly-deep in sticky mud, their eyes pecked out by crows, and killing those poor sightless animals, and dragging maggoty, decomposing carcasses clear of what little water there was left had been enough to turn the stomach.

Val stopped what she was doing. 'What're you thinkin', hon?' She indicated his fingers lightly drumming the table.

He stilled the drumming. 'Just about the drought.'

'Fact of life in the bush, some are worse than others.'

Val was right, they'd seen a few over the years but they had plenty to take their mind off things: their own children, the stockmen, plus the Aborigines down at the camp, whereas for Alice and Jack it had been a lonely existence after the death of their son at Gallipoli, just themselves and a couple of Aboriginal stockmen. It must have been hard.

27

On Jindalee they'd had to reduce their stock holding, but even with fewer cattle they had still lost too many. It was always hard to see dead and dying animals. He could understand Jack's despair, his feeling of helplessness that had caused him to seek a way out. That was one of the problems of living in the outback; it was a harsh, unforgiving place despite its austere beauty. Life in the bush wasn't for the faint-hearted and never would be, and if people thought otherwise then they were deluding themselves.

'What's at Kangaroo Soak, besides Eli Jackson's coolabah tree?'

'You've remembered!'

'Of course I've remembered. That and the one at the green pool are the only two specimens hereabout, at least that's what you once told me, or were you spinning a yarn?'

'No, that's what Jeb Samuel told me the day I signed for this place. He said it was Eli Jackson who planted them.' And he too had carried on the tradition of the first owner of Jindalee. He'd planted specimen trees, jarrahs, from southern Western Australia and, from farther afield, fig, lemon and orange trees and jacarandas. 'No, it's not the flora I want to show you but something else, something I found last February, over three months back now, when I was culling scrub bulls in the breakaways.'

'What is it?'

'I'm not sure really but it's something that needs investigating, you up for it?'

'You know I am.'

'Right then, you tell Yang to organise some tucker for us and get changed, and I'll have a word with Ruby and George. I'll let them know where we're going just in case we decide to camp out tonight.' He knew all too well it wouldn't do to take off into the bush without letting his overseer and Ruby know exactly where they were heading and their likely time of return.

Jon and Val rode out in companionable silence, their swags lashed to their saddles, heading for the breakaways as they did from time to time, to get away from the daily grind of station life. They rode alongside the dry creek bed, travelling in a north-easterly direction, and then took the cut out onto a plain of good grazing when there wasn't a drought. Now, after the scanty summer rain, everywhere still looked dry except for the desert kurrajongs that always remained a startlingly bright glossy green even in the desiccating heat of a drought. The tree was widespread in the semi-arid land of Jindalee and a black fella had once told him that some species of the tree were important sources of water for desert tribes – not that he'd ever had to resort to draining water from a kurrajong to survive.

At midday they approached the range that cut through the north-eastern boundary of Jindalee land. The more fertile plain turned to scrubby country, rocky outcrops and finally the breakaways. They soon found themselves following the section of dried-up creek in a wide gulley that led to Kangaroo Soak, one of the wetter spots that stayed moist even in a dry spell, unless a period of drought was particularly prolonged. When they reached the coolabah tree they dismounted, unsaddled, let the horses drink their fill, and then hobbled them and turned them out to graze on the abundant hay-like grass in the gulley. Jon lit a campfire and put the billy on to boil while Val unpacked their sandwiches. Soon they were sitting with their backs against a rock, eating the pack-up Yang had prepared and drinking black billy tea.

Val finished her sandwiches, wiped her hands and looked about her. 'So, why here?'

Jon indicated along the gulley. 'I found a cave back in the summer.'

'Another one? There must be dozens in this area; I know Ruby's explored several.'

'Not this one, this one was deliberately sealed and a rock fall has opened it up again.'

'Why would someone do that?'

Jon shook his head. 'Dunno, I think it's an Aboriginal burial chamber, there's a pile of bones just inside the entrance and other Aboriginal stuff, but it just doesn't look right. I've been meaning to come back and take a proper look, but you know how it is, I didn't get around to it, and then when Noel suggested we teach the youngsters about Aboriginal beliefs and customs not long after I'd found the cave I thought then I'd better get back here and investigate it properly, and sooner rather than later.'

Val shivered. 'Well, I don't fancy explorin' where there are dead bodies lyin' about.'

'They're just bones, and they've been there a long while. Last time I didn't have a lamp and the tunnel seemed to go a way back, deep into the rock. There may be more bones further into the cave.' He fumbled in his haversack and pulled out two battered torches and an old miner's lamp that used to belong to Stan.

'How did you find it?'

'I didn't, Blue did.'

Val looked at him askance.

'You know what my old cattle dog's like, always poking about, following a scent; anyway, he found it,' said Jon.

They finished their tea, wiped out their pannikins and, with Jon leading the way, walked further along the gulley, through a thicket of mulga until they came to an open patch of ground with the rock fall that had exposed the opening to the cave entrance. Jon took out his torch and Stan's old lamp. 'In case the batteries run out,' he murmured, and together they set out to explore, Jon leading the way.

It was several degrees cooler inside the cave and the fearful sensation of being in a confined space reminded Jon of the tunnel leading to the Perentie-Man Cavern in Paradise Canyon where his Aboriginal mate, Curly, had taken him not long before he died.

'I don't like this much,' commented Val, skirting the pile of bones that appeared to be human with broken Aboriginal artefacts thrown higgledy-piggledy on top of them: woomeras, coolimans, spears and boomerangs all, like the bones, coated in a fine layer of dust and sand.

'Neither do I,' muttered Jon; he'd never been one for confined spaces, even when there was gold in abundance to be had at the end of them, as there had been in Stan's No Hope mine.

The floor of the cave was smooth and sandy and, as they travelled deeper into the rock, Jon shone his torch around the walls and illuminated the primitive drawings in white pipe-clay and red ochre.

'It's definitely an Aboriginal site.' Val shivered. 'Why do you think the bones have been left at the entrance and not carried deeper into the cave?'

Jon frowned. 'I don't know.' He'd asked himself the same thing too. 'Do you fancy exploring further?'

Val switched on her torch. 'Lead on McDuff.'

Jon grinned and shone his in a wide arc, looking for a way forward. The passageway sloped downwards and, after a time, it widened out until, suddenly, they found themselves in a large cavern with a sandy floor. 'Flippin' heck!' said Jon. 'Who would have believed this was here!'

'I should imagine some vast underground river created it, sometime in the Dreamin'. Are there any more drawin's that you can see?'

Jon flashed the torch around the walls of the cavern and there, as in Perentie-Man Cavern, were the drawings, hundreds of them, it seemed. And some were even superimposed over others, as if they'd run out of space and drawn over older ones. The predominant image was kangaroo, enormous images, and smaller ones, walleroos, Jon guessed, the euros common in the area. There were also drawings of snakes, lizards, bandicoot, birds and fish and some creatures Jon couldn't identify.

'Do you think that's the totem animal?' asked Val, inspecting a giant kangaroo in the torch light.

'Probably.' Jon's torch beam revealed more images and drawings showing what appeared to be the animal's internal organs. 'Amazing, isn't it!' he said, awed by the paintings around them. To his mind the art work in this cave was far superior to that in Paradise Canyon. Here, it seemed, the whole of the cave had been illuminated in Aboriginal art, and it appeared to be as fresh as the day it was painted.

Jon wondered why the best Aboriginal art was usually hidden away in secluded places, like the one opposite Stan's No Hope mine at Yaringa and the one in Paradise Canyon. There were other examples as well, like the ones not far from Gilbert's Find and the ones on the rock face overlooking the dried-up lake bed, way out in the desert beyond the stony plain. Perhaps some drawings were more sacred, more significant to Aborigines than others.

'Hush,' said Val. 'Did you hear that?'

'Hear what?'

Val tilted her head. Then both of them heard it, the sound of water dripping. They moved in the direction of the sound and there, under an overhang, was a pool of water that disappeared under the rock.

Jon picked up a stone and lobbed it into the water. 'Seems to be deep.'

'How deep?'

'God knows, a few feet, fathoms perhaps.'

'Is it permanent?'

'I think so, and with all this art work, it's probably sacred.'

'Which tribe does it belong to, d'you know?'

Jon indicated over his shoulder. 'Maybe those back there.' He frowned; he'd never seen Aborigines visiting this part of the station. Did it belong to some tribe that had died out, or been killed back in the early days when the land was acquired by white fellas? Had some of Eli Jackson's men massacred the blackfellas while Jackson was away on his travels and had said nothing to anyone?

'Seems a bit strange to dump bodies in a pile like that,' said Val.

He'd had the same thought. Had it been early settlers who had piled the bones in the cave entrance and sealed it? And what about the lonely grave, not that far away, *D. W. Berridge 1824* burned into the simple wooden cross. Was there a link?

'I wonder if Adie knows about this place?' murmured Jon.

'Why don't you ride over to Jarrahlong and ask him? He may be able to tell you somethin' about the people who used to live here.'

'I might just do that. But there's one thing for sure, the Samuels didn't know about it, if they had they would have found some way of pumping out the water for their sheep and cattle in the droughts.'

Val turned back to the drawings. 'Fascinatin', aren't they? We should make a record,' she said, half to herself.

'Why?'

'Well, they're important, it's part of Australian history; we should make a record of all the other Aboriginal art on the station too.'

Jon turned his torch beam towards her. 'You know what, that is a damned good idea. Maybe I'll have a word with Alistair, ask him to make copies.'

'Perhaps you should invest in a better camera and get Noel to photograph them. You know how keen he is on photography and in all things Aboriginal.'

'You're not just a pretty face are you?'

She grinned as he stepped closer to her.

'And to think you nearly slipped through my fingers.' He leaned forward and kissed her on the lips.

'There was no chance of that,' she murmured in a husky voice, the light shining in her eyes. She took his hand. 'Let's go back to the camp, hon.'

A fortnight later, Jon and Adie stood looking down at the pile of bones. 'What do you think?' asked Jon.

Adie shook his head.

'You ever seen this before?'

Adie shook his head again.

'Any idea whose bones might have been left here?'

Adie scuffed his foot in the dust.

The old Aborigine knew, except he wasn't saying.

'Is this how your people bury their dead?' asked Jon. 'Only it looks like someone just dumped these bones here.' Getting information out of Adie was like pulling a goanna out of its burrow. 'Anyone you know who might know more?' persisted Jon.

'Old fella, over Pilkington way,' said Adie. 'Walter Hayne.'

'Walter Hayne?' repeated Jon.

'Yeah, reckon so,' muttered Adie.

'So what does your mob do when someone dies? Come on, Adie. I can tell from your reaction that this is bad. What do I do to put it right? Where should these people be buried?'

Adie mumbled an answer.

'What did you say?'

'Reckon no one left now.'

Jon frowned. 'You saying the whole mob was wiped out?'

Adie shrugged.

Jon stared at him in disbelief; the old man was definitely hiding something. Now what did he do? Did he just seal up the cave again and leave the bones or did he try and give them an Aboriginal burial? He looked at the remains. It didn't seem right to him to leave them heaped up on top of one another as if the bodies had been discarded like animals. And he couldn't be certain, but he was sure Aborigines wouldn't have dumped the bones of their loved ones at the entrance to what he was convinced was a sacred place.

'I think I'll take a drive over to Walter Hayne's place sometime soon and see what he has to say.' Jon stepped out into the sunlight again with Adie just a pace behind him. The old fella didn't want to be there on his own; Jon sensed his unease. 'We won't mention this to anyone else for now, all right?'

'Okay, boss,' muttered Adie, taking the reins of his horse.

Jon watched as the old Aborigine rode away without looking back. Was Adie right? Was there no one left? Or was Adie wrong? And was he likely to violate some custom or law that would bring vengeance down on his head again, like the last time? Jon flexed his damaged leg where Yildilla, the old Aboriginal kaditja man appointed to mete out Aboriginal justice, had speared him back in

Paradise Canyon when he was still a youth. If he removed the bones would he be risking Aboriginal retribution? He needed to find out, but who could he ask?

CHAPTER 6

A couple of weeks later Jon announced at breakfast that he had plans for the family.

David's face brightened. 'What's that, Dad?'

'We think you're old enough to learn how to build temporary stockyards before you go back to school next week.'

'Do we have to?' grumbled Jamie.

'Yes you do,' said his mother. 'One day you two and Ruby will be runnin' the station and you'll need to know about these things.'

'Girls don't run stations,' scoffed Jamie, looking directly at Ruby who was demolishing a huge plateful of steak and eggs.

'Alice does,' rounded Ruby.

Val laughed at their son's remark. 'Your sister knows more about station work than you'll ever learn.'

Jamie scowled. 'No she doesn't, anyway she's only my half-sister.'

'She's your sister,' said Jon, a warning tone in his voice.

'She's my favourite,' said David.

Ruby grinned at him. 'I'm your only, so I damn-well hope so.'

'Language!' said Val, clearing away the plates.

Later, in the convoy of trucks, bikes and utes driving out to the north-western part of the station, Jon glanced across at Jamie sitting grim-faced beside him. He despaired of the lad, and wondered where he and Val had gone wrong with his upbringing. He was a selfish little brat, except he wasn't so little anymore. It wouldn't be long before he was as tall as him; his twelve-year-old son was already filling out. Perhaps he'd been too hard on his first-born twin, had expected too much of him at too early an age. He stared at the

35

ute ahead of them churning up dust. He was pretty sure David wasn't giving Val such a hard time.

'You'll enjoy it once we're there,' said Jon, forcing enthusiasm into his voice.

'Yeah!' sneered Jamie.

Jon held his temper. 'You like camping out, don't you?'

'No, I don't.'

Jon glanced at him as he drove, noting the sullen look on his son's face.

'Besides, it's boring,' added Jamie.

'The bush isn't boring. There's—'

'Well, I think it's boring.' Jamie clamped his jaws together and folded his arms over his chest as he leaned back in the passenger seat.

'Well, you won't be bored for the next couple of days, there's too much for all of us to do if we're to get the stockyards built before the muster.'

Jon lapsed into silence. Had Ruby been sitting next to him the conversation would have zinged along, she wouldn't have stopped chattering from slamming the truck door shut to opening it again. That was one thing he'd never understand, how it was that he could have such a close relationship with an adopted child when he couldn't with his own flesh and blood. Not for the first time he thanked his lucky stars that Berry Greenall had walked away from his parenting responsibilities; he'd never wished the bloke ill, but, truth to tell, he hadn't shed any tears when he'd heard through the bush telegraph that Berry had ended up dead following a bar-room brawl over some woman he'd been having an affair with. The husband hadn't liked it one little bit and had stuck a blade between Berry's ribs, and that had been the end of Berry.

Jon followed the lead truck at a distance, avoiding the worst of the red backdraught that obscured his vision, and tried to see things from Jamie's perspective. Just because he and Val were happy living on a cattle station in the middle of Western Australia, a three hour drive from the nearest town, didn't mean it would suit their children, even though they did their best to ensure their boys and Ruby were happy.

Val had been right, Jon thought. It had been time for the boys to start boarding school last January. Noel had done an excellent job so far with the fledgling School of the Air support, but the boys had needed more than home schooling could provide. But would they want to come back to Jindalee once they'd finished school? Or would the world beyond Jindalee beckon? Would they outgrow station life?

Jon considered the community they'd created at Jindalee. It suited him and Val, and Ruby seemed happy enough, but the station was a long way from a town of any size. Apart from their immediate family, companionship was limited to the stockmen, the Aborigines living in the camp beyond the creek, George and his family, the youngsters from the orphanages he employed and Noel; then, of course, there was Alice and Alistair over on Jarrahlong who had become honorary grandparents to their three children – not exactly riveting company for twelve-year-old boys. And, if he was honest, station life wasn't an easy option for anyone. There'd been occasions when he'd questioned why they stayed, especially when drought hit as it had in recent years; after all, they had money, there was nothing stopping them moving on to another station with better, more reliable grazing, one closer to Perth. But he knew the answer: he loved the desolate land about him, the saltbush and spinifex and the remote location. And who would look out for the Aborigines if he and Val left and someone like Kit Kennilworth took over the pastoral lease, especially someone who had Ben Nickson in their pocket? No, for him and Val this place was home, but maybe the boys wouldn't see it in the same light once they were grown and had left school. Jamie wouldn't, of that he was increasingly certain.

Jon glanced at his son and saw the tight-lipped look plastered on his face. 'Well, what would you like to do when you grow up if you don't want to work on Jindalee?'

'Join the army,' said Jamie without a moment's hesitation. 'And get away from this place,' he muttered under his breath.

Jon gritted his teeth against a sharp reply. He should have seen it coming the moment Harry Hammond signed up as a regular three years back.

Harry was a bright lad but one of the most difficult to manage. He'd come from the orphanage at Karundah with a huge chip on his shoulder and didn't trust anyone except Val. Jon knew they could never have reached Harry had it not been for Val's patience and sense of humour. Of all the youngsters they had taken on Harry's childhood had been one of the hardest of any he had known. According to the lad he'd been abused by his mother's various lovers for years, and in the end she'd put him into care. Jon didn't know why. He knew nothing of the mother, maybe she'd wanted to protect Harry, but it was more likely she wanted him out of the way: an eight-year-old youngster sees and understands more than a five-year-old child. But, whatever had happened to Harry, he was scarred even before he arrived at the orphanage and, once there, the abuse continued, except then there'd been no escape, just miles and miles of desert scrub that deterred all but the most determined…or lucky.

Jon despaired of the stony look on Jamie's face and his hero worship of Harry. Jamie'd taken to Harry from the first; he'd latched on to him and followed him around the place, and Harry liked the attention, he taught Jamie things: how to wrestle, play cards for money, and steal, which had necessitated a firm-handed approach at the time. Eventually, Harry settled down and, although he wasn't exactly a trusting individual, he learnt he was safe at Jindalee, that no one would touch him, let alone abuse him, and that it would always be a home for him, for as long as he needed one.

Jon had to admit that joining the army had been the making of Harry Hammond. Harry'd returned home on leave a few times over the previous three years and had sat at their dinner table regaling them with tales of army life and it had always been Jamie who had hung on his every word; and now Harry was out in Vietnam fighting the Viet Cong in a war that had gone on far too long, and to which, as far as anyone could see, there was going to be no early end.

Jon changed down a gear and eased the truck through another patch of bulldust. He'd never fully understood the Australian Government's desire to get involved in America's fight against the Communists. He didn't believe the Prime Minister when he spoke of the Reds sweeping down through Indonesia as the Japs had done in the last war when they'd bombed Darwin in '42. If it had been left to him he'd have waited until there was a bigger threat before he'd have sent troops to fight in the jungles and malaria-infested swamps of Vietnam.

'Well,' said Jon, 'I suppose it's as good a place as any to learn a trade. What do you want to be, an engineer?'

'Dunno.' Jamie's face brightened. 'Does it mean I can join up?'

'We'll see nearer the time,' said Jon, praying that Jamie would change his mind sometime over the next few years.

* * *

At midday they arrived at the location Jon had chosen and, while Val organised setting up the camp kitchen with Yang-dhow, Jon, George and the rest of the stockmen started to build the stockyard.

They were planning to muster all the cattle on one of the more remote sections bordering Reef Hill Station, a section which still didn't have permanent stockyards. Creating a temporary yard was time consuming and it was their intention to build permanent yards next to most of the wells and bores one day, but that was in the future, although the sooner it was done the better now that the Western Australian Government had extended tuberculosis testing to beef cattle.

The temporary yard needed to be big enough to manage the animals which were destined for sale at Midland, over Perth way, or for the meat plant. Jon and George had adapted a design George had used when he worked in Queensland. The system worked well and could be easily modified depending on whether they were working with bulls and bullocks or with a cow and calf mob.

The site had been chosen with care, adjacent to Emu Well, one of the wells Jeb and his boys had built back in the early days, approximately twenty miles from their intended starting point, close to the boundary fence, at Fifty-mile Bore.

Jon and George had picked the site the week before, one with the right combination of existing tracks and fences. The line of hills, gullies and creek beds would enable them to drive the cattle with less hassle for them and less stress on the animals. They had chosen the yard site well, the cattle, when disturbed, would naturally run in the direction they wanted them to go, and the driven cattle wouldn't see the yards until they were on top of them: there was nothing worse to handle than a spooked mob that knew what was in the offing.

Jon turned to Jamie and David. 'Well, boys, this is where we are going to build the yards. What do you think?'

Jamie shrugged.

David glanced about him. 'Looks okay to me, Dad.'

Jon nodded encouragement. 'And why is it a good site?'

'It's got water and shade,' added David.

'Good,' said Jon, 'and what else, Jamie?'

Jamie scuffed his feet in the dust. 'Dunno.'

'You can truck in the equipment and easily load up the cattle,' Jon explained, keeping the edge out of his voice. Maybe bringing the family with him hadn't been such a good idea after all!

It took them a day and a half to get the yard up and operational. Once it was completed they sat around the campfire eating Yangdhow's tucker and talked through the muster, the dogs dozing at their feet.

The section they'd earmarked for the muster was rough country, but flatter than the north-east section with its ranges, gullies, breakaways and dense scrub where some cattle had holed up for years avoiding the round-ups and, like the breakaways, it was a part of the station where, Jon suspected, there were still a few scrub bulls that needed culling. Compared to the north-east section the area they'd earmarked for muster was an easy ride. The only problem was the sheer size of it, but that was always the problem for people like them who chose to manage arid country: it took a lot of semi-desert to keep one animal in fodder, three hundred acres per cow, and that was in a good year when the seasonal rains hadn't failed.

Val handed round the mugs of steaming tea to everyone and then sat down next to Jon. 'Do you think it'll be a good muster this time, hon?'

'I hope so. The rainfall's not been good for a few months now but perhaps the new Brahman-Shorthorn-cross bulls we bought a while back have produced some offspring. There should be some prime beef for the taking, but time will tell.'

Ruby leaned back against her saddle, an enamel mug of tea in her hand, gazing into the flames of the campfire. 'Have you considered using a plane to muster the cattle, Jon-Jon?'

Jon glanced at his adopted daughter, rising sixteen and the same age he was when he'd first arrived at Jarrahlong in the middle of a drought.

'You can't use a plane to muster cattle,' scoffed Jamie.

David jumped to Ruby's defence. 'Don't see why not.'

'No runways,' said Jamie.

'The graded road's not that far from here, you could land the plane there,' said David after a moment's thought.

'What, and get flattened by a cattle truck!'

'You do talk a lot of crap,' said David.

'Stop squabbling, you two,' ordered Val. 'What d'you mean, Ruby?'

'I just think we could use a plane, it'd be quicker; we could fly over the whole area with a spotter looking for the cattle.'

'And what about communication?' asked Jon.

40

'Two-way radio, prearranged signals, circling a spot, dipping wings, that sort of thing.'

'And you know all about that, I suppose, being an experienced pilot and all,' mocked Jamie.

'You're only jealous,' said David, 'just 'cos Dad said you're not old enough to learn to fly yet.'

Jamie scowled.

'Paul Johnson says his dad is all for giving it a go,' added Ruby.

'Yeah, well, Sam Johnson's got a Cessna,' said Jon.

'We could buy one.' Ruby's face lit up at the prospect. 'I could fly it now I've got my licence. Dougie says I'm the best pupil he's ever had, and I'm better than Paul and his dad is going to let him try it out on their next muster.'

Jamie looked at his sister. 'Who's Dougie?'

'Dougie Coltrane, the fella who taught me to fly.'

'Oh him!' said Jamie, a sneer on his face.

Jon gave Jamie a warning glance and turned back to Ruby. 'And who'd be spotter? I can't see many being keen to go up in a flimsy plane, tree-top hopping, looking for cattle. I wouldn't.'

'Not with Ruby at the rudder,' said Jamie.

'You won't have the chance, you're away at boarding school most of the time,' snapped Ruby.

'Thank God!' muttered Jamie.

Ruby ignored Jamie's snide comment. 'Tom would be up for it, if I asked him.'

'We'll think about it,' said Jon.

'It's progress.'

'What do you mean?'

'It's not that long ago that we only used horses for mustering, remember? Now we've got a couple of old utes and motorbikes as well as horses. You say yourself that utes are better in some situations.'

'True,' Jon admitted. A truck with a bull bar was invaluable for rounding up a cleanskin bull, especially as the animal could be strapped to the bar until it could be incorporated into the mob and contained. Also, a ute didn't tire of the chase through the bush after a wild bullock, and, so long as there were no staked tyres, there was every chance of running the animal down and rounding it up.

'Using a plane is just the next step. So, why don't we, Jon-Jon? You can see more from a plane than you can from the ground.'

'I said we'll think about it,' repeated Jon.

'Which means you won't,' murmured Ruby.

'We'll think about it,' said Jon firmly. 'Now, it's about time we turned in for the night. It's a fair drive to Fifty-mile Bore. We'll be needing an early start; we've all got a big day ahead of us.'

'I'll take the boys back to the homestead with me in the morning,' said Val. 'It seems to me they've had enough for now.'

'Yeah,' muttered Jamie.

'What about you, Ruby, are you goin' to come back to the homestead with us or are you stayin' with your father?'

'I'm going to stay with Jon-Jon.' She used the pet name she'd adopted as a child, before he and Val were married. 'A few of us like mustering cattle, unlike some I know.'

That night Jon lay looking up at the stars, listening to the snuffles and snores of a sleeping camp, unable to fall asleep himself. When Ruby badgered them about flying lessons a year ago, he'd wondered how long it would be before she'd ask for a plane of her own. He'd never met a more determined, single-minded female than Ruby, except for her mother, and he already knew what Val would say about purchasing a Cessna. She'd reminded him they had more money than they knew what to do with, and why not? – that they wouldn't be having the conversation if Ruby had been a lad, and he guessed she wasn't far wrong. In fact, when it came to ability, gender didn't come into it. Ruby could hold her own against anyone, and, truth to tell, she could run the station as well as he could, and certainly better than most people he knew. She had a good head for figures, and he was forever finding her studying the station accounts, reading up the latest on cattle breeding, improvements in cattle management, and ways of maximising profit. And it wasn't just him she nagged, she wasn't above offering Alice advice on her Merinos, much to Alice's amusement.

Ruby was also right about Sam Johnson. He'd heard rumours over a year ago that Sam was planning to experiment with aerial mustering, the reason he'd sent his son, Paul, for lessons recently. So why shouldn't they give it a go too? But a plane! It was a pretty expensive bit of kit and then there were the other costs. He'd constructed a runway years back, when he'd first bought Jindalee from the Samuels, for the flying doctor, but if they were to buy their own plane they'd need a hangar to keep it in, and it would have to be maintained. The last time he'd been at the stockyards over in

Midland he'd overheard Sam grumbling about having to have his Cessna serviced every hundred flying hours. No, keeping a fixed-wing light aircraft wouldn't come cheap. And then he'd have to get the grader out to cut runways near to the windmills so the plane could land in the bush. It wasn't a cut and dried solution to faster and more efficient mustering, not by a long shot.

Jon pulled the blanket closer. Tomorrow they'd muster in the old way, with horses mainly and the two cattle dogs they'd brought with them – Blue, his favourite and Blue's offspring, Belle – plus the utes, which they'd found were better for dealing with the more difficult animals. There were parts of the station where mustering in the old ways still worked best, especially those sections with gullies and water courses, but even in difficult terrain a fixed-wing aircraft might be useful for spotting cattle.

CHAPTER 7

Jon awoke early, but then he always did. The horse tailer was already busy rounding up the horses that had been out feeding in the bush overnight.

Val and Yang-dhow had been up early too, raking out the ashes and reviving the log used to keep the fire in overnight. Already Jon could smell the billy tea and breakfast. He rolled out of his swag and ate with the others.

After breakfast he tousled David's hair by way of farewell and shrugged when he noticed Jamie was already in the ute passenger seat waiting for his mother and brother. 'See you in a few days, Val,' he said and kissed her.

'Yes, and you take care, hon, especially if you come across a big cleanskin bull, and don't forget to call me. I'll be listenin' on the hour, just in case.'

'Will do.'

Jon opened the driver's side door for her and shut it as she settled herself and started the engine.

A last wave and they were gone, leaving him to the muster.

Once they reached Fifty-mile Bore they set out on horseback to round-up the cattle, while those using utes followed on, mindful of the thicker mulga where it was all too easy to stake a tyre or even a radiator.

Jon opted to ride that day. He whistled for his cattle dogs and headed out to the boundary fence to begin the sweep back to the bore. Almost immediately they flushed out an old and mangy scrub bull, long-tailed and wild, with flaring nostrils and a lethal set of horns that they'd missed on previous musters.

'I've got 'im,' called George, staring the animal down as it swung round to face him, puffing and blowing, and gouging the ground with its hoof.

'Where's Charlie with the bloody ute?' yelled Jon.

'Dunno. Can't hear 'im. What d'ya want to do, boss?'

'You'd better shoot it.'

George raised his rifle and took aim, but the animal was off at a lick, crashing through the mulga, George and the dogs in hot pursuit.

Blast, thought Jon, there was no way there was going to be an easy outcome. He wheeled his horse around and set off after them, listening as George yelled instructions at the dogs even as he urged his horse forward, closing on the animal.

Mulga lashed his face as he chased after George who had a head start on him. He heard the report of a rifle, and another, and hoped George had had clear sight of the bull; an injured animal was unpredictable and dangerous and the mulga thicket wasn't the best killing ground.

Another rifle shot ricocheted around him, then yet another, followed by a piercing yelp. The bull was down, the dogs excited. Jon pushed on through the bush, picturing the scene, until he came upon George standing over the downed bull, his rifle directed at the animal's head. Another gunshot and the animal lay still, its body at George's feet.

Jon dismounted. Belle ran to him and nuzzled his hand as he joined George staring down at the carcass. The animal was over five years old, Jon guessed, and a pretty ropey specimen.

'You're losing your touch, George, five bullets!'

'Four,' said George.

'You can't count either,' said Jon as he remounted. He whistled Blue. 'You seen my dog?' he called when the dog failed to appear.

'Not since before I shot the bull.' George pulled up his horse and whistled the dog. Jon did the same.

'Did the bull trample him?'

'Nah,' said George, 'Blue's a clever bugger, he knows to keep well clear.'

Jon searched the area, whistling the while and found Blue lying stretched out, as if running, the ground beneath him dark with blood.

'Blue!' But Blue didn't move. Fearfully, Jon slipped from his horse and knelt by his dog, putting his hand on Blue's chest, willing a response, but there was no movement, no fluttering heart. The dog was dead, felled by a rifle bullet, the hole in his side clear where the lead had ripped through the ribcage, piercing the heart. Rage welled up, choking him; he'd raised the dog from a pup. Blue was special, a dog he'd developed a bond with, and now he was gone, slain by a careless, stray shot.

He'd been a damned fool! He should never have brought the dogs with him on the round-up, especially Blue, he wasn't a young animal, and now he was dead.

George joined him. 'That Blue?' he asked, his tone reflecting his disbelief.

'You bloody shot him,' said Jon, his voice betraying all the pain and fury at losing his favourite dog.

'He was nowhere near the bull, boss.'

'Must have been, he's dead, right enough,' snapped Jon. He gently picked up Blue as if he were a pup, the body floppy in his arms.

They rode back to camp, not speaking, Jon holding his dog close, barely keeping his grief and anger under control and with Belle trailing behind him. No one, not even Val fully understood him and his relationship with his dogs. Stan would have understood, and the fella over Willicubbin way who'd fallen out with the local priest who'd refused to bury his dog in the cemetery, in the burial plot the old fella had bought for himself. Dogs were often closer than mates to the lonely old men who lived out in the bush for months on end, but not everyone understood or appreciated that, not even blokes who worked with dogs every day.

Back at camp he picked up a shovel, ordered Belle to "stay" and made his way into the bush, alone, to bury his dog.

When Jon got back to the camp, Todd was waiting for him.

George nodded in Todd's direction. 'Mister Kennilworth wants to know if he can borrow a rifle.'

'Why?' asked Jon, his tone clipped, Todd was the last person he wanted dealings with in his present mood.

'Says his is stuffed,' said George.

'Problem?' Todd indicated the shovel in Jon's hand, the hint of a smirk on his face as Jon approached him.

'Why do you want a rifle? What's wrong with yours?' Jon asked, looking pointedly at Todd's horse and the rifle held in the holster attached to the saddle.

'Like yer Abo sez, got a ruddy bullet jammed in the breach, ain't I, and I've got a bull with a busted leg to deal with. It's a long ride back to the homestead. Heard you mustering and reckoned you'd help me out.'

'You did, did you?'

'Yeah, do the same for you sometime.' Todd indicated the shovel again. 'Doing a bit of prospecting, eh?'

'Where's the bull?' asked Jon.

'Not far from Top Well.'

'Go with him, George. Shoot his bloody bull for him.'

'Thank ya, mate,' said Todd.

'I'm not your mate,' snarled Jon, turning his back on Todd. He couldn't stand the bloke and he only half believed Todd was concerned for the welfare of an animal. Knowing Todd, he was probably responsible for the animal's injury.

George returned an hour later.

'Everything all right, George?'

'Yeah, it was a pretty scrubby lookin' animal.'

'And did it have a busted leg?'

'Yeah, but it didn't look like a regular break.'

'I'm not surprised. I wonder what the bloke really wanted.'

'Maybe he wanted a nose around, see what our stock looks like.'

'Maybe.' Jon doubted it though. He was pretty sure Todd had some other reason for his visit.

Jon yawned. 'I'll check on the stock before turning in for the night, it's been a long day.' As he looked over the cattle he contemplated the work ahead and was glad that musters, by and large, ran pretty smoothly.

Satisfied everything was okay he nodded in the direction of the men on night duty and returned to camp. In the morning a couple of the stockmen would move the mob on to the next bore and tail them out to grazing while the rest of them would muster a new section adding more cattle to the mob each day as they gradually worked their way back to the temporary yards at Emu Well.

Jon settled down to sleep, his mind on the work ahead, glad that at least one of his children was interested in station work. Try as he might he couldn't see either of his sons wanting to take over the running of Jindalee with all the work it entailed.

* * *

Once the round-up was complete and the mob safely yarded at Emu Well, the graft began; the men cut out all the cleanskins and set to with the branding. Jon chose their best draught horse that had been trained for the job, a horse that was strong enough to deal with the bigger bulls they occasionally came across in the bush, and essential for those times when it was necessary to brand older animals that had been missed as calves.

Lasso at the ready, Jon rode into the yard, roped a cleanskin bull and, using the strength of his horse, dragged it to the ramp. Once the animal was secured it was branded and castrated, then the stockmen stood back as the enraged animal was released, kicking and thrashing, scattering the stockmen in all directions, before escaping back into the paddock. The animal would need time to recover from its ordeal; maybe by the next muster it'd be ready for sale or slaughter.

Jon did not like castrating older animals; besides, the casualty rate from late castration was higher than he would have liked. When he'd first taken over the property there had been too many older bulls, but over the years they'd eliminated most of them, either to the meatworks or they'd shot them and left the carcasses in the bush. Now, if there were any cleanskin bulls left, they would be found in the more remote areas such as the one they were working in, or over in the breakaways.

After a couple of days they had earmarked the cattle for transport to the sale yards at Midland or for the meat processing plant. That evening Jon and Ruby stood side by side looking at the stock still in the yard awaiting the arrival of the cattle truck. The muster had achieved a mixed bag. The best, maybe a third of them, were in reasonable condition and would be sold, but the majority were pretty ropey looking and no doubt quite a few would end up being condemned at the abattoir.

'Not so good, eh, Ruby?'

'No, they're not, but if we can get rid of all the scrubby-looking bulls and ensure all the cows are served by the new Brahman-cross-Shorthorns then maybe we can improve the stock, especially if we keep the best heifers as breeding animals. Has the vet said when he'll be back for the next TB test?'

Jon groaned. It was fifteen months since Vic Campbell, who had won the TB contract, turned up to test their stock. He'd expected reactors, especially as they'd heard there'd been reactors on Reef Hill, but they'd been lucky. Although, with hindsight, maybe the vet they'd been allocated wasn't as thorough as he'd heard some were. 'Any day, Ruby, word is all cattle have to be tested every two years now, and once the national programme is up and running it'll be every year until they've eradicated the disease.'

'So, according to the vet, we have a clean mob?'

'Yeah, but that doesn't mean it'll be the same next time; you know what the country is like around here, we definitely missed a few, like the scrub bull George shot the other day.' He recalled the scrawny bull with its untrimmed tail hair, a clear indication it had evaded the muster. 'That one wasn't bang-tailed.'

'Well, at least we know to look out for the long-tailed ones,' said Ruby. 'We need to be vigilant, catch those cleanskins and either shoot them or send them to the meatworks. It's best to be ahead of the game.'

Jon couldn't argue with her on that point. It was all right introducing testing for dairy herds and beef cattle on smaller stations in the south, but doing it on a station like Jindalee was a different matter; mustering the wild places and the breakaways was one hell of a job. Finding them to cull was hard enough, and dangerous, but catching all of them was damned near impossible.

Jon remembered all the good horses they'd lost, injured by the lethal horns of enraged cattle; and not just the horses, there'd been injuries among the men too, nasty gashes that needed stitching and on one occasion a punctured lung that required a trip to hospital. Even using a vehicle with strong bull bars for lashing a wild animal to wasn't always the answer either, that was equally dangerous.

'We could bring in outsiders to flush out the scrub stock; Paul Johnson says there are outfits that specialise in it,' said Ruby.

'For a price,' said Jon.

'Well,' Ruby shrugged her shoulders, 'we've no choice in the matter, the Government wants disease free herds so we'll just have to knuckle down and do what they want. It'll be worth it in the long run if we want to sell our beef on the world market and we don't want to be in a situation where we have to de-stock, do we?'

'I don't think it will come to that. We didn't have any reactors last time.'

Ruby flapped her hat at the cloud of gnats circling above them and flopped it back on her head. 'Let's hope it wasn't a fluke, that they just missed the diseased cattle.'

She left him then and went back to the others while Jon continued gazing at the cattle with unseeing eyes, regretting that the muster had cost the life of his best dog.

CHAPTER 8

A month after the muster Jon and George were working up the top
end, near their northern boundary, repairing fencing up beyond
Lake Desolation. They'd brought the old truck laden with the
equipment they needed and had camped out for a few days while
they got the job done. Now they were taking a break, the mid-
winter breeze cooling the heat of the sun, making the day pleas-
antly warm while they sat under a scrubby patch of snap and rattle,
eating damper and sipping the hot tea George had rustled up for
them.

'Well named, ain't it, boss?' said George in a quiet moment
when he noticed Jon staring into the distance, at the light sparkling
on water that wasn't there.

'What do you mean?'

'The lake.'

Jon looked at the lake, at what appeared to be a thin layer of water, knowing that it wasn't real, just a mirage as one frequently
saw. All too often dying men had been convinced there were vast
reserves ahead only to be disappointed when huge clay pans, long
dried of the water they occasionally carried, fooled them, filling
them with hopeful anticipation, only for their expectations to be
cruelly dashed.

He supposed George was right; for most of the time the lake was
dry, but when it carried water the place was transformed, it became
a verdant oasis in the arid semi-desert. 'Aye, you're right about the
desolation out here; she can be pretty bleak, not the best part of the
station, that's for sure.'

George tilted his pannikin of tea towards the eastern edge of the
lake. 'Looks like we've got visitors.'

Jon squinted against the light, not seeing anything in the eye-watering glare. 'How many?'

'A couple, maybe three, hard to tell.'

'Aborigines?'

'Yup, I reckon.'

Jon tilted his hat further back and shaded his eyes with his hand. Gradually his eyes made sense of what he saw, black stick figures, shimmering, the images indistinct, sometimes with heads, sometimes without, as they moved towards them in the hazy light. Two, Jon decided, one smaller than the other. 'We'd better put the billy on, they'll be ready for a brew.'

'It's a woman and a kiddie! Where d'ya reckon they've come from? There ain't anything out there 'cept scrub bush and desert. Leinster?' George speculated, 'Leonora?'

'Bit of a long way to come, winter too, it gets bloody cold at night. Where do you suppose they're heading?'

The two lapsed into silence and watched the pair approach. As they came closer Jon could see that the taller one was a woman wearing a shapeless dress that flapped around her knees. She was shoeless, as was the child who was wearing a similar shaped dress to her mother, made from an old flour bag by the look of things.

The woman stopped a way off and waited. Jon rose to his feet and held out the pannikins they'd been using, both now filled with freshly made black tea. 'Tea?' he called to her. 'Would you like some tea?'

Jon saw the child glance up at the woman. 'Pass me the rest of the damper, will you, George.'

George handed it over and Jon took a step closer to the woman. 'Where you heading?'

'A station.' She nodded in a southerly direction.

'Which one?'

'Don't know name, they's bin got a camp for kids.'

Jon frowned. What the hell was she on about?

'For creamies,' she murmured so low that Jon almost missed it.

He looked at the child again, at her fairish skin and copper-blonde hair that reminded him of Bindi Henderson, the time he'd first seen her when she'd stood watching him as he swam naked in the green pool.

'Jindalee,' he said. 'It's a long walk, you better have this.' He held out the pannikins again and the damper.

The woman watched him with wary eyes, then she took a step

forward and took the proffered damper and tea. She retreated a few paces, putting space between them and sat down on the trunk of a long dead eucalypt. Neither spoke as they ate and drank the tea, their eyes fixed on them as if they were about to be attacked.

'Who told you about the station?' asked Jon when they'd finished eating.

'A blackfella, he say she be safe.'

'He got a name?'

She shook her head. 'Him pretty thin fella.' She shuddered as she seemed to recall the detail. 'An old fella,' she added.

'Scars on his legs?' Jon indicated his thighs to jog her memory.

She nodded.

Was it Yildilla she'd seen? Had the old man come across her and seen the child and recognised her desperation? It was years since he'd seen Yildilla, Bindi Henderson's grandfather. He smiled as he recalled the woman's shudder. The old blackfella put the wind up everyone except Bindi. But Yildilla would have known about Jon's "camp" as the woman put it; Bindi would have told him, she'd have told him that Jon never turned away an Aboriginal family, especially a family with half-caste or quadroon children.

'We're going to Jindalee,' he said. He indicated the truck parked in the shade of the snap and rattle. 'We'll give you a lift.'

The woman stood up, clearly agitated. She took the pannikin from the child's hand and placed it, and her own, on the ground, grabbed hold of the child's hand and set off walking at a rapid pace without looking back.

'She's a pretty scared woman,' observed George. 'She proper worried you'll tek 'em straight to the police in Pilkington.'

George was right; until recently the police had rounded up creamies, as the woman described her daughter. Years ago the Australian authorities had decided that half-caste and quadroon children should be educated into white Australian ways by putting them into settlement schools like the one north of Perth where Bindi had been sent until Alice had rescued her. Neither he, nor Val, agreed with the Government policy, and the desire to "breed out the black" which had led to the children being removed from their families. If the truth be known, it had taken him a while to realise the reason for the antipathy that many whites had towards blacks. It was all tied up with the ownership of the land, the land that had been forcibly taken from the original inhabitants, which had led to, at best, individual killings on both sides and, at worst,

53

massacres of whole communities and which now continued under the more benign guise of "Aboriginal Welfare". It was not comfortable to know that the land that was yours was land that had been taken from others without so much as a "by your leave".

'Bloody government,' muttered George.

Jon glanced across and saw the grim look on George's face and was inclined to agree. She was the second woman to turn up with a half-caste child in recent weeks, even though, as far as he could tell, the assimilation policy had, more or less, ceased to be implemented. But he didn't blame the woman for being afraid; almost seventy years of government policy had taken its toll. Aborigines were understandably wary, terrified their children would be forcibly removed from their care.

Jon watched the pair as they receded into the distance, in the direction of Jindalee. He'd found a place for the other woman; she now helped out with the cooking and the laundry while her child sat in class being educated by Noel Boswell. No doubt he'd end up doing the same thing for the woman and child they'd just seen. Jon smiled grimly to himself. At least there'd be no backlash from Nickson. The constable never visited Jindalee to checking on the Aboriginal children, looking for half-castes to ship off to settlement schools or missions, and had he done so he'd have got short shrift. And Kennilworth's demands that he be charged with abducting Shirley Jones, their house girl, had come to nothing, as he had known it would.

After their tea break Jon collected the pannikins and helped George load up the truck. On the journey home they kept a weather eye out for the woman and her child as they made their way back to Jindalee.

CHAPTER 9

Intermittently, Jon found himself thinking about the Aboriginal remains he'd discovered in the cave near Kangaroo Soak and, in the spring, he decided to pay Walter Hayne a visit to try and find out more about the bones, and whether the soak was the site of a massacre and cover up, or simply an Aboriginal burial ground. As he drove north beyond Pilkington he recalled Adie's reaction when he'd shown him the remains and was convinced it was the former.

Jon frowned, but it wasn't just the bones he'd found, there was also the single marker not that far from the cave, a simple cross with *D. W. Berridge 1824* on it. The wooden marker was pretty battered and had done well to survive the white ants. Question was, were the two linked in some way? And who the hell was D. W. Berridge? Jeb Samuels hadn't known. He'd once said it was the grave of a lone prospector back in the early days, even before the time of Eli Jackson, the first owner of Jindalee. Jon pondered the matter. Would the old prospector, Walter Hayne, know? And if he did would he be prepared to talk about it, or was the past murkier than even he realised? Perhaps the history of the settlement in these parts had been bloodier than people believed.

Finding the bones back in late summer had piqued his interest. The last time he'd been in Perth he'd asked in the library for information about the early days. The reading had been salutary: some settlers reported good relations with the local Aborigines who had helped them to find water and bush tucker, but others spoke of murder and mayhem when they'd moved into Aboriginal territory. An old copy of *The Perth Gazette* reported violent skirmishes between whites and blacks. In one account it said Governor Stirling and his men ambushed an Aboriginal tribe, killing fifteen of them, but others claimed thirty Aborigines had died that day when men, women and children were trapped at a waterhole and massacred in the early 1830s.

The new information that he'd learnt in Perth didn't sit easy with him. The trouble was the time he'd spent with Curly, the first blackfella he'd really come to know well, had taught him to view things from a different perspective. The settlers had been wrong when they believed the land was uninhabited, that it didn't belong to anyone. Just because it wasn't managed in a traditional European way didn't mean the land wasn't harvested.

Jon knew that it wasn't just in the old days that Aborigines were deliberately murdered. Only twenty years back, Buni and his lad, Wally, who'd worked for Jeb Samuels on Jindalee, had been run over on the road near Cavanagh's Creek. Buni's head had been crushed, his blood and brain ground into the dust, and his young, fatally-injured son left to die at the roadside. Jon had been convinced Gerry Worrall was the one responsible for their deaths and he wasn't the only one. Gerry had been killed by an Aboriginal spear soon after and his body left in the bush. Kennilworth, too, hated blacks and often referred to them as vermin, as Gerry had done. There was no getting away from it, when it came to crime and punishment there was still a double standard. Too many Aborigines were arrested for crimes that would only have elicited a warning for whites, and too many blacks ended up dead in custody. As one old timer he'd met in a bar in Menzies, back in the fifties, had said: Blacks don't have no rights. He was inclined to agree with him, nothing much had changed in the intervening years. Would it ever?

Fifty miles north of Pilkington was the hand-painted sign for Walter Hayne's place. People had told him that Walter roamed far and wide in his search for the elusive gold. He was a lone prospector like Stan had been, a chap who had lived all his adult life out in the bush, miles from anywhere, digging and panning for gold.

Jon pulled into Walter's yard, switched off the engine, stepped out of the ute and crossed over to the shack. He hammered on the door and waited. Nothing! The old fella was out then, no telling what time he'd be back.

Jon looked about him at the half a dozen chooks scratching about in the dust, then crossed over to the dilapidated sheds with no fronts and full of stuff that had not been used for years if the layer of dust covering everything was anything to go by. He'd asked

Scally about Walter, but Scally knew nothing more than Adie had told him. Walter had lived in the shack for as long as anyone could remember and fossicked for gold. He sold what he found, bought in the basics and lived a lonely life out in the bush with not even a dog for company.

Jon noticed an old rocking chair on the verandah, and settled down to wait, watching a lone euro that came in to graze over in the scrubby bush beyond the fencing. He set the chair rocking, looking for other creatures and spotted a flock of parrots – twenty-eights. He smiled to himself, wondering who had come up with the name. Whoever it was had an ear, no doubt about it, their calls did sound like *"twenty-eight"*.

Somewhere out of sight came the warble of a magpie. Jon listened for others, but heard nothing. The euro hopped forward, nibbling the better herbage in the open patches where the spring flowers bloomed: vibrant yellow billy-buttons, purple parrakeelya, and everlastings with their papery petals – a patchwork of colour at this time of year. Early explorers and more recent travellers had referred to the landscape in Western Australia as "inhospitable, barren and desolate"; clearly they'd never seen it in the springtime when the colours were at their best, he decided. When it came to flowering bushes his favourite was the grevillea that grew in the more arid parts, and from his chair he spotted one of the larger varieties, now a mass of yellow-orange flowers that, from a distance, looked as if the shrub was on fire. He breathed in the scented air but the overriding aroma was baked earth and peppery, oily eucalypt.

It was a couple of hours before Walter turned up on a battered motorbike with rusting mudguards and equally battered panniers either side of the back wheel. Walter dismounted, pulled the bike back up on its stand and pulled out a canvas bag from the nearest pannier. He nodded a greeting as he ambled across to the shack.

Walter was a frail old fella with a frill of straggly white hair around his bald patch that was as mottled as Spotted Dick pudding. Walter was eighty if he was a day, and Jon wondered how the old fella managed to stay on the bike at his age. He stood and extended a hand in greeting. 'I'm Jon Cadwallader, from Jindalee,' he said, 'beyond Pilkington,' he added.

Walter's handshake was surprisingly firm. 'Eli Jackson's place?'

Jon nodded. 'Jeb Samuels and his missus bought it after Eli died and I bought it off them in December '53.'

'Aye, I did hear that when Eli Jackson's beneficiaries decided to sell the property in the 1920s they sold it to the Samuels, a couple from out east, they say. So, what can I do for you, young man?'

To Jon's amazement the euro he'd spent a couple of hours watching bounded over from the paddock and nuzzled Walter's hand.

Walter felt in his pocket and withdrew what looked like sheep pellets, the concentrate food similar to that sold in Les Harper's Agricultural Stores in Charlestown, and fed her a handful.

Walter fondled the euro's ears. 'Raised her from a pup, found her out on the graded road next to her dead mother, been run over, she had, and this little 'un survived. Made a pouch from an old vest and fed her on powdered milk till she was big enough to fend for herself,' he added.

The animal settled down in the dust at their feet and started grooming the fur on its belly, nibbling for fleas.

Jon turned his attention back to Walter. 'I wondered whether you'd heard mention of a bloke called D. W. Berridge? Only there's a marker on Jindalee with his name on it and the date 1824.'

Walter frowned. '1824 you say?'

'Yeah, that's what it looks like to me.'

'Nah, son, you've got the date wrong, there weren't no whites living this far inland then, wasn't nobody living around Perth until the late 1820s. Me grandfather along with m'grandmother and m'father were one of the pioneering families who settled in York in the 1830s and then, when m'father was in his mid-twenties, he moved farther inland, so the date is a bit out 'cos my old man knew Berridge. They were mates back then.'

'So your father knew what happened to Berridge, yeah?'

Walter ignored the question. 'They were keen to carve out a piece of the wilderness for themselves. My old man eventually changed his mind about Berridge, said he was a wrong 'un; he wasn't the sort of bloke he should have got mixed up with, a rough 'un, and hard with it. By all accounts they hooked up together after Berridge got involved in a fight, a nasty one, according to Pop, although Berridge persuaded him he'd been set up. Anyway, the townsfolk of York kicked Berridge out, told him to sling his hook, that his sort wasn't wanted in the town, so he had to move on, and he persuaded the old man to go with him. They ended up marking out a patch for themselves over Jindalee way, but it wasn't called that then, of course, it was just the bush. I believe it was their plan

58

to go fossicking for gold over in the breakaways.'

'What made your dad change his mind about Berridge?'

'Why d'you want to know?'

'Found something that isn't looking too good.'

'What sort of *"something"*?'

'Bones, human bones.'

Walter gave Jon a long, hard look. 'Y'better take yourself a seat.'
He nodded towards the one Jon had been sitting on, picked up a
kitchen chair for himself and placed it next to the rocking chair.
'Maybe you should tell me what y'found.'

Jon took a deep breath. 'Well, I was looking for poddies on the
north-east side of the station. It's the worst sort of land in that
quarter, all gullies, and breakaways, with a creek that runs through
it and peters out into a soak, when we're not in a dry spell. Do you
know it?'

'Nah, m'father had moved on by then. He'd moved back to York
and settled there for a while, kept his nose clean, made a bob or
two and later married mother and had me.'

'Anyway,' continued Jon, 'the dog I had with me wandered off,
so I went looking for him and found him sniffing around a mound
of bones he'd found in a cave. It seems the entrance had been
sealed, someone had packed it full of rocks, but there'd been a rock
fall and the entrance had opened up again. I realised the dog had
found some human remains. There must be fifteen or twenty bodies, or rather the remains of bodies, you know, just bones and
pieces of cloth here and there, and on top of the bones are artefacts—'

'Artefacts?'

'Yeah, coolimans, spears, woomeras, Aboriginal stuff, all
smashed to smithereens. Well, it's clear it wasn't a burial, not from
the way they're all piled on top of one another, so I had a word
with an old Aboriginal stockman I know from off Jarrahlong Station. He was pretty close-mouthed, didn't want to talk about it, said
to speak to you.'

Walter didn't comment. Instead, he fumbled in his pocket and
pulled out an ancient briar pipe which he proceeded to empty of
ash before repacking it with rough cut. He tamped the tobacco
down, struck a match and sucked on the pipe until the tobacco
caught. 'You mentioned this to anyone else?'

'Like who?'

'The constable.'

'No, can't see the constable being interested. Those bones have been there a long time; there aren't many people left who would know anything about them.'

'No, I don't suppose there would.'

Jon waited while the old man drew on his pipe a few times, ruminating on the past, no doubt sizing him up, wondering how much to tell him. Had it been Walter's father who had done the killing? Had his father killed Berridge too? There'd been more than a few murders over the years, murders that had been concealed like Gerry Worrall's. He and Stan Colley had broken the law, they'd been responsible for disposing of Gerry's body after an Aboriginal execution, and he was sure they hadn't been the first to conceal a murder.

'You've got to remember that we're going back a fair old ways now; in the early days things weren't settled like they are now. The natives didn't take kindly to strangers moving in, using up the scarce resources, especially in a drought. And, according to me father, there was a drought at the time them folk were killed.'

Walter stopped, relit his pipe, and glanced across at Jon. 'Anyway, Berridge and me father had found a soak, then one day they'd gone there to refill their water bottles and found a mob of Abos camped there.'

'Was there trouble?'

'Yeah, you might say there was a bit of a skirmish. Berridge shot one and between the two of them they chased the mob away, but the blacks weren't having it. They came back one night and speared the horses, then melted away into the bush. Me father always said they were watching them, waiting for them to pack up and leave, but Berridge had the bit between his teeth, you might say; he set up an ambush and when the blacks came for water, armed to the teeth with spears, he shot a couple more dead. After that it was war.'

Walter stared into the far distance for quite a while and it crossed Jon's mind that that was all Walter had to say on the subject, that it was the sum total of his knowledge.

'As I said, after that it was war.' Walter drew on his pipe and exhaled a long, slow stream of tobacco smoke. 'The Abo warriors turned up ready for battle and there was a right set-to. Me father and Berridge managed to kill all of 'em 'cept one even though Berridge got speared through his arm. They tracked the one remaining Abo back to his camp and Berridge set about killing the rest of them. Me father tried to stop him, said they were only women, kiddies and old folk. But Berridge slaughtered the lot; he wouldn't listen to reason, said if they didn't kill 'em all they'd bring others back and then there'd never be peace, said it was them or the Abos. Father claimed Berridge was like a man possessed.'

Bloody hell! thought Jon. He'd read of a similar massacre in *The Perth Gazette.* Was it the same massacre, or a different one?

'When did it happen? Was it in the thirties?'

'Nah, much later than that. It would have been sometime in the seventies.'

Jon considered the information. Had he misread the faded date as Walter said, was it 1874 not 1824 when Berridge was buried?

'Who hid the bodies then?'

'Me father. Berridge's wound turned bad, he was burning up for days. Father said he panicked, didn't know what to do. He was afraid more Aborigines would turn up. So he decided to hide all the bodies in a cave they'd found not far from the soak. It was all he could do 'cos Berridge was pretty crook by then, he was in no fit state to help bury the bodies. And it was me father who smashed up the natives' stuff so they couldn't use it again. When Berridge died Father buried him a short way from the others and stuck up a marker for him. And then he skedaddled out of it, terrified of being picked off by the Aborigines. Me father always said he was lucky to get out of it alive. With the horses and Berridge dead he was on his own, and it was a long walk back to the nearest settlement.'

'When did your father tell you all this?'

'Pretty late on, just a couple of days before he died. Seems it had been on his conscience, him being party to Berridge's killing of all them women and their kiddies.'

It crossed Jon's mind that Walter's father hadn't told the whole truth. Maybe he had been more actively involved in the killings than he'd admitted to, but one thing was certain, anyone who did know the truth of it was long dead.

Walter refilled his pipe again and stared out into the bush. Jon sat back in his chair unsure of what to say next. Gerry Worrall had hated Aborigines with a passion, and there were plenty of others who were prejudiced against them. But just how many had been killed on both sides, back in the early days when the land was being settled?

'What are you planning on doing about it?' asked Walter.

'Bury the bones, I suppose. It's a bit late to do anything else. The constable won't be interested in a crime that took place all those years ago.'

'No,' murmured Walter, 'don't s'pose he would.'

Jon stayed a while longer with Walter and shared a meal of bully beef and beans washed down with strong billy tea, similar to the fare Stan had favoured, and then he took his leave of the old fella, leaving him sitting in his rocking chair, the euro at his feet like an old dog, until the two of them were swallowed up in dust created by the backdraught as he drove along the track back to the graded road.

On the long drive home to Jindalee Jon had plenty of time to reflect. Walter's father probably didn't know that the cave was a sacred site or that there was a pool of permanent water further along the passageway. No wonder the Aborigines were determined to protect what was theirs; it wasn't just the water they were protecting but their heritage. He decided there and then that the bones should be given a proper burial but somehow he would have to find out what that entailed. The trouble would be in finding someone he could ask, because Adie wasn't about to tell him.

CHAPTER 10

In the end it was George who helped him bury the bones from the cave near Kangaroo Soak. Together they'd dug the graves in a spot overlooking the ravines under a late spring sky with clouds scudding overhead. When everything was ready Jon wrapped the bones in cloth and laid them to rest. There were seventeen skulls in all, men's, women's and children's. It was impossible to tell the ages of most of the adults, but for some the remains of grey and grizzled hair indicated those aged Aborigines who had been murdered by Berridge all those years ago.

When the graves had been backfilled they marked each and every one with a cairn of stones. As they finished laying stones on the very last grave, Jon turned to George.

'Do you think we'll be punished?'

'For what?' asked George.

'Burying the bones.'

'Nah, it's better than them being heaped up in a pile and forgotten. Besides, didn't the old fella say there's none of 'em left?'

'That's what Adie told me when I last spoke to him. According to his great-grandfather the whole mob was wiped out.'

'It wasn't Adie's mob then?'

'Don't think so, he'd have had something to say about the bones if they were.'

Jon looked back along the valley, to Berridge's grave, and wondered at the nature of a man who could kill kiddies and old folk in cold blood. Not for the first time his Catholic upbringing made him question what the future held in store for those who sinned. Was

Berridge still in Purgatory? And what about Gerry Worrall who had murdered Aborigines? Was there any justice after death? Or had they been absolved of their sins? He wished he knew, logic told him that death was the end, the body returning to dust, that and nothing else, although he conceded that perhaps a belief in an afterlife would be a comfort to the bereaved.

George lashed the picks and shovels to the pack horses while Jon contemplated the future and where he would be buried when the time came. Unlike Jarrahlong Station, Jindalee had no burial ground. There must have been deaths on the station over the years but perhaps the Aborigines had been buried with no ceremony in unmarked graves. Eli Jackson wasn't buried at Jindalee, but that didn't surprise him. According to Jeb Samuels the man hadn't spent that much time on the station; he'd been too busy travelling, collecting plant and tree specimens, to be bothered about what happened in the middle of the outback. And when he died he'd been living out east, in Sydney; no doubt his last resting place was in a cemetery there.

Burying the bones had given him pause for thought; perhaps he should discuss the matter with Val. Maybe they should choose a suitable place where they would both be buried some day, a family plot similar to the one Alice had near to the great jarrahs on Jarrahlong. If Val agreed, he'd mark out a square a short way from the homestead, a plot with iron railings and a seat for sitting and contemplating the dead and the living. He thought about Stan Colley's lonely grave, a stone's throw from Yaringa Creek and within sight of No Hope Mine, and smiled. Stan had wanted a marker that would last. Granite, he'd said, with the words carved deep, and that's what Jon had ordered for him from Mike Tunstall in Pilkington, together with fancy railings and a rigid granite plinth into which he and Scally had set the railings with molten lead. It was a fitting memorial for the old timer who had spent thirty years of his life searching for the elusive gold reef, the gold that had since paid for Jindalee.

'Y'ready, boss?' called George from his saddle, holding out the bridle of the other horse for him to take.

'Yeah.' Jon glanced up at the afternoon sun already casting long purple shadows in the ravines below them. He mounted his horse and they headed for home without looking back.

* * *

The sun had set by the time they got back to the homestead. Val joined him in the yard just as he finished rubbing down his horse. He took in the anxiety etched on her face. 'Anything wrong, Val?'

'We've had a letter from Harry.'

'Harry Hammond?'

'Yes, it's not Harry's handwriting so I think someone must have written it for him. He's been badly injured; it seems they couldn't cope with his injuries in the Australian Field Hospital and he's been transferred to the American one at Vung Tau.'

Jon frowned. It must be serious if they'd shipped him off to an American facility. 'Did they give any details?'

'No, just that he was goin' to be in hospital for a while and he'd write when he could. What do you think has happened to him, hon?'

'Your guess is as good as mine, Val, but if he's been caught by a grenade or been blown up by a landmine he's likely to be in a bad way.'

Jon swore under his breath, life was a bastard for some. He'd worried about Harry from the moment he'd signed up as a regular in the Australian Army, but Harry had been adamant: I want to make something of my life. I don't want to be reliant on others any more, he'd said. Jon had understood, although it wasn't how he saw his relationship with Harry. And in Harry he'd seen himself at that age. But now what? How would Harry cope if his injuries were as devastating as he imagined? There'd been so much in the news about their boys and the American lads being shipped home double amputees and worse, or blinded, or bedridden with injuries from which they'd never fully recover.

'What shall we do, hon?'

'Write and tell him to come home,' said Jon tersely. 'Tell him we want him home.' Jon didn't have a clue about Army protocol when it came to serious injury. Would they fly him back to an army hospital in Australia? Or would they keep him out in Vietnam? And then what? What if they couldn't get him battle-ready again? What if he was a double amputee, or blind, or both? Would it be an honourable discharge on a pension at twenty-one? 'Where's your God now, Father William?' muttered Jon bitterly as he made his way across the yard to the workshop. And he knew he wasn't being fair, Father William had lost his faith too, in the end. He'd lost it long before he'd hanged himself from the cross-beam in the old laundry at Karundah.

* * *

That night Jon and Val were thinking about bed when they heard hammering on the back door.

Jon looked at his watch, half past nine! He opened the door, wondering who the hell was visiting so late, and saw George standing there.

'We got a problem, boss.'

'What sort of problem?'

'Ollie and Ernie Gilbert have been on the grog. Ollie's out of his head, beatin' his wife. There's hell on, you come quick.'

Jon leaned back and called to Val, 'There's trouble at the camp, Val. I need to go.' He grabbed his boots, flopped on his hat and followed George out to the ute idling next to the picket fence.

They drove in silence, Jon recalling his anger when Ollie and Ernie had failed to turn up for the muster a year back. Then they'd both been in town, drinking. So far he'd been lucky with his men, there'd only been one other occasion when a stockman had returned to camp fighting drunk. The fella had been single and when he'd sobered up Jon had told him to pick up his swag and leave. There'd been muttering among the blacks and resentment, they'd argued it was legal for Aborigines to drink, that they had the right, but he'd ignored them, and their grumbling.

When they reached the camp they heard screaming and wailing coming from Ollie's shack. The children were gathered outside in a frightened huddle while some of the women were hammering on the door, yelling.

It was bedlam as Jon shoved his way through the crush and kicked open the shack door.

Ollie's wife was cowering on the floor, her arms held up protecting herself as Ollie laid into her with a stick.

Jon grabbed it, wrenched it off Ollie and pulled the Aborigine away from her. Outside, he could hear George telling the crowd to leave, that they'd sort things out.

Ollie was still in a fighting mood but so uncoordinated he did little damage.

'What do ya want t'do with him, boss?' asked George once Ollie had calmed down.

Jon shook his head. 'Damned if I know. I suppose we could put him in the storeroom; there's a cot in there where he can sleep it off safely. Can't deal with him now, he's far too drunk. Where's

Ernie, is he back yet?'

George shook his head. 'Dunno, boss, but at least he ain't beatin' up a wife 'cos he ain't got one.'

Jon sighed. 'Keep hold of Ollie while I see if his wife's all right.' Then he indicated to the two women standing a way back to follow him and returned to the shack.

Ollie's children were crowded round their mother, fingers stuffed into their mouths, eyes wide with shock, too traumatised to cry.

'You all right?' he asked, helping the woman to her feet and righting an upturned chair for her to sit on.

She nodded.

Jon watched her settle herself and noted the swollen, bloodshot eye, the split lip and the welts across her back.

'Look after her,' he said to the older of the two women, 'and come and fetch me if you need to.'

The women, too frightened to reply, scuttled over to Ollie's wife to do as he'd said.

Neither Jon, nor George got any sleep that night; they spent it keeping an eye on Ollie. In the long hours before dawn Jon raised the growing number of problems they'd been having with some of the stockmen. 'What do we do, George?' he asked.

'Well, for a start, we need to keep that mongrel, Sid Barton, off the place. He's trouble, everyone here knows you don't allow drink but Sid tells 'em you've no right, that the law says they can and it ain't nothin' to do with you. And he tells 'em you're not payin' a fair wage.'

Shocked, Jon glanced at George. 'Not paying them enough! They get paid the same as our white stockmen, they always have on Jindalee, and on Jarrahlong, you know that.'

George looked uneasy. 'Trouble is, boss, some of 'em now believe Sid. They hang on his every word.'

'And what about everyone else?'

George shrugged.

But Jon wasn't about to let it drop. 'You know the situation, George, stations hereabouts are cutting back on employing blackfellas, but we've kept all ours, fed them, even when they're not earning their keep. And we're training some. Wes comes over and teaches a couple of them basic mechanics, and the best of the stockmen are encouraged to learn about stock management, the women too, those like Doris Mandurrin, she's one of the best Aboriginal stockwomen we've ever had on Jindalee. And what about

67

Ollie's wife? She's really taken to painting after Alistair showed your lad and a few others how to do it. Several of the women had a go, you know that.'

'Yeah,' muttered George, his tone less than enthusiastic.

'Look, I know you don't like Tom painting, but he's good, sold a fair number of canvases, he has. And Ollie's wife, she's earning good money too, and although she doesn't paint in the same way as Tom, you have to admit her work is interesting, all those dots and squiggles. I bought one for my study, and Alistair says his agent has a couple on the wall in his gallery.'

'Ollie'll jus' piss it away,' said George.

'Yeah,' said Jon, 'and I believed that giving them opportunities to earn a fair living was the right thing to do.'

George chewed his lip for a moment. 'It's jus' different for blackfellas, they don' see things in white ways.'

'Ya don't say,' muttered Jon under his breath.

'Yeah, some of the mob see, but too much change too fast, boss. Blackfella pride dented by whitefella. It teks time…and a lot a blackfellas are angry.'

'They don't show it.'

'They're angry, right enough,' said George, 'behind the eyes they's angry.'

'So you're saying I'm wasting my time here.'

'No, boss, some blackfellas see what y'doin'.'

'Like you, George?'

'Yeah, and your mate, Bindi, but others don't, still a big lot of bitterness behind what goes on, a lotta mistrust of whitefellas, and that mongrel, Sid Barton, ain't helpin'.'

'So what do we do?'

'Give it to 'em straight and stick to what y'say. They come back drunk and they're out. Same if they don't turn up for the big jobs when they say they will.'

'I don't mind them going walkabout,' said Jon, 'after all it's part of being an Aborigine.'

'Yeah, but they jus' go off when the mood teks 'em; it's different if it's urgent family business, everyone knows that.'

The pale grey light of dawn brightened the small room and the pair of them watched Ollie snoring on the cot, a dribble of spittle running down his chin and pooling on the mattress.

Jon sighed. 'Ollie's a good bloke; trouble is the drink doesn't suit him.'

'It don' suit most blackfellas,' admitted George after a moment or two. 'The old fellas know that 'n' do their best, but young fellas don' listen to the old fellas no more.'

Jon stood up and stretched the stiffness out of his legs.

'What about this fella when he sobers up, boss?'

'We'll give him another chance, there's no other work for him hereabouts, but if he does it again he's off the station for good. I don't want another night like this one,' said Jon, picking up his hat.

CHAPTER 11

It was a full five months before Harry returned to Jindalee, minus both legs that had been amputated below the knees. Jon was relieved that the twins were away at boarding school. He knew Harry wouldn't want Jamie to see him crippled and he worried about how he was going to manage the meeting when the time came.

In March, a month after his return, Harry was still a bitter and angry man and nothing they said or did pulled him out of his depression and despair. Harry flatly refused to speak to anyone unless he had to, to Noel least of all, which had surprised and shocked everyone, but Jon persisted; he insisted that Harry join them for all his meals and refused to take no for an answer.

One night, as usual, almost four weeks to the day since Harry's homecoming, Jon, Val, Ruby, Noel, Harry and Shirley were taking coffee on the verandah after their evening meal when talk turned to the forthcoming muster and the plan to use the second-hand Cessna Jon had been browbeaten into buying for Ruby.

'Who have you got flying spotter?' asked Jon. 'Have you managed to persuade anyone yet?'

Ruby shook her head. 'And Tom won't, he says I'm the last person he'd trust flying a plane, he says it makes him airsick.'

'And does it?' asked Val.

'Too right it does, we ran out of sick bags within the first half-hour the one time I persuaded him to go up with me.' She turned to Noel. 'So, hows about it, Noel, will you be my spotter?'

'Ruby!' said Val.

Noel shook his head. 'I haven't been up in a plane since the Hurricane.'

No one spoke for several moments, remembering how Noel came

by his terrible injuries.

'I'm shocked you even asked,' said Val, a disapproving look on her face.

Ruby blushed. 'Sorry, Noel, I didn't think.'

'That's all right. I would if I could, but too many bad memories...you know.'

'No worries, Noel, I've just realised I've got a spotter right in front of my nose.'

'Who?' asked Jon.

'Harry.'

Harry roused himself at the mention of his name and no one else spoke, waiting for the violent outburst that Harry was prone to of late. He frowned. 'What was that?'

'Spotter,' said Ruby. 'You're going to be my spotter.'

'I'm bloody not.'

'You bloody are,' snapped Ruby.

'Language!' murmured Val.

Harry flung his empty mug into the garden, then tipped over the occasional table as he grabbed at his wheelchair. But he wasn't fast enough; Ruby had already taken possession and she shoved it off the verandah and into the bushes.

'You bitch!' Harry yelled.

'You can swear all you like, Harry, you're flying spotter in the morning whether you like it or not.'

'And how do you propose to get me in the passenger seat?' snarled Harry.

'At the end of my rifle. I'll wheel your chair over to the plane and you can haul yourself up, you're strong enough, and if you can't manage I'll help you, or Tom will, take your pick.'

Jon caught the flicker of a smile on Noel's face as Ruby and Harry glared at each other.

'You can damned well try,' snapped Harry.

'You bet I will, and if you don't I'll shoot you in your best arm.'

Jon bit back a chuckle, and wiped the smile off his face as Harry turned on him.

'Are you going to let her speak to me like that?' he demanded.

'He's a sook, Jon-Jon,' interrupted Ruby. 'He's too scared to be my offsider, that's what he is, scared...scared I'll down the plane with him in it.' She turned to Harry. 'I'm a damn good pilot and if you weren't so wrapped up in yourself you'd know. Besides, anyone'd think you're the only one who's had a rough time of it over

71

in Vietnam.'

'And what would you know about it?'

'At least you're back home and alive, and you've still got two good arms, at least until tomorrow, and a brain, not like Ray Fox's son, he came back in a box. Is that what you wanted? To be buried six feet under? – 'cos if that's the case then let me know, I'll be happy to oblige.' Ruby got to her feet, righted the occasional table and slammed down her empty coffee cup. 'Breakfast is six sharp; you can't fly on an empty stomach.'

No one spoke as Ruby flounced out. When they heard her bedroom door slam shut Jon leaned over to Val, 'Maybe you should have a word with her about her language,' he suggested.

'And d'you think that would do any good when Ruby has her dander up?' asked Val as she fetched Harry's wheelchair from out of the bushes. 'I'm sorry, Harry; I don't know what's got into her these days.'

Harry heaved himself into his chair. 'She needs a bloody good thrashing,' he muttered as he wheeled himself off the verandah and retired to his own room.

Jon glanced across to Noel and Shirley. 'What do you two make of that?'

'I think that is the best move anyone's made since Harry got home,' said Noel.

'Noel's right,' murmured Shirley, 'Harry needs taking out of himself.'

Jon was inclined to agree with them. Harry had been back four weeks and he was like a crazed dingo; everyone was pussy-footing around him while he took out his pent-up frustration on everyone and everything.

'I know where he's coming from,' said Noel. 'I've been in the place where he is, but someone needs to call his bluff. He has to start living again and feeling sorry for himself is no solution. If you want my opinion you need to back Ruby tomorrow, get Harry up in the plane. Flying spotter might just be the ticket.'

Next morning it was Jon who helped Harry into his chair and wheeled him into the kitchen where Val and Shirley were preparing breakfast. Unusually, Ruby wasn't anywhere to be seen and Jon decided that she'd given up on the idea of getting Harry into the passenger seat. But he was wrong. Ruby arrived just as they were finishing their meal, carrying a rifle. Keeping tight hold of the weapon she grabbed the wheelchair handles, swung the chair and Harry around and shoved him out through the kitchen door, down the ramp and across the yard to the waiting plane.

Even from a distance they could hear the heated argument between the pair of them.

'She'll never get him in the plane,' said Jon. 'Harry's not the sort to take orders from anyone except his platoon commander.'

'You puttin' money on it, hon?' asked Val.

'Twenty,' said Jon.

'I wouldn't if I were you,' murmured Shirley, 'you'll lose it.'

'You're on.' Val spat on her palm and held out her hand to seal the deal.

Jon grinned and shook her spitty hand just as the sound of a gun shot ricocheted around the buildings.

They saw horror and then fury spread across Harry's face and Ruby gesticulate with the gun as Tom heaved Harry up towards the cockpit, Ruby holding the gun level with Harry's good arm. Tom manhandled Harry into the passenger seat while Ruby kept the gun trained on him. Satisfied that Harry was finally settled, Ruby handed Tom the rifle and climbed into the pilot's seat.

Minutes later Jon, Val and Shirley watched as Ruby positioned the Cessna ready for take-off. They stood on the verandah listening to Ruby revving the engine, the throttle fully open. The plane rolled forward gathering momentum until, at optimum speed, Ruby pulled back on the controls and the plane was airborne.

Val smiled. 'That's twenty dollars you owe me.'

After a late evening meal Noel and Shirley retired to their beds leaving Jon, Val and Ruby alone on the verandah. Harry had gone to his room straight after the flight and had refused to come out, even for his evening meal and, for once, Val had taken it to him on a tray while the rest of them dined in the kitchen.

'Harry's in a foul mood, seems to me things didn't go so well,' said Val.

Ruby chuckled. 'He'll get over it.'

'So, what was it really like?' asked Jon. 'Do you think it did him any good?'

'I dunno, he called me a cow when I told him where the sick bags were kept,' she said as she sat on the verandah at his feet.

'Did he!' said Jon.

'Yeah, and he said he'd done more flying than I've had hot dinners.' Ruby frowned. 'Maybe I shouldn't have fired that shot; the bullet could have ricocheted off a pebble and killed someone.'

'Well, it didn't. Anyway, how did Harry do, flying spotter?' asked Jon. 'Did he get used to it?'

Ruby shrugged. 'Maybe. He wasn't too bad once he'd stopped being sick. He wasn't keen on flying close to the ground, said a hundred feet was too low.' She grinned. 'His knuckles were white a few times, especially when we were fairly close to a stand of eucalypts.'

'Poor chap,' murmured Val. 'Where did you go?'

'Started off easy at about a hundred feet over the spinifex and saltbush, then moved to the good grazing on the east side, beyond Will's Bore where there are more trees to skirt around. That's when he started to throw up. I told him to look out for cattle and to yell when he saw any, but every time he looked out of the side window he went green around the gills.'

'He's not goin' to make a spotter then?'

'He might, once he gets used to it.'

'I don't think I could do it.' Val sipped her coffee, a frown creasing her forehead. 'I never really liked it the time Merle and I went up in Chips Carpenter's plane. Just lookin' straight ahead made me feel queasy, never mind the fancy stuff.'

'I tried to get him interested, showed him what the plane could do, tree-hopping, skipping over the ground.' Ruby chuckled. 'He wasn't amused when I said she floats like a dragonfly. He was white about the lips and I did wonder whether he'd start throwing up again. By that stage I'd run out of sick bags so I gave him a boiled sweet to suck and that helped.'

Jon smiled. He could just imagine the two of them, Harry's fury at being forced into the plane at gunpoint, and the indignity of throwing up into a paper bag. And he knew Ruby would have taken perverse pleasure at Harry's discomfort, jollying him along the more he swore, doing a few more swoops and dives just to show him she wasn't going to be intimidated by his fury at her treatment of him.

Jon settled deeper into the rattan chair. Would Harry feel differently about giving the spotting job a go once he'd calmed down, or had they done the wrong thing? No doubt time would tell.

The three of them sat together in companionable silence. It was already dark and cicadas rattled in the bush. The night was balmy, the scent of eucalyptus heavy in the air, and the sky was a beautiful rich blue-black with a net of stars brightening the heavens.

Ruby sat on a cushion at his feet, a half-consumed mug of black coffee in her hand. Jon looked down on her auburn hair, burnished copper in the half-light filtering through the gauzy dining-room curtains that billowed in the light breeze. Ruby was well named; she was a beautiful girl with skin that tanned without burning despite having red hair – thick tresses of the kind that Rossetti favoured in his flamboyant art. But, more importantly, she was her mother's daughter. Ruby didn't look like Val or Berry Greenall, her father, but when it came to personality, her open, honest nature, tenacity, and pluck, and in some situations, like today, sheer devilment, she was her mother's daughter all right, she had guts in spades.

He loved his adopted daughter. He'd loved her from the moment she was born, from the moment he had helped her into the world on the hot and humid December night sixteen years back, and he'd never stopped loving her, just as he'd never stopped loving her mother. He loved her as much as he loved his own boys, more, if he were honest, something he'd never really understood. He glanced at Val and saw her watching him. She smiled, leaned across and squeezed his hand while Ruby rested her back against his legs.

'Jon-Jon—'

He waited; Ruby often began with her pet name for him – the name she'd latched onto when she'd first learnt to talk.

'I think we should take Harry to Dougie Coltrane's place tomorrow.'

'Why?'

'He needs to learn to fly.'

Val sat back in her seat and smiled.

'And how will that help?'

'It'll take his mind off things, and he'll be good at it. Once he stopped being sick he forgot himself, and for a while, back there, he forgot he'd no legs.'

Ruby swivelled round and looked at them both. 'Remember that time when we went to England with Alice and Alistair?'

'Which bit?' asked Jon. 'We did a fair bit of travelling then.' He thought back to the time when they'd visited Alice's nephew, Eric, and Francis, his elder son, who now ran the family farm in Lincolnshire. But then his thoughts shifted to Greg, Eric's younger son. Would they ever see him again? He supposed it was a possibility. They'd learned from Eric that Greg was still living in Australia, in Queensland, not the Territory where Alice thought he'd go. Francis had said Greg was managing a cattle station, that he liked the life, was married with a couple of kids, and had no intention of returning to England.

Jon recalled the glance Alice had given him as they'd listened to Francis's description of where Greg lived, that said: I told you so. Maybe Alice had been right; kicking Greg out of Jarrahlong for forging her signature on a bank loan, jeopardizing the station to bankroll a fruitless search for Chips Carpenter's lost gold reef, had ultimately been the making of him. Perhaps Ruby's treatment of Harry would have the same effect, jolt him out of his self-pity, force him to make the best of a bad job, but only time would tell.

Jon pulled himself back to the present, to Ruby's reminiscences.

'Lincolnshire,' she said, 'when we drove past those airbases, Scampton and Waddington, and we went to that village, Scopwick, or something like that, and you had a beer in the pub there—'

'The Royal Oak.'

'That's the one, Jon-Jon, and we got talking to that old man who told us about the graveyard and where that fella was buried.'

'What fella?'

'The Anglo–American pilot, John Gillespie Magee, who flew for the Canadians.'

'I don't remember that,' said Jon.

'You do,' interrupted Val. 'He was the one who was killed on a trainin' flight; he never ever got to fly his Spitfire in battle.'

Jon frowned, trying to bring a vague memory to the fore. 'Anyway, what about him?' he asked, giving up dredging through the grey matter.

'He was a poet.'

'So!'

'Don't you remember? The old fella recited a sonnet he wrote just before he was killed,' said Ruby.

'That's right, "*High Flight*",' said Val. 'The old man said it was called "*High Flight*" and you wrote it down on the back of an envelope because you liked it, because you were obsessed with flying even then.' Val gazed into the darkness for a moment, remembering. 'He was a nice old chap, he'd flown in the First World War and he said he'd been there, in the churchyard, when the Canadians buried John Magee.'

John's face brightened. 'I recall it now. He took us to the cemetery to show us the grave.'

Ruby spun round barely able to contain herself. 'That's right! And there was a quote from the poem on the gravestone: *"Oh! I have slipped the surly bonds of earth...put out my hand, and touched the face of God."* '

Val sighed. 'He was only a lad when he died, nineteen, that's no age is it?'

'Just like Ray Fox's son. He was nineteen too, nineteen! – younger than Harry,' added Jon.

'And there were so many buried in that tiny churchyard, fifty and more war graves,' said Val quietly.

'It's not surprising when you think about it, Val – all those airfields in Lincolnshire, there were a lot of casualties, a lot who died for their country like our boys are doing out in Vietnam.'

Ruby smiled at them both. 'It's my favourite poem; I learned it off by heart: *"Oh! I have slipped the surly bonds of Earth and danced the skies on laughter-silvered wings...where never lark or even eagle flew..."* It really is a beautiful poem and he captures in words what flying really feels like, chasing *"the shouting wind along..."* we definitely need to get Harry up in a plane, teach him to fly. It'll help take him out of himself.'

'I don't know,' murmured Jon. 'It's not that long since he lost his legs. It's too soon.'

'No it's not. Douglas Bader got straight back into the cockpit. He learnt to fly again and he had no legs.'

'Douglas Bader was already a pilot,' argued Jon, 'he didn't just take up flying on a whim.'

'Well, if we don't do something Harry'll kill himself, I know he will.'

Ruby's words jolted him, he felt his heart jump. 'Don't be stupid, Harry would do no such a thing,' he snapped.

'Ruby's right.' Val touched Jon's arm briefly and held his gaze when he turned to her. 'Harry's in a bad place, hon, he has been for weeks and if we don't do somethin' we may live to regret it.'

'Harry wouldn't,' but his tone belied the words.

Val rested her hand on the back of his. 'Get in touch with Dougie Coltrane and arrange for Harry to have lessons. Doug can put him up in that spare cottage of his and if we send Tom as well he can look after Harry while he's learnin'.'

Jon couldn't avoid the worried expression on Val's face, but he was still not completely convinced about Harry's mental state.

The following morning Harry stayed in his room and it was Val who told Jon he had to do something and fast as they sat at the kitchen table with Noel and Shirley, having breakfast together.

'I don't care what it takes, hon, but you get Dougie to start lessons soon, this weekend preferably. Ruby's right, Harry's hit rock bottom. What do you two think?'

'Well, I think he's a lucky fella. I'd jump at the chance to learn to fly,' said Shirley wistfully. 'He'll forget he's got no legs once he's up there flying.'

Noel nodded. 'Yes, Valerie and Shirley are right. There were more than a few I knew who topped themselves or just gave up when they had no purpose in their lives and it wasn't long before they were in their graves.'

'You didn't though, did you?'

'No, I didn't, do you want to know why?'

Jon nodded.

'No faith – that was my problem. I think you get one spin of the coin in life and, when the coin stops spinning, that's it – finito – end of the road as we know it, and with no eternal life to look forward to. That's why I didn't top myself. The worst there is isn't worse than nothing. I'd rather be here, living like I'm living, with this hideous face, than be buried six feet under feeding the worms.'

'Would you believe me if I told you that we don't even notice your scars now?' said Val.

'Yes, I would, because sometimes I forget too,' said Noel. 'It's only when I catch a glimpse of myself in a mirror, or when I meet someone new and they recoil from how I look, or when I'm in a new situation, that I feel self-conscious. That's why I like living out here, "beyond the mulga line", as you call it.'

CHAPTER 12

It was mid-afternoon when Jon, Harry and Tom set off for the air-field a couple of hundred miles away, taking the shorter route on graded roads east of Jindalee. Harry had said nothing when Jon told him of the plan, not a flicker of emotion had crossed his face, and in the days after the subject hadn't been mentioned. Harry was as tight-lipped as ever with a stony look on his face that would have turned milk sour.

Two hours out from Jindalee, Tom, never one to be silent for long, nudged Harry in the ribs. 'How did ya lose your legs, mate?'

Jon held his breath. He'd asked the same question in the early days, not long after Harry came home, but Harry had declined to answer and Val had warned him by one of her looks not to press it. Later that night, as they lay in bed, she'd said Harry would tell them in his own time, when he was good and ready, but how long would that take? Alice had once said that Stan had never talked about his war years, that no one who'd fought in the First World War did, except Stan had, Stan had told him about the Battle of Fromelles and the rest of it, when he'd been in a bad place himself, still in shock from his time out in the desert, the time he believed he was going to die of dehydration after Curly died. And how long had that been after Stan's time at Fromelles? – getting on for thirty-two years. It was a long time to keep silent.

'Y'step on a landmine or summat?' persisted Tom.

Jon was aware of Harry's posture, the stiffened body, his face turned to look out of the side window. He's not going to answer, Jon thought as he hauled on the steering wheel when they hit a patch of bulldust. The steering wheel snatched and the whole vehi-cle yawed until the tyres gripped firmer ground.

'One of Arnie Goldsmith's mates was killed back in August '66 at the Battle of Long Tan,' said Tom, unaware of Harry's silence.

Jon smiled at Tom's laid-back, chatty style and wondered how long it would be before he wore Harry down.

'He sez eighteen Aussies died in the battle, sez our boys managed to wipe out two hundred and forty-five Viet Cong, really rubbed the bastards' noses in it, they did.'

And still Harry didn't speak.

'Some sez it's a bad war, that we should've kept out of it,' said Tom, ignoring the silence. 'According to me dad, that's what Mister Fox sez. That's right, ain't it, Mister Cadwallader? Mister Fox hates the bloody Government for what it did to his lad.'

'Ray Fox is an angry man,' agreed Jon.

Harry said nothing; there was no flicker of emotion on his face as they chewed through more bulldust. Eventually, even Tom gave up and they continued their journey in silence until they pulled off the road to set up camp for the night.

Tom built the fire while Jon made damper, heated the stew he'd brought with them and made a brew. Later, after they'd eaten and were drinking their billy tea looking up into the night sky, Tom pointed at the full moon rising in the east. 'Do ya reckon them Yanks will put a fella on it?'

Jon glanced up at the moon, took in its dimpled surface, the craters visible even from such a great distance. 'That's the plan; we'll know soon enough whether they pull it off. They say they will. And I don't see why not, they've already had men in space and brought them back safe.'

'It's a bit like Noel sez, ain't it?' said Tom.

'And what's that?'

'That what the Yanks and the Russians are doing is like them fellas way back in history who set off in ships not knowin' if they was goin' to fall off the edge.'

'What are you on about?' asked Harry.

'Noel, he sez fellas used to think that the world was flat, that if they went far enough they'd fall off the edge.'

'Yeah, but it wasn't, was it!' Harry couldn't keep the sneer off his face, or out of his voice. 'In any case, going into space is different to sailing across an ocean.'

'Not if ya thought you'd never get back; them early explorers were like our fellas today explorin' space,' argued Tom.

'Anyway, how far is it to the moon?' asked Harry.

'Noel sez it depends on the orbit, but the average is goin' on two hundred and forty thousand miles.' Tom turned to Jon. 'That's right, ain't it?'

Jon shrugged. 'Haven't a clue.'

'Yeah, it is, and accordin' to the paper they're goin' for a moon landin' in July. And that big dish, that radio telescope thing at Parkes Observatory, is goin' to be trackin' it. That's what it said in the paper.'

It's hell of a long way, mused Jon, glancing up at the moon again; it was nine thousand miles back to England and that journey took long enough, even on a plane, so God knows how long it would take astronauts to get to the moon. He suddenly doubted that the Yanks could do it.

'Back in 'Nam there were more than a few occasions when we thought we'd never get back,' said Harry quietly.

Jon held his breath, not wanting to put Harry off.

'Ya mean when y'lost ya legs?' said Tom.

'Yeah, and before that, when we were ambushed by the Viet Cong...the bastards.'

'So, how did y'lose ya legs?'

'Clearing a village of the Viet Cong, the bastards were dug in, weren't they, so we went in with our APCs...'

'APCs?'

'Armoured Personnel Carriers. We fired a round into those houses where the Viet Cong were holed up, and where we had to we fought them hand-to-hand. It was a bloodbath, that I can tell you. There was mortar, machine gun and rifle fire, not the safest place to be by a long shot.' A faint smile creased Harry's face at the unintentional play on words.

'Were ya hit by a shell?' asked Tom.

'Rocket propelled grenade, it landed at my feet and exploded on impact.'

'Cor, mate! So how did ya get outta there?'

'One of the squad pulled me out and then I was airlifted in a chopper back to the field hospital, but there was too much damage for our boys to deal with so they shipped me over to the American medical facility at Vung Tau.'

'I can't begin to imagine what it's been like for you,' said Jon finally. 'But, I'll tell you this for nothing, we're all pleased you survived, legs or no legs.'

'Yeah,' said Harry in a tone that left Jon in no doubt that he wasn't convinced.

'Yes.' Jon's tone reflected the vehemence he was feeling as he glanced at Harry's prosthetics. 'You've lost your legs, and you've still a long way to go, it's going to take time to adjust—'

'It's been over six months already,' said Harry.

'I know, but it could have been worse.'

'Ya reckon?' said Harry, rapping on one of his tin legs with his knuckles.

Jon didn't reply, there was no point, Harry wasn't ready to look to the future yet, he was still coming to terms with the past, and Jon knew better than most that recovery took time. He added wood to the fire to last the night, and rolled out the swags for himself and Harry. 'You need any help?'

'Nah,' said Harry, 'I can manage, thanks.'

Jon lay back, his blanket round him for warmth, looking up at the stars. What was it Stan Colley said? – Life can be a bit of a bastard. Well, Stan hadn't been far wrong.

They arrived at the airfield mid-morning and Jon left Harry and Tom with Dougie Coltrane having arranged to pick them both up in ten days' time.

CHAPTER 13

Four months after Harry took up flying he decided to return home to England, to try and find his mother. They'd all been sitting round the big table in the kitchen eating their evening meal when he broached the subject.

'Don't you think you should send a letter first?' suggested Jon, knowing that Harry had an address for his mother.

'I did, months ago, but she hasn't replied.'

'She might have moved house,' said Val. 'Maybe she got married again, and if she left no forwardin' address they wouldn't be able to deliver the letter.'

Noel caught Harry's dismissive look. 'Anything could have happened. Didn't you say she's from London?'

'Yeah, the East End.'

'Yes, well, you know that parts of it were pretty much blitzed to hell and back in the last war, especially the East End and the dock areas. When you left England it was the mid-fifties, there was still war damage and rebuilding going on, maybe she decided to move away.'

'She won't leave London,' said Harry. 'She's a Londoner, born and bred. She'll only ever leave the place in a coffin.'

'Maybe she died,' murmured Shirley, 'people do.'

'It's a possibility,' Harry admitted after a moment or two. 'And there again she might not.'

'True,' said Jon. 'When are you planning on going?'

'Soon as I can arrange it, early August, I thought.'

'Well, I think you're daft,' muttered Shirley under her breath.

'What was that?' snapped Harry.

'You're daft, Harry. It don't do to go back. You won't catch me going back to bloody England; they can stuff the bloody place up their bloody arses for all I care.' Shirley drew a deep breath. 'None of them ever gave a stuff about me when they shipped me over here.'

Everyone stared at Shirley, their mouths open. It was the most they'd heard her string together in the year and a half she'd been living with them and never had they heard her speak so vehemently about anything before.

Noel grinned, pulling his badly burned face into a gargoyle smile. 'Didn't know you felt so passionately about it all, Shirl.'

Shirley turned on him, her eyes flashing. 'You don't know shit, Noel.'

No one else spoke, even Harry didn't have a comment and he was never one to be short of something to say.

'You like Australia then?' asked Noel eventually, the ugly smile still on his face.

'I didn't say that.'

'Well, what then?'

'I like it here,' she murmured, looking down at her empty plate, her face bright scarlet, 'this place,' she said, tapping the table.

Jon glanced at Val, and imperceptibly raised an eyebrow. Shirley had never given them a hint as to how she felt about living at Jindalee, but she'd never once tried to run away, and seemed happy enough doing the chores around the house – the cleaning, washing and baking, and maintaining the vegetable patch that they expected in exchange for her wages.

'No one beats you here,' she added.

'You mean the Kennilworths?' asked Harry who had heard all about how Shirley came to be living at Jindalee.

'And the rest,' muttered Shirley. She picked up her plate and the empty one in front of Harry, carried them over to the sink, and then cleared away the rest while Val took the fruit pie from the oven and served up dessert.

'Why don't we go with Harry?' said Val.

Jon looked up in surprise.

'It must be gettin' on for three years since we were last there.'

'But you said you didn't want to go back again.'

'Yeah, well, I did say that back then, but that was straight after the damn great row I had with my mother over Ruby, but Mam isn't gettin' any younger, she'll be risin' sixty-five come March.

And life's too short to hold a grudge. What do ya say, hon?'

'I don't need child-minders,' said Harry. 'I'm perfectly capable of getting myself to England.'

Val laughed. 'You dozy idiot, we know that, you could even kangaroo hop yourself there in the Cessna if you wanted, but it'd be nice for us too.' Her face lit up. 'We could stop over in Singapore on the way, it'd be fun. I really like Singapore. Did you ever go there on your leave, Harry?'

Harry shook his head. 'Never got out of Vietnam.'

'That's fixed then, we'll fly and stop over in Singapore for a while, have a proper holiday, go to Raffles for a gin sling and dinner, visit the Botanical Gardens and take a boat ride around the harbour…and I want to visit Little India and buy some more spices, and visit Chinatown. I love Chinatown. Oh, and I want to go to the Thieves' Market on Lavender Street. You'll love it, Harry, it's a bonza place to pick up a bargain.'

Val's enthusiasm was infectious. Noel beamed at her. 'And what about us?'

'I'll bring you back some China tea, from Chinatown how about that?'

'What about Ruby?' said Jon.

'What about her?' said Val. 'Someone has to be here and keep an eye on the place and on the Kennilworths.'

'She's not old enough.'

Harry laughed. 'Ruby's sixteen going on thirty.'

Noel chuckled. 'Harry's right.'

'And what about you?' Val stared pointedly at Jon. 'You were more or less runnin' Jarrahlong when you were her age. And Ruby will be chuffed that you trust her enough to look after the place for a month or so?'

'But—'

'No buts, hon. She's already spent a lorra time runnin' Jarrahlong while Jim Sandy's been recoverin' from his operation, but Jim's back on his feet now, and it's about time she was back home, we've hardly seen anythin' of her these last few weeks.'

'I'm still not sure it's such a good idea?'

'Why? It's not as if it's midsummer, is it? It's winter so it'll be a bit easier to manage things and she's got George, he can run the place with his eyes closed, between 'em they'll be fine.'

Jon knew he was on a hiding to nothing when Val had made her mind up, but he was still not convinced it was the right thing to do, it was a lot to put on Ruby's shoulders.

Val took in the uncertainty on Jon's face. 'Ruby's also got Alice and Alistair to turn to if the worst comes to the worst. And Shirley, Shirley will keep an eye on everyone, won't you, Shirl?'

'Too right I will,' said Shirley, a sparkle in her eyes.

'And Noel, Noel will be here.'

'You betchya,' he said, mimicking Val's accent, 'you won't find me swappin' Jindalee for England any time soon,' he smiled at Shirley and nodded in her direction. 'I'm with her, I like it here.'

Jon glanced at Shirley and saw a pinkish tinge rising in Shirley's cheeks. Not once had she complained when he'd insisted she attend the extra lessons with Noel, alongside the Karundah lads, when she'd first come to live with them. Had he missed something? Surely not! Noel was forty-plus if he was a day. But, there and again, some women liked older men and Val always said he was the last to know what was going on. Was she right? He stole a look at Noel, but Noel's open face, scarred as it was, showed no sign that he'd noticed Shirley's discomfort. One sided then, a pity, thought Jon.

'Are you taking the piss, Noel?' snapped Shirley.

'Good God, no!' said Noel. 'I was agreeing with you, and I mean it, I like it here too.'

Shirley looked at Noel, weighing up his sincerity, then she shrugged and turned back to Val. 'We could always phone you if there's a problem,' she suggested.

'Shirley's right,' agreed Noel, 'so long as you give us a contact number.'

'There's always my sister's, I suppose,' said Val.

Jon scowled; it felt as if he was being railroaded into taking the trip to England.

'So, hows about it, hon? The boys are at boardin' school, Ruby will enjoy the responsibility and the challenge and I'm ready for a holiday. I deserve one, lookin' after you so well for all these years.' She stopped to draw breath. 'Besides I'm fed up with hearin' all the talk about that company drillin' on Wanndarah station. It's all anyone has talked about for the last few weeks.'

'And that's another thing,' said Jon, 'what if they find the nickel they're looking for on Wanndarah and decide to buy the mineral rights on our property? We could get back to Jindalee to find them drilling in our greenstone belt.' Jon frowned. 'I should have done something about it fifteen months back.'

'Well, if they do, they do. We're goin' to England with Harry, I need the break and that's the end of it. If you're really worried you can buy the mineral rights to that greenstone belt just as soon as we get back.'

Jon knew when he was beaten and shook his head in resignation. 'What can I say?'

Val grinned. 'You can try "Yes" hon.' She kissed him on the cheek, then turned and beamed at Harry. 'That's fixed, Harry. You've got company.'

PART II

[August 1969]

CHAPTER 14

Jon, Val and Harry flew into London on a beautiful August day, with the sun comfortably warm like an Australian spring. They took the train into central London and booked into one of the smaller hotels not far from Piccadilly Circus and then, after an early dinner, took in a play, Agatha Christie's *"The Mousetrap"* that Val wanted to see.

The following morning, over breakfast, Jon suggested they take the tube to Forest Gate in the East End and hire a taxi to take them round to the last known address for Harry's mother.

Jon reached for another piece of toast. 'Maybe a neighbour will know where she's living if she's moved.' He glanced at Harry. 'Are you sure you want to do this?'

Harry nodded. 'Sure as I'll ever be. Maybe she's matured a bit, not so brash as she was back in the bad old days.'

'She'll be pleased to see you.' Val rested her hand on Harry's arm. 'I know she will. But it'll be a bit of a shock for her when she learns about you losin' your legs out in Vietnam.'

Harry grinned. 'I can't exactly hide it, can I? – what with the gait I have, and the sticks.'

'She's your mother, she'll just be pleased you're still alive,' reassured Val.

The road was lined with Victorian terraced houses that had escaped the Blitz but some looked drab and uncared for in the summer sun. A few cars were parked in the street, Fords mainly and a Morris or two, but apart from the postman the street looked deserted. They waited for the postman to approach.

91

'Mrs Hammond still live here?' asked Harry.

The postman looked Harry up and down, took in the sticks and the ungainly stance. 'Yeah, Number 28.' He glanced at his watch. 'You'll be lucky if you find her up this early.' And off he went, delivering more letters, whistling as he did so.

Jon glanced at his watch, seventeen minutes past eleven, what sort of woman stayed in bed until almost midday? Was Harry's mother still on the game? He imagined a raddled, forty-year-old slattern with bottle-blonde hair, rouged cheeks and too much cheap perfume. He felt a shiver ripple down his spine. He damn well hoped not, not at her age, it would be too embarrassing for everyone.

'We'll wait in the street,' said Jon. 'It's a bit much if we all turn up on her doorstep.'

Harry hesitated.

Val sat on the low wall next to Number 28. 'You can pop out and tell us if you want us to come back later.'

Harry nodded, made his way to the front door and knocked. After some time, the door opened a crack and a middle-aged woman peered out from round the door. 'Yeah, What d'ya want?' she snapped, a half-smoked cigarette dangling out of the side of her mouth.

'It's me, Harry.'

'Harry?' Mrs Hammond opened the door wider and looked Harry up and down. 'Harry's in Australia.'

'I know, I'm visiting. Can I come in?'

She glanced down the street. 'And who're them?'

'Friends of mine.'

'From Australia?'

Harry nodded.

'I ain't dressed; you'll 'ave t'give me a minute.' She slammed the door in his face and Harry turned back to them and shrugged.

The wait seemed interminable, but eventually the door opened again and this time Mrs Hammond was wearing slacks with a low cut sweater revealing a deep cleavage. 'Ya better come in,' she said, 'and bring ya friends.'

'Not me,' said Jon, 'I'll wait for you out here.'

Val pulled a face, but Jon had already turned away and when he looked back the door was closed.

While he waited, Jon strolled down the street taking in the tidy front gardens, only one or two unkempt and uncared for. The lack of movement on the street surprised him, all these people living in close proximity to each other and yet the place looked deserted. He couldn't remember it being the same in Liverpool when he was a kid. Then, he and his mates would spend hours in the street kicking a football about, or sitting on the kerbs playing jacks and chatting while the women gossiped as they washed the windows or scrubbed the stone steps. There'd be mams yelling at their older kids to look after the younger ones, or shouting for one of their offspring to nip to the corner shop for milk or more bread. No, Liverpool was nothing like this empty street. His mind drifted to the front room not half a dozen houses away, and Harry. He hadn't been convinced that Harry searching out his mother was such a good idea. Leopards didn't change their spots and he was sure it would all end in tears. Val, on the other hand, had been far more optimistic. Some women are not good with youngsters, but Harry's a grown man now, a good-looking bloke, any mother would be proud of him and what he's made of himself. It'll be fine, she'd said, you'll see.

Jon glanced at his watch – half an hour gone; maybe Val was right. The door, two houses along, opened and a bloke stepped out into the street wearing a black overcoat over grey pinstripe trousers, a grey shirt and black tie, and an Astrakhan hat. Jon noted the darker skin tone and the neatly clipped beard. Eastern European, Jon guessed from the look of him. Jon nodded a greeting as the man approached, but the fella looked straight through him as if he didn't exist. Jon dismissed the reaction. Back home even your worst enemy would give you the time of day.

Another five minutes passed and the door of Number 28 finally opened. Val appeared, and then Harry, who pulled the door shut behind him. When Jon joined them Val's smile was forced. 'I think we should go and do some of the sights while we're here, the Tower of London and Buck House for starters,' she said in an over-bright voice.

'How did it go?' asked Jon.

'Not now, hon. I'll tell you later.' She took Harry's arm and turned back to Jon. 'A cup of tea and a toasted teacake wouldn't go amiss either. Keep your eyes peeled for a Lyon's Corner House or somethin' similar.'

Jon took in the warning look in her eyes and didn't argue. 'We'll get a cab at the end of the road,' he said and he fell into step behind the two of them.

* * *

Jon stripped off his underwear and slipped into bed. He lay back watching Val as she brushed her hair and then applied face cream.

'Harry's barely spoken a word all day, so what happened back there in Number 28, Val?'

Val finished rubbing cream on her face, slipped off her dressing gown, got into bed and snuggled up against him as she always did. 'Well, it was okay at first, we all sat down in the sittin' room, and his mother gave us the once over.'

'What do you mean?'

'You know, she looked at what we were wearin', my diamond ring, Harry's watch that we bought him for his twenty-first, our shoes.'

'Shoes?'

'Yeah, shoes, Jon. Shoes are always a dead giveaway…if ya wearin' expensive shoes you're—'

'Well heeled.'

'Exactly, hon. And Harry's and mine, they're the well-heeled type.'

'So, she gave you the once over, then what?'

'She was askin' about where we lived, and Harry told her about bein' in the Australian army and servin' out in Vietnam and gettin' injured, which came as a bit of a shock.'

'In what way?'

'She didn't realise he'd got prosthetic legs.'

Jon sat up in bed. 'But it's obvious, the way he walks, the sticks.'

'I know, but for some reason she didn't put two and two together. Maybe it was the shock of seein' Harry again after so long. Just imagine what it must have been like for her thinkin' her son was livin' nine thousand miles away and him suddenly turnin' up on the doorstep. Anyway, that – him havin' no legs – changed everything. Afterwards, the atmosphere was decidedly chilly, especially when Harry told her he'd been invalided out of the Army.'

'What did Harry say?'

'Well, he sort of ignored the atmosphere and told her he was thinkin' of returnin' home to live in England.'

'He said that?'

'Yeah, said he wanted to get a job flyin'.' Val's face hardened. 'The bitch laughed in his face, told him he didn't stand a cat-in-hell's chance, that no one would employ a cripple when there were

plenty of able-bodied men to choose from. Poor Harry, all the colour drained from his face. He looked winded, as if someone had
punched him in the belly. And then that bloody woman said that if
he thought he could live with her, he'd better think again, that she
wasn't about to start lookin' after a cripple at her time in life, son
or no son. Seems she doesn't want her life ruined because he
hadn't been more careful out in Vietnam.'

'She said all that!'

'And the rest. It all came pourin' out, how he'd been useless as a
kid, that havin' him had cost her two marriages because she'd got
him hangin' off her coat tails. You could say she didn't mince her
words, that's for sure.'

'And that's when you left?'

'Not quite. She looked me up and down again, turned to Harry
and suggested he should keep me sweet, that a rich, older woman
was bound to be lookin' for a bit on the side. And that's when I
slapped her.'

Jon laughed. 'I'm surprised it took you so long.'

'She deserved it.'

'What did Harry say?'

'He didn't say anythin', he just stood up, briefly looked at her
snivellin' on the sofa, rubbin' her cheek, and then we left.'

Jon could picture the scene and the turmoil Harry would have
been going through. The trouble was his mother's reaction wasn't
totally unexpected, any mother who had done to her son what
she'd done to Harry wasn't going to welcome him with open arms,
not unless there was something in it for her. And, as she saw it,
Harry was only going to be a burden. But the fact was Harry would
never be a burden on anyone, he wasn't the type.

'What do we do now?' murmured Jon.

'I don't know, hon. Do you think Harry will come back with us?'

'He's a proud man, he didn't like it when we paid for his flying
lessons. It took me all my time to convince him that he'd find some
way to repay us and it was only because I'd said that that he finally
agreed to give it a go.'

'What about his flyin'. Why don't we set him up so he can develop a business back out in Oz.'

'Doing what?'

'Cattle musters. The Johnson's are doin' it and we've started,
there are bound to be plenty of cattle-station managers that'd give
it a go, I'm sure of that, both in Western Australia and in the

Northern Territory. What if we bankroll him, on a proper business footin', a loan to be repaid over twenty-five years, once he's up and runnin'? And maybe he should consider helicopters as well as fixed wing; we've said ourselves that a helicopter would be better over on the north-eastern side when we're workin' the break-aways.'

'It's a thought,' agreed Jon. 'Maybe a partnership would be better; we provide the equipment, he deals with developing the business and maintenance, what do you think?'

'I think it's a bonzer idea. All we've got to do is sell it to Harry.'

The next morning, at breakfast, Jon broached the subject with Harry.

'What are you going to do now, Harry? Are you still planning on staying in England?'

'Straight up, I haven't a clue; me ma clean took the wind out of me sails. But maybe she's right, getting a job is going to be more difficult than I thought.'

'We've got a proposition to make, Val and me.'

'You don't have to do any more; I'm already in your debt.'

'We don't see that,' said Jon.

'The flying lessons.'

'Right, the flying lessons, which brings me to our proposition, how many chopper pilots do you know, blokes from your army days, who are no longer in the military?'

Harry glanced at Jon and then at Val. 'Only a couple, why?'

'What sort of fellas are they?'

'Well, Chris Sudbury's straight as a die. He pulled a lot of blokes out of sticky situations back out in 'Nam; I heard say that he could turn a bird on a sixpence and fly it through a gap a foot wider than the blade span. Never saw him do it though, but I've heard he's got a job with a firm out east somewhere.'

'And the other bloke.'

'Nat…Nathaniel Gregson, don't know that much about him. He's a bit of a wide boy, the sort that does deals on the side. If you needed something Nat could get it, no questions asked. It was his wheeler-dealing that got him his dishonourable discharge.'

'What's he like as a chopper pilot?' asked Jon.

'So, so. Why?'

Val smiled at Harry. 'We're thinkin' of starting a new business

96

and we're goin' to need your expertise.'

'A partnership,' said Jon. 'You interested?'

'Depends what it is.' Harry leaned back as their full English breakfasts arrived.

Jon sprinkled salt and pepper on his eggs. 'We are thinking of developing the mustering business, offering a service to other station owners, for a price of course. What do you think?'

Harry bit into a sausage and chewed it, thinking.

'As you know, we all muster cattle and sheep at different times, so there's scope for a mustering business especially if we consider mustering in Western Australia and in the Northern Territory.' Jon shovelled more egg and bacon into his mouth, letting the idea develop in Harry's mind.

Val glanced up from her breakfast after giving Harry time to reflect on the offer. 'Would Nat be interested, do you think?'

'Chris might have been, not so sure about Nat. But the cost—'

'Val and I will fund it.'

Harry gave Jon a sceptical look. 'You're talking big bucks; second hand 'copters don't come cheap; and we're already using the Cessna.'

'I know, but Val thinks there's a place for choppers when we're mustering inhospitable terrain. We'd need both, fixed wing and choppers.'

'Kill yourself if you keep swapping from one to the other, ain't good practice.'

'Exactly, that's why we think it'd be best if you do the fixed wing, and someone else the choppers, but you'd manage the whole kit and caboodle. What do you say?'

'I'll think about it.'

'Fair enough, in the meanwhile we'd like you to come with us to Liverpool. We've got family to visit while we're over here, and you can see how the other half live,' joshed Jon. 'And I'll show you where I grew up, until I got shipped out to Australia. As I've told you before, you're not the only child migrant around here.'

Harry wiped his mouth on his napkin and grinned. 'That so! And what about you, Val? Were you a child migrant?'

Jon laughed. 'No, she wasn't, she met me when I was rising seventeen and fell for my blond good looks and charming personality. When I returned to Oz she couldn't live without me, she followed me to Charlestown, and seduced me.'

Val chuckled. 'He's lyin'.'

'Half lying,' said Jon.

'Which half?' asked Harry.

Val smiled. 'Well, I never seduced him.'

CHAPTER 15

In the end they decided against staying at the Adelphi, both agreed it would have been too complicated. Jon was mindful of the half truths he'd told on earlier visits home. Further, he preferred that people believed them to be less wealthy than they were so the smaller hotel on Renshaw Street suited them just fine.

'Yours first or mine?' queried Val as they unpacked.

'Yours.' Jon took out a shirt and hung it on a coathanger. 'Would you prefer to meet them on neutral ground?'

'Like where?'

Jon grinned. 'Dinner at the Adelphi?'

Val smiled. 'I'd prefer a Berni Inn. I like the way they cook their steaks.'

'I'm not sure there is one in Liverpool.'

'Bound to be, they're all over the place.'

It turned out that Val's sister, Evelyn, had other plans: they were invited for lunch in the garden at their brand new home, the one they'd had built over Formby way, and her mother, Mrs Rayner, was going to be there too.

'No one here knows anything about Jindalee, Harry,' said Jon as the three of them sat in the back of a taxi on the way to Formby. 'They know we're doing all right, but that's all, and that's all they need to know. None of them have ever wanted to visit, and I doubt they're ever likely to. Truth be told, and as Val will tell you herself, there's not a lot of love lost between her and her family.'

Harry glanced at Val, simulated zipping his lips, and grinned.

The Franklins' house was constructed of red brick with large bay windows. It sat back from the road at the end of a sweeping drive that curved round a flamboyant ornamental fountain. Either side of the drive were extensive flower beds planted with petunias, begonias, salvias, pansies and nasturtiums that were a riot of summer colour. The taxi pulled up outside the imposing portico and the three of them alighted as the front door opened.

Evelyn stepped out, dressed in her casual best: stone-coloured slacks, cherry-red overblouse and wedge sandals; her dyed copper-coloured hair was combed into a French pleat, and she wore enough gold jewellery to open a shop. Evelyn beamed when she saw them, flung her arms around Val and kissed her, and then did the same to him.

'It's great to see y'both, doesn't seem like three years since y'were last over, does it?' Evelyn hugged Val again. 'I've missed ya, our kid.'

Bob Franklin too gave Val a brief hug, shook Jon's hand and then Harry's when Jon introduced him. Bob turned to present Duane, their only child, but changed his mind.

'Take y'hands out of y'pockets, lad, and wipe that gormless look off y'face,' he ordered.

Duane did as told, his face scarlet.

Jon felt sorry for him, he was only a couple of months older than Ruby, although he seemed younger.

'We're through in the gardin,' chirruped Evelyn, seemingly unaware of the atmosphere around her. 'Mam's waitin' on us there. Her knee's givin' her gyp, the arthritis, y'know.' She ordered Duane to take their coats then led them through into the lounge with a cream shag-pile carpet, leather seating, side tables with larva lamps glooping distorted bubbles through vibrantly coloured oil, and a glitzy mirror-backed bar kitted out with fancy optics, an array of glasses and a plastic pineapple ice bucket.

Val stopped to admire the décor as was expected. 'I like the cream colour scheme.'

'Y'do!' Evelyn beamed, clearly delighted with the comment. 'Bob said I was mad to get the shag-pile, said it'd show the dirt and that I'd catch me heels in it and go flyin'.'

'And have you?' asked Jon.

'Nah, I pick me feet up, don't I. Mam don't like it either, she sez it looks cheap, sez I should have bought an Axminster.'

'Well, it's very nice.' Val sat down on the nearest leather sofa for a moment, then stood up and patted it. 'I like the suite, very smart, and comfortable.'

'Should be, it cost an arm and a leg.' Evelyn giggled. 'I keep tellin' Bob there're no pockets in a shroud when he complains about how much I'm spendin'. Anyway, we'd best go out on to the terrace, Mam'll be wonderin' where we've got to.' She ushered them through the French doors and out on to the flagged patio area where Mrs Rayner sat in a Lloyd Loom chair, her bad leg propped up on a cushioned Lloyd Loom stool.

Val leant down to peck her mother on the cheek and Jon followed suit when he realised what was expected. He noticed Mrs Rayner's rouged cheeks, her plucked eyebrows and pencilled-in arches that gave a permanently surprised look to her face, and the scarlet lipstick that left imprints on the glass whenever she sipped her drink. Mrs Rayner was similarly attired to Evelyn, but to Jon's eye mutton dressed as lamb best described his mother-in-law. He thought no one her age and as broad in the beam as she should wear slim-fitting slacks, or reveal as much cleavage. Old habits, he thought, glad that Val couldn't look tarty even if she tried.

'Nice property,' commented Jon appreciatively after the introductions and the welcoming glass of something sparkling.

'We 'ad it built special, didn't we, hon?' rattled on Evelyn. 'We've got five ensuite bedrooms, all with bidets.'

Harry grinned. 'Bidets!'

'Yeah, a Frog invention for washin' yer bum,' said Bob dryly. 'Don't know how we managed before.'

'And y'should see our dressin' room, it's en..or..mous with a walk-in wardrobe. I bet y'don't have nuthin' like it out in Australia,' she added, her eyes fixed on Jon.

Jon pictured their large bedroom back at Jindalee with an adjacent bathroom and fitted wardrobes – one each – constructed of the finest jarrah wood and finished with polished bronze handles. He inclined his head in agreement. 'You know Australia.'

'Duane sez yous thirty years behind over there.' Evelyn patted Val on the arm, 'Never mind, our kid, one day.' Then her face lit up. 'Maybe we could trot along to Lewis's, y'can order the stuff y'want and gerrit shipped out to Australia. What d'ya say?'

Jon noted Duane's embarrassment at his mother's chatter and changed the subject. 'Trade's good, I take it, Bob.'

'Y'can't go wrong with scrap, mate. That's where all this comes from, and the foreign holidays, and private school for our Duane.'

'And the Jag. Don't forget the Jag,' said Evelyn. 'It's metallic cherry-red with a walnut dash and real leather upholstery. You'll love it, Val.'

Harry chipped in. 'How do you like the motor, Bob?'

'Beautiful, she drives like a dream. Our Evelyn always wanted a Jag, didn't ya, queen?'

Evelyn nudged Val. 'Come a long way from Bridge Street, ain't we?'

'Too right, you have,' said Val with feeling.

'So, 'ow did y'lose y'legs then, my mate?' asked Bob during a gap in the conversation.

'Rocket propelled grenade in Vietnam.'

'Yous a Yank then?'

Both Jon and Harry looked at Bob and then at each other.

'He's an Aussie,' said Val.

Bob looked taken aback. 'What's an Aussie doing fightin' a Yank war?'

'It's our war, too,' said Jon, 'we've had blokes in 'Nam since '62.'

'Well, ya live and learn, don't ya!' said Bob surprise written on his face. 'Did y'know that, son?'

Duane ignored the question and the conversation moved on.

'So what were ya doing out there, Harry? Helpin' the Yanks out?'

'The Government wants to keep the Commies from overrunning the Far East, Bob. Some say if no one stops them they'll sweep down through Indonesia and the Torres Straight and then it'll be Australia next.'

'Well, I'll be damned! I nevva knew we had Aussies out in 'Nam. So what y'goin' to do with y'self now yous a cripple and all?'

Jon winced, when it came to tact Bob had about as much as Val's mother.

'I'm starting up a mustering business.'

'Mustering?'

'Rounding up sheep and cattle using fixed-wing planes and heli-copters.'

'S'pose you'll be helpin' Jon and our Valerie out on their place, then?'

'Yeah,' said Harry, 'that's the general idea.'

Jon glanced at Val and caught the half smile, so they had sold the idea to Harry after all! He turned to Duane. 'What are you going to do after you've finished school, Duane?'

'He's comin' into business with me, ain't ya, son?' said Bob before Duane could answer for himself.

Jon noticed the sullen look on Duane's face and felt the tension between the two of them. 'So, Bob, I take it your business is still expanding.'

Duane caught Jon's eye. 'I want to join the police, Uncle Jon, the CID.'

'Ya what!' growled Bob, his face hardening even as he spoke.

Jon saw a nerve twitching in Bob's jaw, saw the gritted teeth.

'Over my dead body,' snarled Bob. 'We don't want no pigs in this family, and that's that.'

Duane's skin turned white and then flushed scarlet. Without a word, he turned to leave.

'And y'needn't slink off to y'room, kidda, we've got guests, or haven't ya noticed,' snarled his father.

Bob turned his attention back to Jon and strived to lighten the tone. 'Yous got lads, aint ya? S'pose they'll be runnin' the station one day.'

'No,' said Jon. 'Jamie hates the place, he wants to join the army as soon as he's old enough and David hasn't got a practical bone in his body, he'll probably end up an academic studying geology or something similar. No, the only one likely to end up managing Jindalee is Ruby.'

Duane looked up at the mention of his cousin's name. 'She's only my age, isn't she?'

'That's right, a couple of months younger than you,' said Val.

'And you'd let her run Jindalee?' said Duane, a shocked look on his face.

Val smiled. 'Yes, she's runnin' it now; someone needs to be in charge while we're away.'

'Yous gone and left y'daughter in charge!' said Bob in disbelief, his jaw dropping at the thought of a slip of a lass running a station in the middle of the outback.

'Yeah, she's damned good at it, better than me at her age,' admitted Jon, 'and she's got George if she needs advice.'

'Who's George?' asked Bob.

'My Aboriginal overseer.'

'Y'd trust a black?'

'With my life,' said Jon, 'with my life.'

'Can I visit you?' asked Duane.

Everyone focused on Duane for several seconds, taken aback by the request.

Val responded first. 'Of course you can, Duane, so long as your parents don't mind. It'd be nice to have you stay; you can get to know your cousins better.'

'What a good idea!' Evelyn beamed. 'He could go next summer, in the hols, couldn't he, Bob? He gets seven weeks, don't ya, son?'

'And what about the cost? It ain't cheap flyin' to Perth, I'll bet,' grumbled Bob.

'I can use my Post Office savings,' said Duane.

'That won't get you as far as the airport and—'

'Bob, we can afford it, it'll do 'im good. He ought to see a bit more of the world. It'd be an education.'

She's not wrong there, thought Jon.

'I'll think about it,' said Bob.

'Aw, Dad—'

'I said, I'll think about it,' growled Bob.

Lunch was taken on the patio around the expensive new garden furniture that Jon guessed had been bought in especially if the sale's label was anything to go by. Evelyn had ordered in a *"cold collation"*, the description used by the firm she'd ordered it from, consisting of egg and bacon flan, Scotch eggs, vol-au-vents, various salads and beer, and more of the sparkly stuff. Mrs Rayner didn't miss an opportunity to tell them how well Bob and Evelyn had done for themselves. She crowed about the manicured lawns, the architect-designed house, the interior decoration, the new Jaguar, the holidays abroad and the private education for *our* Duane. Finally, Mrs Raynor pointed to Evelyn's new diamond eternity ring that Bob had bought for her.

'Ain't it beautiful, Val? There's one and a half carats in that there ring of our Evelyn's,' boasted Mrs Rayner. 'Bob bought it for their weddin' anni the other week. Yours is nice enough, but fake's always a bit over the top, don't ya think?'

Jon glanced at Val's diamond ring and said nothing – if Val's ignorant mother couldn't recognise quality diamonds then who was he to tell her?

Evelyn was clearly embarrassed by her mother's comment and changed the subject. She turned to Jon. 'I suppose you'll be visitin' y'sister while you're over. Y'know Kathy's divorced?'

'Yes,' said Jon. 'She and Teddy Rawlinson got divorced ten

months back.'

'She still doin' the ballroom dancin'?'

'Yes, but with a new partner, Paul someone, I don't recall his surname, Selman, or something similar.'

'Sherman,' said Val, 'his name's Paul Sherman. They've started up a school teachin' ballroom dancin'.'

'I allus wanted to learn ballroom,' Evelyn's tone was wistful, 'but Bob says it's poncey.'

'I nevva said that,' said Bob.

'Y'did, and y'reckoned no one was going to get ya in a pair of poncey, patent-leather shoes.'

Jon laughed. 'I don't blame you, Bob. You wouldn't catch me in a pair either.'

They left the Franklin family at five o'clock in the taxi Evelyn had called for them. Val waved as the four of them stood on the broad porch steps, waving their farewells.

'They don't change,' sighed Val, turning her attention back to the others, 'but our Evelyn was always good for a laugh, and she always looked out for me when we were kids.'

'Well, I like them,' said Harry.

'Yeah, there's no side to them.' Jon glanced at Val. 'Except perhaps Bob.'

'He has always been one to play his cards close to his chest, hon.'

'It's the company he keeps, Harry,' said Jon. 'Sails a bit close to the wind at times, no wonder he doesn't want Duane joining the police force.'

'Duane a family name?' asked Harry.

'Good Lord, no.' Val chuckled and glanced at Harry. 'It's because our Evelyn's a big Duane Eddy fan, she named Duane after him.'

'Duane Eddy of "*Movin' n' Groovin'*" fame?'

'That's the one. It's not my sort of music.'

'Bob must be doing really well to afford a place like that; did you get an eyeful of the living room?' Harry sighed. 'It must have cost a packet.'

'No expense spared,' commented Jon, 'that carpet was pure wool, and you're right, it's impressive, no doubt about it – if it's to your taste.'

Jon pictured their own homely sitting room back at Jindalee with its fine stone fireplace designed for burning logs in the cast-iron basket; the beautiful hand-crafted wooden bookcases filled with books; the timber flooring covered with Turkey rugs; the soft lighting from the lamps Val strategically placed about the room on occasional tables. Then there were the oil paintings that Alistair had painted for them, as well as those of Aboriginal artists, including Tom's, that they'd bought over the years because they liked them.

'Each to their own,' Jon added, wondering, not for the first time, whether Bob's success in the scrap business was down to his links with organised crime. The last time they'd been over in Liverpool, three years back, the time when the country was going mad over England winning the World Cup, he recalled his childhood friend, Pete McGhee, saying something then that left him wondering about the legitimacy of Bob's business arrangements.

'Will tomorra be as interestin'?' asked Val, changing the subject.

'Your guess is as good as mine.' Jon caught Harry's eye. 'If you'd rather not come with us, we'll understand.'

'In for a penny in for a pound,' said Harry, then realised what he'd said. 'Sorry, Val, no offence intended.'

'It's okay, Harry, they can be a bit over the top at times if you're not used to them.'

'And if you think they're over the top just wait till you meet my Auntie Marg,' said Jon, 'although Harry, Harry Warrener, her second husband's all right, he's quiet, a back-seat kind of fella. You sure you want to come with us tomorrow?'

'Wouldn't miss it for the world.'

'You might live to regret it,' said Jon.

When they arrived back at the hotel there was a letter waiting for them, hand delivered the receptionist said – "a bloke, smart dresser, moustache". Jon frowned as he opened it and saw the signature, Pete McGhee! What did Pete want? And how did he know they were in town? He hadn't told any of his Liverpool mates he was coming and, as far as he knew his Aunt Marg wasn't in communication with Pete or any of the crowd he'd hung around with in the old days.

Jon looked up from the letter. 'We're invited to a party out at Pete's place tomorrow night.'

Val frowned. 'Pete McGhee?'

'The very one,' said Jon dryly.

'Who's Pete McGhee?' asked Harry.

'A mucker from the old days, when I was still a kid, before I was shipped off to Oz.'

'Pete's what you might call a spiv so watch yourself, Harry,' said Val, her frown deepening. She turned to Jon. 'Do you think Merle'll be there?'

'It's a possibility, that's if she still lives in Liverpool.'

'And Merle?' queried Harry.

Jon grimaced. 'Pete's twin sister.'

'Exotic sort of name,' commented Harry.

A wry smile replaced Val's frown. 'She's an exotic sort of woman, and a bit of a man-eater, so watch yourself there an' all, yeah!'

'So we're going then?' said Jon.

'Indeed we are, but I'm goin' to need a new frock.'

Jon grinned. 'What's wrong with the one you're wearing?'

'Not exotic enough,' said Val in a deadpan voice.

CHAPTER 16

The McGhees had moved to a much larger house further out of town, another Victorian property similar to the one they'd owned before but with a more impressive conservatory and imposing formal gardens to the front and sculptured informality to the rear.

The guests wandered out onto the terrace from the conservatory, and down towards the lily ponds that were well stocked with koi carp. On the terrace a sumptuous buffet had been laid out on long trestle tables covered in starched white tablecloths. Waiters and waitresses circulated, offering sparkling wine and canapés. At the back of the house the trees and shrubs around the lawn were festooned with twinkling lights and on the tables were lighted candles protected by glass.

Val accepted a flute of champagne from a waiter and followed Jon and Harry out on to the terrace.

'Bloody hell!' she murmured. 'So this is how the poor live!'

'He a millionaire?' asked Harry.

Jon nodded.

'How did he make his money?'

'He married money and is into real estate, Pete's words not mine,' added Jon hastily.

'The landed gentry?' asked Harry.

Val chuckled. 'That's a good one, Harry; you wait till you meet Daffers.'

'Daffers?'

'Daphne, she's a good 'un, bit ditzy, but a heart of pure gold, pity about the hus—'

'Jon! Valerie! It's good to see you both again.' Pete looked Val up and down, took in the elegant evening dress in midnight-blue shot silk that enhanced her colouring, the expensive shoes, the cashmere shawl draped over her shoulders against the evening chill and kissed her on the cheek. 'You're looking very…'

'Nice?' supplied Val.

'Elegant,' finished Pete.

'Thank you,' she murmured.

Pete turned to Jon and clapped him on the back. 'Pleased you could come at short notice.' He gave Harry the once over. 'And who's your friend?'

'Harry, Harry Hammond.'

Pete extended a hand to Harry. 'See you've been in the wars.' He said, indicating Harry's sticks.

'You could say that,' agreed Harry, 'Vietnam.'

'And what's an Aussie doing in Vietnam?'

Jon looked at Pete, surely Pete knew, the Aussies had been out there long enough.

'Of course, how stupid of me…Vietnam!' Pete turned back to Jon. 'How long're you over for this time?'

'Not long, it's just a flying visit, to see the family.' Jon caught a glimpse of an anxious Daphne heading towards them. 'Lovely party, Daphne.'

'Nice to see y'both, we're glad you could come, ain't we, Pete?' She forced a smile and glanced at Pete as if for approval.

'And the weather couldn't be better,' said Val, kissing Daphne on the cheek and offering hers. 'Daphne, this is Harry, he's a friend of ours and a business associate.'

Pete raised an eyebrow. 'You a station owner too?'

Harry shook his head. 'Mustering, we're going into the mustering business using planes and helicopters, at least that's the plan.'

Jon could see Pete had already lost interest. 'Much money in it?' he asked, the look on his face indicating that he didn't really care about the answer.

'Time will tell,' said Jon.

'Have y'brought the family with ya?' asked Daphne.

'No, the boys are in boardin' school and Ruby is holdin' the fort back home.' Val took a sip of champagne. 'And what about Kenneth? How is he these days?'

'He's doin' real well.' Daphne beamed at Pete. 'You're hopin' Kenny'll go into the business with y'once he's finished school, ain't ya, darl?' She glanced at Pete as if waiting for confirmation but Pete had already moved on. Daphne, still clearly anxious about the party, and Pete, indicated the laden tables behind her. 'Help yerselves to food, there's loads.' She looked away, searching for Pete. 'Must go, Pete likes me t'circulate, sez it helps oil the wheels of business...' Her voice trailed off. 'I'll catch up later, yeah!' A brief smile and she was gone, tripping along the terrace after Pete, spilling her champagne on the York stone as she scurried after him, to where he was greeting some new arrivals.

'What do you make of that?' asked Jon.

Val pondered for a moment or two. 'Maybe they've had a row.'

'Don't think so...no, definitely not, that's how they always are, Pete treats her like a doormat and she lets him.'

'She doesn't talk like gentry,' said Harry. 'Didn't you say Pete had married money?'

'He did, her dad has a construction business; he made a packet after the war. He now has one of the largest companies in the UK and has diversified into building motorways.'

'New money,' added Val, 'just like us.'

'What do they know about Jindalee?' asked Harry.

'Not much.' Jon's tone hardened. 'They think it's paying its way with enough spare for a trip home to see family and friends every three or four years.'

'Why don't you tell them the truth?'

Jon considered the question. Why had he never told them? He realised he couldn't answer that except that it was none of Pete's business, and besides, what Pete knew, Merle knew, and he'd rather Merle knew as little as possible. 'It's complicated, Harry.'

'When do you think Merle'll turn up?' asked Val.

Had she read his mind? But Val wasn't looking at him, she was too busy scanning the crowd, looking for Merle's distinctive auburn hair, the elegant dress. Jon smiled, no wonder she'd wanted a swank new outfit. 'You know, Pete was right.'

'Right about what, hon?'

'You look stunning in that outfit, the best dressed woman here.' Jon grinned as she blew him a kiss and he thought she'd never looked lovelier.

'Thanks, hon, it's nice to be appreciated.' She turned to Harry. 'You ready for a bite to eat 'cos I'm starvin' and I can see others are already tuckin' into the buffet.'

'Too right, I am, Val.'

'You two go ahead,' said Jon. 'I think I'll take a stroll around for a bit and get a feel for the lie of the land, so to speak.'

While Val and Harry headed towards the buffet, Jon took the broad steps leading down to the garden; he crossed over the lawn, close mowed and clipped to a velvet sward. At the pond's edge he looked down at the carp and then turned back to look at the terrace where most of the guests were talking and laughing, while in the background came the sound of a band playing the Beatles' *"Hey Jude"* and other favourites. There was no doubt about it, Pete had done well for himself, but at what price, for him and for Daphne? Of the two it was Daphne he felt sorrier for, Pete could be a bit of a bastard; hard, was the word, and single-minded. Jon suspected love hadn't come into it when Pete had married. But would he dump Daphne once the right woman came along? Or would he have affairs like other blokes – a wife at home and a mistress ensconced in a maisonette somewhere? Maybe, knowing Pete, he was already leading a double life.

'It's an agreeable property, don't you think?' said a cultured voice.

Jon turned, took in the fella standing behind and to the left of him and smiled. 'You're not wrong there.'

'An Australian!' said the bloke.

'Liverpudlian.'

'Really!'

'Yeah, but I've lived in Australia for most of my life.'

The bloke switched his glass to his left hand and extended the right. 'I'm James Glengarry.'

Jon shook it. 'Jon Cadwallader.'

'Are you a friend of the McGhees, or a business associate?'

Jon hesitated. Pete wasn't a friend as such, at least not anymore. 'Friend, I suppose, at least we were when we were kids. We don't have that much to do with each other these days.'

'Are you the chap with the cattle ranch out in Western Australia?'

Jon sipped his champagne. How did the bloke know that? And why would Pete have told James about Jindalee? 'Station. They call them stations.'

'So they do. Peter said he had a friend in Western Australia who owns a cattle ranch…station,' he corrected.

'Are you a mate…friend of Pete's?'

'Business associate.' James didn't elaborate.

Jon suddenly had an image of Curly – the Aborigine's irrepressible smile absent for once, and he wondered why Curly had sprung

111

to mind at that moment when he was nine thousand miles away from home, in a Liverpool back garden on a summer night, talking to a bloke who knew more about him than he knew about the bloke.

'You known Pete long?' asked Jon.

'A few months or so.'

Jon absorbed the information. He was on boggy ground, he knew he was. He wished Val were with him, Val would have the bloke sussed faster than anyone else he knew. If Val liked him that would have been good enough for him, as it was he felt vulnerable, and didn't know why. Had they been invited to the party for a reason? Did Pete have an ulterior motive? Was that why Curly had sprung to mind, unbidden? Was it a subconscious warning? He changed the subject.

'Do you live locally?'

'Cheshire, we have an estate in Cheshire.'

Jon racked his brains, "estate", did that mean farm? – or was the bloke from the landed gentry? Jon glanced at him, took in the expensive suit, the starched white shirt, the flower in his lapel, and the shoes, expensive by the look of them, probably bespoke, definitely well heeled then, and he smelt good for a fella, and it wasn't *Old Spice*.

'Are you in Liverpool for long?' asked James.

Jon shook his head. 'No. We're just visiting family, we fly back next week.' He spotted Val heading in their direction. Relief flooded through him. He smiled, it wasn't the first time she'd turned up at an opportune moment; it was almost as if she'd read his mind.

'Try this, hon, it's absolutely delicious.' She held out a canapé for him to taste.

Jon smiled. 'What is it?'

'A blini, smoked salmon and caviar – taste, you'll like it.' She glanced at James. 'I should've brought two, shouldn't I? You'll have to take my word for it, they're delicious. I'm Val.' She extended her hand, shook his and beamed at him. 'And you are?'

'James,' said James.

'Are you a friend of Pete or Daphne?'

James beamed. 'Peter, I haven't had the pleasure of meeting his wife yet.'

Val turned to him, full on, appraising him openly. 'Haven't you? Well, I'll tell you this for nothin', she's lovely, no side to her at all, it's just a pity—'

'James has an estate in Cheshire,' interrupted Jon.

'My father does,' corrected James.

'Second or third?' asked Val.

James frowned, and Jon gave her a nudge.

'Son?' she added.

James laughed. 'Second.' He turned to Jon. 'You didn't tell me you have a clever wife… and direct too, I like that in a woman.'

'You married?' asked Val without a trace of a smile on her face.

James smiled. 'Not yet, I'm looking for someone like you.'

'You'll have no problem then.' Val's tone was dry. 'There are plenty like me in Liverpool.' She briefly rested her hand on Jon's shoulder. 'I'd better be gettin' back to Harry. I left him with a man-eater.'

Val smiled at Jon's quizzical look, mouthed *Merle* at him and made a moue. She leaned forward and kissed him on the cheek. 'Take care, hon,' she whispered, and she was gone, tripping over the lawn in her expensive shoes.

James watched Val make her way along the terrace. 'You have a lovely wife, and I see she knows Merle.'

'Thank you,' said Jon, conscious that James had picked up on Val's parting shot. He'd been right to be wary, James wasn't the sort to miss anything, of that he was increasingly certain. 'She's the salt of the earth, I'm really fortunate and, yes, she does know Merle, they were in school together.'

'Yes,' said James, 'Peter told me.'

'Told you what?'

'About Valerie, and that you were once engaged to his sister.'

'Yeah!' A frown creased Jon's brow. He and Merle had never been properly engaged, she hadn't said yes on the occasions he'd asked her to marry him. 'That was a long time ago.'

'She's at the party, have you met her yet?'

'No,' admitted Jon, 'but I'm sure I will,' he added, and wasn't a bit surprised to see Pete and Merle crossing the lawn towards them.

'Speak of the devil and the *"man-eater"*,' murmured James. He greeted Pete and smiled at Merle. 'As lovely as ever,' he said to her.

'Thank you, James.' Merle kissed him on the cheek and then turned to Jon, leaned forward and kissed him too.

Jon felt her hot breath caress his face and the warmth from her body as she pressed against him even as he tried to avoid contact

113

with the woman he'd once wanted to marry when they were both still young. How could he have been so naïve? Why had he never seen her for what she was? – or seen how she concealed her manipulative, callous ways, keeping them well hidden behind a carefully cultivated façade? He tensed and she pulled away.

'I've already met Val, she's busy chatting to the Galsworthy girls; and, it seems, they've taken a shine to your protégé, Jon.'

'Harry?'

'Yes, he's a nice chap, pity about his legs.'

Jon didn't comment, just fixed her with a contemplative look. The woman never ceased to surprise him. How could she, a doctor, take such a cold, dispassionate view? He pulled himself up, maybe that was how doctors coped with life's tragedies. 'You still working at the hospital?'

Merle laughed. 'Hell, no, I'm in private practice, on Rodney Street.'

Pete grinned. 'She's making more dosh than me, and that's saying something.' He smiled at James. 'I see you've already introduced yourself.'

'That's right; Jon and I have exchanged pleasantries. Nice party... as always,' James said. 'Where's Daphne?'

'Looking after the plebs,' said Pete.

Jon didn't comment, whatever had he admired in the man? He was a nasty piece of work, as cold and calculating as his sister, and if James Glengarry was anything like Pete he'd do well to steer clear of him too.

Merle smiled at James as she laid an elegantly manicured hand on his arm. 'You know Jon owns a cattle station in Western Australia, don't you? It's a very nice property.' Her tone was warm and husky. She turned to Jon. 'How is Jindalee?'

'So, so,' answered Jon, aware that Merle was up to her old tricks, trying to charm James, still convinced she was irresistible. 'It's been pretty dry over the last few months.'

'I was telling James how big your station is, a million acres, that's right, isn't it?'

'Not quite, nine fifty or thereabouts.'

'And what about Wanndarah?' asked Pete.

Jon glanced at him. 'What about Wanndarah?'

'I gather Alexandros Bartokas has had enough, decided to move back to Greece.'

How the hell did Pete know that? And the Bartokas family moving back to Greece! – that was news to him. 'There's not much in the bush that would interest you, Pete. There's no scope for building motorways in the middle of the outback at the moment, or hotels and housing estates, come to that.'

Pete grinned and, for once in more years than he cared to remember, Jon saw the kid in him, the enthusiasm when he'd talked about making a million.

'It's James and his business partner who bought the mineral rights on Wanndarah Station over a year ago.'

Jon nearly choked. He took another sip of champagne to cover his surprise and confusion. So James was the co-owner of the company that had started drilling on Wanndarah a few weeks back, taking core samples from the south-west quadrant of the station, not far from the Jindalee boundary! He swore under his breath. He should have checked out the situation over a year back, taken out mineral rights on Jindalee then. 'Is that so, James?'

'Indeed it is,' agreed James. 'We live in exciting times, do we not?'

Jon's mind raced. 'Who's your business partner? Anyone I know?'

'Patrick O'Shea, have you heard of him? The company is based in London, but we have offices in Perth and Kalgoorlie.'

Patrick O'Shea! The name rang a bell, but Jon couldn't put a face to the name. Jon kept his features bland, his mind churning. So Glenshea Holdings belonged to James Glengarry and Patrick O'Shea. No wonder no one back home knew who owned the Pommy-based company with their state of the art drilling rigs, who were sinking money into the area as if there was no tomorrow. It must have been Patrick who had employed the prospector, Gus McDonald, who'd been seen in and around Charlestown over fifteen months back. He remembered Wes mentioning him, not that anyone had known what he was looking for then, although there had been speculation it was nickel he was after.

'I've bought stock in James's venture,' said Pete.

'And me,' interrupted Merle.

'We're investing in James's nickel mine, getting in early while shares are rock bottom.' Pete's face brightened. 'James says the core samples are some of the best they've ever seen in the area and that before long there'll be a mad scramble to buy and the price will rocket.'

'I gather you know a bit about mining,' said James, 'Patrick says that is where you made your fortune…in the goldfields…or so he was told.'

'Nearly cost you your life, didn't it, Jon?'

Merle's words pulled Jon up sharp and he noticed she also had James's full attention. 'How did you know that?'

'The sister in the hospital told me all about it.'

'Sister Lewis?'

'That's the one, Liz Lewis. She really fell for you, you know, until I told her you were spoken for.'

'Well, tonight isn't the time to talk business,' said Pete. 'How about you meet up with us tomorrow, Jon?'

'Can't do, we're spending the day with my sister.'

'Rearrange it,' said Merle.

'I've already rearranged it once to come to this party, and I'm not calling off again.'

'Monday then,' suggested James. 'Why don't you all have lunch with me and we can talk it over then, my father can join us too, he's interested in investing.'

Jon looked at the three of them; there was no way he was going to go into business with any of them, not now, not ever. But it wouldn't hurt to find out more about their plans, especially as they'd be drilling on land adjacent to Jindalee. 'All right,' he said.

'That's fixed, then,' said Pete. 'I'll pick you up from your hotel at eleven-thirty Monday morning. Now, I must get back to my other guests.'

And circulate, thought Jon sarcastically. 'And I'd better go and find Valerie,' he said, half to himself. He left them then and strolled, unhurriedly, across the manicured lawn to join Val who was chatting to Daphne on the terrace.

CHAPTER 17

On Monday morning Val fixed her eyes on Jon over the breakfast table. 'I don't want to go, hon, the three of them, they're...they're dangerous and Merle's always tryin' to get her talons into you.'

Jon laughed. 'You're not jealous, are you?'

Val ignored the question.

'If you don't want to go, Val, we could have a look around the city. You can show me the sights,' said Harry between mouthfuls of eggs and bacon.

'I want you both there.'

Harry stopped eating and looked at Jon. 'Both of us?'

'Yeah, both of you, I want you to be my eyes and ears, listen and look out for what I miss. We need to know what their plans are, especially if they go ahead and mine the greenstone. It's close to our boundary and the stratum continues on Jindalee land.'

Val added milk to her coffee. 'Will Daphne be there?'

'I very much doubt it. I can't see Pete involving her in anything to do with business.'

'You know, hon, she's not stupid, she said a couple of things the other night that made me think.'

'Like what?'

'Veiled comments about Pete. If you ask me, Daphne's got his measure.'

'She's lived with him long enough. Do you think she knows anything about the business?' asked Jon.

'I doubt it, Pete's like Daphne's father, an old-fashioned type; he reckons women, like children, should be seen and not heard. He certainly doesn't rate Daphne's intellectual ability, that's for sure.

117

More fool him,' added Val under her breath before sipping her coffee.

'So Pete won't be taking her along for support,' said Jon.

'Not if he's got Merle with him, hon.'

Pete's Bentley purred along Cheshire back lanes, between thick hedgerows already changing colour and laden with hips, haws and crab apples, until they reached the gatehouse. Then came the long avenue, flanked on either side with ancient lime trees, two hundred years old if the building ahead of them was anything to go by. The hall was built in the Georgian style of warm red brick with stone detailing, and along the roof line were statues of legendary creatures: gryphons, dragons and wyverns.

'Smart pad,' commented Harry.

'So this is where James lives?' murmured Val.

'Yes, he has a flat here, but it's his brother, Ralph, who will inherit,' said Merle from the front seat.

'How did you two come to meet James?' asked Jon.

'There was a piece in one of the investment papers I get about a British mining company starting up exploration in Western Australia, looking for nickel.' Pete glanced at Jon in the rear-view mirror. 'There's a world shortage, you know. And then, by chance, I heard about James's operation through a mutual friend with insider knowledge. He'd seen the data from some core samples that had been sent in.'

'Is this information reliable? It sounds a bit dodgy to me.'

'Totally reliable. Apparently it's the richest site they've found to date. It's going to make everyone involved dollar millionaires. Anyway, I got in touch with James through this mutual friend and James got back to me, made me an offer I couldn't refuse.'

'So you don't know that much about him.'

'He's from a very good family, if that's what you mean,' interrupted Merle.

Jon wasn't about to let the matter drop. 'What about his business acumen?'

'He's a wealthy bloke,' said Pete.

'That's not what I asked. How much experience has he in the mining business, and of Australia?'

'Enough. And he's got good advisers behind him.'

'I suppose you mean Patrick O'Shea,' said Jon.

'Yes, and in any case his sort don't risk family money lightly,' said Pete.

Val dug Jon in the ribs and mouthed at him to shut up. 'I hope the grub's good,' she said and smiled when she saw Merle stiffen at the coarse word.

The butler met them and showed them into the library, a long oblong room flanked on the right-hand side by three pairs of French windows that led out onto an ornate terrace. Apart from the carved grey-marble chimney breast the rest of the room was lined with floor-to-ceiling bookcases housing leather-bound books that looked every bit as old as the building. Evidence of travel books, autobiographies, and novels, of the sort he and Val had in their study back in Australia, were in short supply. A log fire smouldered in the grate, barely warming the chilly air despite the warmth of the August day outside. What was the point of having a mansion like this, thought Jon, if you couldn't afford to heat it?

Harry crossed to a circular mahogany table and glanced down at the chart displayed there. 'Geological map...Western Australia,' he mouthed at Jon when the others weren't looking.

The door opened and in walked James. 'Good to see you again,' he said as he strode over and shook hands with each of them in turn.

'Nice place you've got here,' commented Jon.

'Yes, it's been in the family for a couple of hundred years or so, a relative won it at cards. The previous owner gambled the family fortune away.'

Was James about to do the same with his nickel mine? Jon wondered. Or was he only risking other people's money?

'Ahh, Harry, I see you've spotted the map.' James crossed over to the table and stood next to Harry. 'Are you familiar with the geology of Western Australia?'

'Not really. I can recognise a breakaway when I see one and that's about it,' said Harry, not committing himself.

James smiled at Merle. 'Would you like a drink? – whisky, gin, brandy, or vodka?'

'I'd like a gin and Dubonnet, please.'

James nodded at the butler who'd discreetly followed him into the room. 'Valerie?'

'Whisky and soda, if you don't mind.'

'Whisky on the rocks for me,' said Jon.

'And I'll have the same,' said Pete.

'Any chance of a beer, mate?' asked Harry.

'I'm sure Watson can find you a bottle. And I'll have a whisky neat, thank you, Watson.' James turned to Jon. 'Perhaps you'd like to see where we are drilling on the map over here.' He walked round to the other side of the table and unrolled a second map of Western Australia, while Watson served up the drinks and backed out of the room.

'This is the area for which we acquired the mineral rights several months ago now.' James pointed to Wanndarah Station to the north-west of Jindalee. 'And, as I'm sure you know, we now have men test drilling in this region, taking core samples and, to date, they're looking very promising, very promising indeed.' He swept his finger along the south-eastern boundary of Wanndarah that bordered Jindalee, west of Lake Desolation.

Why was James telling him all this? Surely he knew that all the locals were well aware of where the test drilling was being carried out. It was the main topic of conversation locally, in Charlestown, in Pilkington, and on all the stations thereabouts, and Glenshea Holdings was the company that had hired equipment from Wes Chapman, a grader amongst other things, to cut tracks deep into the bush for the rigs to reach the chosen drilling sites.

Merle strolled over and stood next to Jon. 'What's the country like there, desert?'

'Well, it's not the best, semi-arid, with a ridge of rock running on a diagonal alignment, crossing the station boundaries, exactly the sort of territory a mining company would be interested in, I should think.'

'It's a greenstone belt,' said James.

'Haven't a clue what sort of stone it is,' lied Jon, having already been told what the rock composition was by Alex Bartokas when the mining company finally started drilling several weeks back.

'Greenstone's good for gold and nickel apparently. Some mining companies have already eyed out greenstone belts around Wiluna and then there's another belt east of there at a place called Mount Fisher.' James tapped the map laid out before them. 'Here and here, no doubt you are familiar with these locations.'

'Why the interest in nickel all of a sudden?' asked Harry.

Pete laughed. 'That's a good one coming from you.'

Val glanced at Jon, querying Pete's reaction.

'What do you mean?' asked Harry.

'Nickel's gone through the roof these last few months; there've been companies opening up nickel mines in Kambalda, near Coolgardie; at Laverton, north of Kalgoorlie; and in the Kimberleys; wouldn't surprise us if nickel doesn't peak at seven thousand pounds a ton soon. Have you heard of Poseidon?' asked James.

'No, should I?'

'It's a mining company selling shares as fast as they can print the certificates; they have a mine not far from Laverton, a place called Windarra.'

Jon kept quiet. There'd been a lot of talk about nickel; the "new boom" people were calling it.

'But why is there such a big interest in nickel?' repeated Harry.

'Demand for it on the back of the Vietnam War – the United States can't get enough of it. Then there is the trouble in Canada – a major producer there is stymied by industrial action. It's a great opportunity for Australia.' James strolled over to the fireplace and pressed a button set in the wall.

Within seconds Watson had reappeared to refill their glasses.

'Nickel's a rare commodity still, but massive deposits have been found in your bit of the outback, nickel's the new gold, the area will be booming again like it was in gold-rush days. There's a packet to be made for those prepared to invest,' said Pete, 'that's right, isn't it, James?'

'Yes, some believe that Australia will be a major world producer of nickel within a decade. They estimate that the country has getting on for thirty to thirty-five per cent of the world reserves and the bulk of that is believed to be in Western Australia.'

'Where do we come into this?' asked Jon.

'Backers, investors – drilling is an expensive business,' said James.

'Tell me about it!' Jon sighed. 'The last bore we sank cost us a packet.'

'So we are offering shares in the company. As I said earlier, initial samples are looking good, very good, and those who get in early can buy at a preferential rate, the cost of the shares can only rise once our findings are made public.'

'We can't lose with nickel being the price it is,' added Pete.

'Pete and I have bought stocks and shares in Glenshea,' said Merle. 'And we wondered whether you'd be interested in buying too, before the company publishes the results from the core sam-

121

ples, especially as you know the region well, know its potential.'

'Think about it.' James rolled up the map sensing a less than enthusiastic response. 'Let's have lunch and take a break from business talk.' He took Val's empty glass and placed it on the side table, 'Tell me, how do you keep yourself sane in the outback? Merle tells me it's a pretty bleak place. She says you both nearly died out there when your plane went down in the desert, is that right?'

'That's true, but Jon found us, didn't you, hon? And to keep myself busy, I knit.'

Jon heard Harry choking on the last of his beer and smiled to himself. He didn't dare look at Val; he knew he'd spoil it all by laughing. He half expected Merle to make a scathing comment about the ridiculous image of Val sitting on the back porch, knitting, but she didn't. Maybe that's what she wants to believe, he thought as he followed the others through into the dining room.

Back at their hotel, over dinner, Jon, Val and Harry discussed the day's events.

'Knitting,' muttered Jon, 'you can't even sew, never mind knit!'

'I can too, me mam taught me French knittin'.'

'French knitting?'

'Yeah, hon, you take an empty cotton reel, hammer four little nails in the top and you keep hookin' the wool over each nail in turn until you end up with a thin, knitted tube, and then you can stitch it together to make table mats and other useful things.'

Harry grinned. 'They believed you, you know?'

'Yeah,' said Val, 'how about that!'

'So, what do you think?' asked Jon.

'I'll have the Dover sole, hon.'

'No, you galah, their offer.'

'Wouldn't touch it with a barge pole, but I think you were right, we should take out a mineral lease on that part of Jindalee close to Wanndarah boundary before they extend theirs. We wouldn't want James and his mate drillin' on Jindalee land, would we, hon?'

'If we do that we'd have to start mining ourselves.' Jon frowned as he considered the implications; it was an aspect of taking out a mineral lease that had put him off doing anything about it earlier.

'Well, why not? It doesn't have to be a major effort, we could play at it, do just enough to keep the licence. That greenstone goes straight through our least productive land, and if we decide to do it properly we could make a killin', hon, we'll be dollar million-aires,' she said, mimicking Pete's delivery, 'what with nickel goin' through the roof and all.'

'What do you think, Harry?' asked Jon.

'I'm with Val, I overheard James with his father; he thinks he's got you both hooked.'

'Like the other two.'

'Yeah, if you ask me Pete and Merle are being taken for a ride. But it wouldn't hurt to do a bit of research into this company, Glenshea Holdings, or whatever it's called. Isn't there somewhere where you can look up who owns what, what the shareholding is, managing directors, that sort of thing?'

'Companies House,' said Val, 'that'd be the place to start.'

'What do you know about Companies House?' asked Jon.

'Only what I read in the library early this mornin'. I decided to do some research of me own before lunch.'

'And there was me thinking you were having your hair done.'

Val ignored the comment. 'Companies House keeps a record of all limited companies in the UK and those overseas with a branch or place of business in the UK, which I should think covers James's business. They have to be registered there, file annual re-turns and company accounts, and provide a list of directors and so on. All we need is a few details about the company and we can look 'em up on the register. We can also find out if James is on any other company boards.'

'Clever girl,' murmured Jon.

Val frowned and chewed her lip. 'Do you think we should ask around at home?'

'What do you mean?'

'Do you know anyone in the mining industry who might know a bit about Glenshea Holdings and this nickel situation? Someone with real insider knowledge?'

'Can't think of anyone offhand,' said Jon.

'James and Pete are right, you know. I've been readin' the finan-cial pages in the paper since we've been here. It seems everyone's goin' mad over nickel stock, but, if you ask me, it can't last.'

'It can if there's a world shortage and we've got the mineral de-posits,' said Harry.

'Yeah, well a lot will depend on the quality; there've been enough people who invested in gold mines on the strength of "promising" samples only to end up buyin' a duff pup.'

Jon glanced at the waiter hovering at his side. 'Two Dover soles please.' He turned to Harry. 'What're you having?'

'I'll have the turbot.'

'And a turbot,' said Jon. 'And we'll have a bottle of Muscadet too.'

'Certainly, Sir.'

'Thank you.' Jon turned back to Val and Harry a frown on his brow. 'Strange Pete didn't realise that Aussies have been in Vietnam since the early sixties, but he knew about the price of nickel and the link to the war.'

'Some fellas are like that, hon, they only take in what they think is useful. Aussies fightin' in Vietnam doesn't mean anythin' to the likes of Pete, but the price of nickel does if he's thinkin' of investin'. If you ask me, James has Pete wrapped around his little finger.'

The following morning Jon told Harry they were going to show him their old stomping ground, South Street and Bridge Street.

As they drove along South Street in a taxi Harry took in the narrow street. 'It's pretty much like where I was brought up in the East End.'

'Yes, it is,' said Jon, 'that's why I wanted you to see it. We have more in common than you thought, haven't we?'

'Yeah,' Harry hesitated, 'remember when I first moved to Jindalee?'

'Yes, I do, vividily in fact.'

'Well, I didn't really believe you when you told me you were a child migrant, I thought you'd just said it to make me feel at ease.'

'Well, that wasn't the case, Harry. We've always been up front with you and we always will.'

'Well,' said Val, 'on a lighter note, compared to South Street and where you were brought up, Harry, Bridge Street is even more down market, we didn't even run to front gardens. My mother, Evelyn and I lived at Number 20 and Jon's grandma lived at Number 27. It was when he visited back in 1947 that I first met him.'

'Sefton Park, said Jon, 'that's where I first saw you.'

Val chuckled, 'And you thought I was brash, and I suppose I was back then.'

'I don't believe you were brash,' said Harry.

'Yeah, well, I was, and I came from a pretty rough family.'

'They're not that bad!' said Harry.

'Yeah, well they were, so don't you go beating yourself up about your mother, yeah!'

Jon glanced at Val, surprised she'd said as much as she had. He recalled the first time he'd seen Evelyn dolled up to the nines, heading for a night out on the town. Back in those days both Evelyn and her mother were on the game. He reckoned they'd done well to turn their lives around.

'So where did Pete and Merle live?' asked Harry.

'South Street,' said Val, 'same as Jon. They were both ambitious even then and it didn't take Pete too long to buy himself a nice property in a better part of town. He was a spiv even as a kid and was making more money from black market deals than blokes could earn in regular employment.'

'He hasn't changed then?' said Harry

'No, he hasn't changed,' agreed Jon.

As they drove along Bridge Street back to their hotel and lunch Jon thought it unlikely they'd visit this part of Liverpool again – no one he knew lived here any more. 'You know, we did have some happy times as kids. We all knew each other and if you were in trouble then everyone would muck in to help out. As I recall there was a real community spirit about the place.'

'It was more or less the same in London,' said Harry, 'not that I can remember that much; like you I was shipped off to Australia at a pretty young age.'

'Yes,' said Jon, 'but you know what, we haven't done so bad, have we?'

Harry laughed. 'I reckon we've done pretty well, considering.'

Val grinned. 'And once our musterin' business is up and runnin' we'll all be dollar millionaires in no time!'

'You reckon?' said Harry.

'Yeah,' said Val a smile on her face, 'I reckon.'

PART III

[September 1969 – July 1970]

CHAPTER 18

Jon looked out of the cabin window as the Boeing flew out of London, reflecting on their brief visit back to the Old Country. Seeing his sister, Kathy, had been an anti-climax; they no longer had anything in common. He had no interest in dance schools and she none in cattle stations and she had absolutely no desire to fly out to Australia for a visit, but at least she'd appreciated their offer to fund the improvements she and Paul Sherman had in mind for the dance school, and he'd been glad to help.

'What's wrong, hon?' asked Val.

'Sorry?'

'I said, anythin' wrong?'

'Why?'

She indicated his hands resting in his lap. 'You're tapping.'

'Tapping?'

'Yes, you always do it when you're distracted. So, what's on your mind?'

'Just thinking about this and that.'

'My lot or yours?'

'Mine, I haven't that much in common with them anymore, have I?'

'Did you ever? – 'cos I didn't with mine, especially my mother.'

Too right, thought Jon, but family was family at the end of the day and one made an effort.

'I must admit it was nice seein' our Evelyn so happy,' rattled on Val. 'And Duane, he's a good kid. I think he'll make somethin' of himself, and it won't be in the scrap trade.'

'Yeah, I think you're right,' said Jon, 'but there is no way Bob is going to let him join the police force, that's for sure.'

129

Val glanced across at Jon now twiddling his thumbs. 'Is that all that's botherin' you?'

'You don't miss much, do you?'

'It was that phone call, wasn't it?'

Val had got it in one. The call came through to the hotel as they were leaving – Pete phoning to wish them "bon voyage" and to tell him the "good news".

It was anything but, reflected Jon. He recalled their conversation: We'll be in your neck of the woods, old boy, Pete had said. We're visiting our investment at Wanndarah – all right if we call at your place while we're over? You and James? he'd asked. And Merle, Pete had added.

Pete had been full of himself, his words brimming with bonhomie, the clipped Queen's English accent he'd worked so hard to cultivate letting him down – the Liverpool intonation too difficult to lose completely.

'Did he tell you you'd be an idiot not to invest, that it was the opportunity of a lifetime?' asked Val.

'Yeah, something like that. He said Patrick was publishing the core sample findings next week. According to him if we buy now we can't lose, joked that if we weren't careful we'd find ourselves dollar millionaires in no time.'

Val chuckled. 'He'd have a shock if he knew we already are.'

Jon frowned.

Val patted his restless hands. 'Don't worry about it, hon. We're not investin', but they can stay a couple of days. I can just about cope with that, no worries.'

When Jon, Val and Harry arrived at Jindalee Station there was hell on. Charlie, one of the Aboriginal stockmen, met them as they stepped out of the ute.

'There's trouble over on the Reef Hill boundary, boss. Mister Kennilworth and his men're causin' trouble. Miss Ruby and George, they're tryin' to sort it out, told me to fetch a couple more fellas for backup.'

'That bad, Charlie?'

'Yeah, boss, it's turned nasty, right enough.'

'Where exactly?'

'George sez near the last trouble, the fence is down again.'

Jon swore under his breath. Kit Kennilworth was forever causing strife. 'Give me a minute, Charlie; I need to change out of this gear. Start up the truck, will you?'

Jon turned to Val and Harry. 'I'd better go out and see what it's all about.'

'Do you want us to come with you?' asked Val.

'No, it'll just be the usual stand-off; you know what Kit's like. It'll be a case of driving our cattle back onto Jindalee and repairing the fence. There'll be a bit of cussing and shouting…nothing for you to worry about.' Once indoors he stripped off his travelling clothes and dragged on working ones. On his way out he stopped by the gun room and took out his rifle – the Remington Val had bought him for his birthday a couple of years back – and hurried over to the truck, already idling in the yard. 'Thanks, Charlie.'

'Y'want me along, boss?'

'Aye, it wouldn't hurt to have an extra man to help with the round-up.'

Neither spoke as they drove out toward Twenty-five Mile Bore over on the west side of the station, bordering Reef Hill land. As they approached the boundary fence closest to the bore they heard rifle shots echoing across the scrub.

'Bloody hell!' muttered Jon, his stomach in knots as he pictured Ruby and George dealing with their maniac of a neighbour. As they pulled out on to more open ground Jon could see the fence smashed down as if a herd of cattle had stampeded through it. Beyond, on Reef Hill land, next to the creek, was the station truck that George used. Ruby and George were standing next to it, immobile, Todd's gun trained on them. Even as Jon neared the scene more shots rang out and he could hear Ruby screaming at Todd and Kit to stop.

Jon pulled up behind George's truck, killed the engine and stepped out, his own gun in his hand, followed by Charlie. 'What the hell's going on here?' he yelled.

Ruby spun round. 'Jon,' she screamed, 'they've shot them! They've shot the lot!'

Jon struggled to take in her words until he rounded George's truck and saw the carnage – cattle, his cattle, dead and dying along the edge of Reef Hill creek: cows, heifers, young bulls and calves, shot where they'd been standing.

'You bastard!' yelled Jon. 'What've you gone and done that for?'

'I've warned you to keep your cattle off my land,' snarled Kit.

'We damn well have. We're forever repairing the boundary

131

fence, but someone keeps cutting it and tampering with the water supply. Some mongrel is turning off the water to our troughs.'

'Well, it ain't me, you want to look to your own.'

'And what do you mean by that?'

'Them Abos you employ – they're troublemakers, they don't like fences, they don't. Well, this is Reef Hill land, mine! And, just in case you've forgotten, we're in the middle of a dry spell so it certainly isn't me cutting the fence. I'm giving you fair warning, Cadwallader, I'll shoot anything that shouldn't be here, your bloody cattle, or your bloody Abos. Anything, you hear me? – anything trespassing on my property.'

Kit signalled to his son and his men and they retreated to their utes, rifles still trained on the four of them.

Kit leaned out of his side window as he pulled away, 'And you can take those animals off my land. I don't want rotting carcasses contaminating the water.'

The four of them watched the convoy depart, leaving only the dust and the sound of the engines fading as they drove back to Reef Hill homestead.

Ruby sank to her knees. 'They shot 'em, Jon, even the calves. They wouldn't listen. They threatened to shoot George too, and they meant it.'

Jon walked over to the bodies of his cattle and shot those animals that hadn't been killed outright in the slaughter. Then he roped the dead animals to the towing hitch and started dragging the carcasses into the bush on to his own land. There were too many to bury, it would be a case of letting nature take its course.

Once all the animals had been removed from Reef Hill land and the fence repaired, Jon sent George, Ruby and Charlie on ahead in the other ute, back to the homestead.

He watched them leave and considered the problem he had with Kit Kennilworth. Kit had a point, there was no way he would have deliberately cut the fence, or tampered with the water supply at Twenty-five Mile Bore, not in the present situation. Jon cast his mind back over the confrontation and recalled the look on Todd's face – satisfaction, that had been what lay behind Todd's half smile, he was sure of it. Had Todd been the one to snip the wire? But why? Todd knew the problems of raising beef on semi-arid land; he knew the desperate need for water in times of drought. So why would Todd put their own cattle at risk by letting Jindalee animals water on their land?

Jon drummed his fingers on the steering wheel. Ruby had once said Todd hated station life, had been filled with envy when Harry joined the army and went to Vietnam. Was that the reason? Was Todd trying to undermine his father's work? Was it an underhand way of getting his own back on a domineering and controlling father? It beggared belief, but the theory made sense. But how did he stop the mongrel from breaking down the boundary fences so giving Kit the legitimate right to shoot Jindalee cattle, claiming he was the one sinned against, the victim of *"bloody Abos"* as he described them?

Jon sat in his cab watching the flies settling on the carcasses and the braver crows already approaching lured by the smell of blood and dead flesh, and remembered the bones of the Aborigines he'd found in the cave over at Kangaroo Soak: they'd been massacred, a whole tribe wiped out according to Walter Hayne. And here he was, almost a hundred years later, listening to Kennilworth as he threatened to shoot not just cattle but any Aboriginal stockmen trespassing on Reef Hill land. Jon shook his head. How did you deal with men like that? But he already knew the answer, and he knew that Wes Chapman was right to warn him against throwaway comments, said half in jest, about handing back the land they owned to the Aborigines one day. Wes was right; he'd already had to put up with criticism for employing too many blacks and for paying them a fair rate for the job, so suggesting the land should be returned to the natives would only add fuel to the fire.

Jon started the truck and rammed it into gear, recalling as he did so what others like Eyre had said about the plight of the dispossessed Aborigines in journals written over a hundred years back. It seemed to him attitudes hadn't changed that much in the intervening years.

As he drove, he looked about him. Jindalee land wasn't the best. It was semi-arid and even back in the late 1800s, before there was white settlement in the interior, it wasn't the sort of land that would have had had settled Aboriginal communities – the land was too poor. The natives in this area would have had to cover vast distances leading a semi-nomadic existence, travelling from soak to soak, waterhole to waterhole, staying a short while at each before moving on: it was the nature of the land out here, and care had to be taken not to overuse it if they were to survive in the long term. It was still the same, thought Jon, in times of drought they had to reduce their stock holding and could only carry the number they did because of the wells and bores that had been dug and drilled over the years. Curly had once told him that in the Big Dry his people had had to turn to the white men for sustenance or die because the nature of the land had been changed by the introduction of white men's cattle and sheep, not to mention the feral camels, brumbies and goats, and the subsequent overgrazing that destroyed the native flora and drove the wildlife away.

The fact was, the best land for the white man was the best land for the Aborigine, and the white man settled where the water was depriving both Aborigines and the native wildlife of access to the soaks, springs and gnamma holes they'd relied on for millennia.

Jon could picture it all, just as Eyre had, the Aborigines retreating in the face of the white invasion, waiting for the intruders to leave, and when they didn't, returning to their own tribal land for the seasonal food they relied on, or for cultural and religious purposes. But by then the land was considered settled. Confrontation had been inevitable, and bloody and brutal in some cases. But even where the settlers had treated the natives well the result was still the same for the original inhabitants – dispossession.

When Jon arrived back at Jindalee, Ruby and Val were waiting for him.

Val handed Jon a mugful of tea. 'Ruby says Kennilworth has killed some of our cattle.'

Jon nodded, a grim look on his face.

'Do you want me to call Nickson out?'

'It'd do no good; Nickson and Kennilworth are thick as thieves.' Jon's voice tightened with sarcasm. 'I can't see Nickson doing much other than taking a trip over to Reef Hill and tapping Kit on the wrist for being a naughty boy. No, we're going to have to find some other way of fixing the Kennilworths, something that will stop this petty warfare they've been subjecting us to.'

'Yeah,' agreed Ruby, 'and the sooner the better, because the situation is getting worse. We no sooner fix the damn fence than it's breached again.'

Jon slammed his empty mug down on the kitchen table. 'We'll sleep on it, see if we can come up with something that will stop this once and for all.'

CHAPTER 19

A week after their return to Jindalee, George and his family set off for Queensland to visit traditional sites important to them. Jon, still concerned about Kennilworth and the boundary fence over near Twenty-five Mile Bore, decided to ride out and check whether the repair he, George and Charlie had made was still intact.

'Do you want me to come with you?' asked Val, over breakfast. They were alone for once, Ruby was at Jarrahlong, helping Alice, Harry was in Darwin trying to persuade Nathaniel Gregson to fly choppers in their new mustering business, and Shirley had temporarily taken over May's responsibilities.

'No need. I was thinking of riding the boundary up there; it's a while since I've done that, and it'll do me good, give me time to think things through.'

Val smiled. 'Which problem is that? – Kennilworth or James, Pete and Merle?'

Jon grinned at her. 'Both, but now you mention it, what are we going to do about the McGhees and James Glengarry when they arrive?'

'Wing it, but at the very least you need to peg out a square and get over to Pilkington to take out a mineral lease on that land west of Lake Desolation. You'd be pig-sick if James's mate, Patrick O'Shea, beats you to it.'

'You're right, as usual; I'll do it as soon as I get back.'

'How long will you be gone?'

'Three days I should think. I'll ride over to the bore, check the fences between us and Reef Hill, camp out for the night and then ride the rest of the northern boundary.'

'I'll get Yang-dhow to pack up some tucker for you while you sort things out with Charlie and get saddled up, and when you get back from your trip I'll cook us your favourite dinner.'

'Corned-beef stew and damper,' he quipped.

'No, hon, Scouse.'

It was nine in the morning before Jon left the homestead on his favourite horse, Beauty, a dun-coloured mare, similar to the one Ty Henderson had ridden the first time he'd met him back in the late forties when the dogger had ridden into the yard at Jarrahlong to sort out the dingo problem they'd been having. That was the first time he'd seen a dun-coloured horse. He'd been taken with the honey-coloured coat, the black mane and tail and darker shading on the head and legs, and he'd vowed then to have one one day.

Jon patted the horse as he rode out and looked about him, seeing the place with fresh eyes after his trip to England. Despite the drought, it was a pretty fine spring, usually the nicest time of the year – unless it was blowing up a storm – when the temperature didn't get too hot. The day was perfect; a breeze was scudding the clouds along with just enough edge to dry the sweat, and all about him were wild flowers – a Persian carpet of colour that never ceased to delight – the purple parakeelyas, green and purple mulla mulla, yellow billy-buttons and pink and white everlastings.

To his mind, this land beyond the mulga line was a bonza place and it was his, his and Val's. They'd raised their children on this land, they'd grow old together on it and then, in time, they'd be buried in its soil, in the plot they'd selected overlooking the creek, on one of the most beautiful parts of the station – a stone's throw from the homestead. Mike Tunstall had already made the fancy wrought-iron railings with a pretty arched gateway to mark off the square, and they'd planted scented roses to grow over the arch. He'd wanted to seed the ground with drought-resistant grass, watered by a trickle pipe laid from the main water tank, but Val had laughed at him. What's wrong with the red earth, hon? she'd asked. She'd been right, as usual. There was nothing wrong with the red earth, it was just that he'd wanted the green, a reminder of England, a nod to his heritage, but in the end, he'd left the land as it was.

He whistled as he rode, easy in the saddle, and content. An hour out from the station he spotted a lone dingo watching him from the ridge. A pure-bred, he noted, not one of the feral half-breeds that, like dingoes, often travelled in packs killing sheep and calves, the reason for employing the dogger on stations like Jindalee and Jarrahlong. He watched the animal watching him and admired the look of it, its reddish sandy coat merging with the colour of the sandhills behind it. He didn't particularly like killing dingoes, or any animal come to that. To his mind they all had a place, but it was a question of balance, it didn't do when their numbers were such that musters produced reduced numbers of calves. The same was true on Jarrahlong – when dingo and feral dog numbers were up lamb numbers were down, and the situation was exacerbated during droughts.

And it wasn't just the dingoes and feral dogs that were a problem; the rabbits had devastated the land in the outback, driving men to bankruptcy. Jon concentrated on riding for a while, letting his horse have her head over the rougher ground, mulling over the situation. At least rabbits weren't a problem on Jindalee, but the bloody camels were, especially in droughts, and so were the brumbies to a lesser extent.

There was no doubt about it, the effect of the white settlers on the indigenous population, dispossessing them, bringing in livestock that ultimately decimated huge tracts of the bush, had been badly managed. And it wasn't just the supposedly useful species they'd introduced either, he thought. There were the foxes brought in for hunting, and cats that preyed on the smaller marsupials. No, the influx of the white man had changed large swathes of the outback forever and devastated many species of indigenous fauna.

The trouble was people never learnt, he mused; only the other week there'd been a piece in the paper about cane toads brought in from tropical America to control a beetle attacking the sugarcane in Queensland. That would probably end up being a problem as big as the rabbits in the end, he'd put money on it.

Jon dismounted at one of the permanent soaks on the station and let the horse drink while he built a fire to boil a billy of tea, wondering if there was any chance of getting back to some of the old ways. But deep down he knew it would be well-nigh impossible, an uphill struggle at the very least, even if people had the will.

He sat on a log, watching the mare graze on the wanderrie grass, waiting for the water to boil. It was cooler in the shade of the gimlet and he was conscious of a flock of zebra finches flitting through the bushes, attracted by the water. That was one thing about the finches, they were never far from water: see them out in the bush, follow them and they'd save your life, if you let them. That's what Val had done the time she and Merle were stranded out in the stony desert after Chips Carpenter had had to do a forced landing in his plane. He pictured Val as he'd found her all those years ago, with Yildilla's help. She'd been painfully thin, standing between two scrubby bushes, holding a goanna she'd caught for breakfast. It was then he'd realised it was her he loved and not Merle.

He brushed the memory aside, threw a handful of tea leaves into the billy and then poured himself a pannikin of black tea sweetened with sugar. He wondered how long it would be before Pete, Merle and James turned up in Charlestown – any day, if what Pete had said was anything to go by. He could have done without the added complication of the three of them on his patch.

Val was annoyed about it too, not that she'd said anything, but his past with Merle was always between them and although Val said she believed him when he said he'd never slept with Merle he wasn't sure she'd completely accepted it. Whatever Merle had said to her the time they'd been stranded had left its mark. Val still half believed he felt something for Merle even though she joked about it. Jon swore under his breath. How on earth had they managed to get themselves lumbered with the three of them?

Jon sat back and sipped his tea, enjoying the breeze ruffling his hair, listening to the calls of the wedge-tailed eagles high above, but it wasn't long before his thoughts drifted back to the present and the impending visit. He really could have done without Pete, Merle and James at Jindalee but, with luck they wouldn't stay long, a couple of days at most and then they'd be rid of them for good. Pete would be in for a shock though, that was for sure.

Jon finished his tea and threw the dregs into the dust. He'd had a lucky escape. Had he married Merle it would have been a disaster: she wasn't the type to be happy living in the bush. She would have nagged him to sell up, use his wealth to buy an estate like James's back in England. He couldn't think of anything worse.

As the sun reached its zenith he doused the fire with sand, wiped the pannikin clean, and whistled Beauty. Even in spring the sun bleached colour at midday; in the distance the greens and blues had melded to aqua and the rich, red earth had paled to honey-gold. He squinted against the light, tilted his hat lower, shading his eyes against the glare and mounted his horse. They set off, picking their way between the tussocks of spinifex grass and prickly curara bushes.

138

Overhead, the pair of wedge-tails he'd heard earlier soared in the heat of the day, riding the thermals, their mewing calls drifting on the warm breeze. Wedge-tails always reminded him of Yildilla, Bindi's grandfather – it was their gimlet eyes, watchful, all-seeing, and inscrutable. He shuddered. It was years since he'd seen the old kaditja man, fourteen or so, the time when Yildilla led him to Val and Merle out on the stony plain after the plane crash. More recently he'd wondered if it was Yildilla who'd told the woman with the half-caste child that they'd be safe at Jindalee. But, other than that possible connection he'd only heard occasional reports of him living in the desert, in the old ways, only visiting white communities to buy tobacco and other necessities. Was the old man still alive? Jon supposed he was, otherwise he'd have heard. But Yildilla would be in his eighties by now, although it was hard to tell, he reckoned Yildilla had been born old.

The wedge-tails mewed again, pulling him out of his reverie; he banished thoughts of Yildilla and concentrated on checking the boundary fence.

Jon followed the fence and reached Twenty-five-Mile Bore in the late afternoon. He was relieved there were no breaks and that the cattle were well spread out in the bush, not seeking a way through onto Reef Hill land. He unsaddled the mare, watered her, hobbled her for the night and left her to browse before gathering a pile of wood to see him through till morning. By the time his meal was ready it was dark and the stars were out in the night sky.

Jon settled back against the saddle, his feet towards the fire, gazing into the flames as he ate the food Yang-dhow had prepared for him. He'd always enjoyed camping out, especially on spring nights when it was cool but not cold enough to chill him to the marrow. Tonight, a single blanket would be enough to keep him warm with just a couple of mulga roots as "keepers" to maintain the fire through till morning. Usually he had company; George or Val would be with him, or the stockmen if they were on a muster, but sometimes it did a bloke good to be on his own, it gave a fella time to think, to sort out priorities – like what to do about the bloody nickel!

The more he thought about it the more he knew that investing in James Glengarry's nickel mine was a bad idea. He didn't know why, it was just a gut feeling, but a strong one. When James arrived in Charlestown with Pete and Merle he wouldn't shilly-shally, he'd tell them straight that he wasn't interested. He had all the wealth he needed from Stan's gold and he owned Jindalee. To get involved in buying shares in a mining operation, even with insider knowledge, wasn't for him, especially considering the people involved and he knew Val agreed. Truth to tell he wished the core samples had been duds, with only enough nickel to register but not enough to make the operation economical. They could do without all the muck and noise a mine would create. One only had to take a look at the big gold mining operations in the goldfields to see what mining did to the land.

Jon woke with a start in the small hours of the morning sure he'd heard the report of a rifle. He sat bolt upright, but heard nothing more except the sounds of small nocturnal marsupials and mice scuttling about in the grasses and dried leaves. Had he dreamt it? After a moment or two he settled down again but was unable to sleep, instead he lay there, listening. Almost an hour later came a second shot followed soon after by another rifle crack, but this time the sound came from a north-easterly direction, the sound carrying on the cold night air.

It was impossible to calculate distance, especially at night when sound seemed to travel further, when there were no competing noises and the air was cold and still. Whoever had fired the rifle could well be many miles away. He could tell from the night sky that there were two or three hours to go till dawn, and until there was light it was pointless attempting to investigate. But still, who was out and about at three in the morning with a rifle? Was it one of Kennilworth's men shooting Jindalee cattle? Then he dismissed the very idea; Kennilworth was a bastard right enough, but even he wasn't that foolish. The other possibility was an Aborigine out hunting, although he wasn't convinced.

He breakfasted early and by first light had eaten, doused the fire, and found and saddled his horse. The rifle shots had come from the direction of the breakaways, over on the north-eastern side of the station, a fair old ride at the best of times, but it wouldn't do to ignore what he'd heard. It might not be a fella out hunting but someone in trouble, the rifle shots a desperate call for help from a bloke badly injured and stranded in inhospitable territory. Even as he rode there came a fourth rifle crack then, soon after, a fifth report – was the person travelling east looking for human habitation? Was that why the sound always seemed to be ahead of him? He was glad he'd had the foresight to refill all of his water bottles and the water bag around the horse's neck; whoever was out there would probably be ready for a drink.

For once he didn't notice the countryside; he was too busy concentrating on finding the fastest, safest route for his horse. He skirted the worst of the spinifex and curara on the more arid land and then took the short cut along a dry creek bed as soon as he came upon it.

By mid morning he'd reached the breakaways and paused, listening. After a few minutes he yelled, calling to whoever had discharged the rifle, listening for the echo to die away. But there were only the familiar birds chattering in answer. He rode his horse deeper into the gorges, scanning the territory the while. When the route narrowed and divided into two he took the most likely, stopping to listen and calling from time to time, but to no avail. He gave the horse her head and let her pick her way over increasingly difficult terrain. Surely whoever had fired the shots wouldn't be this deep in the breakaways, there was no reason for them to be here, unless it was a lone prospector looking for good auriferous country? Or was it someone from the mining company following a hunch, looking for greenstone and the nickel it contained? – someone who was now lost and panicking.

'Anyone about?' he yelled.

A rifle shot came by way of an answer. Close by, Jon calculated and near enough to make the horse jump, then came another and his horse crumpled under him.

CHAPTER 20

The horse falling caught Jon unawares. Time slowed. He could smell the warm scent of the horse's skin as the air was sucked out of his body. He fought for breath as his mount dropped beneath him, dragging the reins from his fingers as he catapulted over the animal's head, arms flung out to break his fall. But it was too late; he hit the ground with a sickening thud. For a split second came flashes of spinning light...blackness, and...

....his skull throbs, nausea rises like the tide; his ears ring and a metallic taste in his mouth sickens him.

'Who've you upset, mate?' comes a familiar voice.

Who...? – his head aches...who is it? What sort of question is that? He wants to brush his face...the fluttering, like moths, distracts him, but the sensation fades and then comes the smell – earthy, musky... acrid warmth...

...Oh God! – he'd wet himself! – and his world was spinning, a nauseating sensation accompanied the rushing sound clamouring in his ears. Had he had too much grog...was that it? Was he drunk? Bile rose up and burning, choking bitterness splattered the rocks as he retched.

But whose voice was it? And why? Or was it all imagination, or a dream? He hated the nightmares that disturbed sleep far too often – even after all the years at Jindalee – the unexpected sense of helplessness, of being trapped, unable to escape from some un-named horror, as if his brain had no will of its own.

Thinking made the head ache more, but he couldn't work it out, his addled brain fuddled thought and the blackness crept up like soupy fog rolling in over the turgid Mersey River on miserable November mornings...

'...Y'can't stay here, mate,' comes the voice again from the depths, that familiar voice that he can't identify.

Why not? he thinks, not wanting to think of anything, the effort too much for his throbbing head. Strewth, he feels ill, worse than before. Is this still a nightmare? Is that it? Is he sick? Does he have a fever?

'Nah, mate, it's no dream.'

Loose rock clatters, Perentie Man looms over him wearing a hat, shading him from the sun, the reptilian skin glistens in the bright daylight, the scales gleam like beaded cloth. Curly's totem animal lashes out, a few sharp kicks to his ribs, then it bends down for a closer look, its hot, foetid breath wafts on the air like a stinking zephyr. Its tongue flicks; a smile breaks on its ugly face...

...He closed his mind to the images, to his throbbing head. It was a nightmare! Curly's totem animal was in a dream – as happened sometimes. But why so vivid, so close...the stench of it...the roughness of reptilian skin pressing against his cheek? Was it a nightmare? Horror swept over him and then came blessed oblivion...

...Later, he woke conscious that time had passed – an hour? – a day? – he wasn't sure, was never sure about the stuff in nightmares. Time was elastic in dreams, it stretched and contracted, as if stitched together in a loop from which he can never escape...as now, when the voice he knows and doesn't know comes again in his ear...together with the nauseous, spinning sensation. He gritted his teeth, fighting the drift...

'...Wake up y'bloody fool!'

Curly! He knows it's Curly this time – the familiar dialect, the exasperation behind the words. What are y'doin' here, mate? he tries to say, but the words won't come.

'Tryin' to save y'bloody skin, y'drongo. Wake up!' orders Curly as if he's heard every word.

He tries to open his eyes, but the throbbing in his head is too much. The nausea engulfs him and he dreams of vomiting, the slick, acrid stench filling his mouth and spewing from his lips, running down his cheek and over his chin.

'Up!' orders the voice...

...He scrunched up his cheek, the one without the vomit, and felt the skin tight and hot, and peered out of the other eye. He blinked, not sure of what he'd seen, and looked again...rock and something unrecognisable, glossy black, and above the black, beige – a stick was it? No, not a stick but dun-coloured hair...a horse's leg and hoof! What was he doing sleeping next to his horse? He made to reach out, perhaps if he...

'...Don't even think about it, mate,' growls Curly, 'and y'close yer eyes again 'n' y're dead meat.'

...But it was no good, the slipping...fading sensation had returned...the light was turning black again...What did Curly mean? Why can't he sleep...? Why...?

'...Hon!'
Val...? What is she doing here?
'She's worried about ya, mate.'
'Why?'
''Cos y'didn't go home,' says Curly.
'What d'you mean?' He thinks he shrieks, his voice fading even as he speaks...

...Scuttling, scrabbling sounds woke him; sharp little claws dug at an eyelid, then came a nip, teeth! He jerked and whatever it was fled. When he shivered he couldn't stop; chattering teeth echoed through the bones in his head. He wasn't drunk, even though he still felt sick and dizzy; he knew he wasn't drunk despite the smell of vomit coating his cheek and mouth. And his head ached. He opened an eye, and saw the horse's hoof and fetlock. This time it made sense, it was his mare. Was she dead? She must be, he'd been lying next to her long enough to get chilled to the bone. Had the horse stumbled and broken her neck? Had he broken his? He concentrated on his head, tried to lift it, but couldn't...his fingers, could he twiddle them? His toes? A hand that didn't seem to be his patted the pain where his head ached. Wincing as he did so, he probed a blood-encrusted gash and the matted hair around it. No

144

wonder his head ached!

And where was he? Why wasn't there someone hauling him up? Yelling for help? Yelling at him to get to his feet and to stop wasting everyone's time?

Concentrate, he told himself again. Think! – where had he been before the accident? – before the horse stumbled?

Liverpool! It was Liverpool! – a party, the lights, the champagne…but there was no horse there, was there? Horses and rocky ground weren't Liverpool, he was on Jindalee somewhere.

Jon opened his good eye again and squinted in the bright morning light. The breakaways! He was in the breakaways! What the hell was he doing in the breakaways with only a horse for company?

He could see the cloudless sky, the sun casting long shadows on the far side of the valley. Then he remembered – he'd been on the other side of the station checking the fencing near Twenty-five Mile Bore. That's where they'd start searching and then they'd follow the boundary fence; no one would think of looking this far to the east, they wouldn't consider seaching the breakaways; it was the last place they'd look! Worse, no one would know he was in trouble, at least not for a couple of days, not until he failed to return and only then would they start to worry. He'd been an idiot, a prize idiot! No one should ignore the primary rule: never deviate from the plan without informing someone or leaving a message. He, better than anyone, knew that the bush was a dangerous place, even at the kinder times of the year when the temperatures stayed well below a hundred degrees. At least it wasn't midsummer, he was thankful for that.

Jon stared at his dead horse, at the blowflies clustering around her eyes, nostrils and mouth, saw the yellow seed-like eggs that would hatch into maggots. A few days and the carcass would be a seething, heaving mass of engorged, wriggling larvae consuming the animal in days rather than weeks; soon she would be a dried out shell of bones and skin – all that would be left of the finest animal on the station. He wanted to weep but had no tears, his mouth and eyes were swollen and dry, his tongue already cleaving to the sides of his mouth as flies settled on him looking for moisture, for places to lay their bloody eggs.

Later still and delirious, with both water bottles missing and the canvas water bag around the horse's neck ripped open, panic rolled over him like a tide and he knew he was in serious trouble. Already the symptoms of heatstroke were apparent: throbbing headache, hot, dry skin, nausea and vomiting, and worse, he couldn't think straight. He knew he had to leave the breakaways and find water, it wasn't an option.

Somehow, he pushed himself upright and waited until the dizziness subsided then looked at the horse. "Beauty" he'd called her, because she was, had been, beautiful. Now her eyes were opaque, dried by the sun and the flies feeding on the moisture, and on the gaping wound below her ear. He sat back on his haunches, squeezing his eyes shut, trying to make sense of the injury…a bullet hole!

Someone had shot the horse from under him!

Shocked by the realisation, he peered at the wound again. A bullet hole, for sure. Death would have been instantaneous. The animal hadn't stood a chance. He couldn't recall a rifle shot before the horse collapsed, but there and again they'd been crossing rocky ground, and his memory was hazy.

But why? Why had no one come to help him, only Perentie Man? He recalled the sensation of Curly's totem animal leaning over him, the sour breath, had it really been a dream? Or had someone been there checking he was dead? He didn't know, couldn't think, couldn't remember.

Jon squinted at the midday sun. He must have drifted off again. That would explain why time seemed to leap forward between blinks. He tried to lick his lips and couldn't. Water, he needed water. He looked about him trying to pinpoint where he was, trying to remember where the waterholes were, the soaks. Kangaroo Soak was the closest, and the sacred cave where the Aboriginal bones had been, but how far, half a mile perhaps? Tears pricked his eyes; he'd never make it, the state he was in.

'Ya bloody have to, mate.'

Curly! Curly was dead, had been dead for years. Jon scanned the valley, but there was only the dead horse, the scrubby bush, and a thorny devil basking on a shaley mound, warming its body in the sun's heat. He drew his arm across his hot, dry brow. His Aboriginal friend was right; if he wanted to survive he had to reach water, waiting for a relief party was foolhardy, by the time they found him he'd be dead, the flesh mouldering from his bones.

He dragged himself upright, catching his breath, the effort agony as broken ribs grated. Every gasp of breath sent shock waves through him, spiking his brain. Had it been the fall or had he been kicked as well? Then there were the missing water canisters. Had Perentie Man not been a dream but someone intent on ensuring a death in the outback, miles from home?

Walking in the heat of the day was a lunatic thing to do, but waiting for the cooler hours wasn't an option. He looked for a suitable pebble to suck, to hold the thirst at bay, a trick Curly had taught him the time they'd journeyed to Paradise Canyon, and he kept his eyes skinned the while for a kurrajong with its precious store of water.

Jon kept to the shady side of the gorge, avoiding the needle-sharp thorns that could shred skin faster than a filleting knife, resisting the urge to strip off his shirt and discard his hat. He'd been in the same position once before, had been delirious enough to discard his clothes in the belief that he would be cooler; it was the act of an idiot, and was a lesson he wouldn't have to learn twice.

Walking jolted his memory – he'd been riding the boundary, had camped out for the night and then there'd been the gunshots. Investigating them had seemed the right thing to do. Is that what the fella who'd shot his horse had assumed? – that he'd check things out? Someone had lured him into the breakaways and had lain in wait. Was he one of Kennilworth's men, or was it Todd?

The more he reflected on it the more convinced he was that the Kennilworths lay behind it somewhere. There'd been the cattle they'd shot, the running feud over the broken fences, and their anger over Shirley Jones. His relationship with Kit Kennilworth had never been good and had deteriorated since he'd taken Shirley into his household. Kit never had been one to give any ground on anything, and that maniac of a son, Todd, well, Jon was convinced the bloke was dangerous, a fella who couldn't be controlled or trusted.

Every now and again he stopped and listened for an aircraft, unsure in his befuddled state of how many days he'd been unconscious in the gorge, praying that Ruby or Harry were out searching for him in the Cessna, quartering the country, looking for a needle in the proverbial haystack. And the men would be out too, in utes or on horseback, covering the ground over on the west side. And they'd have Charlie with them – Charlie was a good tracker, he'd be able to follow the route taken....unless the bastard who'd killed the horse had obliterated his tracks, scrubbed them out with brushwood, and maybe leaving a false trail away from Twenty-five Mile Bore.

147

But listening was futile – there was only the familiar sounds of the bush, the occasional scuttling and rustling as small reptiles and rodents took cover behind rocks and thorny bushes, and high overhead the shrill call of a wedge-tailed eagle circling on a thermal, watching as he stumbled along. He struggled to keep to a line, his mind increasingly sluggish as dehydration set in. For the first time that day he felt afraid. How long before the urge to strip off his clothing become unbearable? How long before his mind went completely and he'd do just that, throw off his shirt, kick off his strides and his boots, as he'd done back on the plain after Curly died?

A dry sob caught in his throat, he missed his footing, staggered, and fell heavily, knocking the air out of his lungs. The pain made his head spin and brought with it blessed oblivion…

….Jon came to, choking on the pebble he'd been sucking on; he hadn't been out of it for long. Next time he might not be so lucky! He eased himself onto his side, holding back the black with sheer determination, concentrating on the sparkles of light circling behind his lids. He leaned against a boulder and gathered himself, knowing he needed rest, if only for a few minutes, conscious of the wedge-tail following his feeble efforts.

As he watched the bird became a speck in the sky, soaring on the thermals, waiting for the cooler hours when creatures came out to feed. At least there wasn't a mob of them. Pastoralists and cattlemen hated them: they shot and poisoned them in their hundreds to protect their animals and collect the five-shilling bounty the government paid for each bird killed. He recalled the time he'd been with Adie and they'd seen several birds attack and bring down a fully-grown kangaroo.

He shuddered at the memory, would it swoop down and feed off him? Would it peck out his eyes once he was too weak and feeble to protect himself?

He closed his mind against the image and rested awhile, the pain in his ribs a throbbing ache. Revived, he pushed himself up, and leaned against the rock for support, afraid of taking a step in case he keeled over.

Bile rose in his gullet and filled his mouth. He spat out the bitterness, gritted his teeth and thought of Kangaroo Soak – there'd be water there. If he could reach it he'd survive long enough to be found. He had no doubt he would be found, Val wouldn't rest until he was.

It was hard to see through gritty eyes. Was he developing sandy blight? He'd heard of blokes having to be led by mates, and Lasseter had spoken of being blinded and driven crazy by gritty eyes. His head throbbed. He was in a bad way, "crook" was the Aussie word. He tried to laugh but all that came from his mouth was a croak – blind, dumb and crippled with pain, he was a bloody useless specimen, he'd be better off dead! But he knew he was kidding himself. He felt his mind drifting.

'Where are you, hon?'

The breakaways he tried to say, the words just thoughts.

'She can't hear ya, mate,' came Curly's voice in his head.

You can, he thought, so why not, Val? And he imagined he could hear Curly chuckling.

One foot, and then the other, he told himself, focusing on feet that didn't seem to belong, ignoring the sun beating down on his head and back, and the bloody eagle high overhead, and Curly muttering in his ear.

One foot and then the other...one...foot...and...then the other. It's not the first time he's had to concentrate on walking, but he can't recall the occasion.

'Ain't y'got no pituri on ya, mate?' asked Curly.

Pituri! He knows the word. Where's he heard it before? And then he remembered the narcotic Aborigines used for dulling the pain of circumcision, for giving them stamina, and for lacing the water at waterholes to drug the game.

'Y brain ain't gone yet, then,' quipped Curly.

Curly was wrong, his brain was sluggish now, remembering the pituri had been hard, dredging the depths to recall the detail... and soon it would be worse...soon his mind would shut down altogether.

'You dozy idiot, hon,' said Val. *'George says you're not at Twenty-five Mile Bore, so what've you gone and done? You fancied a day trip to Kal, or somethin'?'*

Jon heard the worry behind her words and the false cheerfulness. The sun dropped beyond the ridge, and he shivered, his skin burning up from sunburn and heatstroke.

'Hang on, hon, we'll find you...everyone's lookin'.'

He held on to the words he believed he'd heard, knowing it was the delirium talking, merely imagination, hearing only what he wanted to hear.

'*Y've still not learnt, 'ave ya, mate?*' said Curly in his ear.

'*Learnt what?*' he thinks he said, but can't be sure. Nothing seemed real any more, neither the conversations in his head nor his feet shuffling across the stony ground.

Jon reached the soak at dusk after stumbling over rocks and scratching through the brush surrounding the damp patch. He tried to make a depression to collect the muddy water, but in the end he just buried his face in the wetness of it and rested, what little moisture he could suck up revived him but he knew it wasn't enough. He slept then, lying flat out on his stomach, a cheek resting on the muddy sand.

Later, when the moon was overhead silvering the land, he came to, and knew he had to reach the water; it was his only chance, except in the cave he couldn't be seen from a plane or by anyone searching at ground level. Would anyone think to look in the cave with his horse half a mile away?

He hoped so.

Jon concentrated on the task ahead, creating an image of what he needed to do, preparing for the superhuman effort it would take. How far to the water? – fifty, sixty yards perhaps. Could he manage that? "Could" wasn't an option, "must" was the word he was searching for in a brain muddled by heatstroke. The place had been a grave for a mob of Aborigines; would it end up being his?

'*Might be, mate, if y'don't get a wriggle on,*' murmured Curly in his ear.

He saw Curly in his mind's eye, the lanky youth who had taught him to love the outback, the land that could easily be the death of him if he didn't get himself together. Curly had been a good-looking Aborigine, pretty for a fella, with an irrepressible gappy grin, sun-bleached copper-blond hair and an indomitable laid-back spirit. A sob caught in his throat. He'd loved Curly like a brother; the pain of his death was still sharp in his breast, the hours it had taken Curly to die, the gangrenous flesh poisoning his body and his brain. It was no way to go, not for anyone, and not for someone as young and vibrant as Curly had been.

'*I'm still with ya, mate, if y'let me,*' came Curly's words in his head. '*Y'can't get rid of a mate that easy. Now, pick y'feet up, y'drongo, and get a drink.*'

Making the move was hard, his leaden feet wouldn't respond,

and then he felt it, a sharp kick on the backside. The pain made him gasp.

'Get up ya lazy bastard.'

Somehow he got to his feet and staggered over the loose rockfall to the cave entrance; he flopped onto cool sand under the overhang and dragged himself like a king brown deeper into the cave, over the dry, soft sand, and rested.

'Light a fire, hon' came Val's voice. *'We'll see the smoke, everyone's out lookin'.'*

Light a fire! He couldn't even drag himself to his feet never mind gather the wherewithal for a bloody fire!

He closed his eyes and rested his forehead on his arms. Somewhere deep in the cave water dripped into the pool of crystal clear water that he'd found, water that would have helped save the Samuels' sheep had they known of its existence. Life was a bitch, no doubt about it. Who'd told him that? He dredged his muddled brain for the answer.

'I did.'

The new voice dragged him from the depths. Who was it? Who'd spoken?

'Yer old mate...Stan.'

Was he dying? Was that why he'd heard Curly speaking to him and now Stan? But it didn't make sense. Val had spoken to him too and she wasn't dead. Had he gone mad? Was he delusional? Was it dehydration? Fever? In the blackness behind his eyelids an image formed – three people sitting in a row, like the "see all, hear all, say nowt" brass monkeys Gran had on the mantelshelf in her kitchen. Except these weren't monkeys, they were his nearest and dearest: a dead gold prospector, a dead Aborigine, and Val, his own, very much alive, wife.

Stan chuckled. *'A ruddy monkey, you reckon!'*

Jon felt himself smile even though his lips hadn't moved, couldn't move. The moment passed. He had to get to water or he'd die. He staggered to his feet and stumbled deeper into the cave. The distance in the dark seemed interminable, but he remembered the way – there were no forks, just the straight passage down towards the pool. He blocked his mind to the effort and concentrated on reaching the life-sustaining water.

Time was meaningless. He had no way of gauging how long it took but at some point he found himself kneeling at the water's edge drinking deep draughts of cool, sweet water. Gradually the swirling lights behind his eyelids faded, exhaustion overwhelmed him and then came the blessed comfort of sleep as his body claimed the rest it needed.

CHAPTER 21

He knew he was dreaming. It was always the same, he was never conscious of people physically talking in his dreams, but talk they did, the words seeming to float in his subconscious. And people in them were how he remembered them which was why it was odd talking to a mother who was younger than he was now. He hadn't realised how pretty she'd been, prettier than his Aunt Marg, which was odd too, his mother had always said Marg was the good-looking one, but not to his eye. But there and again, maybe he was biased, she was his mother, and when all was said and done mothers were beautiful to their sons, weren't they...?

'...Australia!' Mam says. 'Who'd have thought it!' Her face darkens. 'They said you'd be looked after, son. It never occurred to me they'd send you half a world away, to Australia.'

'It's okay, Mam,' he hears himself say, 'it all worked out in the end.'

'I thought my sister would take you in when your gran was so sick, but, it seems, you can't rely on your nearest and dearest. Marg isn't much better than that ne'er-do-well father of yours.'

'She looked after Kathy well enough,' he says.

She sighs. 'She never did take to you, did she?'

Jon chuckles. 'She said I was a snotty-nosed kid with my arse hanging out of my britches.'

'She said that!' says Mam. 'You were never snotty nosed and you never had holes in your britches, never!'

'I know, Mam, but the bottom line is, she never liked me. And that's all right; I always considered her to be a bit of an old cow.'

The background seems to shift and change and suddenly his

153

mother is gone and instead there are the three brass monkeys ex-cept they are not monkeys but Stan, Val and Curly.

'I see you came to ya senses and married the right gal,' says Stan.

Val glances at Stan and smiles. 'She's still on the scene, Stan. She's not an easy woman to get rid of.'

'Merle?' queries Stan.

'The one and the very same. She's sleepin' in the spare room,' Val says in a clipped tone.

'What do you mean?' asks Jon. 'What's Merle doing visiting our place?'

'Have you forgotten?' said Val. 'She's visitin' the outback to look at the damned nickel mine along with Pete and James.'

'What nickel mine?' asks Curly.

The figures blurr and swim, shapeshifting into the drillers at the mining lease over on Wanndarah, the generator powering the drilling rig, working twenty-four hours a day, whining in his ears even as he looks down at it – an eagle's-eye view.

'You reckon you should invest, son?' asks Stan. 'Val here sez that according to Merle you'll all be dollar millionaires. Don't think Val's that convinced though.'

'You're not wrong there, Stan,' says Val.

Jon smiles grimly. 'Val's right, invest in that and you'll lose your shirt, Stan.'

'Wes sez the core samples are bonza according to your mate, Pete. Wes sez they're the best this side of Laverton, sez he's going to buy some shares. Word is it's a rich seam.'

'He'll be an idiot if he does,' mutters Jon to no one in particular.

Stan smiles. 'And what does Alice say?'

'Same thing, Stan.'

'Well, you listen to what Alice sez, she don't often get things wrong...'

...Time passed, how much time there was no way of telling; it was pitch dark in the cave, not even a sliver of reflected light coming from the cave entrance. He still felt nauseous and shivery – per-haps he was still concussed from the fall, from the gash in his scalp, it would explain the blackouts, the confusion, the times when it seemed he'd been dreaming of dead people speaking to him...and Val! He frowned; Val wasn't dead so why had she been in the dream?

Was it telepathy?

He remembered the other time he'd been dehydrated and dying in the desert, his desperation when Jimmi turned up. Jimmi had heard him, knew where to find him.

He fixed his mind on Val, willing her to hear him, trying to picture the cave to give her a clue. But the effort made his head ache and spin, sparkles of light swirled around like midges on a summer evening and he vomited until his belly ached, bringing up nothing but watery fluid. He rolled over on his back and rested, thinking of Val, listening for her voice that he'd heard earlier, in a quiet moment, when his mind was empty, telling him to light a fire, a signal for them to see.

The night Ruby was born Val had called to him in desperation, and he'd heard her then, in the twilight between slumber and wakefulness, so why couldn't he hear her now? He had earlier and, more to the point, why couldn't she hear him when he willed her to listen? Why couldn't she sense his desperation? But he knew the answer – they'd all be busy back at Jindalee. Val would be co-ordinating the search, she'd be out in the ute or on a horse, just as he would have been doing if it had been her lost in the bush. Other things would be impingeing on her mind; she needed the silence, and an empty mind to hear him.

Feelings of panic and despair engulfed him and he bit back a string of expletives. Swearing wouldn't help, it never did. He concentrated on the throbbing head, willing the blackness to stay away, but he could feel himself slipping...slipping...

....He's flying, high up, almost as high as the wedge-tails, and he laughs as he remembers Ruby's favourite poem, "High Flight". What were the words again? – something about eagles' wings, and chasing the wind along, but he can't think, and anyway what does it matter?

He shrugs off the memory and, without warning, he's kneeling by Matt's side in the middle of a cyclone looking at the Cafferty twin's ruined skull scythed in two by a piece of tin sheet. Tears roll down his cheek as he stares at the mess through the rain; and then he is running, running through chest-deep water, his clay feet treading the gushing torrent and getting nowhere. The frustration is a heavy lump in his chest...he flails his hands, but they meet no resistance, they windmill like kites in a spin, twisting and turning, and he

155

hears himself calling, but no sound emerges from his parched lips. Who is he shouting for? He can't think.

O'Leary, the bastard priest from Karundah, dressed all in black, like a crow, is looming over him, patting him on the head. And, even as he looks up into the priest's moon face, the image slips and changes into Perentie Man, the massive monitor lizard with its foetid breath and scaly skin catching the light and blinding him. The reptile's mouth opens wide, and he feels himself sliding into its stinking maw, his fingers scrabbling on the rocky ground, fingernails tearing, ripping, bloody...staining the rock, resisting...and the screaming, screaming...screaming...

'...Gently,' he heard someone say, warm breath wafting over him as he is lifted – two people, or is it three? A light swept the cave roof, a beam of light that didn't stay still long enough to make sense of where he is.

'Is he still with us?' came Val's familiar voice.

A male voice muttered a reply he didn't quite catch, but he guessed it was Charlie; it sounded like Charlie, the voice was deep enough.

'Jon, you're safe now, hon.'

His heart lifted. She'd found him! She'd heard him!

'Can we carry him between us, Charlie?' Ruby's words came through clenched teeth as she took the strain.

'No worries,' grunted Charlie. 'How come he found this place?'

'There was a rock fall, and his dog led him into the cave.'

Jon remembered as Val spoke, relieved that he still had all his mental faculties, even if his body was in bad shape.

'This where he found all them bones he buried?' asked Charlie.

'Yes. He said they'd been massacred. Walter Haynes, the old prospector over beyond Pilkington told him it happened way back, in the early days, before the land was properly settled,' said Val.

'Yeah,' grunted Charlie, 'y'mean when it was still ours.'

'Sorry, Charlie, no offence intended.'

'S'alright missus, we knows you is more understandin' than most, especially that bastard Kennilworth. Y's'pose he's got anything to do with killin' the horse?'

'I really don't know, but someone did.'

In a hazy world of tidal nausea Jon listened to their conversation as they carried him from the cave out into the bright sunlight – the light behind his eyelids turning from midnight blue to scarlet as they emerged from the gloom.

'Jon,' came Val's voice. 'Can you hear me, Jon?'

His mouth seemed to form an answer but nothing came from his lips and he came to the conclusion that he'd only imagined speaking.

'He's still out of it,' came Charlie's voice. 'We need to get 'im to the hospital pretty damn quick.'

'It'll take an hour and a half for the flying doctor to get to the station, then another hour and a half to Kal. It'd be quicker if I fly him there,' volunteered Ruby.

'Yes, hon, but they're trained, and he'll be flat out on a stretcher in the plane not slumped in the passenger seat in the Cessna. The flying doctor is our best bet.'

Jon smiled to himself, trust Val to consider all the options and go for the most sensible. In any case another couple of hours either way wasn't going to make much difference to the outcome.

CHAPTER 22

They kept Jon in Kalgoorlie hospital for a week. Sister Lewis, who'd nursed him after his mining mishap years earlier, told him that it was about time he took more care, that nasty accidents out in the bush were the surest way to a short life.

Once he'd been given the all-clear Ruby came for him in the Cessna and in what seemed a remarkably short time he was back home again, sitting around the family dining table with Val, Ruby, Alice and Alistair, Harry, Shirley and Noel.

'So,' said Alice, 'apart from dehydration and exhaustion, what was wrong?'

'Apparently, the bullet left a crease in my skull and fractured the bone, Alice.'

Val carried in a tray of cups and saucers and started to pour out the coffee.

'What bullet? You didn't tell us someone shot him, Val? Who did it?' demanded Alice as she accepted a cup of coffee.

Jon answered before Val had a chance to speak. 'I haven't a clue, Alice. I didn't see anyone, only heard a few rifle shots over to the north-east of Twenty-five Mile Bore. So I headed in that direction but the shots seemed to come from even further east, which is how I ended up in the breakaways.'

'Todd,' muttered Shirley as she helped herself to sugar.

'What about him?' asked Val.

'It'll have been Todd.'

'What makes you think that?' asked Jon, interested in Shirley's point of view; it was one that he'd considered himself. He didn't like Todd, but would Todd go as far as to shoot him and the horse from under him? And if he had, why?

158

'He's evil,' said Shirley

Jon looked over at Val and raised an eyebrow.

'Is Todd the one who...molested...you?' Val's voice was gentle and she deliberately chose a less emotive word than rape.

Shirley's face whitened and then she flushed scarlet. She nodded swiftly without looking at any of them.

'I'll kill him,' muttered Harry, 'just see if I don't.'

Shirley stopped fidgeting with the hem of her dress and glanced at each of them in turn. 'He shoots things. He likes killing, likes seeing things suffer.'

'What do you mean?' asked Jon.

'I saw him shooting station dogs, he used to aim at them and shoot 'em in the leg, and he'd laugh when the poor things cried. Then when he'd had enough he'd shoot 'em in the head. Gabe reckoned—'

'Gabe?' queried Noel.

'Todd's older brother,' said Jon.

Harry's brow cleared. 'Oh, you mean Gabriel.'

'Gabe reckoned that when Todd was younger he used to take birds from their nests and pluck 'em alive and he did it to the chooks too.' Shirley shuddered. 'There ain't nobody nastier than Todd. He ain't safe to be around, and he's vindictive too, he won't rest 'til he's punished you for taking me in.'

Val stopped stirring her coffee. 'What about Kit? Can't he stop him? Or his mother?'

Shirley shook her head. 'They dote on him, they do. Todd can't do nothing wrong in their eyes. They taught him you have to be tough in the outback; they think Gabe's a bit of a girl.'

'I'm not surprised giving the bloke a name like Gabriel,' commented Alice tartly. 'He's probably sensitive about it.'

'Todd bullies him,' added Shirley.

Harry caught Shirley's eye. 'Can't see that, Shirl. Gabriel is four years older and about a stone heavier.'

Jon noted Shirley's unease. 'She's right, Harry, according to Todd, Gabe isn't all there. Todd makes fun of him, calls him slow, says that's why the old man has no time for him. Not that I agree. I think Gabe is all right, he's just quiet, and next to that brother of his he does seem slow.'

'Are they ashamed of him?' asked Alistair.

Jon pondered a moment. 'I hadn't thought to look at it like that,' he admitted.

159

'Sometimes that is the case, especially if you've sired a son who doesn't exactly live up to your expectations,' said Alistair.

'Do you think Shirley's right?' asked Noel.

'About what?' asked Jon, leaning back in his seat.

'Shooting you and the horse and leaving you out in the bush to die.'

'It's a possibility. It's true that Todd didn't like it when we brought Shirley here to live with us, and his father was furious when we showed Constable Nickson the doctor's letter.'

'There's another nasty piece of work,' commented Alice. 'Kit and him are big mates, have been mates since they were kids, they still go drinking together.'

Val topped up Alice's cup. 'I think we should change the subject and talk about something pleasanter, don't you?'

'Yes,' agreed Alice, 'and we've some news, Alistair's received a commission to paint a portrait.'

'Good for you, Alistair, anyone I know?' asked Jon.

Alice chuckled. 'Your old beau.'

Jon frowned.

'Mercenary Merle,' jumped in Ruby, 'she saw the painting Alistair did of Mum and was as green as those eyes of hers, couldn't wait to have one done of herself, could she?'

Alistair's face flushed with embarrassment. 'I didn't want to do it, but I ran out of excuses.'

'She's had one sitting already.' Alice patted Alistair's hand. 'But, I have to say it's not your best work, is it, dear?' She turned to the others. 'His heart isn't in it.'

Val smiled. 'Not like mine. You've made me look serene and quite beautiful, Alistair.'

'You are beautiful,' murmured Jon.

'More beautiful than that snake,' agreed Ruby.

'I take it you don't like the woman,' said Noel.

Harry laughed. 'That's an understatement if ever there was one, you know what Rube's like when someone upsets her, look how she pulled a gun on me that time and made me fly spotter in that damn plane of hers.'

'What's she done to upset you, Ruby?' asked Jon.

'She has a sharp, sarcastic tongue, and she's definitely one for the put-down comments, if you ask me she doesn't like female competition. That's why she can't stand Mum.'

'I think you've just about summed her up,' said Alice. 'She

didn't like it when your father turned her down flat after she finally decided he was the one she wanted. It was the second most sensible thing your father ever did.'

'Was it, Alice? And what was the first?' asked Jon.

'Marrying Val,' said Alice tartly.

Val laughed. 'There you go, hon! You listen to Alice, she's never wrong.'

Jon grinned. 'Don't I always? Anyway, weren't the McGhees going to stay here while they were over.'

'They were, but you goin' missin' put paid to that plan. They got fed up hangin' around here on their own while we were out lookin' for you, so they decided they'd be better off in Charlestown. They ended up rentin' rooms in The Grand instead.'

'I bet that was a relief.'

Val smiled. 'Not really. I was too worried about you to be bothered about them. Merle was disappointed that you weren't here, but they didn't have plans to stay long; their new pal, Patrick O'Shea, was expectin' them in Perth. He invited them to the launch party he's organisin' for the nickel mine and they accepted, after that their plan is to fly home and then maybe visit later in the year once the mine is up and runnin' and makin' a mint.'

'They're still drilling over on Wanndarah, then,' said Jon.

'Too right they are,' said Alice, 'and they've been trying to talk me into buying in.'

Ruby chuckled. 'Promised you'd be a dollar millionaire, didn't they?'

Alice tutted. 'If you ask me, people are going mad over this nickel, it's like it was in the old days over gold, everyone rushing to the next find. Les Harper says there are prospectors out all over the place, and that they've started test drilling over Laverton way. Word is that a mining company has found a rich seam at Mount Windarra.'

'You mean the Poseidon Company?' said Jon, recalling James Glengarry mentioning it.

'Yes, that's the one,' agreed Alice. 'According to Les shares are going up fast, says you need to buy in early if you want to make a killing. That's right, isn't it, Alistair?'

'Yes, and they're also sinking mines out at Leinster and at Kambalda, it seems everyone is out to make a fast buck, as the Yanks would say. One wonders how it will all end.'

'There'll be those who make a fortune and those who lose one, it was like that with the gold,' said Alice.

'We should stick to cattle,' said Val, 'at least we know where we are with cattle.'

'What about the greenstone belt you pegged and registered?' asked Alice.

'Oh, that, that's only to stop Patrick O'Shea and his mob applying for a mineral lease on it. We wouldn't want that lot on our land, would we, hon?'

'At least there'll be plenty of new jobs,' commented Alistair.

'But not for blacks,' said Alice. 'You know what people are like about employing blacks around here.'

Ruby's brow knitted. 'They don't know anything about mining though, do they?'

'That's only because they've never been trained,' interrupted Noel. 'Ernie Gilbert's boys, Merv and Mal, have picked up car mechanics pretty quickly. And you told me that Wes is impressed by Merv, that he's one of the best apprentices he's ever had, didn't you, Jon?'

The talk moved on to Race Day in October and the Cathay Cup – the race to end all races according to Alice, when half a dozen bullocks were ridden flat out, chewing up the racecourse in a free-for-all that was as exhilarating to watch as it was dangerous to participate in. Jon left them arguing over which bullock was set fair to win the Cathay Cup and retired to a more comfortable seat in the sitting room to reflect on the earlier talk about nickel. Trust Val to get things organised. She hadn't wasted any time while he was laid up in hospital. She'd pegged the greenstone outcrop on Jindalee – an extension of the greenstone belt on Wanndarah – and registered it. As she said, they could play at mining, and as long as it appeared active their lease wouldn't lapse and if Wanndarah was a rich seam then it would prevent Patrick O'Shea, or anyone else, laying a claim to the mineral rights on what appeared to be the most promising section of Jindalee.

Jon smiled to himself, there was still scads of gold down Stan's No Hope mine at Yaringa Creek, but that was backfilled now so that a lone prospector noseying about was unlikely to discover it. They still panned for alluvial gold and used the dry-blower to keep the lease ticking over which meant the valley and its Dreaming was safe from a gold rush.

He thought about what they'd achieved at Jindalee, employing as many Aborigines as they reasonably could, teaching them about blood lines and animal management as well as training up one or two in truck maintenance with Wes's help. Was there more to be done? Should they explore the possibility of developing a nickel mine? It was poor land for cattle and had no Dreaming associated with it, no sacred places or burial sites. What if they did develop it, bring in the best engineers, train their younger men in the newest mining techniques? Was it a goer? And besides, David said he wanted to be a geologist and work for a mining company one day. Raising cattle bored David, but a nickel mine wouldn't.

Jon imagined Kit Kennilworth's reaction if he sank a nickel mine on Jindalee and employed blacks. Kit was already pretty vocal about the use of Aborigines as stockmen, said they were lazy, but he was wrong; a good Aboriginal stockman was the equal of a white stockman any day of the week, often better.

'What are you doing sittin' in the dark?' asked Val, kissing him on the forehead.

'Thinking.'

'That, in my experience, is a very dangerous thing to do. Come on, hon, it's time for bed, the others all turned in half an hour ago.'

CHAPTER 23

The race meeting in Charlestown had increased to a three-day event by the beginning of the 1960s with additional attractions to draw the crowds. Wes, Connie and Les, who more or less formed the town committee, had bought bunting and proper booths for those merchants who wanted to take advantage of the crowds that descended on the town for the festival weekend. Most people arrived on the Thursday and set up camp on the edge of town, only leaving late on the Monday morning after a heavy night of drinking and dancing.

Over a few hours the town with a population of about twenty souls became a heaving mass of several hundred, many of them driving in from beyond Kalgoorlie and Merredin for the festivities. Over the years it became known that Charlestown knew how to party and party they did.

Friday night the main entertainment was the film show in the town hall, and on the Saturday a matinee for families, followed by an early evening showing for youngsters and then a later evening viewing to cater for adults.

Saturday was racing and a kids' rodeo, and on the Sunday there was a rodeo for adults, followed by the final race of the meeting – the Cathay Cup – which had been switched to the Sunday afternoon. The whole weekend finished with a dance in the town hall on the Sunday night.

Two-up ran in Les's lean-to over the whole weekend and Connie was busy in The Grand serving meals and beers as if there were no tomorrow. Out on the edge of town people had already set up camp, lit their fires, chucked steaks and snags on the griddle and then, after their meal, they'd bed down in their blueys, looking up at the stars, as prospectors did in the old days. Jon envied them as he drove past those already tucking into their suppers. He'd rather be sleeping out under the stars than suffering a hot, stuffy room in The Grand.

Jon nosed the ute through the crowd and parked as close to The Grand as he could. As he stepped out of the vehicle he chided himself for being such a misery. It was party time and he should make an effort or Val would give him what for! He opened the ute door for Alice and glanced down the main street heaving with with people. The place had changed quite a lot over the years. Simpsons was now a dress shop with the menswear transferred to a new store next to The Grand. There was a hairdresser and a barber's shop, a hardware store and a new grocery store with refrigerated units so people could treat themselves to an ice cream and other dairy products, the supply maintained by the fortnightly refrigerated lorry that kept the town adequately stocked. Les Harper's Agricultural Stores was busier than ever, as was Wes's garage on the edge of town.

'It's a bit crowded,' commented Alice as she gathered herself and their overnight bag which she handed to Alistair to carry. The four of them had their usual rooms booked in The Grand, while Ruby was staying with the Hendersons.

After they'd settled in Val, Jon and Ruby met up at the racecourse to enjoy the first snags of the meeting, down beers and circulate amongst the people they knew from the local stations. It was quite a party and the main topic of conversation was the nickel boom.

Jon made an effort to enjoy himself; he joined in conversations, watched Val laughing at tired jokes, and was relieved that Merle and Pete had returned to England. Having to entertain them on his own patch wasn't something he'd relished. He wasn't comfortable with their hard-sell approach that he'd heard about, how they'd encouraging others to invest more than they could reasonably afford in Glenshea nickel stock.

The bloody nickle trade! Bottom line, he was afraid for his friends and neighbours. There was something about the whole operation that just didn't stack up. As he chewed over the problem he spotted Wes Chapman heading in their direction. He put down his beer and clapped Wes on the back.

'Nice to see you, Wes. Can I shout you a beer?'

'Wouldn't say no,' said Wes. He turned to Val after a moment or two. 'I take it Jon's fully recovered from his ordeal.'

Val smiled. 'Pretty much, Wes.'

Jon handed Wes a beer. 'How're you doing? I haven't seen you around for a while.'

'Been on me holidays, ain't I.'

'That's a first, can't ever remember you going anywhere except to Kal for spares,' said Jon.

'Where did you go, Perth?' asked Val.

'Alice.'

'Alice?' queried Ruby who had just joined them.

'Yeah, Alice Springs – for the regatta.'

'What regatta?'

Wes tilted an imaginary straw boater, a broad smile on his face. 'The Henley-on-Todd Regatta, that's what.'

'I've heard about that,' said Jon. 'It started a few years back, '62 if my memory serves, there was a piece about it in the paper as I recall.'

'What made you decide to go there?' asked Val.

'A mate from me school days lives there now, he was back visiting family over Merredin way, we met up for a beer and he invited me, said it was worth a look so I decided it was about time I took a break.'

Ruby looked puzzled. 'Pretty dry place, the Alice.'

'True, the Todd's as dry as a bone mostly, but my word those folk know how to float a boat. You should have seen them. I ain't seen anything like it before, talk about laugh, seeing those lads on the Todd.'

Ruby frowned. 'How does it work? Do they tow the boats or push them?'

'They cut the bottoms out of the boats and carry them – flat out they go, crew pitched against crew. By the time they get to the finish the sweat's pouring off them, and they're the colour of Kit Kennilworth's racing silks – scarlet.'

'It takes an Australian to come up with such a mad idea,' said Jon.

'Aye, started as a fundraiser for charity, so me mate says. The Rotary Club wanted to raise some money and a fella called Reg Smith came up with the idea.'

'And I thought this place was mad holding the Cathay Cup for the fastest bullock on the course,' said Jon.

'Talking about peculiar races, there's talk in Alice of holding a camel race.'

'When?' asked Jon.

Wes shrugged his shoulders. 'Dunno, but there were a couple of fellas who were of the opinion they could race camels along the Todd, said if it was okay for bottomless boats then it'd be marvellous for camels. They'd had a skinful mind, but it wouldn't surprise me if there isn't camel racing in Alice before long.'

'If I had my way we'd cull the lot of them, there're too many and they do a lot of damage, particularly at wells and bores, and to the fencing,' said Jon.

'Talking of racing, are you planning on laying a bet on the Melbourne Cup next month?'

'I usually do, Wes. Les Harper sees to it for me.'

'There's a prime favourite this year just on the name alone.'

'You don't say!'

'Aye, "Rain Lover". You heard the story about him?'

'No, can't say I have, but didn't he win last year?'

'That's right. Won it as a four-year-old stallion. Mick Robbins owns him, Mick made his money from mining coal, he did, says the horse is set fair to win again and if he does he's planning on putting him out to stud.'

'Well, with a name like "Rain Lover" there'll be a good few rooting for him. You putting money on him?' asked Jon.

'Sure am.'

'Well, let's hope he wins and brings the rain with him, we could do with some.'

'Aye,' agreed Wes. 'I can't remember it being this dry even at the beginning of the decade and it was bad enough then.'

'Are you two ready for a feed?' called Val who had wandered over to one of the griddles. 'There's some pretty good grub over here and I'm starvin'.'

'We'll be with you now,' answered Jon. 'Come on, Wes, after you, I'll shout you a snag.'

'Where's Alice and Alistair?' asked Wes.

'The Grand,' said Jon. 'They're having tea there tonight.'

Saturday morning they were out early with Ruby who'd entered her best horse for the barrel racing and, later in the day, the camp drafting.

167

The barrel race had been set up beyond the airstrip, the barrels laid out in a clover-leaf design. Spectator stands provided a good view of the course and the horses and riders. Everything was ready and so was the time keeper.

Barrel racing was all a question of skill and speed and when it came to Ruby she was one of the best. Jon and Val made their way to the stands and watched as Ruby took her horse around the course in record time, circling each barrel in turn until she'd completed a perfect clover-leaf. A cheer went up as she rode through the finish in the best time of the morning and then it was a waiting game as the rest of the riders completed the course.

'Do you think she'll take the cup, hon?' asked Val as they watched a woman from over Pilkington way ride her bay around the barrels like a pro.

'Dunno, there're a few good riders out there this year.' Jon nodded at the woman as she rounded the third barrel, clipping it as she did so, making her horse stumble. 'She had the beating of Ruby had she kept her horse true.'

Val and Jon eyed the clock and breathed easier when she came home two seconds over Ruby's time, but ten minutes later, when the second-to-last rider clocked an equal time, it was clear there was going to be a decider.

They reached the main enclosure just as the announcement came over the loudspeaker that the decider would commence shortly.

'We thought you'd got it,' said Val as Ruby walked her horse over to them.

'So did I,' the wry smile on Ruby's face said it all, 'but Beryl McBride is one of the best, she won the Quartermaine Cup last year.'

While they were chatting, killing time, Wes Chapman strolled over. 'Nice to see they've introduced a few more events for the gals, you did pretty well there, young lady.'

'Thanks, Wes.'

'You'll have her beat, no doubt about it.'

Ruby grinned. 'I hope so; I fancy that silver cup on our mantelpiece.'

'Hey up! Do you hear that, Ruby?' said Val, tilting her head to listen to the latest announcement. 'You need to be gettin' along to the collectin' ring.'

* * *

Ruby won the Barrel Race Cup and Jon shouted them all a beer in the bar at The Grand to celebrate.

They hadn't been there long when Kit Kennilworth and his lad, Todd, arrived. Kit shouted a round for his mates and then caught Jon's eye. 'I hear you've had a bit of a do; word is you very nearly bought it falling off that horse of yours. You should be more careful in them breakaways.'

Jon frowned then turned to face Kit full on. 'You've got your facts wrong, Mr Kennilworth, some mongrel shot my horse and had a go at me too.'

Todd sneered. 'That's your story and you're sticking to it, eh!'

'That's right, and one of my men found the empty cartridge cases to prove it. Whoever it was didn't bother to clean up after himself.'

Todd scowled. 'It don't mean a thing. No one picks up spent cases.'

'You had us all worried, word was out on the schedules; I even considered sending our boys over to help look for ya,' joshed Kit.

Jon glanced at the pair of them, faces bland with just the hint of a grin; it was the last thing they would have done. The Kennilworths weren't known for helping anyone.

'Well, as you can see, I survived and no doubt whoever did it will give themselves away before too long, and when they do I'll be ready for them.'

Val leaned towards him. 'Leave it be, hon, they're not worth it,' she murmured in his ear.

'What's the low-down on all this drilling they're doing over on Bartokas's place, then? I've heard the find on Wanndarah is the best this side of Kal. And Todd here says they've pegged the greenstone on your place.' Kit chuckled. 'They'll be drilling on Jindalee before you know it and investors will be making a packet out of your nickel within the next eighteen months.'

Jon ignored the comment.

'Me and my boys are thinking of investing. Could be we'll make a killing. Might even make enough to buy you out.'

'You'll never have enough dollars to do that, Kit, and if I were to sell Jindalee it wouldn't be to you.'

'We'll see, never yet met a fella who could turn his back on a good profit.' Kit moved along, having said his piece, and ordered another round of beer.

'Do you think he's right?' asked Val.

'About what?'

'The nickel.'

'Your guess is as good as mine. I do know the Poseidon share price on nickel stocks is going through the roof. And if there is nickel on Wanndarah then there's no reason why there shouldn't be nickel on Jindalee, it's the same rock strata. It's a damn good job you pegged it and took out the mineral lease for us.'

'Yeah, but I reckon Kit thinks it's Glenshea Holdings who have taken out the mineral lease on our land, don't you?'

Jon grinned. 'He'll be pig sick when he learns otherwise, won't he.'

Meeting up with the Kennilworths really put a dampener on the rest of the weekend for Jon. He watched the racing in the afternoon, put bets on the Charlestown Gold Plate and the Silver Plate, but for him the best race of the day was the Squatters' Tin Cup, a race over four furlongs and open to anyone local with a nag fit enough to compete. It was a race like those in the early days, when he'd first come to Charlestown, when it was still an amateur meeting run by "Rafferty's Rules" rather than those of the Australian Jockey Club, with not enough prize money to attract serious interest. The Squatters' Cup was the last race of the day on the Saturday and was a bit of fun for everyone. Unlike the early days though, the horses had been groomed within an inch of their lives, their coats shone and most of the riders had begged or borrowed racing silks to look the part.

The betting opened an hour before the race and every man and his dog had a dollar on the outcome. As the jockeys gathered their horses at the starting line the crowd jostled for the best positions. Jon joined Val, Ruby, Alice and Alistair in the stands where they were still busy studying form, wondering whether they'd placed their money on the right nag.

Before Jon had settled himself, they were off, nine horses pounding down the track, hell-bent on winning the tin trophy, the fifty dollar cash prize, and the promise of as much beer as the winning owner could drink in The Grand in one calendar month. Dust flew as thirty-six hooves hit the dirt, the shouts from the people in the stand was deafening as each and every one of them yelled for their horse to win the half-mile race.

Twice round the track and Alex Bartokas's grandson, Andy, came in first on Alex's best mare. Jon smiled, pleased that the Bartokas family had won the best race of the meeting as far as he was concerned. The win would be a small boost for Alex who, everyone knew, was struggling to keep Wanndarah going in the current drought.

That night Jon stayed in the bar drinking beer with Noel Boswell instead of playing two-up, or attending the film show with Val.

'You don't fancy the film, Noel?' asked Jon as he set down a couple of glasses of beer.

'No, I've already seen it, and I'm not much of a gambler. Never was any good at tossing coins when I was a kid, so I'm not going to be any better at it now.'

Jon caught the glances as, every now and again, a visitor to the town caught a glimpse of Noel's badly burned face. 'How do you cope with it, Noel?'

'Everyone looking? You get used to it after a while. The people who matter to me live here and they don't really notice the scars anymore unless someone points them out.'

Jon nodded his agreement. Noel was right. Jon stared into his beer. Noel was a nice bloke, but would he ever find someone to love him? He doubted it, there weren't that many unmarried women in the area of Noel's age who would be prepared to overlook such disfigurement and consider marriage...except perhaps Shirley. He recalled the occasion, just before their trip to England, when he'd suspected she had feelings for Noel. 'Are you staying for the Cathay Cup tomorrow?' he asked.

Noel shook his head. 'No, I'm driving home tonight; I don't think I could cope with the dance afterwards.'

'If you give me an hour, I'll see Val and square things with her and catch a ride home with you. I've had enough of the spring meeting; all anyone can talk about is the bloody nickel boom.'

CHAPTER 24

One night, a couple of months after the race meeting, Jon lay in bed unable to sleep. Val rolled onto her side and snuggled up against him. 'Somethin' worryin' you, hon?'

'Just thinking.'

'About what?'

'The drought, the barometer's still high.'

'It can't last forever.'

'We said that before and it lasted six years.'

'True, maybe you should order in more feed and ship a few more cattle out to agistment.' She rolled back and lay beside him staring at the ceiling as he was doing. 'I've invited Merle and Pete for Christmas.'

'Why did you go and do that?'

'Well, with them back visitin' their investments again and stayin' in The Grand we can hardly ignore them, can we?'

'Don't see why not.'

'Well, there're only the two of them. It seems their pal, James, prefers to spend Christmas at the family pile back in Cheshire.'

Jon recalled the sinking feeling in the pit of his stomach when they'd walked into the saloon in The Grand a week back and had seen Merle, Pete and Patrick O'Shea propping up the bar. Pete had been full of himself, talking about Glenshea nickel stock at every opportunity while Merle had been flirting with Patrick O'Shea. But it was the timing of their visit that had surprised him with Christmas only ten days away.

Val gave him a bemused look. 'They're your mates.'

'They were mates,' muttered Jon. For a while now he had questioned what it was he'd liked about Pete, and when it came to Merle, well, he'd really misread her! She was still stunningly beau-

172

tiful and charming when out to impress, but deep down she was a nasty piece of work. 'I don't know why they're back, Pete's got a wife and son in Liverpool; you'd think he'd want to be with them for the festive season.'

'That was a marriage of convenience if ever there was one,' said Val. 'I feel sorry for Daphne. If she's any sense she'll find herself a new fella and ditch Pete. Anyway, I've invited them and that's the end of it. It won't be for long, just a few days; we'll kick them out straight after New Year, if they're still here. Besides, they'll be too preoccupied countin' the money they're makin' and visitin' the mine on Wanndarah to bother us. Did you know those nickel shares have gone up fifty dollars since last week?'

Jon groaned. 'Don't tell me! I'll bet most of the people in Charlestown have bought stock, the figures being as high as they are, and especially with Pete, Merle and that Patrick O'Shea fella in the bar every night talking it up.'

'Maybe it'll all come good.'

'I damn well hope so because if it goes belly up there'll be a lot of bankrupt people around here.' Jon rolled onto his side, pulled her towards him and kissed her. 'Can you stand Merle and Pete for a few days?'

She pulled a face. 'Of course I can, hon, it's not exactly a life-time, is it?'

He propped himself up on one elbow and looked down into her smiling eyes. 'I love you, Mrs Cadwallader.'

She giggled. 'How much, Mr Cadwallader?'

'Come here, Mrs Cadwallader, and I'll show you.'

Christmas was always a happy time at Jindalee. The boys were back from boarding school, Alice and Alistair drove over from Jarrahlong and stayed for the whole holiday period, Ed Scally, Rachel and Ty Henderson and their two children, Joe and Amy, drove over for Boxing Day, and then there were the rest who lived at Jindalee. Those child mirgrants who had once lived with them but who had since moved on to other jobs also knew they could turn up unannounced, that Jindalee was their home for as long as they wanted to call it home. For that reason, Jon had bought extra transportable accommodation: dongas – ensuite bedrooms plumbed in for water and to the septic tank. At other times of the year mining companies hired them for their surveyors and prospectors when they were working in the area, and they also came in useful when they needed to employ extra stockmen at the busy times.

Despite Christmas being at the hottest time of the year Val insisted on having a traditional British Christmas dinner, roast rib of beef and all the trimmings: Yorkshire puddings, horseradish sauce, roast potatoes and vegetables followed by an enormous plum pudding laced with brandy and carried, flaming, to the table amid cheers from the assembled guests. Jon wondered what Pete and Merle would make of it.

Pete and Merle arrived on Christmas Eve in time for the barbecue. The bough shed had been prepared well in advance. It was far too hot to eat indoors or out in the full sun so a few years back Jon had built a "cool room", a brush shed based on the Coolgardie Safe principle, a construction of double wire netting walls stuffed with dried spinifex and roofed with woven bamboo. Drip-feed water pipes had been fitted across and along the roof edge to keep the spinifex permanently wet, the evaporation keeping the edge off the heat by up to twenty degrees. Any breeze wafting through the open sections was an additional blessing when the temperatures could easily top forty degrees centigrade. They could seat twenty-four at a push but usually there were fifteen or so for dinner on Christmas Eve, Christmas Day and Boxing Day.

Val and Jon were having a drink with Alice and Alistair when Ruby brought Merle and Pete round the side of the homestead to the back garden.

Jon stood to greet them and heard Merle catch her breath as she took in the scene before her, the riot of colour from the shrubs and plants growing in profusion, maintained by the hidden self-watering system Jon had rigged up for Val. The jacaranda tree was magnificent, so was the bougainvillea that grew along the verandahs. Roses, together with the most beautiful native plants, edged the lawn. Chinese lanterns glowing in the trees and also along the verandahs added to the spectacle.

'It's stunning, Jon.' She turned to Pete, 'And it's nicer than your place, and bigger,' she commented. 'Who does all the gardening? Is it you, Val?'

Val smiled, ''Fraid not, a couple of the Aboriginal women keep it in trim, and Shirley,' she indicated Shirley sitting at the next table with Noel and Harry, laughing at something one of them had said.

'Shirley's a natural when it comes to gardening, and she's a damn good cook too. We're lucky to have her. Anyway, can I get either of you a drink?'

'Beer please,' said Pete.

'Do you have whisky?' asked Merle.

Val smiled. 'Of course, Scotch or bourbon? and do you prefer ice or ginger ale?'

'Scotch, straight with ice, please.'

Jon tapped Pete's arm. 'How are you at cooking steaks?' He indicated an old forty-four-gallon oil drum that had been cut in half lengthways and placed on steel legs with a gridiron at one side and a hot plate on the other. Bone-dry wood was already burning away, building up a layer of hot ash over which the prime steaks and snags would cook.

'Can't say I've ever tried it.'

'Well, there's always a first time. Gets a bit warm though, glad to see you've come in casual, not the sort of do for your best bib and tucker.'

Everyone was on their best behaviour that night; Alice chatted with Merle even though Jon could see she found it hard work; Pete turned out to be a dab hand at cooking the steaks and actually enjoyed himself; Ruby, Harry, Shirley, Graham, Bertie and Noel spent the evening telling each other jokes and then made their way down to the creek that Jon had dammed for swimming.

'No skinny dippin',' ordered Val. 'We've got visitors.'

Merle glanced at her, askance.

Alice laughed. 'Val's only joking, Merle. Do you fancy a swim?'

Merle shuddered. 'No thank you, I only swim in proper pools.'

'She's scared of catching something nasty,' said Pete, a wide grin on his face.

'The worst you could find in there are a few yabbies, if you're lucky.'

'Yabbies?' queried Merle.

'Fresh water crayfish,' said Alice. 'We don't run to crocodiles in this stretch of the bush.'

CHAPTER 25

Early in the New Year Jon was in town for stores, and all Les Harper could grumble about was the mistake he'd made selling his nickel stock in the middle of December.

Les ran through the list selecting the items Jon wanted, bitching about what an idiot he'd been selling when he did, that if he'd hung on for another couple of weeks he could have sold at fifty-five dollars more per share.

'Bird in the hand, Les,' said Jon as he loaded up the station's five-ton truck with staples, fencing wire and all the other paraphernalia he needed to complete the task of fencing off the breakaways. 'You've made a fair profit on your money, haven't you?'

'S'pose so,' grumbled Les. 'Coulda doubled it if I hadn't lost me nerve, never was such a sook in the two-up ring. "Nerves-of-steel", that was me moniker back in the old days.'

Jon grinned at him. 'And what would you have done with all the extra cash? I thought you'd got enough put by for your old age. You can't take it with you, mate, and there's a limit to how much you can spend out here. Or are you thinking of retiring to the bright lights of Perth, planning on finding yourself a fancy woman to spend the rest of your days with?'

'Less of the cheek! Far as I'm concerned, you're still wet behind the ears, and what's it to you what I do with my money?'

'Nothing at all, Les. If you're one of those types who gets satisfaction from counting his cash then good on you. Just never took you for a "king-in-his-counting-house" type.'

Les scowled.

Jon clapped him on the back, 'Count your blessings, and if you run short let me know and I'll bail you out, no worries.'

'Clear off, you smarmy bastard, and let me finish making up your bloody order.'

Jon smiled and left him to it. Les was in a pig of a mood about the money he reckoned he'd lost and it was best just to let him simmer down and begin to see reason. He headed over to The Grand, strolling along the covered walkway, keeping out of the heat of the day.

Outside The Grand he looked in vain for the utility that Pete and Merle had rented and he wondered where they'd gone. He still couldn't understand why they'd bothered to fly out to Australia just before Christmas to see their investment only three months since their initial visit back in September. Now, as then, all they could talk about was the price of nickel so he'd been glad to see the back of them when they'd decided to fly to Perth to spend New Year with Patrick O'Shea. Jon frowned, but now they were back in Charlestown, had flown in two days ago according to Wes. Was there a problem at the mine?

Jon entered the cool of the hotel foyer and pushed through the double doors into the saloon. Connie smiled as he crossed over to the bar and ordered a beer. Jon nodded a greeting to the pair of old diggers leaning against the counter and did the same.

'You have a good Christmas, Jon?' asked Connie.

'My word, yes, one of the best. You know Val and Christmas; it's her favourite time of the year. We have to do it the traditional way, a roast dinner and plum duff; it makes me sweat just thinking about it.'

Connie polished another glass. 'I hear that on the coast everyone goes down to the beach and has a picnic.'

'Sensible thing to do in this heat, but, knowing Val, we'd still be having roast and all the trimmings, and plum duff to boot, even if we lived on the coast.'

'You in to see your friends?'

'No, Les is making up an order for me, but he's in a pig of a mood, thinks he sold his nickel stock too soon, says the price is still going up and looks set fair to rise another fifty dollars. He's crying over all the money he says he's lost.'

'You know they're back in town?'

'Yeah, Wes said. They've hired a ute off him again.'

'They weren't so chatty this time, seems something's bothering them, they were off early this morning, out to the drilling site. They had another fella with them, a bloke they'd brought out from Perth. They spent all day there yesterday, as well.'

'Did they, now!' Jon took a long pull on his beer and wiped his mouth. 'Maybe, they're planning to extend the drilling.'

'Maybe,' said Connie.

Jon was half way through his steak dinner when Pete and Merle arrived. They didn't see him sitting over by the window as they took seats by the far wall, well away from the bar. Connie carried over the whiskies they'd ordered and left them to it.

Jon watched, unable to hear their muted conversation, but was intrigued by the grim look on Pete's face and Merle flapping her arms up and down whenever she spoke. Something had upset them, that was clear. He finished his steak, mopped up the juice with a heel of bread, washed it down with the last of the beer, picked up his hat and covered the distance between them, picking up a chair on the way to sit on.

'Can't keep away from the place, eh?' he said, smiling to soften the comment.

Pete scowled. 'What do you want?'

Jon sat back on his seat, ignoring Pete's grim face and the sour words. 'Just being friendly.'

Pete got to his feet. 'Well, I'm not in the mood; I've a phone call to make.'

'Trouble back home?' asked Jon, taking in Merle's stricken look. 'Is Daphne all right?'

Merle laughed mirthlessly. 'Oh Daphne's fine, sitting pretty you might say.'

'So what is the trouble?' Jon glanced up just as Connie appeared.

'The pilot rang, says he'll be here first thing,' said Connie. 'Will you let your brother know?'

Merle nodded. 'He'll be back in a few minutes; he's making a phone call.' After Connie left she looked at Jon for a moment or two, chewing her lip. 'Patrick's done a bunk,' she said finally.

'What do you mean?'

'We came down to breakfast four days ago and he wasn't around. His maid said he'd left early in the morning with cases, half a lorry load of them. We're not sure but we think he's offloaded all his nickel stock too.'

Jon whistled long and low, already ahead of the story.

'We were out at the drilling site yesterday and again today. It seems no one out there has been paid for weeks, the company that supplied the drilling equipment say they haven't been paid either, so they're busy dismantling the rig. Pete has phoned the Glenshea Holdings company number but no one is answering. It seems Pat left owing a small fortune,' said Merle.

'What are you planning to do now?'

'We're going back to Perth, we have to find out how we stand, and we'll need to let James know the situation too.'

For Jon the writing was already on the wall. By now anyone in the know would have sold their stock and got out while prices were at a premium, anyone else left holding shares would have worthless pieces of paper, their initial investment vanished without trace into Patrick's off-shore bank account, no doubt. He realised that for once Les had fallen on his feet, not that he knew it yet.

Pete came back into the saloon still looking grim. 'The so-and-so's cleared out with our money and, according to someone in the Glenshea office, the shares have tumbled, they're not worth the paper they're printed on.'

'You mean we've lost everything?' whispered Merle.

Pete nodded grimly. 'Every last dollar.'

No one spoke as Connie appeared. 'Can I get you a drink, anyone?'

'Double whiskies all round,' said Pete.

'Can we afford it?' muttered Merle, her face grey.

'I'll pay,' said Jon.

'Is there a problem?' asked Connie.

Pete glanced up at her. 'You could say that.'

'Anything to do with the nickel?'

'Yeah, it seems Patrick O'Shea has stitched everyone up. He knew the core samples weren't good but he talked them up, told everyone, including us, his partners, they were the best in the area,' said Pete, bitterly.

'How much have I lost?' asked Connie, her face ashen.

'How much did you invest?' asked Jon.

'More than I should have.'

'Well, you can kiss it goodbye,' said Pete, 'join the club.'

Connie stared at the three of them, 'Surely not!' She licked her lips when no one spoke. 'Is there no hope?'

'Well, there is nickel,' said Pete, 'but not as much as we'd been led to believe, and it's deeper than we expected so it'll be more expensive to get at it, and it might not even be worth the effort.'

Connie stood there for a moment, clearly taking in the situation and the atmosphere, then, tight-lipped, she turned on her heels, fetched the drinks and slammed them down on the table. Pete downed his in one.

Jon watched Connie toss her apron onto the counter and disappear through into the back of the hotel. 'What about all the people around here who've invested?'

'What about them?' said Pete.

'Well, they only bought shares because—'

'It's their own damned fault,' snapped Pete, 'we're in the same boat.'

'Not quite,' said Jon, 'you've still got a business back in Liverpool and Merle is a qualified doctor. For the older people around here, like Connie and Wes, it'll be their life savings.'

'What are we going to do, Pete?' whispered Merle in a stricken voice.

'Go back to Liverpool and start again,' muttered Pete bitterly. 'As Jon has pointed out, you'll be okay, you've got a profession, you'll soon get a new position, you won't starve.'

Jon glanced from one to the other. 'How much did you invest?'

'Everything,' said Merle. 'We both did. I sold the partnership I had and invested the lot. I was planning a life of luxury, on taking a world cruise aboard the Queen Elizabeth once the nickel came in; instead, like Pete says, I'll have to start all over again.'

'It's not over yet,' growled Pete, 'Patrick can't be too difficult to find, I'll make the scoundrel pay back our investment.'

'How, if you can't find him?' asked Jon.

'I'll find the scumbag; somehow, I'll find him.'

'I'll go and pack,' said Merle.

'No,' said Pete, 'it'd be better if you stay here.' He glanced at Jon. 'Can Merle stay at Jindalee while I contact James and try and sort out this mess and minimise our losses?'

Jon kept his face deadpan. He couldn't see how that was going to be possible and he certainly didn't want Merle back at Jindalee, it had been bad enough putting up with the pair of them over Christmas and Merle staying for a protracted period wasn't a good idea, the woman was trouble, always had been, except he'd been blind to the fact when he was younger. 'Yes,' he murmured, wishing he had a good enough reason to say no.

CHAPTER 26

When Jon turned up with Merle and all her luggage Val raised a questioning eyebrow, saw the look on Jon's face and said nothing.

While Jon settled Merle on the verandah with a glass of Val's home-made lemonade Val went to make up a bed for her in the spare room. Jon followed her into the bedroom.

'What's happened? Why have you brought Merle back here?' asked Val as she shoved a pillow into a pillowcase and thumped it hard a couple of times. 'Well!'

'Patrick O'Shea has done a runner leaving behind a lot of unpaid bills; apparently the Glenshea nickel shares have taken a tumble.'

'I'm not surprised, the rate they've been going up, they had to start to slow at some point, any fool could have seen that.'

'It's not that, Val, it seems they've crashed. The Glenshea stock isn't worth the paper it's written on.'

Val stopped what she was doing and looked at Jon. 'You mean they're bankrupt? Oh my God, that means all our friends will have lost their money too!'

'Yes, it looks like it. Let's hope they didn't invest too much. I bought a copy of the *Pilkington Gazette* and it seems nickel stock in Glenshea Holdings has gone from a high of two hundred and seventy dollars a week ago to less than forty dollars now and, if you ask me, it's likely to drop even further once word gets out. Seems that the core samples weren't as rich in nickel as they'd anticipated and Patrick knew it wasn't, but he talked it up to get people to invest then sold off his own stock at the top end of the market and bolted leaving everyone else high and dry, and a lot of unpaid bills to boot.'

'That's terrible, Jon.'

'Aye, I know. Wes won't have been paid for his grader, the drillers haven't been paid, neither have the blokes working at the site,
and any shares bought are next to worthless, or they will be in a
day or two.'

'Poor Daphne.'

'And that's another matter, things don't seem quite right between
Pete and Daphne.'

'Well, I'm not surprised,' said Val, 'it was common knowledge
that Pete only married her for her father's business contacts.'

'Maybe Pete's father-in-law will bail you out,' said Jon over dinner a few days later.

Merle laughed mirthlessly. 'No chance.'

'Why not?' asked Jon.

'O'Shaunessy was incandescent when he learnt Pete had borrowed against his share in the family construction company to raise
the funds he needed to invest in Glenshea nickel. He said too many
people had lost money in worthless gold mines in Australia in the
past and Pete was a bloody fool to speculate on Australian nickel.'

'Well, O'Shaunessy is right on that point,' said Jon. 'You can't
blame him for being cautious.'

'But that wasn't all of it. Daphne had signed over her twenty per
cent holdings in the family company to Pete, which was sensible;
you know what a dimwit she is.'

'Daphne's never seemed particularly dumb to me,' said Val.

'She can hold her own on fashion and knitting,' said Merle, 'not
that you need much between the ears for that.'

Jon noticed the flush creeping up Val's neck and expected a reaction to the veiled insult but she let it pass.

'When her father found out he was furious, he sent a pair of
heavies round to Pete's house with his solicitor and forced Pete to
sign the holding back leaving Pete with a mere five-per-cent share
in the company that O'Shaunessy had given him as a wedding present.'

'At least he didn't strip the lot off him,' said Val, 'he could have
done.'

Merle scowled.

'Then, when the old man offered to buy Pete's holding back for a
fair price Pete took the offer and that's what he used to buy into
Glenshea nickel. Anyway, not long after that Daphne filed for di-

vorce and put the family house up for sale. Pete got a measly fifteen per cent.'

'So Daphne got eighty-five?' said Val.

'No, she got fifteen per cent too, the old man had the rest, seems he owned the bulk of it anyway.'

Jon whistled long and low. 'So Pete lost everything too!'

'Sounds to me that Mr O'Shaunessy didn't much like or trust Pete,' said Val.

'Rubbish,' snapped Merle, 'that's what the bloke is like, a controlling megalomaniac.'

Val raised an eyebrow.

'That's why this investment was so important to Pete,' Merle continued. 'We thought we couldn't lose and Pete wanted to recoup what he'd lost when Daphne's father forced him to transfer Daphne's stock back to O'Shaunessy Construction. The old man's a racketeer,' she muttered. 'I told Pete he was a fool to get himself involved with that criminal, and marrying his daughter was one of the daftest things he's ever done.'

Val, seated at the opposite end of the dining table, said nothing but Jon could tell she didn't agree with Merle. Daphne was a nice woman and they both believed she was the one who'd been hard done by, not Pete. Had he been Daphne's father he'd have done exactly the same thing. You looked after your own at the end of the day, and Pete had been a fool not to see it.

'Didn't you realise that you were risking everything?' asked Jon.

'We did our homework if that's what you mean. James showed us the reports on the core samples, we're not complete idiots, but we weren't to know the results had been falsified.'

'Falsified?' said Val.

'Yes,' said Merle bitterly, 'the results were skewed to look better than they really were.'

'And what about O'Shea, did you check up on him?'

'James did, he said Patrick was an honest businessman and a self-made millionaire, that he knew about mining and all it entailed.'

'Who did he check with?' asked Val.

'I don't know.'

'And James Glengarry?' asked Jon. 'Has he lost everything too?'

'I suppose he must have.'

'But you don't know for definite.'

Merle shook her head.

'Has he been in touch?'

'No.'

'Have you tried to contact him?'

Merle frowned. 'Pete has, several times but, according to the butler, James is out of the country on business.'

I bet he is, thought Jon. He glanced at Val and caught the look. James would have fallen on his feet, he'd put money on it. 'What will you do now, Merle?'

'I don't know, Jon, I really don't know. But the one thing I do know is that I'm sick to death of the subject.' She stood up, picked up the book she'd been reading and stalked off to her bedroom.

'You should give her a break,' said Val. 'You wouldn't be very happy if you'd just lost everything.'

'But she hasn't, has she? She's still got her medical qualifications and she's fit and healthy. She's not exactly had a tough life; she'll soon find a well-paid job and get back on her feet.'

'Are you going to bankroll her, help her set up a clinic in Rodney Street like she had before?'

Jon looked at Val, surprised. 'Why would I do that for her after what she's been like towards you?'

'Yeah, well, she's not exactly happy at the moment, is she?'

'I wouldn't want to waste our money on her,' said Jon. 'But I'd be happy to pay for her ticket home on a boat.'

'Steerage?' quipped Val a big grin on her face as she cleared away the lunch plates.

Jon picked up his glass and headed out to the verandah overlooking the garden Val had created. Steerage, she'd joked, which was about right. He smiled. There wasn't a bad bone in Val's body, she was one of the kindest, most generous people he knew, and she always had a smile on her face. Stan Colley had seen it as soon as he met her, long before he'd realised that Val was pure gold.

He wished Pete would hurry up and get back. Merle was a pain in the neck, and he was sick of her company. The sooner the pair of them went back to England the better.

Another week passed and Pete was still in Perth trying to get a lead on O'Shea. But, according to Merle, no one was keen to speak to him. Jon wasn't surprised; Poms weren't exactly popular in Australia and Pete had a knack of rubbing people up the wrong way.

Meanwhile, life at Jindalee continued. Jon and his stockmen had spent weeks mustering the breakaways in the lead up to Christmas, marking and culling cleanskin bulls that had evaded previous round-ups, often living for years without ever seeing the inside of a stockyard or a race.

The new fencing they'd started to put up straight after the muster was almost complete and, once the final section was in place, it would prevent animals disappearing back into the gorges. It had been a long and expensive job, but one that had needed doing.

Jon rode into the yard at Jindalee, looking forward to tea with the family while his stockmen completed the last section of fencing. Merle, when she heard of the project and fed up with homestead life, asked to ride out to see what all the talk had been about.

'There's not much to see, Merle,' said Jon who didn't think it such a good idea. 'It's pretty harsh terrain and there isn't anything for you to do, you'll soon get bored.'

'Can't be any more boring than sitting around here all day.'

Val let the insult pass and refilled Merle's coffee cup from the percolator.

'I'd still like to go,' persisted Merle, 'you always said I'd fall in love with the outback if I gave it a chance.'

Jon knew that was true; he'd written that often enough in his letters when he'd still considered her to be his girl, words she'd always chosen to ignore until now. He didn't answer, he didn't want her out with them in the bush, she'd be a liability, someone would have to be with her at all times to ensure she didn't get into trouble.

'Well?'

Jon shook his head. 'It's a long way, Merle, and it's not suitable for a ute.'

'I can ride.'

'Since when?' asked Val.

'Since I had riding lessons once,' snapped Merle.

'We'll have finished the fencing in a day or two. If you like I'll drive you and Val into Kalgoorlie, we'll ask Alice to look after our boys and maybe we can take in a show at the theatre there. You'll like it, Merle; it's a big Victorian theatre with ornate decoration, built in the days when there was plenty of money around and people wanted some culture in their lives.'

Merle made a moue. 'I can go to a theatre back home. We've got theatres in Liverpool for God's sake.'

'You'll be camping out with the stockmen,' said Jon knowing exactly what Merle thought about the Aborigines he employed.

'You don't want me to go, that's it, isn't it?'

'No,' said Jon, lying through his teeth, 'it's not something you'd like.'

'Yes, I will. What time do we leave in the morning?'

'Dawn,' said Jon, his tone clipped.

Val caught Jon's eye. 'You'd better saddle up extra horses, hon, for me and the boys, we'll ride out with you too. It'll be nice for them, and it means we can spend a bit more time together before I take them back to school next week.'

Jon smiled at her, pleased he wouldn't have to deal with Merle all on his own.

They breakfasted early and left at first light, under a sky banded in peach and turquoise. He'd saddled up their own horses and a quiet, older mare for Merle, not trusting Merle's assurance that she was a passably good rider, and was somewhat surprised to see her coping better than he'd expected.

'It's a long ride, Merle. You'll be stiff by the time you climb out of the saddle.'

Merle ignored his warning. 'If Val can do it then so can I.'

Neither he nor Val commented. Both of them rode extensively most weeks and were used to hours in the saddle, and the boys had been born to it. Merle would find out soon enough that Jon wasn't exaggerating.

'Remember that time we were stranded out in that desert after Chips crashed the plane, Val?' said Merle. She chuckled. 'We managed then, didn't we, even though I'd broken my leg?'

'Yes,' said Val, 'I didn't think we'd get out of that alive.'

'I did, I knew someone would find us, never doubted it for a moment,' boasted Merle.

Jon glanced across at Val but her face gave nothing away. That wasn't what Val had told him. Keeping Merle's spirits up had been the hardest part, that and putting up with Merle's constant complaints about the quality of the water, the bush food Val had managed to find for them, the hot temperatures by day and the freezing ones at night. It never ceased to amaze Jon how some people had the capacity to change the facts to suit themselves and were selective in their recall of events.

'I've kept my friends entertained for many an evening, telling them about those weeks in the outback, how useful my medical knowledge was in saving us.'

Jon saw Val brace herself for a sharp reply and then she clearly reconsidered and buttoned her lip. Merle'd been a self-centred woman then, and full of herself, and nothing had changed in the intervening years.

'Not very good land around here, is it?' commented Merle. 'You must find it hard to make a living sometimes.'

'Actually,' said Jon, 'the grazing here is pretty good.'

'It doesn't look like the farms back in England.'

'No, it doesn't, but the nutrition in the grazing here is adequate, and we've drilled a few bores on this section of the station so the cattle have enough water, except in the very worst droughts.'

The bush opened out until they were in kinder country, the land as far as they could see to the west covered in leafy low-growing bushes. Closer to them were patches of mallee and mulga – the eucalyptus and acacia – which provided shade from the heat of the day.

'What are they?' asked Merle, indicating the long seed pods of the acacia.

'They're wattle seed pods,' said Val.

'You mean those trees covered in yellow pompom flowers that we saw when we were here in September?'

'Yeah, they're the ones,' said Val.

'Well, they're pretty enough I suppose, but I still don't see what it is you love about this place, though. If you ask me it's pretty desolate for the most part, isn't it? – and remote.'

'You get used to it,' said Val, 'and it does have a beauty all of its own.'

'If you like this sort of thing,' said Merle. 'I prefer my land-scapes a bit greener. And driving for three hours just to go to a dance or see a film isn't exactly my idea of fun.'

'Me neither,' said Jamie who had ridden up with David to join them.

'You don't like living in the outback, then?' queried Merle, glancing at Jamie as he rode alongside her.

'Not much.'

'What do you plan to do when you grow up?'

'Join the army,' said Jamie.

187

Merle looked over her shoulder to David. 'And what about you, David? Are you going to run Jindalee for your dad?'

David grinned at her. 'No fear. No, Ruby'll do that, she likes the bush, not like Jamie and me.'

'You going to join the army too?'

'No, I'm going to university, get a degree in geology and land a job with one of the big mining companies.'

'Seems neither of your boys like station life as much as you two do.' She grinned. 'And here I was thinking it was just me who couldn't stand the place.'

Jon rode ahead, sick of Merle's comments about the land that he loved. Why did she want to camp out in the bush if she hated it so much? He glanced up at the wedge-tailed eagles circling overhead in a cerulean sky, the patchwork of cloud creating matching shade on the landscape, and felt his heart lift at the beauty of it all. Val felt the same way; she loved this land every bit as much as he did, but both of them understood why their boys were so disenchanted with station life, the isolation and the sheer hard graft the place entailed was not for everyone. He tilted back his hat and felt the breeze on his face, drying the thin film of sweat on his brow, as he listened to Val's monosyllabic replies to Merle's incessant chatter about what she didn't like about the outback. He reined in his horse feeling guilty for leaving her to look after Merle alone and waited until they caught up with him.

As they rode they disturbed a mob of feral camels. The animals set off at an ungainly gallop, kicking up red dust as they went.

'I didn't know you had camels on the station, Jon,' called Merle. 'What do you do with them?'

'Shoot them,' said Jon without turning round.

'Why?'

'Because they're a damned nuisance and they compete with the cattle for grazing.' And it wasn't just the amount they ate, he mused; worst was the sheer volume of water they drank often leaving their cattle short in droughts.

'How did they get here?' asked Merle.

'They were imported from Afghanistan along with Afghani cameleers, back before the days when we had trains and trucks. Some bright spark thought that with them being desert animals they'd be ideally suited to life in the bush.'

'Well, they are, aren't they?' said Merle.

'Yeah, they are, the problem is that when people no longer

needed them they just turned them loose and they've thrived, there're thousands of them in the outback, gone feral, and they're a bloody menace,' said Jon.

'It's not just the camels,' said Val, 'there're feral goats, not to mention foxes, cats and—'

'And don't forget the brumbies,' called Jon.

'What are brumbies?' asked Merle.

'Feral horses. We usually see a few about the place when we're checkin' the wells and bores; they need water just as much as the cattle,' said Val.

They arrived at the camp by midday just as Yang-dhow was making a brew. Jon watched as Merle slipped from the saddle and walked stiff-legged over to the cook's wagon and a welcome mugful of tea. He waited for the complaint about saddle sores, but there was none. He didn't comment about the abandoned horse, just caught the bridle and led the animal to the corral and unsaddled her, along with his own and Val's horse. Val smiled at him and murmured her thanks but he knew she was still irritated with him for inviting Merle to stay and he felt bad about leaving her to entertain Merle while he'd been away working with the men. At least it wouldn't be for much longer. Another few days and Merle would be going back to Perth when Val took the boys back to school there, and good riddance, he thought as he downed his tea.

While the others sorted themselves out at the camp, Jon saddled up a fresh horse and rode out to where the stockmen were finishing off the fencing. George grinned at him as he approached.

'Like y'timing, boss.'

'You've just about finished, have you?'

George held out his hands, revealing blistered palms. 'I'll be glad when it's done.'

'Unfortunately the government hasn't left us a deal of choice. Those scrub bulls are a liability, we either test 'em for TB or shoot them,' said Jon.

'Yeah, well, it's been a helluva job sweepin' the breakaways, the boys have been chasing them rogue bulls for the last few days, reckon we've got 'em all now, but they're a pretty lively mob, some we shot, there weren't anything else for it.'

'What's the quality like?'

George took off his hat and mopped his brow. 'Fair, I'd say, considering the dry conditions, but wild, my word they're wild, and dangerous. Some of them bulls have never seen the inside of a race, and they've been fully growed these last four years.'

George wasn't wrong; cornered they'd turn and fight, charging at the men on their horses, and even those in trucks and utes. 'Four years you say!'

'Yer, reckon it'll be the meatworks and a tinned-dog job for most of them – or meat extract, 'bout all they'll be good for.'

'How much longer do you think it'll take to finish this stretch?'

George scratched his scalp and slapped the hat back on. 'Day after tomorra maybe, if the posts don't take too much sinkin'.'

Early the next morning Val joined Jon as he saddled his horse. 'Much fencin' left to do?' she asked.

'A day, day and a half perhaps…it's taken longer than we expected.'

'You still all right for our picnic?'

'I'll be back mid-morning, Val, promise.'

'See you are, hon.'

'How about we go to Kangaroo Soak, show Merle the coolabah tree, have a bite to eat and then ride up to the place where George and I buried the Aboriginal bones? You get a good view of the breakaways from there. It looks pretty spectacular, and if that doesn't impress her then nothing will.'

'I wouldn't hold your breath, if I were you.'

Jon grinned at her. 'You're developing a sarcastic streak.'

'Do you blame me?'

'No, she's a bitch, no two ways about it.'

'What about the cave? We could show her those Aboriginal drawings.'

'No, that place is sacred.'

'You showed me.'

'Yeah, but you love this land, you like the Aboriginal people. She doesn't. All she'd see would be primitive drawings, not Aboriginal belief. In any case I've no secrets from you.' Jon sighed, 'One thing's for sure, Val, I'll be glad to see the back of her.'

'You invited her to stay with us,' she teased.

Jon pulled a face. 'Don't I know it! I'm sick to the back teeth of her, and of having to watch what I say all the time. It's hard work.'

'Tell me about it!'

Jon hitched up his britches and planted a kiss on Val's cheek
'See you later,' she said, patting the horse on its rump.
'Yeah,' he said, 'mid-morning.'

Three hours later Jon took his leave of George and his men and set off back to camp anxious not to be late after promising Val he'd be there to go with them to Kangaroo Soak. As he rode he counted his blessings. He was a lucky so-and-so; circumstances had sent him to a land that he'd initially seen as the back of beyond, a harsh place that he'd hated with a passion when he was still a kid. In those days he'd been bitter, eaten up by resentment and hatred, hatred of the Superintendent at the orphanage in Liverpool who had sent him to Australia, hatred of the Catholic Brothers, particularly Father O'Leary, into whose care he'd been placed, into the care of men who had betrayed trust in the most unspeakable ways; and hatred of almost everyone else he'd met back then, because trust had been broken once too often.

Jon guided his horse along a gully, letting it pick its own route, recalling an earlier time when he could barely sit on a horse, when he'd first met Alice. What's your name? she'd asked. Jon, he'd said. Jon who? she'd replied, and he'd said just Jon, and ever since then she'd called him Jon Just for his habit of using "just" too often. Over the years he'd learnt to avoid the word, even so Alice still called him "Jon Just" occasionally. But it wasn't only Alice who had saved him, there had been Stan, the grizzled old prospector who had pulled a double-barrelled shotgun on him when he'd found him with O'Leary's unconscious body at the mouth of the mineshaft after he'd decided killing the bloke wasn't worth it, not that Stan knew that at the time.

Alice and Stan, two curmudgeonly old folk, had been the saving of him, they'd helped him turn his life around when he was still a bitter kid of sixteen, a kid who'd hated everyone and everything.

Stan had once said something about Alice…what was it? Jon dredged his memory of Stan reminiscing about the love of his life. Suddenly he remembered exactly: It takes a special sort of woman to be happy in the outback, Stan'd said, and on reflection Stan was right. Val was like Alice, "a special sort of woman", a woman happy to live the frontier life, far away from the luxuries of urban living. Merle certainly couldn't, Merle was too highly strung for the bush.

Movement away to his right caught Jon's attention. He shielded his eyes against the light and caught a glimpse of a goanna, or bungarra as they were called locally, disappearing into a hole in the sandbank. He smiled to himself as he recalled his time with Curly, his Aboriginal mate, who'd shown him a different outback. Curly had liked bungarra, he'd liked them roasted in hot ashes.

When Jon got back to camp the horses were already saddled, a pack-up prepared, fresh damper wrapped in a cloth and the billy hitched to the saddle.

Val looked at her watch. 'On the dot, hon,' she said, laughter in her voice.

The five of them set off and, in no time at all, they had reached the soak, hobbled the animals and turned them loose to graze. The boys were sent to collect firewood and soon the campfire was lit on an open patch of sandy ground well away from combustible material. A bush fire started by a carelessly lit campfire was the last thing they needed, thought Jon. Before long the billy was boiling and they were enjoying a picnic meal in the shade of the coolabah, a warm breeze playing over their faces.

CHAPTER 27

Jon wasn't used to sitting for so long. 'How about a ride up to the high ground overlooking the ravines?' he suggested, after they'd eaten.

'What for?' asked Jamie.

'We can show Merle the Aboriginal burial ground, and take a look at the view while we're up there.' He turned to Merle 'You can see the whole spread of the breakaways laid out below. You'll like it, Merle, and it'll be cooler in the breeze.'

'Is it a long ride?'

'It'll take ages,' grumbled Jamie, 'and there's nothing up there except scrub and, anyway, I hate burial grounds.'

'I think I'll give it a miss. I'd rather stay here,' said Merle.

'I want to go,' said David. 'I want to check out the rocks up there, see if there are any fossils.'

Jon and David saddled up their horses and soon they were heading back into rough country, making their way through the labyrinthine gorges up to the burial ground overlooking the ravines to the north-west, and the arid semi-desert to the east.

Once they reached the high ground they sat in companionable silence for a while, catching the cooling breeze that took the edge off the midsummer heat, enjoying the view and listening to the calls of the wedge-tails soaring high overhead. Even as they rested they heard Val's voice echoing through the ravines, calling to Merle and Jamie.

'They must have gone for a ride after all,' said David.

Jon frowned. Why was Val calling them? If Jamie was with Merle she'd be safe enough, they wouldn't get lost, Jamie knew the area well. It was more or less his backyard. Jon glanced at his watch, almost three o'clock, but Val wouldn't be calling to them unless she was concerned.

'Come on, David, I suppose we'd better return to camp.' He grabbed his horse's bridle and mounted, deciding to take the longer but faster route back, approaching Kangaroo Soak from the far end. As they rode along the top edge of the great gashes in the rock he kept looking down, scanning the gullies that he could see from above; then, when they reached the farthest one, he gave the horse its head and allowed it to pick its own route down to Kangaroo Soak, David following behind.

When they arrived at the camp there was no sign of Val, Jamie or Merle. Their horses were also missing, but Jon noted they'd taken time to extinguish the campfire. He listened for voices but heard nothing. Maybe Merle and Jamie had ridden off together and Val had gone to find them. It made sense.

'You stay here, David, I can't be worrying about you as well as them, okay?'

'All right, Dad, I'll pack up, it's about time we were going anyway.'

Jon set off, searching the ground for hoof marks, irritated at having to go looking for them, but at least there weren't that many places they could be. Jamie would have kept an eye on Merle. He would have made sure she didn't ride off to explore alone. In any case, he was sure Merle would have the sense not to wander too far from the camp. She'd been stranded in the outback once before so she knew the dangers. Besides, Val would have caught up with them by now; they'd probably be making their way back to camp, having a good old natter. Jon listened again, but heard only the clip clop of his horse's hooves and the silence of the rocky places. He slowed the pace of the horse, keeping his eyes peeled for signs of passage and sounds that would give away their location.

Jon continued at walking pace, urging the horse forward, listening, then he heard Val calling in the far distance. It seemed to him to come from the direction of the ghost-gum gully, but sounds were often distorted as echoes bounced along the irregular rock faces, the distances deceptive. He heard a scream away to the left, along a wide gully in the gorge side that petered out to a dead end. So that's where Jamie had taken Merle, to show her the Aboriginal rock art! And then came another scream – more panicked this time – Merle's – it certainly wasn't Jamie's voice. A snake? Pound to a penny she'd seen a snake and knowing his luck it would be one of the venomous varieties. The rattle of the horse's hooves on stony ground blotted out further sound as he pushed on along the gorge in the direction of the scream, convinced that her fright would have been caused by something ordinary, at worst a death adder and at best a harmless thorny devil that she'd spotted basking in the sun – they were startlingly ugly little beggars if you'd never seen one before.

As he rounded a spur in the rock he saw Merle in the distance standing rigid next to a clump of saltbush, her back to him. What the hell had the woman done with her horse? And what had made her scream? He scanned the gully and then spotted the problem and a shiver rippled through him. There, beyond her, backed up against the breakaway, was a bull, its escape route blocked by her presence. He slowed, it wouldn't do to spook the animal, but even as he checked his horse Val cut in ahead, riding flat out in Merle's direction.

Before he could call to her she'd reined in, making her horse skitter and slither over the rough ground.

Jon urged his horse forward, his eyes fixed on the bull. Its flared nostrils, its lowered head, the way it raked at the rocky ground with its hoof told him that Merle was in mortal danger.

Merle stood rooted to the spot, terrified, as the bull, only feet away from her, prepared to charge, its sides heaving as it puffed and blowed.

What on earth was Merle doing on foot? And Jamie? Where the hell was he? And then Jon saw his son slipping and slithering down from the ledge where the Aboriginal art was to be found.

'Stay there!' yelled Jon, his hand raised in warning.

Jamie continued his descent.

'Bloody fool!' muttered Jon. Hadn't Jamie heard the warning shout? Or was he ignoring it in his hurry to reach Merle? Couldn't Jamie see the bull? Didn't he realise the rattling stones were making the animal nervous?

Jon cursed himself for not bringing his rifle as he edged his horse forward, intending to put a barrier between Merle and Jamie and the bull, but he was still too far away from them.

Jon glanced at Val. One false move and she too would be at risk; even at the best of times it was dangerous to approach feral cattle, but now, after a week of mustering, the bull would be on its mettle.

Jon breathed easier for a moment; Val was ahead of the game, it was clear that she too had assessed the situation and was pushing her horse over the rocky ground, determined to distract the animal.

'Cut round him,' he yelled. 'Let him past you. Don't block him.'

'Got you, hon,' she called back.

She was closer and better placed. Val was no fool, she'd turn the bull away; the horse she was riding was one of their best stock horses, a horse with plenty of energy and strength, well used to cattle, even difficult ones like scrub bulls, but momentarily neither of them had been watching Jamie, and now they both spotted their son approaching the bull.

'Jamie!' they yelled simultaneously.

'You fool!' hissed Jon. 'Go back!' he yelled. 'Go back!'

But Jamie wasn't listening.

The unnatural quiet was deafening, just the soft sluff...sluff as the animal panted, the air flapping through flared nostrils, and the buzz of insects circling his own sweaty head. Jon tried to think, could he use his horse as a diversion as Val was attempting to do? He urged his horse forward, faster.

An ear-splitting yell ricocheted around the canyon. 'Do something, Jamie,' yelled Merle, waving her arms frantically in the air, screaming over and over, 'For God's sake, do something! Do something!'

Jon watched, horrified, as the animal tensed, the energy transferred into the powerful leg and neck muscles. Then the startled bull surged forward, its head lowered for the attack.

To Jon's ear the sounds seemed strangely muted, his focus on the scene before him.

Val forced her horse to leap like a cat over rocks and then she pushed it through the brush towards the bull, wanting to spook it, to make it take the easy route to freedom. But the enormous clean-skin stood its ground and, with a sudden vicious swipe of its massive head, its horns gouged a groove along the flank of Val's horse, flipping it over, unseating her.

'Va...aall,' he screamed while all around him the air seemed to sparkle, splinters of light flashing as sunlight caught the diamonds in her ring, refracting shards of brilliant colour.

Val, he tried to shout, his throat tight with fear as the bull spun, following the line of Val's body arcing through the air.

Jon heard the sickening thud as she hit the ground, and Merle screaming and screaming.

The enraged animal lowered its head again as Val's horse struggled to its feet, blocking Jon's view.

'No...oo!' screamed Jamie, covering the short distance between himself and the bull, drawing its attention away from his mother as she gathered herself.

'No...oo!' yelled Jon, kicking his horse forward even as the lethal horns scythed through the air again, catching Jamie in the midriff, impaling him.

The animal tossed its head, flinging Jamie's body up and away, like a rag doll.

Jamie's body seemed to hang momentarily in space as Jon's shout ripped though the air. But the bull wasn't finished. The minute Jamie's body hit the ground the bull went to toss him into the air for a second time.

Jon rode his horse directly at the animal, knocking it off the attack. Deflected, the animal fled, missing Jamie's inert body as it bolted.

Jon leapt off his horse and covered the ground between himself and Jamie who lay motionless, the ground turning red as he bled out onto the rock beneath him.

'Jamie!...Oh, Jamie!' cried Val.

Even as Jon felt for a pulse, Val brushed him aside and gathered Jamie's head to her breast and it was then he saw the great rent in Jamie's belly, the bloody garments caked in dust, his bluish-white intestines spilling out of the gouged flesh.

'Merle!' Val screamed. 'Merle!'

Merle didn't move, she stood staring at the three of them, ashen faced, and then her legs buckled and she sank to her knees, sobbing.

'You're a doctor,' Val yelled. 'Do something!'

When Merle didn't move Val lowered her son's head to the ground and stood up, but Jon was quicker he yanked Merle to her feet and dragged her over to Jamie.

'Do something, for God's sake,' he snarled as he stripped off his shirt, bunched it up and pressed the wadded cloth against Jamie's lacerated and bleeding stomach.

'It wasn't my fault...it was the bull,' wept Merle. 'You said it was safe,' she said as she knelt, shivering, before the boy. 'You said it was safe,' she repeated in a whisper.

It was then Jon realised that it was up to him to try and save his son. He grabbed Merle's hand and forced her to hold the wad in place in an attempt to stem the bleeding and hold the intestines within the body cavity. 'Stay here,' he ordered even as Val knelt

197

down at Jamie's side to take his place. 'I'll get help.'

He snatched at his horse's reins, swung himself up into the saddle, kicked it in the flanks and rode back to camp, relieved to see the stockmen were still there.

'George!' he yelled as he approached the camp. 'George!'

They all turned at the fear in his voice.

'Rig up the transceiver and call for a doctor, tell them we need one at Jindalee, fast.'

'What's wrong, boss?' said George, discarding his fencing pliers even as he stepped towards Jon.

'Jamie, he's been gored, it's bad.'

Within seconds the other stockmen gathered together what they needed and followed him, carrying stretcher poles and the canvas they used for transporting the injured.

The men bore the unconscious Jamie back to camp and placed him on a truck's flatbed, layering their jackets under him to cushion against the worst effects of travelling over rough ground.

'The doctor's on his way,' said George quietly.

Val knelt at Jamie's side, holding his hand while Jon kept the blood-sodden shirt firmly in place. George climbed into the driver's seat, started the engine and set off back to the homestead leaving the rest behind to pack up the camp.

As they drove away Jon saw Merle standing with the stockmen, wringing her hands, useless in the crisis. It was then he remembered David.

'Get David,' he shouted at the stockmen left behind with Merle, 'he's at Kangaroo Soak...and get the horses.'

Jon saw the stricken look on Val's face. 'Don't worry, we'll have Jamie home soon, the doctor's on his way.'

But her eyes said it all. They both knew the situation was hopeless. The blood-soaked shirt told them so. The injuries Jamie had sustained were fatal, he'd seen others gored by bulls, and if the blood loss didn't kill him then the shock and septicaemia would.

The journey back to Jindalee seemed interminable even though George drove as fast as he dared, finding the smoothest route out of the breakaways and through the thick bush. Jon sat in the back next to Val, holding his son, wishing he'd never agreed to let the four of them join him so deep in the outback

At the homestead a crowd met them alerted by Charlie who had gone ahead to prepare the landing strip. Shirley and May had organised a proper stretcher and had made up a cot on the verandah overlooking the airstrip.

Gently and together they lifted Jamie onto the stretcher, carried him over to the verandah, and laid him on clean sheets that soaked up the fresh blood instantly turning the white cotton crimson.

Shirley brought a bowl of water, a cloth and a towel and Val wiped Jamie's face free of blood and dust as he lay on the makeshift bed. But Jon could hear Jamie's laboured breath, shallower now, the pulse weaker and he knew in his heart that the doctor wouldn't arrive in time, and even if he did, there was nothing to be done to save the life of his first-born son.

Noel, Shirley, George and May also sensed it and withdrew a distance leaving Jon alone with Val and their child.

Jon stood by Val's side, as she held their son's hand in hers.

'You hear me, Jamie?' she said. 'The doctor will be here soon, you'll be fine,' she jollied, keeping her voice light, refusing to acknowledge the alternative. 'You stupid, brave boy, hon,' she murmured in his ear. She kissed his brow and his hand that she was holding, 'She wasn't worth savin', Jamie. You should have left her to the wretched bull.'

Jamie's eyelids flickered open for a moment and Jon thought that he'd been wrong, that there was hope.

'I'll be all right, won't I?' mouthed Jamie.

Tears rolled down Val's cheeks, 'Of course you will my lovely,' she lied, plastering a smile on her ashen face so Jamie couldn't see her despair, but his eyes were already shutting, his head lolling on the pillow.

'You should've left her to the wretched bull, y'hear me?' Val repeated. 'You hear me?'

But Jon knew all of them would have done the same, Val, David and especially Jamie who had never cared for his own safety.

Val violently brushed away fresh tears that filled her eyes as Jamie's short breaths became shorter still, his breathing shallower as Val gathered him to her breast.

In the distance they heard the drone of the De Havilland as the flying doctor prepared to land, but already Jon knew it was too late. Jamie had slipped away from them even as Val held him in her arms, his blood-soaked clothing staining hers as she cradled his broken body and cursed the God who had allowed him to die. Sobs convulsed her as the aircraft taxied to a halt.

Jon looked at Val, their dead son in her arms, and heard Val's animal howl that seemed to tear at his soul, a sound that ripped through his body, and left a terrible ache, like a vice, around his heart. Tears rolled down Val's cheeks, as she held her son close, rocking him like a baby, the howl replaced by sobs of despair and anguish. Out in the yard, beyond the fence, the others just stood, listening, hats in their hands, not knowing what to do or say.

Jon disengaged Val's arms from their son and drew her to him and, for a moment, she sank against his chest, her body racked with pain, her hair soft against his cheek. He lifted his hand and caressed her hair, smoothing, soothing, as if she were a child, his own throat tight and constricted as he struggled to hold back his own tears.

He felt Val tense and suddenly she shoved him away. He turned to see what she was looking at and saw Merle stepping from the cab of a station truck and then stand immobile, wringing her hands as their other son, David, joined her, white faced and shaking at the tableau before him.

He turned back to Val and saw a range of emotions sweep over her features, her face hardening as she fought back tears.

'You should never have brought that woman into our home,' she spat, 'she's nothing but trouble, this should never have happened.'

Even as she spoke George led the doctor over to them. Jon, conscious that David too needed comfort, acknowledged the doctor's presence and shook his head. Understanding flickered over the doctor's face.

'I'll still need to examine him,' he said gently.

Jon nodded and stepped away from the cot while Val, her face a mask of pure hatred and rage, strode over to Merle and, without a moment's hesitation, slapped Merle hard across the face and then took David into her arms.

The damage was plain to see as the doctor examined the body. Jamie's clothes were saturated in blood where the lethal horns had gouged and ripped the stomach. The injury was not survivable, even Jon could see that; the gut and the bowel were irreparably damaged, the blood loss alone would have been enough to kill him. Val sobbed behind them. Jon turned, took her arm and led her and

David into the kitchen while the doctor finished examining their son.

'He's dead?' said David, his face a mask of shocked disbelief.

'Yes,' said Jon, 'just a few minutes ago.'

Shirley, her face white and drawn, put on the kettle for tea and then poured out three stiff measures of brandy. She gave each of them a glass, including David, and for once Jon didn't comment, but knocked the liquid back in one gulp, letting the brandy burn its way down into his stomach and suffuse his body with heat. David coughed as he drank his, then he slammed his glass onto the table and ran out of the kitchen and across the yard.

'Don't worry about David,' murmured Shirley, 'I'll look after him.' And she was gone, following David across the yard to the barn.

Everything passed in a blur, in no time at all the doctor was speaking to him, giving him the death certificate, examining Val and prescribing a sedative from the medical chest. And then it seemed the doctor was gone, without Jon even noticing, and they were left to pick up the pieces.

CHAPTER 28

That night Jon lay on the bed next to Val, so close that he could feel the warmth from her body and yet she could have been on the other side of the world. She had gone to bed before him but when he'd joined her, her back was stiff and unyielding, he knew she wasn't asleep, he could feel her silent sobs even through the mattress and when he'd tried to take her in his arms to comfort her she'd shrugged him away. About three o'clock he felt her body soften in sleep as exhaustion overtook her, but sleep eluded him; he lay still, gazing at the ceiling with sightless eyes. His body was racked with pain and he couldn't understand how that could be – how emotional pain could be so physical, but it was, the lump in his chest was heavy, choking, unbearable, and his head ached.

Jon's thoughts drifted to earlier, to when the two of them had gone into Jamie's bedroom together with a bowl of warm water to wash their son's body, and prepare him for burial.

It was the second time he'd carried out such a task and he remembered the first time, when Stan died. He'd been the only one there then, and he had done it alone. He remembered it as clear as if it were yesterday, washing the old man's sunken frame, drying him, dressing him in clean clothes and combing his wiry, white hair that usually stuck out at all angles.

But bathing his own son's body had been different; seeing his son's battered body lying there, his horrifically gored belly, had been too much to bear, but Val hadn't flinched.

Together they'd removed Jamie's bloodstained and dusty clothes, and then they'd stood a moment looking down at their son's torn and battered body.

Val had not hesitated; she'd wrung out a cloth and tenderly washed her son, caressing his arms, legs, chest and belly as she

202

gently washed away the blood and the gore before handing the cloth to him to rinse every now and again, and all the time she talked softly to Jamie, telling him how much she loved him, how much they both loved him.

As Val bathed him she recalled happier times, his first steps, and his first word, "durs".

Jon smiled at the memory; it had taken them ages to realise what Jamie was really saying. He'd been watching ants scavenging on the verandah and had pointed at them, as they scurried to and fro to their nest, and said "durs". For months they'd all called ants "durs" until one day they'd realised that Jamie had been saying "there" when he pointed, that he hadn't meant "ants" at all.

Then, after Val's early memories came the recent reality. Jon listened as Val told their dead son he'd been a pain in the backside at times, that he was always the one to fall out of a tree, or cut his knee, or have an argument with Ruby, but that they wouldn't have wanted it any other way, that he was a wonderful son, a son destined to grow up into a fine young man, a son who had selflessly sacrificed himself to save another, a son of whom they were exceedingly proud.

Her voice had caught then and she'd choked back sobs, knowing that they would never see Jamie grown up, or married, or meet his children, and all the while he'd stood next to Val ready with the towel she'd need to dry their boy.

Just thinking over the events of the evening brought fresh pain and he gulped back the urge to weep and rage as Val had done when she'd realised Jamie was dead.

Val had wanted their son's wounds bandaged.

He hadn't seen the point, but he'd said nothing; he'd waited patiently while Val fetched the medical chest and then he'd helped her bandage Jamie so that the gaping wounds were no longer visible. Then they'd dressed him in his best clothes, and when they had finished Jamie lay as if asleep had it not been for the unnatural pallor of his skin and the emptiness in his face as if the soul was no longer there.

Hot tears seeped from under his eyelids, trickled down his cheeks and into his ears. He blinked fresh ones away and turned his thoughts to Ruby. Tomorrow he'd have to drive over to Jarrahlong and break the news to her. She'd be devastated, she and Jamie squabbled over every whip and toss, but deep down they'd loved each other, despite the rivalry between them.

And still he couldn't sleep.

At four o'clock he rose and crossed the yard to the shed. There he found the items he needed and, by the light of the moon, he rounded the homestead and made his way to the spot he and Val had chosen for a burial plot, over a year back, when they'd first heard about the injuries Harry had sustained in Vietnam. It was then they'd decided to plan ahead and pick a spot, somewhere they both liked, and as they'd mapped it out and planned the layout they'd laughed about who would use it first. Val had told him what she wanted, should she die before him, and he'd joked that she should make sure she dug his grave deep enough because he didn't want his long sleep disturbed by dingoes.

He choked back tears, and now here he was about to dig a grave for his first-born twin. It was all wrong, parents weren't supposed to bury their children, it should be the other way around, and years down the line, when they were both old and grey and had lived their three score years and ten; then, that was the time for burials, not now, not for a child, a child not yet in his teens.

He swung the pickaxe violently, into the spot he'd chosen for the grave, with all the pain and anguish in his heart, oblivious of the night noises and scents wafting on the summer air. Through hot tears he hacked at the earth like a man demented, huge great sweeps as the metal head sliced through the silvered light and hissed through the softer soil, as he brought the pickaxe down with every ounce of strength he possessed.

When he'd loosened the top layer he grabbed a spade and began digging, and soon a pattern was established. Inch by inch he dug the grave and as he dug the sky lightened to the east and he could hear the station dogs stirring, the occasional yaps and yelps, and the rooster greeting the morning, a morning that his son would never see.

Sweat trickled down his forehead and stung his eyes but still he dug. His son would need to be buried; it wouldn't do to leave a body long in summer heat.

Jon was so engrossed in digging he didn't hear, or see, George approach. The Aborigine touched him on the shoulder and Jon looked up, startled, his face tight with pain and exhaustion.

George held a mug of coffee, the hot drink steaming in the chill morning air. George offered his other hand, pulled Jon out of the grave, took the pickaxe from him, gave him the coffee, and indicated the carved stone seat for him to sit on, the seat that he and

Val had commissioned from Mike Tunstall, the stonemason in Pilkington, the man who carved all the gravestones in the area.

Suddenly, exhaustion overtook Jon, and, bone weary, he sat while George jumped down into the half-dug grave and continued the task.

Half an hour later, Val joined them. She sat beside him watching George prepare Jamie's last resting place. Neither spoke but when he took her hand she didn't pull away. His heart ached for their shared suffering and he wondered whether they would ever come to terms with their loss.

The sky brightened as dawn gave way to daylight and in time the grave was prepared.

George mopped his face and propped the digging tools next to the railings. 'Reckon it's deep enough,' he said.

'Thank you, George,' said Jon and turned to Val. 'When do you want to do it, Val?'

She looked up, confusion on her face.

'I'll go and fetch a priest for the burial; you'd like that, wouldn't you?'

She shook her head, 'I don't want a priest, we can bury him ourselves, our prayers are good enough, aren't they?'

Her answer troubled him, Val was a Catholic, as was he, although he'd given up his faith years ago, but Val hadn't, he'd find her from time to time reading a bible, she'd want a priest, he knew she would. 'But—'

'No buts, Jon. He's our son, we'll do it.'

'I've a prayer book we could use, but it's not Catholic,' said George. 'Will it do?'

Val smiled a tremulous smile, 'Thanks, George, it will do very well.'

'The stockmen, they've asked if they can come.'

'Come?' said Jon.

'You know, to the burial,' murmured George.

'Of course they can,' said Val, running a hand over her forehead even as she spoke, her eyes filling with tears. 'We'll have the service tomorrow afternoon, when Ruby, Alice and Alistair arrive,' she added.

'We better tell them, they don't know.'

'They do, Jon. Everyone knows.' She picked up the empty mug and left them then, a lonely figure walking back to the homestead with all the cares of the world on her back.

* * *

From mid-morning onwards friends and neighbours arrived in cars, utes and trucks from Charlestown, Pilkington and from off the local stations. Harry flew in, in his Cessna. The day before the funeral Charlie and Noel had driven into Pilkington to pick up the coffin and by the time everyone had arrived for the service it was resting on the heavy mahogany dining table ready for the final journey to the burial ground overlooking the homestead.

Jon could hardly bear to look at the polished wood coffin that held his son's body. He stepped through the French doors and headed down to the creek, needing to get away from the oppressive atmosphere, to breathe. He stood by the water where the twins and Ruby swam, watching butterflies flit amongst the flowering bushes on the far side of the creek, and sensed someone else's presence. He swung round, thinking it was Val.

'Oh, it's you!' he said to Merle, rage welling up as he turned away, not wanting her to see the pain and anger in his eyes.

'I've asked Connie if she will give me a lift back to Charlestown and she said she would…I'm going back to Perth.'

Jon stood ramrod straight, his back to her.

'I'm really sorry about Jamie, Jon.'

Jon didn't comment, knowing he wouldn't be able to keep a civil tongue in his head. But then the words just tumbled out. 'What possessed you to wander off like you did?'

'I wasn't to know you'd got wild bulls roaming around in those gorges. You said they'd all been rounded up,' she added, the tone petulant, accusing. 'It wasn't my fault.'

'Not your fault!' he yelled in fury. 'Not your fault! You did nothing to help him. You're a doctor for God's sake; you just stood there and let him bleed to death.' He knew he wasn't being fair, that no one could have saved Jamie, but she could have done something, she could have tried to save him.

'You're being unreasonable,' she snapped, then she turned on her heels and left him standing there, tears streaming down his face.

Val was seated next to her son's coffin when Ruby, Alice and Alistair arrived from Jarrahlong. Jon held himself in, keeping tight rein over his emotions, as he hugged Ruby, letting her sob against his shoulder. Alistair offered his condolences while Alice, tears rolling down her lined face, took Val in her arms. Alice then took his hands in hers and told him to be strong, that one day the pain would ease, that life could be lived again. Jon bit back a sharp retort, it didn't feel as if he would ever get over Jamie's death, how could he, loving his son as much as he did. Then he remembered that Alice was speaking from experience, she too had lost a young son.

When the time came, Jon, Wes, George and Noel carried the coffin from the house, crossing the back lawns, the garden beyond and up the hill overlooking the homestead, to the burial ground.

Alistair led the service and read from the bible and prayer book that George had provided. Jon and Val stood side by side with Ruby and David next to them, surrounded by those who they'd become close to over the years, while the Aborgines from off the station watched from a distance. Connie stood next to Alice, holding her up when the emotion of the moment threatened to overwhelm her, and Jon nodded his thanks to Connie after the service, knowing how hard it was for Alice who regarded his children as family, the grandchildren she'd never had.

The rest of the day passed in a blur. Yang-dhow, May, Shirley and Connie prepared refreshments and served up copious tea, while George and Charlie backfilled the grave and placed the flowers that Val had picked from the garden on Jamie's last resting place.

By dusk most people had left, including Merle. She'd sat stiff-necked in Connie's ute and didn't even nod goodbye as Connie pulled out of the yard. And good riddance, thought Jon as the ute vanished in the backdraught of red dust. Merle's rant by the creek had been unexpected. He'd believed she would acknowledge her part in his son's death; instead, she'd only been concerned about herself, she'd barely given Jamie a mention, hadn't acknowledged his bravery in saving her life.

Jon retreated to his study, topped up the whisky tumbler, glad to be alone, grateful that Noel had taken Graham Eastman and Bertie Grey under his wing. He couldn't cope with their shock, not when he'd got David and Ruby to think about. He took a long draught of the fiery drink, glad of the heat in his belly. He didn't want to go to bed yet, he didn't want to lie sleepless next to Val, Val with her back turned to him, her hurt and anger a barrier between them. Did she blame him for Jamie's death too? Merle did and, if truth be told, if anyone was at fault then it was him for agreeing, against his

207

better judgement, that Merle could stay at Jindalee. He should have said no when Pete asked. Merle could have gone back to Perth too and then none of it would have happened.

Up on the hill he could see the railings around the burial ground, and out in the bush came the soft night-time noises of the nocturnal creatures one rarely saw in daylight hours. Even as he stood near the open door, looking out into the silvered landscape, there came the soft *'oom-oom-oom'* of a frogmouth owl out in the bush.

It was a clear, cloudless night, soft and still with no breeze to stir the trees, just the warm scent of the bush and baked earth carried on the air. Without even thinking he stumbled across the verandah, the tumbler of whisky still in his hand, and walked across the lawns, through the shrubs and upwards to the burial ground. He unlatched the gate and crossed over to the stone seat overlooking the grave that he and George had dug for Jamie.

He sat staring at the red earth, almost grey in the moonlight, letting the pain of loss mingle with the heat of the alcohol in his belly, thinking about how his life had changed so dramatically in a mere fifty-odd hours.

His thoughts were skittering over the events leading up to the tragedy when his attention drifted to the bush, bush that led to the ridge overlooking the shallow valley through which the creek flowed. Stan had always said the semi-arid land beyond the mulga line was truly the back of beyond, that it was a harsh place to live and not for the faint-hearted; that it was a cruel place, red in tooth and claw, and he was right. That's the nature of this land, Stan'd said once, you have to live with it on those terms and not try to mould it to your will.

He'd understood what Stan meant after Curly's death, and again in the days after Matt Cafferty lost his life in the cyclone over Leonora way. But this felt different; it felt as if his beating heart had been ripped from his chest; he felt like drinking himself insensible so he wouldn't have to live with the pain of his loss, except he couldn't, too many others were relying on him to be strong.

He smiled grimly when he remembered what Alice had said – that pain eases with time. He couldn't see it at the moment, but he supposed she knew having lost her son at Gallipoli, but her husband hadn't coped, Stan had said, he said Jack had taken to alcohol to deaden the pain, regularly drinking himself to the floor in The Grand.

Jon took another slug of whisky, and understood Jack's need to drink himself into oblivion. Stan had spoken of driving Jack back to Jarrahlong and helping Alice put him into bed. Reading between the lines Jack had never got over his son's death either, so would he get over Jamie's?

He shivered then, and looked about him, half expecting to see Val or Ruby. But there was no one there, except he was convinced there was, that someone was watching from a distance, from beyond his sightline in the moonlit night.

Was it Jamie's spirit?

Some people believed that the souls of the dead stayed around for a while after death. Was it Jamie out there, watching him? 'That you, son?' Jon murmured, feeling a fool for asking, but there was no reply save for the soft *'oom-oom-oom'* in the bush, the frog-mouth he'd heard earlier.

Unsettled, he picked up his empty glass and made his way back to the homestead and bed.

CHAPTER 29

The days came and went in the six months following Jamie's death and Jon had no real recollection of them. Station work kept him busy: boundary riding, cattle mustering, checking the wells and bores, repairing fencing and general maintenance. Val always chose to drive David to and from boarding school alone, refusing all offers of company. She stayed over in Perth on each occasion, shopping, she'd said, but he'd never noticed anything new upon her return and he guessed her heart hadn't been in it.

Since Jamie's death it seemed to him as if the whole household wore his and Val's misery like a shroud. He glanced up at the winter sky. Where had the autumn gone? But he knew the answer – work! It was work that was keeping him sane. He returned to the task in hand, reset the auger on the back of the truck and chewed out another post hole, repositioned the truck and cut another, his mind miles away from the job. The mindless, repetitive task of replacing weakened fences ripped out by the camels that had come in from the desert in the dry conditions, suited him; he always left early, even before the stockmen were awake, not wanting company, liking the isolation. And, as usual, his thoughts drifted to what bothered him most, the dilemma of belief versus unbelief.

After Jamie's death he'd often wondered about his Catholic upbringing and Catholic belief in the afterlife. He worried about Purgatory, but he worried more about the lack of it. There had been no priest present when Jamie died, and no priest attended at the funeral. Jamie hadn't been given the last rites and it had crossed his mind that that was partly the reason he and Val were finding it so hard to come to terms with their son's death. According to Roman Catholic doctrine those who didn't die in a state of grace and had not had their sins forgiven were burdened by them and must be purified before entering Heaven. The trouble was he didn't know whether Jamie had died in a state of grace. How could that be when the way in which he died had been so sudden and so horrific? And what did the words mean exactly? Jon knew that Val regularly prayed for Jamie's soul, and so did he, sort of. But was it enough? Would their son one day enter Heaven, or was he destined to spend an age in Purgatory? And what about Hell? A frisson of fear rippled over him. Could children be cast into the fiery furnace? Surely not, children were children; surely the sins of a child could not be equated with the sins of an adult?

Thinking about it made Jon's head ache. Night after night he wrestled with the problem, and it didn't help that, logically, it was all bulldust; it didn't make sense that there was existence after death – but that is what *he* believed, or what he thought he believed. And, he'd more or less been happy with that belief, even when Curly died he hadn't really changed his mind about it, or when Matt Cafferty died. But now it was different, what if his unbelief affected his child? The sins of the father and all that – he remembered a sermon on the subject at Karundah, O'Leary pronouncing on the wages of sin, on hell-fire and damnation, the sins of the fathers being visited unto the third, fourth and fifth generation. Or at least O'Leary had said something like that, he hadn't been listening, he'd been too busy watching the corellas squabbling on the half-built church wall across the way from the makeshift chapel they worshipped in. O'Leary's sermon had been the last thing on his mind at the time.

Mid-morning he downed tools and built a fire. As soon as the billy boiled, he made a brew, sat back against the truck wheel sipping the hot tea – black and sweet, just as he liked it – and brooded over his other worry: Val.

Things were strained between them; it seemed as if the happy laughing woman he'd married had gone forever. They no longer talked about things, and they were the sort of couple who had always shared everything. They'd always had something to say, something to discuss, but no longer, it was almost as if Val could no longer bear to be in his presence. He guessed she half blamed him for Jamie's death, for bringing Merle to Jindalee. Val believed that without Merle's presence the tragedy would never have happened, and she was right. Had Merle not been staying at Jindalee they wouldn't have ended up in the breakaways and Jamie wouldn't have found himself in the position of trying to save Merle from a fully-grown, enraged feral bull. Val had never said it, not in so many words, but the reproach was there in her eyes and at night, in bed, she turned her back on him. It was weeks since he'd felt her arms around him. They'd rarely made love since Jamie's death and when they did it had been a need thing for him, and for her, and only briefly had she fully responded before pulling back, as if ashamed of her desire with their son not long buried. She always pushed him away afterwards, tears streaming down her cheeks and often she wouldn't allow him to hold her or kiss her, except for the odd perfunctory peck on the cheek for appearances' sake. Sometimes the yearning to take her in his arms was almost too hard to bear; he wanted the closeness they'd always had, the loving, tactile relationship they'd shared. And sometimes he wondered whether they'd ever get through this trough in their marriage, whether they would ever be a couple, in the real sense, again.

It was the loneliness that was getting to them; neither of them seemed able to talk about their grief. He even found it impossible to talk to George, and before he and George had been able to talk about most things. Was it guilt? Was Val right, that he was to blame for bringing Merle back into their lives? It was true the woman had been nothing but trouble. It had been Merle's demands that Val go with her on that fateful flight with Chips Carpenter that very nearly cost them their lives along with that of Chips, and now Merle had been central in Jamie's death. She had been a blight on his life and he rued the day he'd ever set eyes on her and been smitten by her seductive smile, her long dark hair and emerald green eyes. She was like the siren who sat on the Lorelei rock in the middle of the Rhine, the siren who led men to their destruction. Now it felt as if he were being led to his and there didn't seem to be any way he could stop it.

Overhead, a wedge-tailed eagle circled on a thermal and even as he struggled with his conscience he watched the bird drop like a stone on some unsuspecting prey. Death in the morning, mused Jon, it was surely a harsh and brutal existence for all who lived in this God-forsaken place. For weeks now the land had given him no joy or pleasure, he did the work that needed doing and slept a troubled sleep at night. His pride in Jindalee had gone; it was just a station, with all the heartbreak living in such a place entailed.

For the first time he debated whether he and Val should sell up and move to gentler country, where life wasn't lived on the edge, where it wasn't necessary to own three hundred acres to sustain one cow, where stations were not calculated in thousands of acres or square miles, as Jindalee and Jarrahlong were. As he packed away the gear and prepared to return to the homestead he decided he would broach the subject with Val, ask her if she too would rather leave Jindalee and start afresh, somewhere kinder, in the southern part of the State.

CHAPTER 30

When Jon arrived back at Jindalee Alice and Alistair's ute was in the yard and so was Ruby's. Jon parked up the truck, emptied out the fencing gear and stashed it in the store before making his way over to the homestead. In the kitchen, Shirley was busy preparing tea as usual.

'Smells nice, Shirley.'

'Mutton,' said Shirley, a smile on her face. 'Alice brought it, said it would roast up nice with a few spuds and carrots, and she said I wasn't to forget the mint sauce.'

'How long?' asked Jon.

Shirley blew air up her face and glanced at the clock. 'An hour, the mutton went in late.'

'So I've time for a shower.'

'Plenty. Oh! …and Val says will you open a couple of bottles of wine, she says you'll know the ones we need.'

Jon left Shirley sweating in the kitchen and headed for the bedroom conscious of the low conversation coming from the verandah on the west elevation, their favourite spot of an evening.

Jon whistled to himself as he showered. It was weeks since Val had organised a dinner for Alice and Alistair, maybe she was feeling better, less depressed. He hoped so. The last few months had been pretty grim. He washed off the grime of the day and his own ennui, hoping that they'd reached a turning point. It seemed to him they had spent six months in limbo, unable to address the agony of their loss which still felt like a stone grating and grazing his innards with every breath. He knew it was the same for Val; it showed in the dark circles under her eyes, in her skin that carried a careworn, grey hue and in her eyes that no longer sparkled with mirth when something amused her. Truth to tell neither of them smiled much any more and he couldn't remember the last time he'd heard a belly laugh from Val, a deep chortle that was so infectious everyone else laughed along with her even when they didn't know what she was laughing at.

Jon stepped out of the shower, dried himself, pulled on a clean shirt and trousers and looked in the mirror as he combed his blond hair. Shocked, he took a step back, hesitated and then moved closer to the glass. For an instant he hadn't recognised himself. His frown lines were deeper and his grey eyes looked wary even to himself, but it was his hair that had pulled him up short. He'd gone grey at the temples. Grey! For God's sake, he was only thirty-nine! Grey! Is this what grief did? Had Val gone grey too? He stepped away from the mirror again. When had he last looked at her, really looked at her? He couldn't remember – probably sometime before Jamie died. And then it came back to him. They'd been in Kalgoorlie, had stayed for a few days in early December, taken in a play at the theatre there. She'd dressed in her midnight blue silk dress, the one she'd worn at Pete's party in Liverpool. He'd kissed her, told her she was beautiful and that had been their undoing. Mutual desire had swept them along, and they'd made love, making them late for the play. But they'd had the devil's own luck, aisle seats on the balcony, so they'd been allowed in. Desire flooded through him at the thought of her body, her soft breasts and belly, her creamy white legs encircling him, drawing him into her. It had been a while since they'd been so close. He adjusted himself, finished combing his hair and took a couple of deep breaths, thinking of other things, allowing his ardour to abate, then, after a few minutes, he joined the others on the verandah.

He ruffled David's hair, gave Val a perfunctory kiss on the cheek, then Alice, and patted Alistair on the shoulder by way of greeting. 'Nice to see you both.' But his mind was on Val; her hair was greying too, like his, at the temples. Why had he not noticed? And the lines on her face! They'd both aged! 'Where's Ruby?'

'Having a bath,' said David.

'She's been hoggin' the bathroom for over an hour, she'll come out lookin' like a prune,' said Val.

Alice laughed. 'No, she won't, a bit crinkled on the fingertips perhaps, but definitely not prune-like. Where's Noel tonight?'

'Charlestown,' said Val, she glanced at her watch. 'Either in The Grand or playin' two-up by now I should think.'

215

'How are things at Jarrahlong?' asked Jon.

'They're fine especially now Jim Sandy's made a complete recovery from the appendicitis operation he had over a year ago. And Ruby, well, its always a pleasure having her over at Jarrahlong. She and Jim Sandy make a damned good management team. We're really glad you can spare her as often as you do. As you know it's all too much for me these days. I'm not as young as I was and that's true of Adie too, not that Adie was ever any good on the management side of things.'

Conversation flagged and Jon was conscious of Jamie's absence at the gathering, his ghostly presence in all of their minds, putting a dampener on what should have been a carefree party.

Jon refreshed everyone's glasses and remembered Shirley's request to see to the wine. He excused himself and made for the dining room to choose a couple of suitable bottles to go with the roast mutton, the smell of which was drifting on the air. Alice liked a full-bodied red but Val preferred white no matter what the main course. He selected one of each, opened them and left them to breathe, although he'd never seen the sense in it, but there and again he wasn't a connoisseur when it came to wine, he usually opened a bottle of beer for himself and one for Noel who wasn't keen on wine either.

He glanced at the dining table already set with the best china, cutlery and napkins and with a centre decoration of roses from the garden and pictured Jamie's coffin resting there. He quickly pulled himself back to the present and glanced out of the French windows to the burial place on the hill overlooking Jindalee homestead, the hill for which the station had been named way back in the early days. Was Alice right? Would things get easier with time?

When he rejoined the others he noticed that Alice was watching him, deep concern in her eyes, and he knew something was on her mind.

'Alistair and I have been thinking.'

Here it comes, thought Jon. 'Oh, yes?' he said, his tone wary.

'Yes, we think it would be a good idea if the four of you had a holiday together while David's on his July break from boarding school. Maybe a trip to Darwin, or perhaps you might like to take a holiday over in the Whitsundays.'

'What are the Whitsundays?' asked David.

'Small islands just off the Queensland coast near the town of Bowen,' said Alistair.

'Midway between Rockhampton and Cairns,' said Alice.

David's face lit up. 'Are the Whitsundays near to the Great Barrier Reef?'

'Yes,' said Alistair.

'Goodie!' said David. 'I've always wanted to see the Great Barrier Reef. Did you know it can be seen from space?'

'Can it really!' said Alistair. 'I didn't know that.'

Out of the corner of his eye Jon could see the stony look on Val's face. She wasn't keen, which was a pity, they could all do with a break from Jindalee, and a family holiday was just the ticket. Jon felt his enthusiasm wane. He was the last person Val would want to spend time with at the moment. Over the months since Jamie's death she'd become even more withdrawn. Some nights she didn't even sleep with him, he'd find her in the morning slumped on Jamie's bed, the pillow soggy with her tears. From earlier conversations he knew she blamed herself as much as him for the tragedy, for acquiescing in allowing Merle to stay at Jindalee.

'Well, think about it,' said Alice. 'Alistair and I can stay here and oversee things for you, and you've got George, between us we can run things on a temporary basis so long as there are no big musters in the offing.'

'Thanks, Alice, we will,' he said and changed the subject.

That night, after the others had gone to bed, he watched as Val sat at the dressing table brushing her hair.

'What do you think about Alice's idea?' he asked, making his voice sound enthusiastic, knowing she wasn't keen. 'A break from this place will be good for all of us. We could go further afield if you prefer, Fiji perhaps, or Hawaii, or somewhere else exotic. We could do with a change of scene; we haven't had a family holiday in a while.'

He saw Val's chest and back expand as she sucked in a deep lungful of air, and a chill rippled over him. She didn't want to go.

'I've already booked a trip.'

The silence between them seemed to stretch as she sat at the dressing table, hairbrush in her hand, barely moving as if holding her breath.

'What do you mean?'

She turned to face him. 'What I said. I've booked a trip to England…for David and me.'

217

Jon felt the colour drain from his cheeks. She'd never done such a thing before; they'd always talked over anything major that impinged on the family, and now this! 'Without discussing it?'

Val shrugged, the colour on her cheeks heightening even as he looked at her.

'When were you going to tell me...or weren't you?' He could feel his anger rising; what was she doing to them going off to England alone...with David? 'And what about Ruby?'

'Ruby'll be fine, she's got you.'

'Have you asked her?'

'Ruby loves it here; she's not interested in visitin' England again, at least not at the moment.'

'And David is?'

'David's in a bad way, Jon. You know that. He's taken Jamie's death hard. His teachers say he's withdrawn. I told you.'

Jon looked at her, still in shock. She was right; she told him the same thing every time she took a trip to Perth to see their son.

'And Ruby's okay, you know she is; besides, she and Jamie were never that close.'

'Yes, they were,' said Jon. 'She loved Jamie every bit as much as she loves David.'

'Maybe,' conceded Val, 'but she was always closer to David, you know that – less rivalry between them. And Ruby's accepted Jamie's death, David hasn't.'

'And neither have you,' murmured Jon under his breath.

'What was that?'

'I said, and neither have you.'

Val looked at him, her face a picture of sadness. 'I don't suppose I have; can anyone come to terms with the death of a child?'

Jon had no answer. 'So, when are you going?'

'At the end of the school holidays. It'll give me time to organise things. I've already spoken to David's headmaster and he thinks it will do David good...and so do I.'

'I see you've thought of everything,' said Jon tersely. 'Do you have to go so soon?'

She didn't comment, and refused to look in his direction.

'Where in England?'

'Liverpool.'

'Liverpool?'

'Yes. We'll stay with our Evelyn. David can get to know his cousin, Duane.'

Jon looked at her askance. Had she lost her mind? She couldn't stick Evelyn and Bob, and her mother would drive her up the wall.

'We'll come with you, Ruby and me. George can manage the place. We can go for six months, a year if you like; it'll do us all good.'

She didn't answer and Jon felt his heart beginning to beat faster, she didn't want to go with him, it was written all over her face. 'And how long are you going for?' He held his breath fearful of her reply, beginning to wonder whether this was the end of them as a couple.

'A couple of months, maybe three.'

Three months! Three months was an age, they'd never been apart for so long, not since they'd been married. 'Are you planning on coming back?'

She hesitated and ice seemed to chill his blood, he couldn't bear the thought of never seeing her again. 'Is it me?'

'No, it's me. I can't face living here any longer.'

'We'll sell up then. We can move to the southern part of the state.' He caught the look in her eye. 'Or go east. We can go to New South Wales or Victoria. We can go back to England if you want. I don't care where we go, just so long as we're together.'

She looked at him with sad eyes.

'It's me, isn't it, you still blame me?' said Jon.

'And myself, Jon, and myself.'

The silence seemed to stretch again and the distance between them became a chasm.

'We can get through this, Val. We just need time, like Alice said, we're still grieving.'

'I know, Jon, I know, but I need to get away for a while, from Jindalee, from you. I need space to think, to come to terms with what's happened. It'll do us good.'

Bitter laughter exploded from him. 'Do us good! Do us good, Val! We should be working this out together.'

She didn't reply and he knew the argument was lost. She'd already made up her mind.

PART IV

[September 1970 – April 1971]

CHAPTER 31

In the six weeks following Val and David's departure for England loneliness wrapped around Jon like mist on a Mersey morning. Ruby was sick of him and went back to Jarrahlong. Even Adie is better company than you at the moment, she'd said from the ute as she'd pulled out of the yard.

Jon couldn't understand it, he'd been a loner most of his life until he'd married Val. He'd had friends: Curly, Stan, and Alice, and he regarded Wes as a mate, but he hadn't come to rely on them and need them as he had Val. And even among the mob of people who lived at Jindalee the loneliness persisted. He was poor company for everyone.

The stockmen went about their business, giving him a wide berth whenever a black mood descended; only George and Noel persisted in engaging him in conversation. Shirley had taken to spending more time over at the Aboriginal camp, and Harry kept in touch on the radio schedules or by letter. Every week Jon drove to The Grand in Charlestown and waited for Val's call on the telephone there but their conversations were stilted – yes, everything was fine in Liverpool, no, she wasn't ready to return yet, and, yes they were both well, but the tone belied the words and Jon knew that Val was as miserable as he.

Station life followed its pattern; the regular trips out to the wells and bores became more frequent in the protracted drought.

'It's lookin' set to be another bad 'un,' said George as they checked Emu Well, making sure the water was flowing. 'How many months is it – twenty or more?' he asked as they dragged the carcasses of a dead cow and a couple of brumbies that had succumbed in the exceptional dry spell, further out into the bush.

'Too damned long,' said Jon, 'seems no one has seen it this dry this fast, in living memory, even Alice says it's exceptional.'

'Y'think we're headin' for another six-year drought like we had in the early sixties?'

'I hope not,' muttered Jon, 'and Kit Kennilworth and his sodding son don't make life any easier, cutting the fences.'

'Why do they do it?'

'God only knows. It doesn't make any sense. No one in their right mind would cut a boundary fence in a drought. Kit insists it's not him, he says it's the Aborigines or the camels, but I can't see it myself.'

'Nah,' said George, 'it's not Abos.'

The two of them finished up at Emu and set off for the next well. 'At least we're better placed for water since we ploughed the profits back into drilling new bores,' said Jon. 'Tapping into the aquifer should sustain us, unless it gets really bad.'

'Does the missus know it's still severe?'

'No, I don't want to worry her.'

'She bin away long time, gettin' on six weeks gone, y'reckon she'll come home soon?' asked George.

Jon shook his head.

'She still not herself?'

'No.'

'Give her time, she'll be right.'

'I'm selling the place, George.'

George stopped what he was doing. 'Why?'

'Too much has happened. Val and me, we're both in a bad place. There're too many memories. Perhaps we can move on if we start somewhere new.'

'What about the stockmen?'

'You'll be all right. I'll put in a word, good overseers are hard to find, at least ones prepared to live in the back of beyond.'

George disregarded Jon's reassurance. 'Depends on who buys the place. They won't keep on all the stockmen. You know that. No one employs as many blackfellas as you do, boss.'

'Yeah, well, my mind's made up. If they want a job bad enough they'll find one. And you know what the situation is like; most aren't as reliable as they once were – it's the drink, and Sid Barton stirring them up doesn't help, telling them blokes like me are taking advantage, that they can earn more in the towns.'

'Have y'told Missus Macarthur?'

'No, I'm planning on going over there tomorrow.'

'And what about Ruby? Y'know how she feels about the place.'

'She'll settle once we've got a new station someplace else, she'll be too busy to fret.'

Jon drove into the yard at Jarrahlong the following morning. Alice was sitting in her favourite chair, smoking a cheroot while looking across towards the shearing shed where Jim Sandy and Ruby were repairing the pens with a couple of stockmen.

'Morning, Alice, I see you're taking it easy.'

'Reckon I'm entitled at my age.'

'Where's Alistair?'

'In Perth consulting with his agent. Why?'

'No reason, just wondered whether he was out painting.'

'You fancy a coffee?'

'Yes, Belle's already making one for us.'

'So what brings you to this stretch of the bush? It's been a while.'

'You know how it is.'

'Aye, I do. How's Val?'

'Not good.'

'When's she coming back?'

Jon shrugged. 'She says she's not ready.'

'Give her time.'

'That's what George says, but she's been away too long, that's why I've decided to sell Jindalee.'

'Why, for God's sake?'

'Jamie.'

'Jamie? What's Jamie got to do with it?'

'We can't live there any more, Alice, too many bad memories. Val can't face it and, if I'm honest, neither can I.'

'You're not the only ones to lose someone dear in the outback,' said Alice.

'It's different when it's a child.'

'Is it? Seems to me it won't matter where you live, the memories will go with you.'

'Maybe, but there isn't much room for error if there's an accident out here.'

'Accidents happen the world over; others have had to come to terms with death in the bush, the Brysons—'

'No they didn't, Alice. You told me the mother ended up in a mental institution.'

'That was because they never found the little lad's body. It was the not knowing that drove the poor woman mad. It's bad enough not having a body to grieve over, but at least I know where my son's grave is even if I wasn't there when they buried him.'

Neither spoke for a while, both lost in their thoughts.

'And then there was Jack,' said Alice. 'I know it's different when it's a child but when someone takes their own life, for whatever reason, it leaves those left behind with the *"what ifs"* and the *"if onlys"* and the guilt, whether it is deserved or not. I've often asked myself whether if I'd gone with Jack that day it would have made a difference. Alistair says not, he says Jack would have found some other time and place, but I don't know. I should have seen it coming, seen the depression, the despair, it was clear enough...the drinking...the sleepless nights.' She pulled herself together. 'So don't you go thinking moving away will make it any easier. It won't. All you'll be doing is separating yourself from your friends, those who are here for you when you need them most.'

Jon pressed his lips together. He wished Alice would shut up, his mind was made up. He and Val needed a fresh start, somewhere else, a place where memories would be less raw, the pain less acute.

'You haven't heard a word I've said, have you?'

'Yeah, I have, but—'

'But you've made up your mind to go.'

Jon nodded.

'And what does Ruby think?'

'I haven't told her yet.'

'She won't like it.'

'I don't suppose she will.'

'When will the advert go out?'

'Any day, Alice, any day.'

CHAPTER 32

Two months after Val had left for England, sleep continued to elude Jon; instead, he cat-napped, catching up on lost rest whenever he could. Often, in the small hours, he'd make his way to the burial ground high on the hill overlooking the homestead and there he would sit on the stone bench keeping Jamie company, or so he imagined. While there he'd find himself talking to Jamie in a way he'd never done in life, sharing his worries, his shattered dreams, his regrets. Sometimes he believed Jamie was out there, in the bush, watching and listening, and then he'd tell himself off for being fanciful, that it was all down to too vivid an imagination as Gran always said he'd had, even as a kid, when he'd still lived in Liverpool with his mam and sister.

One night when Jon was whiling away the small hours sitting next to Jamie's grave, his mind occupied and brooding about the fate of Jindalee, a shadowy figure appeared just out of clear sight-line. At first Jon thought it was his imagination and then he realised it was Yildilla, standing a way off, on one leg, the foot of the other leg resting against his calf as he leaned on a staff, watching him. A frisson rippled over him when he realised who it was. Just how long had the Aborigine been watching him? Had the times he thought it was Jamie really been Yildilla all along?

At first Jon ignored him, and as soon as he sensed the old man's presence Yildilla would leave, but every night, at some point, Yildilla would appear. He seemed to arrive when Jon least expected him and his behaviour was always the same, silently watchful, as if he were some sort of guardian keeping vigil over both him and Jamie.

Jon's feelings about Yildilla, Bindi's Aboriginal grandfather, were mixed. The old fella inspired awe, fear and respect in equal measure. It was impossible to regard him in any other way. For a start he always dressed native style, a belt around his waist with modesty tassels, and on his chest and arms, cicatrices – the raised scars formed as a result of some ancient cutting ceremony in his youth. On his forehead was a woven band of animal hide, probably opossum plastered with gypsum, or pipe clay, and on the flattened surface were painted designs in red and yellow ochre: circles, straight lines and spots. In addition were a couple of feathers that fluttered in the breeze. Yildilla's skin was dark and weathered, and his hair more grizzled – almost white in parts – than when Jon first met him.

One night Jon glanced up, aware that the old fella had appeared yet again, standing as usual on one foot, the other foot tucked behind the knee of the leg upon which he balanced, his hand holding a staff, steadying himself. And then Jon frowned, convinced that Yildilla had spoken to him, except he'd heard nothing, the words just seemed to be in his mind: *You bin come with me.*

Jon tilted his head to listen, not sure of what he'd heard, but the words did not come again and the solitary figure did not move, blink, or in any way indicate that some form of communication had passed between them.

Sod it, thought Jon, angry when he found himself looking for the old fella, but every successive night, in the small hours, came Yildilla's words in his head: *You bin come with me.*

Jon wondered where Yildilla was living. He asked George and Charlie but neither of them knew. And when he'd told George about the old fella and their mutual history George told him to be careful, that Aboriginal lawmen were dangerous and he'd never heard of one seeking out a white fella for company before.

Jon considered the situation; the old bastard had speared him in the thigh and left him in Paradise Canyon, or the place Jon had named Paradise Canyon. At the time he'd believed he was going to die and he still limped from the terrible wound he'd suffered, but then, later, he would never have found Val and Merle on the stony plain without Yildilla guiding him. Maybe the old fella was sorry for what he had done to him when he was still a youth. Maybe the Aborigine wanted to make amends before he left Jindalee forever. Was that why Yildilla was back? – at the worst time in his life, Jamie dead, Val in England with David, and him in a wilderness place, bereft and worried for his future, his wife, whom he loved beyond life itself, seemingly lost to him.

After a fortnight of Yildilla's nightly visits, Jon decided to speak to Alice and Alistair.

'You're going to do what?' Alice said, her face a mask of incredulity.

'I think Yildilla wants to take me into the desert, I'm not sure but I think he wants to show me something.'

'A bloody grave,' she muttered. 'You're an idiot,' she shouted. Her lined face, brown as a banksia nut, creased into an impressive frown. 'How do you know he'll not abandon you to a certain death if the mood takes him? It's not as if you're a blood relative of his, is it? And you know the vagaries of the desert better than most Poms,' she added sarcastically.

'I don't know for sure, I've just a feeling it'll be all right.'

'And what about Ruby?'

'I want you and Alistair to keep an eye out for Ruby, maybe visit a couple of times while I'm gone, make sure she's okay, not that she needs a deal of looking after. George will help her run the place while I'm away and she's got Noel and Shirley for company. She won't be alone.'

'And what about the buyer you've got lined up for Jindalee? Isn't he on the brink of signing for the place?'

'He is, but a week here or there isn't going to make much difference. We've agreed a price, the fella isn't going to back out now just because I want to go walkabout for a few days or so.'

Alice harrumphed. 'Seems to me you're not as keen to sell as you thought you were.'

'No, I'm selling, right enough.'

'What does Val say?'

'I've written and told her. She'll be fine about it, she'll be happier living someplace else.'

'How long will you be gone?' asked Alistair.

'Dunno for sure, a few days.'

'And what if Val comes home and finds you've gone walkabout, what will she think?' said Alice.

'I dare say not a lot, after all she's on her own walkabout, isn't she!'

Alice ignored the statement. 'It's not exactly the best time to be out in the desert, it's been pretty dry these last couple of years, two of the driest for a while. What if you can't find water?'

'Yildilla will find water. According to Bindi no one knows and understands the desert better than he does.'

'Just because he's a black doesn't mean he's infallible, not all blacks are good trackers you know, or can read the counrty, and if you're travelling outside his patch, well, anything could happen. You could end up a desiccated carcass like them brumbies we find, or the sheep and cattle, stinking piles of skin and bone and not much else.'

'Thanks for that, Alice.'

'I'm not happy about this. And if anything happens to you then it'll be me who has to deal with Ruby, Val and David, you'll be well out of it.'

'I know all that, Alice, but something is telling me I need to do this. It's years since I last saw the old fella, fifteen or more, since before Val and I got married. There must be a reason he's been visiting me nightly. Yildilla doesn't strike me as the sort to do things on a whim.'

'How do you know what the old man wants if he's not spoken to you?' asked Alistair.

'It's just the words that come into my head, always the same: *You bin come with me.*'

'Have you ever had a conversation with the bloke? Do you know what he sounds like, the sort of words and phrases he uses?'

Jon looked Alistair in the eye and shook his head. 'No, never.'

'Can you trust him?'

'Not sure, Alistair, but Bindi does.'

'She's his granddaughter. You're not exactly a blood relative.'

Jon smiled briefly. 'No, that's for sure.'

'And what do we tell Val if she gets back before you?' asked Alice.

'Tell her I love her,' said Jon simply.

The next night Jon returned to the burial ground and sat on the bench seat, peering into the dark, trying to make sense of the patterns as cloud intermittently obscured the moon. In the distance he heard the mournful howl of a lone dingo, the sound, to his mind, reminiscent of the imagined banshee wail of a lost soul. He closed his ears to the spine-tingling howl and glanced down at his rucksack. He'd come prepared and had packed a change of clothes and spare boots, along with flour, salt, dried meat, sugar and tea. He'd also brought with him a couple of water canisters.

When the cloud cleared briefly Jon saw the Aborigine, watching, and then came Yildilla's words in his head: *You bin ready then?*

The old fella knew! Could the old Aborigine read minds or had one of the stockmen back at the homestead told him?

Jon stood and shrugged the rucksack on to his back. *I'm ready, old fella,* he said, just thinking the words, directing them at Yildilla.

We bin long way travel tonight. The old fella silently replied, waiting, his face impassive, just the feathers attached to the head-band on his brow fluttering in the breeze.

When Jon reached him Yildilla still didn't speak. Then, without so much as a moment's hesitation, the Aborigine turned on his heels and made off along the ridge, heading east.

And Jon followed.

They travelled without stopping until the sun reached its zenith and then the old fella settled himself under a shade tree.

Jon offered him water and one of the sandwiches he'd brought with him.

'Where are we going?' Jon asked after they'd eaten.

'Walkabout, maybe us bin visit ancestor place.'

Jon looked at the old fella, open-mouthed. How long had he known the old Aborigine? Twenty years? More? The old kaditja man had never spoken directly to him before, but on the few occasions he'd heard Yildilla's deep voice it had never ceased to surprise him. Yildilla had always been as thin as a lath, and yet his low-pitched voice seemed to reverberate within his chest, adding depth and solemnity to it. It was a voice that couldn't be ignored, a voice that sounded as wise and as old as Methuselah's.

'Paradise Canyon?'

Yildilla didn't answer.

CHAPTER 33

For ten days or so they travelled through the bush, crossed the main Kalgoorlie-Wiluna road and avoided the township of Leonora and the mines in the area. They skirted homesteads and steered well clear of outstations, travelling on beyond dried-up lake beds, always heading east in the direction of the Great Victoria Desert. During the day they exchanged few words and, come the evening, they'd light a campfire and roast bungarra as the locals called the goanna that Yildilla invariably caught for them – the flour and tea Jon had brought with him long gone.

One night they sheltered under a rocky overhang, the land below and before them spinifex plain, and barren. Yildilla appeared to be asleep but Jon knew that if he moved the old man's eyes would be on him, ever watchful.

Jon gazed up into the night sky and cursed himself for not keeping a note of the days travelled. Somehow he'd lost all track of time and distance. What had happened to him that he had let himself be seduced by the old fella? Setting out on a journey to God knows where and for God knows what purpose? He hated not knowing exactly where he was, being reliant on the old fella sleeping silently beside him, except Yildilla wasn't sleeping, he was just dozing – of that Jon was certain. The other worry was the direction they were travelling, towards the prohibited sites where the Government had been doing nuclear testing, the area where Jimmi and his wife, Molly, and their family had spent time when they fell ill. Everyone knew it wasn't a safe place to be.

Jon remembered the state of Jimmi and his family when they'd returned to Jarrahlong, the time when Alice's great-nephew, Greg, had refused to have them on Alice's land, so he had taken them to

232

live with him at Jindalee. Molly had died three years after the first sickness afflicted them, cancer according to the doctor, and Jimmi was chronically ill. Their children, adults now, were still prone to bouts of sickness. Alistair said it was the effects of the fallout from the atomic bomb testing in the 1950s. There was still a God-Almighty row going on about the contamination of Australian land by the British Government, but not a lot of that appeared in the press, the details hushed up by the powers that be.

Jon tried to recall what Alistair had told him about the half-life of plutonium, strontium, uranium and the other nasty things that had contaminated the desert testing sites at Woomera and Maralinga. Was that where they were going? Was Yildilla taking them deep into his traditional lands that they'd been denied access to for so long? Is that what he meant by "ancestor place"? Or had he misunderstood?

Jon looked up into the clear night sky, at the net of stars, some of them dead suns according to Alistair, stars that only existed in the light that was still travelling to earth. Alistair also said that new stars were constantly being formed in the great spiral nebulas; it was all beyond his understanding. All he knew was that somehow the patterns in the night sky brought him comfort and he hoped that Val too was contemplating some of the same constellations: Orion, Ursa Major, Cassiopeia, although he knew his favourite, Crux – the Southern Cross – couldn't be seen from the Northern hemisphere. Was Val missing the huge starry diamond which hung in the night sky, the constellation that had been a constant in the whole of their married life, the constellation they looked up at of an evening as they planned the next day's, month's, year's work on Jindalee?

But where did they stand now? They were half a world away from each other, their marriage riven by the loss of their first-born twin, their plans for Jindalee as dust. Together they'd created a different sort of station, a station that enabled Aborigines to earn a decent living on the land that was originally theirs. Black stockmen working on Jindalee now knew as much as they did about raising prime beef, and some had been trained to strip down engines, replace gearboxes, gaskets or sumps. Would the new owner continue along the same lines? He doubted it. Ben Saxby had different ideas for Jindalee. So why was it he no longer cared? But he knew the answer to that too, the harsh land had sucked the lifeblood from him. He no longer had the will to fight for Aboriginal rights, not when the very people he was fighting for didn't seem to care, when most of them preferred grog and walkabouts to regular meaningful employment, and he suspected it was the same for Val.

Val's absence was a constant nagging ache in his heart, now there was a great vacuum within him, an emptiness he couldn't fill. Had he got it all wrong letting her go travelling alone with just David for company? Perhaps he should have insisted on going too and to hell with everything else.

Jon closed his eyes against the night sky and felt the breeze ruffle his hair, evaporating the film of sweat on his brow, cooling his skin, his mind drifting to his other worry – the changing attitudes among the Aborigines. There were stirrers coming in from outside, men like Sid Barton, telling the men they were hard done by, that they should be paid more, that it was, after all, Aboriginal land that had been stolen from their people. Jon had sympathy to a degree; the Aborigines had been dispossessed and it was true some station owners paid a pittance, arguing that board and lodge was adequate recompense, but that hadn't been the case at Jindalee. They'd always paid their men and women well, the going rate for the job, and educated their families. And then there was the drink. New Government legislation meant Aborigines could buy alcohol and increasing numbers did, coming back to the station worse for wear weeks after they'd left for a trip into town, all their savings gone and with a craving they couldn't slake.

Jon's head spun just thinking about it all. Now was the right time to leave, a time for him and Val to make a new start some place else, where arguments over land rights and pay and liquor legislation didn't exist – and there were no terrible memories. Maybe they should abandon Australia and emigrate to New Zealand. Tom Gregson had done that. According to Harry Hammond, Tom'd got himself a job on a sheep station on the South Island and loved the place. Jon was still mulling over his problems when sleep claimed him.

Jon woke at dawn; the morning breeze chilled him, pulling him out of troubled sleep. The campfire had been replenished, but Yildilla was gone, just the slight depression in the ground where he'd slept a reminder of his presence. Fear twisted Jon's gut. Had Yildilla abandoned him? He took several deep breaths, controlling the panic and his pounding heart. He was an idiot – the old fella would be back and as soon as he was he'd tell him he was ready to go home to Jindalee, that he'd been away too long already, that there were things he needed to do.

Above him the eastern sky took on the cool purple blush of dawn – the sky as stippled and mottled as mackerel skin; when the sun rose, breasting the horizon, it would turn the whole sky a lurid red. Jon recalled his grandmother's favourite saying: Red sky in the morning shepherd's warning, red sky at night shepherd's delight, and couldn't think for the life of him whether the old adage applied to the southern hemisphere too.

Finally, stiff from sleeping on the hard sand, he rolled out of his swag and put a billy on to boil with just enough water for one brew from the canister they'd replenished at a soak two days back. Once the water boiled he threw in tea leaves, let the concoction steep for a while, then tapped the sides of the billy to settle the leaves. When the liquid was cool enough to drink he took it straight from the billy straining the leaves through his teeth, spitting out the bigger bits as he downed the hot, black tea.

Yildilla returned not long after the sun was fully up, the carcass of a half-grown euro, one of the smaller, rough-coated, grey kangaroos that were prevalent in the country they were currently travelling through, slung over his shoulder.

'Him pretty fine tucker,' commented Yildilla as he let the carcass drop onto the ground between them.

'I want to go back, Yildilla, back to Jindalee, today.'

The old fella just stood, staring at the dead animal.

Had Yildilla heard him? Or was he just ignoring him? 'It's time,' said Jon. 'I've been out here too long,' and then in a lower voice, almost to himself, '…can't think what I'm doing here in this God-forsaken place, anyway.' He looked about him and saw the out-back as he'd once seen it – hostile – and for a fleeting moment wondered how he'd ever come to love such an arid land. But he didn't love it now, did he? It had taken almost everything he held dear, stripped him of his self-satisfied contentment and made him look at himself with a cold eye. He'd been an idiot!

'When him good and ready,' muttered Yildilla already preparing the gutted animal.

Jon glanced at the old Aborigine. Who was Yildilla referring to, the ruddy kangaroo or himself? In the end he shrugged off his irritation and made Yildilla a pannikin of tea.

Yildilla tossed the offal on to the hot ashes to cook while he stitched together the stomach incision with a thin piece of stick. Yildilla removed the offal once it was cooked then threw a bunch of brushwood onto the ashes. When the whole was burning fiercely the old Aborigine took the animal and dropped it into the flames, turning it several times to singe off the hair. Then he excavated a pit in the ashes and laid the euro in the hole on its back with the knee joints already broken, and along with the tail that he'd hacked off with an ancient hunting knife. Sand and hot ashes were piled up over the carcass so that only the rear feet and front paws protruded from the pit.

While they waited for the euro to cook they shared the roasted liver and lights for breakfast washed down with another pannikin of tea.

A few hours later and long before the animal was properly cooked to Jon's taste, Yildilla pulled it from the pit.

Typical! thought Jon, as he watched Yildilla brush the hot ashes off the flesh with the one remaining leafy branch not consumed by the flames. He'd noted before that when it came to cooking food blackfellas merely warmed it through, leaving the flesh bloody and chewy. He smiled as he recalled something Stan had once said of Aboriginal cooking: *A good vet'd bring it round.*

Yildilla tore and cut the animal, pulling the joints apart. Without standing on ceremony the old fella began to eat and indicated Jon should do the same.

Jon knew from experience that if he wanted the better-cooked meat he should dive in, and soon he was chewing and slurping alongside Yildilla, the hot juices running down his chin and chest and down his arms. The hot meat tasted good after the meagre diet they'd been living on – of goanna or rabbit, and edible roots, berries and seeds, when they could find them.

All too soon Jon felt bloated and he lay back against a rock and belched to ease the ache in his belly. He watched as Yildilla continued to eat and wondered how they would preserve the leftovers for another day without the carcass spoiling, although, he supposed, it wouldn't matter too much. They'd be going home just as soon as they'd eaten and, after a meal like that, it wouldn't matter if they didn't eat for a week.

He dozed for a while and when he woke Yildilla was still eating. Jon forced himself to eat more and then gave up, his belly uncomfortably full, worried that if he wasn't careful he'd probably vomit up all the food he had eaten. It was only then that he found himself watching Yildilla in horrified fascination. He just couldn't believe how much the old fella could pack away, in fact how much he had already packed away, and he was still eating! It was like watching a skinny jackal devouring a zebra on the Serengeti Plain – a documentary he'd once seen on the Pathé News in the cinema in Liverpool when he was a kid and he and Billy Wainwright used to go to the Saturday matinée.

By the time Yildilla had finished eating there was not that much of the animal left. The old fella lay down next to the remains of the campfire and slept as the sun began to set and to Jon's eye the old fella looked almost as thin as when he'd started eating, just a small paunch perhaps, but not as if he'd eaten three-quarters of a half-grown euro, not by a long shot!

When he next woke Yildilla was eating again, sucking out the marrow from the long bones of the legs and gnawing off the last of the flesh from the joints. The offer of an unsucked long bone turned Jon's stomach. He still felt uncomfortably full, the rich meat sitting heavily in his stomach. Instead, he rolled up his swag and started to ready himself for the journey home, already mentally preparing for the long flight to England and his overdue reunion with Val and David.

Jon looked up from his packing, suddenly aware of Yildilla's eyes fixed on him.

'What?' demanded Jon, his voice hostile with barely contained irritation.

'Too soon,' said Yildilla.

'What do you mean, too soon? We've been in this goddamn place too long already, it's time to go. I've things to do.'

'Too soon,' said Yildilla, his eyes slits as he stared at Jon without blinking.

'I'll go on my own then,' muttered Jon, stuffing his pannikin into the swag, but he knew it was foolhardy, he didn't know the route and water had been scarce. They'd only got this far because Yildilla knew where the permanent water was.

'We go to Jindalee soon,' offered Yildilla, 'y'be ready then, after.'

'After what?' demanded Jon.

'You see.'

Jon didn't see; he'd been stupid to even consider travelling with Yildilla deep into the desert and for no purpose that he could fathom. At least on earlier occasions he'd had a reason. There'd been the journey into the desert with Curly to avoid Gerry's wrath and then later to return the tjuringa, and the last time, when Val and Merle were lost and Yildilla had guided him to them. Yildilla hadn't let him down then even though, at the time, he hadn't known where Yildilla was leading him. That had worked out all right, hadn't it?

He glanced across at the old Aborigine still gnawing on a bone. Perhaps he should trust him for another couple of days or so, and in any case, did he have a choice? 'All right,' he mumbled, 'a couple or three days, no more.'

CHAPTER 34

After a further two days' journey Jon and Yildilla approached an Aboriginal camp somewhere on the Nullarbor, Jon guessed. To his eye the camp appeared to be permanent or at least semi-permanent and it was shocking to behold. Compared to how the Aborigines lived on Jindalee, what lay before him looked more like a waste-land, and the people themselves looked listless and dull-eyed, and many, he noted, were suffering from red-eyed conjunctivitis. So why had Yildilla brought him here? It wasn't as if they could do anything to make these people's miserable lives better.

They passed by family groups gathered around the ashes of campfires, empty tins, pieces of cardboard and the discarded bones from butchered kangaroos and other animals scattered about them. Amongst it all some dogs slept, noses on paws; others were awake, heads raised, ears flattened, a low rumbling in the throat as they watched their approach.

Yildilla stalked past small gatherings of individual families, look-ing neither to the right nor to the left, and settled himself by one of the older inhabitants next to a pitifully small campfire some dis-tance from the others. Jon sat down to wait while Yildilla spoke to the older man, an Aborigine with a similar pattern of cicatrices on his upper body, his lower half clothed Western style in tattered, filthy strides.

Later, they were offered roast rabbit and damper which they ate as dust swirled around the camp filling their nostrils and eyes with ash blown up from the remains of old campfires. Fine sand and ash filmed the food they were eating and Jon wondered how the people could bear to live with the misery of it all.

The next day, after some of the women had wandered off to

search for bush tucker and the younger men had gone in search of kangaroo, and for want of anything better to do with his time, Jon tackled Yildilla and his ancient companion about the community, who they were and what they were doing living such desolate lives in the desert.

The old fella, who called himself Tom, turned a rheumy eye in Jon's direction. 'Government want 'im blackfella off the land, send whitefellas, patrol officers they call 'em, to put 'im in camps over Cundeelee way. Blackfellas not allowed on ancestor land no more, live on what government gives 'im, old ways forgotten by young blackfellas.' He stared into the ashes of the campfire and chewed on a plug of tobacco, spitting out the brown saliva that stained his teeth and made his breath stink.

Jon considered what the old fella had said; Cundeelee was over a hundred miles east of Kalgoorlie but still well into Western Australia. It was an Aboriginal community with a ration depot and an Aboriginal Evangelical Mission where blackfellas could get food and be converted to Christianity but it was miles away, well west of where he calculated they were.

'Where is your ancestor land, Tom?'

'This um.' The old fella indicated the soil beneath him.

Jon remembered the time Jimmi and his family had turned up at Jarrahlong, sick and ill, after spending time at Emu Field. They had been moved off their ancestral land by patrol officers about the time they were testing atomic bombs in the area. Then, more recently, there'd been more testing at Maralinga also east of where they were now camped. No doubt these Aborigines had been displaced then. Had they been moved because further tests were due to commence at Maralinga?

'So, they've let you back on your own land, have they?'

Tom shook his head. 'Them don't know we's here.'

Jon frowned, dredging his memory for something Alistair had said, that Aborigines were agitating for the right to return permanently to their tribal lands in the prohibited area. As it was they'd only been allowed to make brief visits to look after their sacred sites and places of importance. Jon could see that for people like Yildilla that wasn't enough, but it was complicated too, some Aborigines were fearful of the contamination they'd been told about. They believed the Dreaming had been destroyed, the soaks and waterholes violated and the land spoiled. But Maralinga was some distance away, although, as far as he knew, the area was still Gov-

240

ernment land, the people still prohibited from returning to their tribal territories.

Jon looked about him while Yildilla and Tom yattered on in their own language. The part of the desert they were in was predominantly flat, the stony plain covered in the native grasses, blue bush, and saltbush. Water was scarce and, by and large, too brackish for drinking; the soaks and rock holes that provided the only fresh water had been few and far between. It was clear that it was a harsh life for these people. Hunting and gathering would have consumed large parts of their day, unlike Aborigines who lived in lusher landscapes. He felt sorry for the community; their land had not been the best even before the Government got their sticky fingers on it for their weapon testing, but it had been theirs and they had learned to live with the vagaries of its climate, moving across its vast area, making the most of the seasonal produce, teaching the next generation where and how to utilise the available bush food. But now, dispossessed, the younger generation had been denied the chance to learn how to live off the land as their ancestors had done, something that had happened all too often in the past, and which had resulted in apathy amongst Aborigines who had been denied their birthright. Many had ended up bereft of a reason for living which led, in part, to the drunkenness and inertia that now affected those who no longer had purpose in their lives.

Was this what Yildilla wanted him to see? His tribe reduced to living a wretched life, their traditions interrupted? And so what? What was he supposed to do about it? He'd had enough problems at Jindalee with stockmen who had once been reliable but who now drifted off to local towns and came back the worse for wear and belligerent, demanding their rights, accusing Jon of stealing their birthright. He couldn't cope with some of his own stockmen so what was Yildilla expecting him to do about these people? He turned away, hiding his anger and confusion.

That night the wind got up. The humpies they'd made from brush wood offered no real protection and when daylight came it was clear everything was covered in a thick layer of sand and ash. Dust storms were a fact of life out in the bush, but back home it was easier to shelter from the worst of it, although the clean-up was a time-consuming process; the sand got everywhere necessitating much sweeping, dusting and washing after a bad blow. But this, deep in Aboriginal tribal land, was as bad as a dust storm got, the wind whipped through the camp carrying the stinging sand with it,

241

obscuring everything further than a few paces. Then, just when it seemed it was never going to end, the wind dropped and everyone was left to sort themselves out.

Over the next few days people drifted in from the desert. They built themselves humpies and settled down to wait, or so it seemed. Soon there were family groups encamped along what Jon took to be a track through the desert.

'What's going on?' he asked Yildilla.

'Him corroboree,' muttered the old fella.

'For what?'

Yildilla didn't reply and Jon could tell he'd get no more out of him until he was good and ready. Jon was still no wiser as to why the old kaditja man had brought him into the desert to stay with a bunch of dispossessed Aborigines.

And then, soon after, while the men in the tribe were busy decorating themselves with paint and feathers, Yildilla came for him, telling him to leave his swag behind and follow. As they walked, the old kaditja man carried a fire-stick, swinging it as he led the way, keeping the ember glowing. They walked for four hours deeper into the desert, heading east again and, as the sun reached its blistering midday heat, Yildilla stopped and indicated the ground a dozen paces ahead.

There, in the red earth, was a sinkhole approximately six feet across and roughly hexagonal in shape. Jon peered down into the gloom. Where was Yildilla taking him? – to shelter from the sweltering heat? – to an underground water supply? Without a word Yildilla climbed down into the blackness, indicating that Jon should follow and when he did so Jon could see that the floor of the opening sloped steeply, leading into a natural tunnel in the limestone. Yildilla stooped and tilted his body, first this way, then that, as he negotiated the narrow passageway.

It was cool inside the tunnel and dark. Jon strove to listen and followed Yildilla, scenting the odour of the man he could no longer see clearly in the gloom as he led them deeper into the bowels of the earth.

The glow from the fire-stick increased suddenly as Yildilla swung it, his body blocking the light with each pass of the stick and Jon recalled a similar occasion, way back, when he was a kid of fifteen, following Stan Colley as he'd led the way down an adit into No Hope Mine, to the lightning-strike cavern where, eventually, Stan had discovered gold.

But this wasn't a mine, this was a natural cave created in the Dreaming, it was sinuous and snake-like, an ancient watercourse, perhaps, but to where?

It grew cooler as they travelled deeper into the cave and eventually Jon sensed the tunnel opening out into a vast domed space, a great cavern deep under the Nullarbor. Yildilla motioned him to squat and while he waited Jon listened to the old fella moving about in the dark, just the blur of the fire-stick as Yildilla searched, but searched for what?

And then came the flair as spinifex ignited, Jon blinked, the brightness dazzling after the pitch black of the tunnel. Yildilla fed the flames, adding dried wood, and Jon guessed that somewhere there was a stockpile. Soon the initial flames died back and the fire took on a more moderate conformation, like a campfire, and as Jon's eyes accustomed to the gloom he noticed the smoke from the fire swirling about them as if caught in a backdraught, as if they were in the centre of a vortex, but never once did the smoke make his eyes stream, nor did he cough.

'Where are we?' he asked.

'Nullarbor,' said Yildilla.

Jon looked about him. Was this the only cave or were they in a labyrinth of subterranean limestone passages? And, if so, where did they ultimately lead? He tried to recall what he knew about limestone and guessed that the subterranean tunnel and the cave they were in would have been carved out by water, long gone, perhaps when the continent was young, when it still had rivers and abundant water, back in the time of the Aboriginal Dreaming. It was probably part of a whole caving system, the network stretching for miles, like the potholes and underground rivers he'd read about in the Peak District in England. He smiled at the thought – a maze of limestone caves under the Nullarbor. How many other people knew of their existence apart from Yildilla and his people?

He envisaged the desert above him where life was harsh and wildlife scarce, just a few dingoes, emus, camels and kangaroos and the occasional wombat. Yildilla had pointed out their tracks as they crossed the land, but apart from rare tracks they'd only caught glimpses of emus and camels in the far distance and now and again a kangaroo. The area was treeless for the most part, even the mallee that grew just about everywhere struggled in the desert above him, mainly it was just the spinifex, blue bush and saltbush that Yildilla had used to light the fire. Nullarbor! The place had been well named by someone in the past. It hadn't always been like that though if the stockpile of wood in the cave was anything to go by. There must have been trees aplenty once upon a time. He couldn't see Aborigines carrying in wood from far afield, not in the present conditions and just how old was the timber, a hundred years, a thousand, was there any way of knowing?

'Why are we here?' asked Jon, glancing at Yildilla who was sitting on the other side of the blazing timber throwing aromatic leaves onto the flames.

Yildilla didn't reply, instead he wafted a leafy branch through the smoke dispersing it still further. As Jon breathed in the pungent scent his thoughts drifted, and he was conscious of a disembodied calmness settling over him…

…Time is elastic, he realises, day and night meld into one, figures flit in shadows and ghosts of people he's known hover at the edges of his vision – the ghosts of people he's loved: his mother, his gran, Stan, and his son, Jamie. And then Curly appears and smiles.

'What are you doing here?' he calls, delighted to see his old friend, noticing once again how Curly hasn't aged, as he has done. Curly is still as handsome as ever – his white teeth with the gap between the front two, catches the firelight. His skin shines like burnished copper and his curly, chin-length, dark-blond hair gleams as he tilts his head in greeting.

'Y're in a bad place, Jon.'

'You said that before.'

'Still true,' says Curly. 'You lost y'way.'

'Is that what Yildilla reckons?'

Curly nods. 'Yildilla's right. He's always right.'

'Why am I here?'

'To renew y'spirit, make y'one with the land again.'

He shakes his head. 'No, Curly, too much has happened.'

'Yer son,' says Curly, 'he's back in the land now, his spirit's waitin'.'

'What do you mean, waiting?'

'Waitin' for a woman to step his way, then his spirit enter her, then he'll be born again.'

He frowns at the words he doesn't believe. He shakes his head, denying the concept.

'Curly's right,' murmurs Stan from the shadows.

'That you, old man?'

'Aye, it's me, right enough,' says Stan, leaning forward, the fire-light illuminating Stan's lined face, spiky white hair, blue eyes and his weather-beaten skin. 'Abos believe babies are conceived when a woman passes the right spot, where there's a waiting spirit. The waiting spirit enters the woman's belly and then, in time, after the spirit has grown, the child is born. That is what Curly is saying, that your son is in a sort of limbo, a spirit child in waiting.'

'You mean Curly believes in reincarnation, is that what you are saying, Stan?'

'Somethin' like that,' mumbles Stan. 'That's right, ain't it, Curly?'

'If y'say so, Stan,' murmurs Curly, frowning at the unfamiliar word.

He breathes in more smoke, letting the narcotic essence befuddle his brain. 'It's better if I go,' he says to no one in particular.

'Better? For who?' asks Curly. 'Y'belong here, 'n' what happens when y'leave? – Jindalee just another station, like Reef Hill, with fellas who don't love the place, or the people – my people. They've had enough trouble; they can do without fellas like Kennilworth, and that bastard son of his. He kills and rapes as he likes and no one stops him, 'cept you and y'missus.'

'The missus has gone, Curly. She can't take Jindalee anymore, not after Jamie.'

'She'll be back,' murmurs Stan, 'give her time, she'll be back. The place is in her blood, like it is for you...'

Jon pulled himself out of his reverie and stared into the flames, reflecting on all that had happened to him and Val, and on Jamie's death. He didn't believe Stan's words. Things could never be right again, the pain was too raw, too new, even now. He understood why Val couldn't stay, why she wanted to leave. He wants her back but knows things must change.

'You're wrong, Stan,' he said, half to himself, but Stan and Curly had gone, there was just Yildilla sitting before him adding more leaves to the flames.

'Why am I here, Yildilla?'

'For y'to see,' answered Yildilla, echoing Curly's words as he threw more twigs and leaves onto the flames.

'See what?'

The dry twigs burned bright, flaring upwards with a pale bluish smoke that seemed to fill the chamber with a scent Jon had never smelt before. It wasn't sandalwood, or eucalypt, or the raspberry-jam scent of jam wattle, or of any plant he was familiar with. He felt himself drifting as a warm sensation flooded his body. He relaxed in front of the flames; it made a change from the interminable journeying across the sandhills, the desert and the vast stony plains that dominated the landscape in the areas they had travelled through.

Jon turned to Yildilla, about to suggest they put on the billy and found himself watching, mesmerised, as Yildilla's form slipped, his shape shifting into the unfamiliar, his body elongating, his legs and arms growing shorter, stubbier, and his face also slipping, the upper lip lengthening and the jaw and nose flattening, the deep-set eyes becoming reptilian in shape on the side of the head and his skin taking on the appearance of beaded cloth in the half light. Jon blinked and shook his head; it was the heat and tiredness affecting his imagination...

...How do you do that, Yildilla? But the question is merely a thought, the words unformed, no sound emanates from his lips. The figure continues to shift and change until he recognises it – Perentie Man! Curly's totem animal, the monitor lizard, the drawing in the cave back in the place he thinks of as Paradise Canyon, the Aboriginal ancestor that has manifested itself to him before in delirium, out on the stony plain, after Curly died, and again when he was buried beneath the rock fall in the Deborah Mine.

But why now? Why here? He isn't sick. He doesn't have a fever. His situation isn't desperate as it had been back then.

'It is, mate,' says Perentie Man in Curly's voice. 'Y're at a crossroads. Y've lost y'way.'

That's Yildilla for you, he thinks, Yildilla's the bastard who brought me here. Why is Perentie Man mimicking Curly's voice? he wonders. He looks at the reptile sitting across from him, but its face is blank, not a flicker of expression mars its countenance and he wonders where Yildilla has gone.

And then he's no longer in the cavern. He and Perentie Man are running side by side, across the desert, the spiky spinifex, the gibbers, sharp, cutting the soles of his feet, making him gasp as he keeps pace with the reptile.

'Where are we going?' he asks.

Followin' the footprint, he thinks he hears.

The formless land stretches before them and they traverse the desert and when he turns around to see where they've come from the landscape has been transformed. There, behind him, where once there was nothing is the vast tapestry of the outback as if viewed from above. There is sand and gibber plain, claypans, salt-pans, and squiggles of rock, like the king brown rock, and huge plateaus with gorges carved deep into the strata, and waterfalls and pools of crystal clear water. As his eyes sweep over the land, he sees the sandhills, miles and miles of sandhills, stretching as far as the eye can see, parallel dunes that wash across the land like waves. Then there are the rivers, sparkling ribbons of silver blue that cut through rock creating more gorges, or sinking through the sand, creating dry riverbeds, grinding and dissolving the rock as the water finds new routes deep beneath their feet. Even as he looks, the land becomes alive with wildlife; animals: kangaroo, wallaby, opossum, echidna, bilbies and other marsupials; birds: emus, magpies, corellas, frogmouths, budgerigars and finches; insects: dragonflies the size of a handspan, butterflies – myriads of them – beetles, and ants – whole battalions of ants marching across the land in columns – and termites frenetically building their cities in towers of dark red earth...and flies, everywhere, flies. Then there are the reptiles: snakes, geckos, goannas and per-enties. And all about the eye-watering backcloth of colour – rust red earth, cobalt sky, grey-green herbage with splashes of brilliant colour from the wildflowers: the crimson sturt pea, the green and the purple mulla mulla, purple parakeelya, yellow billy-buttons, white and pink everlastings and orchids. There is colour too from the grasses, flowering trees and bushes. It is a wild and tumultuous Eden, shifting and changing even as he looks, the land slipping and sliding as if time is speeding, forming itself into the more familiar, harsher patterns he is used to. He marvels as the primordial land shimmers and changes into the present, into a landscape he knows, or thinks he knows, and his heart lifts at the glimpse he has been granted of the outback in the Dreamtime when Perentie Man, Curly's ancestor and totem, traversed the hinterland creating that which he has claimed for his own.

He laughs with delight, and he hears his own laughter ringing in his ears as he runs alongside Perentie Man. His heart leaps at the freedom he feels, the sense of belonging, running like a child across the vast expanse of land, his land, realising that he too has the knowledge as Curly had and as Yildilla has. Never again will he be lost in this Eden, not while he remembers the words: the footprint. The words will guide him as he follows Perentie's footprint from the Dreamtime.

He turns to Perentie Man and the vision fades, he finds himself back in the cavern sitting by the fire, gazing, as Yildilla is doing, into the flames. He turns to Yildilla, looks into his ancient, lined face, a face as old as Methuselah's, and opens his mouth to speak, but Yildilla holds up a restraining hand, stopping the words he is about to say.

White smoke drifts around them, swirling, enveloping them in its soft haze, the scent of it taking him to a dreaming place, where mind and body are as one. He accepts the roll-up Yildilla offers and draws on the Aboriginal tobacco knowing what it is he smokes from the time Bindi gave him some to dull the pain in his damaged leg. He inhales the smoke deep into his lungs and holds it there, letting the drug take effect, enjoying the sensation of being at once in the cavern and yet everywhere. From the depths he thinks he can hear chanting and guesses it is Yildilla singing the Footprint as Curly has done, and then comes the narration in a language he's never fully learned, able only to pick out odd words and phrases as the epic tale of the Dreamtime unfolds.

At some point comes the cutting and the blood flowing down his chest and over his belly, the warm stickiness of it, the metallic smell, and the ash stinging as Yildilla rubs it into the cuts, an action he knows will ultimately form the distinctive cicatrices, the raised scars on his body, and somehow he knows he has done enough to bridge the divide between whitefella and black. He's been accepted by the ancient people who have occupied the land from time immemorial. The chanting continues, and the beat of clapsticks keeps the rhythm in his head, he lets it all flow over and through him as the sounds trail off and die…

Jon shivered, suddenly aware of his surroundings and the smoky atmosphere pervading the cavern.

He glanced at Yildilla but the old Aborigine appeared lost in thought. Jon stretched his legs, stiff from sitting for so long, and the movement made him catch his breath as a sharp pain, like a knife, sliced through him. When he looked down he saw the cuts on his chest, parallel lines etched deep in the flesh, and ash and blood mixed, staining his trousers.

'What have you done?' he shouted, rage welling up like bile from his belly.

When Yildilla didn't answer Jon leaned across and shook him violently, forcing the old man to listen. 'Why?'

Yildilla looked back at him through hooded eyes. 'You ready. You one of us now.'

'What the hell are you saying?'

'You part of my people.'

Horrified, Jon glanced down at his chest, ran his fingers over the tender flesh. 'You should have asked first,' he raged, angry and confused.

Over the next few hours Jon's fury gradually abated. Yildilla was impervious to his rage, and ranting at him served no useful purpose. Jon realised the damage was done; he was forever marked in the Aboriginal way and, once he'd calmed down, he realised that despite the pain and discomfort the scarring didn't matter; the cuts would heal, but what he didn't understand was why? Why had Yildilla chosen the present time to mark him out? It was years since their last contact, so why now?

When Yildilla indicated it was time to go Jon followed, his thoughts in turmoil as they retraced their route back to the Aboriginal encampment.

It was dark when they arrived and from a distance Jon heard the chanting and saw the flickering light from the fires. Everyone was out, men, women and children; the men were dressed decoratively, their bodies painted in white pipe clay and red ochre. Groups of people intoned an Aboriginal song as they performed ritual dances, animal hunts out in the bush by the men, digging dances by the women imitating the hunt for witchetty grubs, the fat, white grubs of moths and beetles that infested the roots of the witchetty bush, and other desert delicacies.

The next morning the men gathered out in the desert not far from the camp and there they proceeded to clear a patch of ground of stones, saltbush and grassy tussocks until a circular space was prepared. Some of the men cut themselves and sprinkled the ground with their blood, whilst another one carried a larger version of what Jon knew as a tjuringa, a sacred tribal object similar to the one Curly had entrusted into his safe keeping just before his death from snakebite. Jon noticed that the markings on the wood were, as far as he could remember, almost identical to those on Curly's tjuringa and he guessed that he was being allowed to observe and maybe even take part in a sacred ceremony to honour the tribe's totem, Perentie. Other men, suitably decorated in white pipe clay and red ochre, took sticks and drew images in the earth, distinctive parts of Perentie, the tail, the head and the feet, but there were other symbols, or stylised sketches Jon did not recognise, long sinuous lines, intestines, maybe, and circles, eggs? It was difficult to know, but he was told all parts of the creature were sacred and represented in the sketches.

Once the drawings were complete they were covered with leafy branches and then the sacred tjuringa, that recorded tribal history from the dreaming, was carried forward with great ceremony, the leafy boughs removed and the wooden object placed at the side of the drawing. Tom, the eldest man in the tribe and the leader of the group for the ceremony, then squatted as did the other men. There followed a monotonous chanting with Tom periodically pointing to one part of the animal or another. Clearly, even to Jon's untuned ear, the history of the totem was being related, the significance of the various parts of the animal described. And so it continued, the men gathered around the ceremonial drawing, chanting the story of the ancestor animal, recounting their tribal history throughout the rest of the day and night.

At dawn, a smaller version of the wooden tjuringa was hung around Jon's neck with great solemnity and he realised that all that had happened under the Nullarbor, and the ceremony he'd been allowed to watch, had been preparation for this moment although why Yildilla and his tribe had chosen this time to bestow such a great honour on him was beyond his understanding. As he mulled over all that had happened, was happening, the younger men were dispatched to the women's camp. When the women and children arrived they were allowed to stand at the edge of the ceremonial site and watch as three men began to mime the Perentie, their arms crooked at the elbows, their fingers splayed like the toes of the creature, their backs bent forward, their bodies held low to the ground. They imitated the staccato movements of a giant monitor lizard crossing the land, their tongues flicking as they swung their heads from side to side, smelling and tasting the air about them.

Jon shivered as he recalled the last time he'd seen such a mime, the time Yildilla did it when he and the men from Jarrahlong were camped out in the bush, when Yildilla had come in search of

Curly's tjuringa.

With a curious jerky movement the "creatures" circled the camp. The women and children watched, mesmerised, then, when they least expected it, the "perenties" lunged at them making them turn and flee, screaming, back to their own camp.

Satisfied with the outcome of the mime the three men slowly shook off their perentie personas and rejoined the group, where they remained until the end of the ceremony when the drawing of Perentie was scrubbed out.

Throughout the long ceremony Jon was aware that he had been allowed to observe sacred rites and rituals, that he had, as an honorary member, been accepted as one of Yildilla's tribe, that he would, forever, be linked to these people, whether he wanted to be or not.

He glanced about him, at the people around him – would there be a price to pay? And, if so, when would the first dues be called in? Or had they already been paid? He didn't know and he sensed it was pointless to ask.

CHAPTER 35

After the ceremony, Yildilla accompanied him across the desert as far as the town of Leonora and then left him to make his own way home. Jon looked down at his clothes, bloodstained and tattered after his time in the desert and the beard he'd grown while away with Yildilla. He looked like a swagman, and to make matters worse somewhere along the line he'd lost the money he'd had with him.

He supposed he could go to the bank and argue the case but the thought depressed him. Instead, he hitched a lift from one to the drivers of a delivery truck heading to Kalgoorlie. In Kal he went to his own bank, withdrew some money, then made his way to the nearest hotel where he took a room, had a bath and a shave, a meal, and a good night's sleep. In the morning he paid the bill and walked to one of the truck stops where he found a driver going to Perth and cadged a lift as far as Southern Cross.

'Where you bin?' the driver asked.

Jon fixed his eye on the horizon. 'You wouldn't believe me.'

'Try me,' said Walt Robinson, 'there ain't much I haven't heard over the years from the lifts I've given. Woman trouble?'

Jon smiled wryly, he wasn't about to go down that route. He shook his head, conscious of the partially-healed wounds on his chest. 'Nah, I've been walkabout…out east of here.'

'Like those Abo fellas?'

'Yeah, that's right.'

Walt took his eyes off the road. 'Ya don't look the type, mate. What do ya do for a livin'…when yer workin' that is?'

'Got a station up beyond Charlestown, a ways north of Southern Cross.'

'So what happened? Station owners are rich cockies, aren't they? You find station life too easy, wanted a bit of a challenge, is that it?'

'No', said Jon, deciding to tell the truth and get the bloke off his back. 'Lost a son a few months back, just needed to get away from the place, get myself straightened out.' It was close enough to the truth if truth be told.

'Straight up?' asked Walt.

'Straight up,' said Jon.

'Strewth, mate, that's a toughie!'

The revelation had the desired effect. Walt shut up and left Jon alone with his thoughts. As he sat in the warm cab, resisting the temptation to scratch the scabs on his chest, he wondered whether it had all been worth it, whether going with Yildilla had given him a new perspective and wasn't sure that it had. There was one thing about the death of a loved one; it certainly put a different slant on what was important and what wasn't. Jamie's death had soured all that he had, the wealth he and Val had accumulated, the station, all of it he would give up in the blink of an eye if it would bring Jamie back. But it wouldn't, nothing would, and he didn't care what Curly and Stan had said during his hallucination back in the cave under the Nullarbor about Jamie's spirit returning to the earth to await a new birth. He didn't believe all that rubbish, just as he didn't really believe in Purgatory, or a life in Paradise for those who had faith in Christ and lived by His tenets…although he could be wrong, maybe there was something in the Catholic idea of Purgatory, except for him Purgatory was in the here and now.

Almost as bad as Jamie's death was the rift, a great chasm, between him and Val, and somehow, and soon, he needed to bridge it and bring her back to him. He needed Val by his side, he felt lonely without her. She made him laugh at himself and she kept him from his worst excesses, she gave him pause for thought, and support when he doubted himself and his ability to do his best for those he loved.

In the weeks after Jamie's death Val had withdrawn into herself. She wouldn't talk to him, he'd known how she was feeling but he didn't really know what was going on in her head, what she was thinking. He did know that she didn't want to live after Jamie died, but David and Ruby kept her with them. Had she not had them to consider then he would have been fearful for her life. As Stan had once said, there are worse things than death, and out in the desert when Curly had been dying in agony, he'd learnt the truth of that. Perhaps Alistair was right when he said it was harder for a mother to lose a child, than for a father. Maybe carrying a child and giving birth created a bond that was stronger and therefore more devastating when it was broken. When he'd seen the suffering in Val's eyes, and the heartbreak, he'd wanted to crush her to him, hold her and comfort her, but she'd pushed him away, unable to contemplate comfort from him or anyone else.

He turned his face to the side window and watched the landscape slip by, thick bush, predominantly tall eucalypts with the scrubby mallee undergrowth, and in the open spaces the yellowish grass, dotting the red earth. Sometimes it's nice not to think, he thought, but just letting the mind slide into neutral was hard, his shoulder muscles felt tense and he questioned whether he'd ever get back onto a surer footing. For the first time in ages he thought of Alice – what she'd say when she saw him? There'd probably be a tongue lashing, but there and again she could take one look at him and order Belle to make some tea, or if he looked really crook it'd be half a tumbler of bourbon whiskey – Alice, better than anyone, knew what he and Val were going through.

It was early evening by the time a driver dropped Jon off in Charlestown. The sun had already set and the lights from The Grand spilled across the road from the saloon. He could hear outbursts of raucous laughter from the bar – the shearers were in town. The weekend, he realised, and smiled wryly. That was one thing about living out in the bush, you lost all sense of time; time was measured by the turning of the earth around the sun and the movement of the moon around the earth. Days, months and years were all that mattered, everything else was immaterial.

He stood on the walkway, under the verandah that provided protection from the sun, and hesitated. The landlady, Connie Andersen, would make him welcome; he knew that, she'd also find a bed for him even if the hotel was full. She was that sort, but somehow he couldn't face the conviviality of the crowd that would be gathered in the bar. There'd be the questions and the sidelong glances from those who knew him well, they'd be wondering about him and Val and how he was coping now one of his sons was dead, and his wife and other son gone walkabout in England. There'd be questions too about the sale of Jindalee and the new owner. He knew that people meant well, but he just wasn't up to it; things were still too raw, too painful to even think about, never mind talk about. Instead, he turned on his heels and continued down the street, away from the hotel, past the groups of Aborigines lounging in doorways, one or two already drunk despite the early hour. Scally! Should he turn up on Scally's doorstep, or Wes's?

Jon knew that Scally would be pleased to see him. Scally still missed Rachel and her children, ever since she and Ty Henderson had built their own place further down the road on a block of land Scally had bought for them. True they were only a step or two away but it wasn't the same as having family under the same roof and although Tom and Amy spent half their time at their grand-dad's place, there were still the lonely times, and evenings stretched – something Jon had learnt since Val and David's departure for England.

But somehow Scally's company didn't appeal. Scally held a few opinions Jon didn't share – his attitude to Aborigines for one – so he decided to call on Wes. Wes Chapman was a mate, and a bonza bloke, the salt-of-the-earth type who didn't make demands and who could be relied upon when the chips were down. He wasn't brash in any way and people confided in him, shared confidences that they knew would go no further. He didn't pry, he'd just ask you outright and if you wanted to tell him something he'd listen, if you didn't then that too was fine.

Wes was good at small talk, and there wasn't much he missed working in the garage as he did and, besides all that, he served up a pretty mean bully-beef stew. He kept a pot on the stove that was never dry; he'd add a bit of this, a dash of that, and throw in another block of bully when the meat content got a bit lean. Jon was of the opinion that Wes had lived on bully stew, damper and strong tea for nigh on sixty years, and he marvelled that the mechanic had never tired of the diet. Wes was a fella with modest needs, a man at ease with himself, a fella one could trust with a confidence or a life.

The moon was low in the sky when Jon reached the outer edge of Charlestown. The huge double doors of the garage Wes owned were closed and the rusting corrugated iron fronting the building was more or less as he'd first seen it back in 1946.

Jon smiled, nothing changed. In all the years Jon had known Wes someone would arrive with a new poster and Wes'd point to the glue pot and the fella, it was usually a fella, would pick up the glue pot, smear a few dabs on the back of the poster and plaster it on over the old so adding a dash of vivacity and colour to the garage frontage. The posters, and the ancient red and cream petrol pumps that had an art deco look about them, were images that Jon would forever associate with the little town he'd come to think of as home.

Jon skirted the building, picking his way though the backyard and the sprawling collection of partially cannibalised lorries, utes and trailers, until he came to Wes's home.

Jon knocked on the door and waited. Inside he heard Wes's old mongrel's rumbling growl.

'Hush, Samson,' Wes yelled from somewhere in the back of the building. Then came Wes's lumbering footsteps and the plank door's screech as he dragged it open over rough flooring.

Jon saw Samson's nose first and then Wes's slippered feet. As his eyes swept upward he took in Wes's belly spilling over his or-nately-tooled leather belt, his checked shirt and then Wes's ruddy complexion with the surprised look as he recognised his visitor.

'Well, I'll be damned, where have you bin these last few weeks? We've been worried about ya.'

'Walkabout, Wes.'

Wes yanked the door even wider and shoved Samson out of the way with his foot. 'Come in, come in. You eaten yet?'

Jon shook his head.

'You're just in time, the usual?'

'That'll do nicely, you make the best bully stew in the State.'

Wes grinned. 'Less of the flattery, young fella-me-lad. We both know I've had plenty of practice, if I can't make a passably good bully stew by now I never shall.' He gave Jon a friendly slap on the back as Jon stepped through into the main room in the wood and tin shack that Wes called home.

On top of the black rectangular stove, not dissimilar to the one Stan had had in his place at Yaringa Creek, stood an equally black cast-iron cooking pot. And next to that was a cast-iron griddle with the damper already cooked to perfection and smelling wonderful to Jon's hungry senses.

'Help yourself to bully and damper,' said Wes, picking up his own plateful already half eaten.

Jon did as bid and soon the two of them were tucking into Wes's famous stew, with Samson spoilt for choice. The old dog's eyes flicked from one plate to the other, saliva dribbling from his mouth onto the rough timber flooring, as he awaited an empty plate to lick.

When Wes finished his he belched and then lowered the plate to the floor for Samson to finish off the gravy smears and a bit of damper that he had purposely left for the dog.

'How is she then?' asked Wes, not beating about the bush.

'Last I heard she was still in Liverpool, her and David.'

'You're a bloody idiot. If I were you I'd get on the first plane out of Perth and fetch her back. She belongs here.'

Jon couldn't argue with that. He was of the same opinion. He couldn't believe he'd been daft enough to think a temporary separation would solve anything.

'Take it you haven't been back to Jindalee yet?'

'No. Why?'

Wes let out a long sigh. 'A lot has happened while you've been away.'

'Like what?'

'Don't rightly know, Nickson's been investigating, he's none the wiser either, but that gal of yours is in the thick of it.'

'Ruby?'

'No, the other one.'

Other one? Jon couldn't think for a moment, the only girl who sprang to mind was Ruby, and Ruby wasn't the sort to get herself into trouble. 'I don't know who you're talking about.'

'Sharon...I think that's her name.'

'Oh, you mean Shirley.'

'Aye, that's the one.'

'What about her?'

'She's a good-looking gal, and sparky, by all accounts,' said Wes avoiding Jon's piercing gaze.

'Come on, Wes. What have you heard?'

'Seems she's shacked up with one of your black stockmen.'

Jon frowned.

'Aye,' said Wes, 'the trouble is she wasn't discreet about it. At the dance last Saturday they were both in town, the Abos were standing around the Town Hall drinking, as they do, and Sharon—'

'Shirley.'

'Aye, Shirley...Shirley was sitting with them, laughing and joking as youngsters do. You can imagine the situation, can't ya?'

Jon could imagine. Aborigines weren't exactly popular in town and since the drinking laws had been relaxed the tensions had increased. The alcohol coupled with increased rights that Aborigines were demanding meant you had problems. And now this!

'Seems Kit's son, Todd, was at the dance and he took umbrage. There was a bit of a dust-up on the dance floor and in the end Les threw them all out and called the police, but by the time Nickson arrived Shirley and her fella had gone.'

'So was that the end of it, or did something else happen?'

'Well, Nickson said he'd have a word with you about the gal, tell you to point out to her the error of her ways and all that, that consorting with blacks isn't the done thing, that the locals take exception to white women going with blackfellas, and—'

'And this was last weekend, you say?'

'Yeah.'

Jon shook his head. It was the last thing he needed at the moment. But he wasn't surprised Shirley preferred the company of blackfellas especially after all she'd suffered at the hands of Todd and his family, and it wouldn't have helped that he and Val hadn't been in any fit state to look out for her in the months since Jamie's death.

'I'll have a word with her when I get home.'

'Trouble is that wasn't the end of it,' said Wes. 'Sometime during this last week the young black fella and a mate were driving along the old droving road to Pilkington when someone shot 'em. When they didn't come home your overseer sent a couple of stockmen to look for them.' Wes hesitated and glanced at Jon.

'Dead?'

'Yes, dead right enough. One of them was sitting in the driving seat in the burnt out cab, charred pretty bad, he was. Nickson says he'd been shot through the windscreen, bullet to the head. The other was shot in the back. Looks like he'd tried to run away. They found his body in the bush a few yards from the ute.'

'Todd,' said Jon without hesitation.

'Nickson says not. Kit says Todd was with him at the time of the murders and Ned Ackroyd has vouched for him too.'

Wes busied himself pouring out a couple of quart pots of tea. He handed one to Jon.

Jon drank down the scalding brew barely noticing the heat as he gulped the bitter billy tea that Wes preferred.

'Can I borrow a truck, Wes? I'd best be getting back.'

'Course you can, mate, but it's a bit late to be driving now, you'd spend half your time dodging 'roos, you'd be better leaving at the crack of dawn, you can be back by the time the station rises and you won't have lost a deal of time.'

Jon knew Wes had a point, even so his mind was in turmoil worrying about this new development. He sat back in his chair unsettled by Wes's news. Had it been a white fella going with one of the Aboriginal women no one would have given it a thought, Aboriginal women were still regarded as fair game. Not that long ago he'd heard talk of a walk-out on one cattle station where the black stockmen were fed up with being sent out to look after the mob every weekend so the white stockmen could knock off the women in their spare time. And then there were the half-castes, all, as far as he knew, with black mothers and white fathers. He'd never ever heard of a half-caste kid with a white mother and a black father.

Now, two of his stockmen were dead, killed in cold blood by the sound of it. Here he was running a station in 1970 and it was almost as bad as it had been in the early days, blacks being murdered for no good reason.

But if it wasn't Todd, then who was responsible? There were enough people out there who would tolerate most things, but over the last ten years or so, attitudes towards the blacks had hardened. People who hadn't voiced an opinion before were vocal against Aboriginal Land Rights, a growing issue in Western Australia, and everyone seemed to have a view on it. Then there was the problem of black stockmen demanding equality and the Government legislating for it. It had caused a lot of bad feeling among some pastoralists who had got away with paying their Aboriginal stockmen a pittance for years.

'I could have done without this.'

'Aye,' said Wes, 'that's what Connie said.'

CHAPTER 36

Dawn was still a pink blush on the horizon when Jon arrived back at Jindalee in one of Wes's trucks. He didn't bother going into the homestead but headed across the yard to where George lived and was pleased to see the kitchen light on as he'd expected.

He hammered on the door and waited.

May opened it, took one look at Jon and called over her shoulder. 'Mister Cadwallader for you, George. Come in,' she added, stepping aside to let him through into the kitchen.

George looked up from his breakfast.

'Hello, George, Wes tells me there's been a bit of bother.'

'Pretty bad business, boss. Atmosphere over in the camp's pretty bad too, no one's prepared to work, they's convinced the police ain't doing nothing. Fellas out here sez no one cares about us blacks.'

'Slow down, George, start at the beginning.'

'You had breakfast?' asked May.

Jon nodded, 'Yeah, with Wes, thanks...so what happened, George?'

'Don't rightly know. Miki Barker and Albert Cooper—'

'Albert, you mean Charlie's son?'

'Yeah, anyway, last Tuesday they went off to Pilkington in the old ute, said they'd pick up a few things we'd ordered from the stores there and have a night out with some mates from over on Harrison Station. Trouble is feelin's were already runnin' high with the blackfellas 'cos Todd and his pal, Nick—'

'Nick?'

'Yeah, Mister Kenton's son. Anyway they'd been out to the Abo camp over on the Harrison and shot all their dogs a couple of

260

weeks back. Mister Kenton sez the dogs were killin' his lambs, but I don't reckon that was the case. Old fella Kenton's too mean to pay a dogger and the dingoes and wild dogs are out of control over there, can't hardly blame the blackfella's dogs for that, but y'know Todd and Nick when they get together.'

'What's that to do with our boys?'

'I'm tellin' ya, boss, I'm tellin' ya. As I said feelin's were already runnin' high over the dog killin' when Shirley decides she and Albert should go to the dance in Charlestown last Saturday night.'

'Didn't anyone say anything to them?'

'Yeah, Charlie told Albert not to be an idiot, that he'd get himself into a fight, and Ruby sez she told Shirley she was askin' for trouble, that Albert wouldn't be allowed into the dance, but neither of 'em listened, they counted on it bein' a'right, it being in a public place an' all.'

Jon could picture it, white and black stockmen would have turned out in force for the social event of the month, there'd have been plenty of drinking as well as dancing, plenty of blacks hanging around on the fringes getting pretty well-oiled.

'Anyway, it seems Shirley sort of listened to Ruby's advice and decided to stay away from the dance and hang around outside the Town Hall with the blackfellas, trouble was Todd spotted her and took exception, her bein' with the blackfellas and not with 'im.'

'Didn't anyone step in to stop the trouble?'

'Nah, boss, it all happened too quick. Todd grabbed hold of Shirley and dragged her into the Town Hall and onto the dance floor. She shoved him off and he laughed, said she was nothin' but a whore who'd drop her knickers for anyone, and he didn't want to dance with a bitch who shacked-up with blacks.'

'Where was Albert?'

'Right there, boss, in the doorway, he heard it all and had to be held back from givin' Todd a thrashin'. And he could have done it too, Albert was a big fella, six feet two and well built, and he'd always had a fiery temper...took after his old man, he did.'

Jon whistled, long and low.

'Aye,' said George, 'and that wasn't the end of it. Todd told Albert's mates to keep their mongrel under control or he'd shoot 'im like he did all Abo mongrels, especially them as violated white women.'

'And no one tried to calm things down?'

261

'As I said, boss, it all happened so fast, Les Harper told Albert and his mates and Shirley to go home. And they did but not before Shirley screamed that Todd was nothin' but a bloody rapist, that he didn't care who he attacked, white women or black women, that if she had her way she'd chop his donger off. I'm tellin' ya, boss, if Les Harper and Al Green hadn't stepped in there'd have been blood on the dance floor, no doubt about it.'

'She said all that?'

'Too right she did, she was still screamin' at Todd as Al Green and Les Harper dragged her outside and shoved her in Albert's ute.'

Jon could just imagine the scene, all Shirley's pent-up anger bursting out, but at what cost? Did Saturday night's incident have a bearing on the murders? 'Who do you think did it, George?'

'That drongo, Todd, if y'ask me. Whoever it was had a repeatin' rifle, only way he could've got two of 'em so quick, either that or there was more than one of 'em. We found a couple of spent cartridge cases at the scene and handed them in to Nickson, said he should be able to find out whose rifle they'd come from.'

'What did Nickson say?'

George snorted. 'Nickson, he don't want to know; and he's thick with that mongrel, Mister Kennilworth.'

'What about the spent cases?'

'Nickson said there weren't anythin' distinctive about 'em, said they could've come from any gun, but I don't know so much, there was a distinctive crimp on 'em.'

Jon frowned. He'd found spent cartridge cases with distinctive crimping in the breakaways near where he'd been shot. Were they from the same rifle?

'What do you think?'

'I can't see Nickson makin' much of an effort to find the killer.'

Jon knew George wasn't far wrong. Nickson was a bit of a lazy sod, anything for a quiet life. When there had been a problem over Shirley running away from the Kennilworth place, Nickson hadn't really wanted to know about that, and he'd never exactly been quick to investigate crimes against Aborigines either. Nickson had done bugger all when Buni and his son, Wally, were run over at Cavanagh's Creek way back in the late forties: bottom line, Nickson didn't rate blacks.

'I suppose I'd better get over to Pilkington later and have a word, see what is happening. Where are the bodies, do you know?'

'Pilkington cemetery.'

'How are the families?'

'Still grievin'. It ain't a place for white fellas to be right now. Charlie's mutterin', reckons if Nickson don't find the killer then he will, sez he's not lettin' this go.'

'I don't blame him,' said Jon. 'I'd do the same. Changing the subject, how did Ruby get on while I was away?'

'Y'know Ruby.'

'True, was she a pain in the backside?'

'Nah, she's gotta real feel for the place and she gets on well with the stockmen, seems they recognise a good 'un when they see one.'

'Was she all right with you? She didn't try and pull rank, did she?'

'Ruby's not like that. Tell ya what though, she's good at pickin' brains, wants to know everything, got Charlie to show her the best way to break in a brumbie. You know what Charlie's like with horses, seems to be able to read 'em, has 'em eatin' out of his hand in no time.' He chuckled. 'Took Ruby a while to get him to tell her but, my word she listened when he did, she's almost as good as he is now, and she ain't afraid of anythin' ain't that girl of yours.'

Jon hid his pleasure; it didn't do to be overly proud of one's children. But proud he was, it was just a pity his boys…boy wasn't interested in station life.

'I better be getting home to see how she is. You saying we can't rely on the stockmen for any big jobs at the moment, is that it?'

'Yeah, that's right. There's still a lot of bad feelin' over at the camp.'

'There's not a lot I can do about that, George.'

'Give 'em time, boss, give 'em time…Oh, and Mister Saxby was around a few times, wonderin' where you'd got to. Sez he wants things done and dusted sooner rather than later.'

Jon dismissed the message. He couldn't be bothered with Ben Saxby right at the moment. The business over his men being murdered needed sorting out before he even considered finalising the sale of Jindalee. Ben Saxby could whistle for a bit and if he didn't like it, tough!

CHAPTER 37

Jon took his leave of George and May and headed over to the homestead, wanting to see Ruby and dreading his meeting with Shirley. He really wished Val were home, she'd know how to tackle the delicate situation.

If Wes was right then Shirley would be in a bad way following Albert's death. So just how close had the two of them become while he'd been away? And how long had the relationship been going on for? Val hadn't mentioned it, and he hadn't noticed anything, but there and again both he and Val were too preoccupied with their own grief to notice what Shirley was up to.

When he reached the house the place was silent. Usually he would have expected Shirley to be up and in the kitchen helping Val prepare breakfast for the family, for Noel and for any visitors staying at Jindalee. Noel would still need breakfast even if there was no one else to feed.

He made himself a coffee and waited, listening for movement from the rest of the house. He checked his watch. Six o'clock, both the girls should be up by now, but he couldn't hear any noises from the bathroom.

Jon pulled the kitchen door open and listened, cocking an ear first for sounds from Ruby's room to the left and then Shirley's room at the far end of the corridor, next to the utility and gun room.

Nothing!

When he finished his coffee he went looking, first to Ruby's room. He knocked on the door and waited, when there was no reply he opened the door and saw the mound of bedding.

'Ruby?'

Ruby flung off the top sheet and sat up, still dazed from deep sleep. 'What...?' Then she realised who it was and flung herself out of bed and gave him a hug. 'Jon-Jon, when did you get back?'

'Last night, but it was late so I stayed over with Wes. And what about you, stay-abed?'

She yawned. 'Noel and me, we sat up late discussing things.' She looked him in the eye. 'Did Wes tell you?'

'About the killings?'

'Yeah, and Shirley and Albert?'

'Yes, he told me about that too, and George filled the rest in for me. What does Noel think?'

'Same as everyone else, people aren't ready to deal with white women going with black men; it was bound to cause trouble. Noel says the same thing happened back home in England with the Yanks in the last war; the Yanks didn't like it when their blackfellas got off with British women, caused fights over there too. But he reckons the Brits weren't that bothered about it, at least not so bothered as the Yanks were.'

'Well, you're not the only stay-abed this morning, Shirley isn't up either and Noel will be over any minute for his breakfast.'

'I'll be two ticks. Oh, and that so-and-so, Benjamin Saxby, has been sniffing round.'

'Yes, so George said.'

'I don't like the man. He'll be no good for Jindalee. If you must sell, can't you find someone better than him?'

'Not now, Ruby, I've got other things on my mind.'

He shut the bedroom door and walked down the corridor to Shirley's room, knocked on her door, waited, listened and knocked again. Still nothing! He tentatively opened the door and looked into the bedroom and saw her bed hadn't been slept in.

He took in the rest of the room but everything seemed pretty normal. Clothes strewn over a chair, hairbrush on the dressing table, lipstick, a threadbare teddy on the pillow and a couple of women's magazines on the floor at the side of the bed where she'd dropped them.

Jon frowned. Where the hell had she gone? He closed the bedroom door and returned to the kitchen to find Noel already making himself a fry up of steak and eggs.

Noel jumped when he heard Jon's tread, 'Good God, Jon, I didn't know you were back! I thought you were a ghost.' He took the pan off the heat. 'I don't know where everyone is.' He glanced at his watch. 'It isn't like Ruby or Shirley to be late up. Have you eaten?'

'Yeah, but a while back. Ruby's getting dressed. I don't know where Shirley's got to.'

Noel crossed over to the refrigerator, took out another two steaks and threw them into the frying pan.

'Have you seen Shirley, Noel?'

'Isn't she in her room?'

'No.'

'Bathroom?'

'Don't think so.'

Noel shrugged. 'Haven't got a clue, as I say she's usually up and cooking breakfast by this time. You can usually set your watch by her.' He flipped over the steaks and added eggs to the other pan. 'It's nice to have you back. Did you find what you were looking for?'

Had he? Right at the moment things didn't seem to be any clearer in his head, and he still wasn't completely sure why Yildilla had taken him on walkabout. Had the long walk through the desert, his experience in the cavern under the Nullarbor, the corroboree and the gift of the tjuringa, changed him?

'I don't know, but it seems an old Aborigine I know decided I should learn more about the Dreaming.' He didn't elaborate; his experiences were still too new to properly assess what had happened. It certainly hadn't eased the pain of his loss, but his attitude to the outback had softened, he no longer felt so ambivalent about the place as he had in the weeks and months since Jamie's death.

Noel plated up the steak and eggs and handed Jon his.

'Maybe I'd have done better to stay around. We wouldn't be in this mess if I had.'

'Maybe,' agreed Noel, 'and maybe not. If you ask me, the pair of them were pretty strong-willed, and Shirley had really taken a shine to Albert.'

'Aye, so George says,' said Jon.

According to Ruby, Shirley returned mid-morning, spent over an hour in the bathroom and then went to her room where she stayed for the rest of the day.

'Have you spoken to her?' asked Jon later that evening.

'Briefly,' said Ruby, 'I shoved my head around the door about teatime but she told me to go away, said she was still tired.'

266

'She say where she was last night?'

'No, and I didn't ask, she'll probably tell us in the morning when she's had a good night's sleep.'

If she stays in her bed, thought Jon. He walked over to the sideboard, switched on the lamp and poured himself a whisky, then he returned to the easy chair and settled down next to Ruby.

'George says you did a good job while I've was away.'

'That so?' Ruby's voice was flat, and Jon sensed she didn't care what George had said.

'You still going to sell Jindalee?' she asked.

'Yes.'

'Well, I think you're wrong, moving away won't make any difference. Jamie will always be a big hole in our lives no matter where we live.' She hesitated a moment. 'Did you find what you were looking for, then?'

Jon glanced across at Ruby and saw her watching him. 'You been talking to Noel?'

'Why?'

'He asked the very same question this morning.'

'Well?'

'I don't know, but now I'm back it seems to me I'd have done better staying put than going off with Yildilla. Maybe we wouldn't be in this mess if I'd stayed.'

'Yeah, I suppose you're right.'

Jon gazed into his tumbler and swirled the last of the whisky around before swallowing it down.

'Are you and Mum going to get divorced?'

The question came as a shock. 'Of course not, why do you think that?'

'Mum's not happy, neither are you and you haven't seen each other for over three months now. Mum going off with David to England, and you off on your own with Yildilla, and your plans to sell Jindalee, it just seems the family isn't a family any more.'

'You could have gone with your mother, you know that, Ruby.'

'What? – and leave this place for months on end to go gallivanting around Liverpool, living with Auntie Evelyn's mob? No thank you.'

Jon didn't comment, there didn't seem to be anything else to say about that, Ruby had just about summed up the situation, and the scathing tone said it all.

'Your mum has been in a bad place since Jamie's death.'

'It's been hard for all of us.'

'I know. You loved your brother as much as we did, do, but Jamie's death was tough on your mum. She blames herself.' And she blames me, thought Jon.

'It wasn't her fault; if anyone's to blame it's that Merle woman.'

'Your mum doesn't see it quite like that; she thinks we are partly to blame for bringing you up here, in this environment. She says, and she's right, that the bush is a hard place to live even if you love it and your mother does love it, but she's not so blind as to see that it can come at a cost for all of us.'

'I know she loves the bush,' said Ruby. 'She once said it was almost as if she'd been born in the wrong place, that arriving at Jarrahlong that first day was like coming home for her. She said it was a balmy evening and the earth smelt hot and Alice's old silver gum was rustling in the slight breeze.'

'That's right,' said Jon, remembering the moment, his feelings of shock and horror at the sight of her.

'Mum says she was wearing white suede shoes that attracted the red dust. She laughed, said they'd cost her a week's wages back in Liverpool, and that when she'd tried to brush off the dust with sweaty hands it made them worse. She said they were ruined.'

'Yeah, they were.' Jon laughed. 'She tried washing them but that didn't work either.'

Ruby glanced at Jon. 'And she said you were furious with her for turning up, but that she knew you were the one so she ignored your temper tantrums until you came to your senses.' Ruby gazed into the distance for a while, reflecting, and then stirred herself. 'Mum says you can conquer the world with the right pair of shoes.'

'She does, doesn't she?' said Jon a half smile on his face, remembering the half a dozen pairs of fancy shoes Val had in the wardrobe alongside the soft leather boots she usually wore with the khaki strides she favoured when they were out in the bush.

Ruby grinned, 'Too right she does.' Then the smile left her face. 'Will she come back?'

'Of course she will.'

'She won't decide to stay in England?'

'With her sister!' said Jon. 'No chance, they'd end up killing each other.'

Ruby giggled, 'She left her carving knife at home.' Then, solemn-faced, she asked, 'What was my father like?'

Jon hesitated.

'Berry,' Ruby avoided looking at him, 'I know you are my Dad…but the other one, Berry…did my mother love him?'

Jon didn't know how to answer. He hadn't given any thought to Berry Greenall for sometime. 'Berry and your mum were together for quite a while, but I suppose when you came along it was difficult, being on the shearing circuit isn't easy for a family man…'

'He was quite the lad though, wasn't he? He'd already had a bit of a fling with Aunt Rachel.'

"*Bit of a fling*", Jon supposed that was as good a way of describing the relationship as any.

'Well, I…'

'And there's my half-brother, Joe; Berry didn't marry Aunt Rachel, did he?'

'No, but by the time Joe was born your Aunt Rachel wouldn't have married him even if he'd asked her.'

'Mum thinks he couldn't help himself, that he was one of those men who like the ladies; she says he ended up dead because he had an affair with a married woman.'

'Look, Ruby, your dad wasn't a bad man. He was one of the best shearers in the State and he was a good mate by all accounts. He was what some would call a man's man, perhaps he wasn't cut out to be a husband and a father; some blokes aren't.'

'That's what Mum said.'

'Yeah, well, as we said earlier, the outback is a tough place for everyone, so I don't think you should think too badly of Berry.' Jon glanced at his watch. 'I think it is time you went to bed; I don't fancy cooking my own breakfast in the morning.'

Ruby laughed as she hauled herself to her feet, 'You didn't cook it this morning, Noel did.'

'Less of the cheek, young lady.'

'You'll write to Mum, won't you? Ask her to come home.'

'I already did, while I was in town the other day. Wes said it would get there in two shakes if I sent it airmail, so I did. She'll be home before we know it.'

Ruby leaned over and kissed him on the forehead. 'Night-night.'

'Night-night, Ruby,' murmured Jon.

CHAPTER 38

The police station and lock-up in Pilkington were located three blocks from the only remaining hotel in town, the Commercial. Like Charlestown, Pilkington was an old gold-mining town and its heyday too was long over; now, it supplied the townsfolk, all twenty-two of them, and the men off the local stations, with a place to drink away the dust and a store where they could buy the basics. There was also a garage, a post office, a health clinic, a fire station, a church and a town hall that looked too ornate for the place as it now was. On the outskirts was the cemetery, bigger than the one in Charlestown, and testimony, if it were needed, to the size of the gold rush back at the turn of the century. It also boasted a cricket pitch out in the bush, within sight of the church, which had been used right up until the First World War when Pilkington challenged Charlestown to the Pilkington equivalent of the "Ashes". Some wag had carved a tiny replica cup in wood as an "Ashes" trophy that was presented after the first ever cricket match held in 1898 when the town was in the thick of gold-fever and boasted a population of one thousand four hundred souls, approximately three hundred more than Charlestown of the same period.

The tradition had died out with the loss of men in the First World War. There were enough listed on the war memorial next to the church to have decimated the cricket team. But that didn't explain why no one had bothered to revive the annual event until eighteen months back when a few of the locals had arranged a friendly, but it hadn't been a success. The turnout had been low, bad planning, he guessed, and bad timing; three of the Charlestown team hadn't been available, Harry had been over in Vietnam and George and his son, Tom, had been visiting family in Queenland.

The Charlestown team had taken a thrashing which hadn't helped. Maybe he should talk to Mike Tunstall and Les Harper, see whether, between them, they could get a couple of teams together and give it another go, and advertise it better.

Jon smiled as he recalled the stories he'd heard of friendly rivalry and dirty doings between the teams. That was one thing about old mining towns, their varied and fascinating history. But today wasn't a day for reminiscing. He stepped into the police station and saw Constable Curran, Nickson's offsider, working at his desk.

'Nickson about?'

Curran indicated the inner door and returned to his paperwork.

Jon knocked and entered.

'Take a seat?' said Nickson somewhat flustered by the unexpected visit.

'I gather that a couple of my stockmen have been murdered,' said Jon not bothering to waste time on niceties. 'Have you found out who did it?'

'No,' said Nickson, 'there were no witnesses. Doubt whether we'll ever get to the bottom of it. Bad business, though,' he shook his head, 'a bad business.'

Jon took in the bland look on Nickson's face. 'And what about the spent cartridge cases?'

'What cartridge cases?'

'The ones my overseer, George, gave you.'

'Oh, those!'

'Well?'

'Well, what?'

'Significant, don't you think? It shouldn't be too difficult to compare them to those from the rifles of your suspects. My overseer says they're distinctive.'

'We haven't got any.'

'Any what?'

'Suspects.'

Jon jiggled the spent cases in his pocket, the ones he'd found in the gully not far from his dead horse, debating whether to show them to Nickson. 'Are they like these?' He took them from his pocket and held them in the palm of his hand.

'Where did you get 'em from?'

'Over in the breakaways, from the time someone shot my horse from under me and left me for dead with a crease in my skull. These are pretty distinctive too, maybe you should see if they

271

match the ones my overseer gave you.'

'Wouldn't make any difference if they did. Whoever owns the rifle will have it well hidden by now.'

'Not if they're convinced no one's going to come looking,' said Jon.

'Anyway,' said Nickson, 'we haven't any suspects.'

'That's not what I've heard, Constable.'

'And what have you heard?' The sneer was there in the tone.

'That Todd Kennilworth was heard to threaten Albert Cooper on the Town Hall steps in Charlestown on dance night, not that long before Albert and his mate, Miki Barker, were shot?'

'There wasn't nothing in that, just a lot of hot air.'

'You reckon? As I've heard it there's a fair bit of animosity between Todd and the blacks at the moment over a dog shoot on Harrison Station,' said Jon.

'Are you saying a station owner has no right to protect his property?'

'No, all I'm saying is that Todd isn't exactly known for his love of blacks.'

'Can't argue with that,' said Nickson, 'and he's not the only one. If you ask me the blacks around here are getting too big for their boots with all this Government legislation. They reckon they've got the same rights as whites, and they haven't.'

'No, they haven't…yet,' said Jon, dryly. 'So where was he when my men were shot?'

'Who?'

'Todd.'

'At home, his Dad has vouched for him, and so has Ned Ackroyd.'

'Ned?'

'Kit's…Mr Kennilworth's head stockman. He says it's probably an Abo thing, you know what they're like?'

'No, tell me.'

Nickson sighed. 'Albert had likely been…' he hesitated, 'messin' with another Abo's gin, seems to me it was tribal punishment, you know better than me what they're like.'

Jon gave him a long look, the disgust clear on his face and was pleased to see Nickson redden.

'So you've no intention of taking this further?'

Nickson shook his head. 'Not unless you, or someone else, comes up with some real proof, not just a couple of spent cartridge cases…that, or someone confesses, and I can't see that happening, not over a couple of blacks.'

'What about the bodies?'

'What bodies?'

'My men, Constable.'

'We buried 'em. Can't keep corpses in this heat, you know that.'

At Jindalee most of the black stockmen remained in the camp. Only George and his son, Tom, and Ruby drove out daily to check the bores and wells in the drought conditions and Jon was glad that there was no muster scheduled for the coming month. The homestead, usually busy with men repairing equipment, breaking in new horses to replace older stock, and all the other jobs that needed doing, was quiet.

Since Jon's return he'd seen neither hide nor hair of Charlie Cooper. George said he'd gone walkabout soon after it became clear that the police were doing nothing to find his son's killer. Word was he'd gone to consult with the elders of his mob, that if white fellas wouldn't punish the killer then he'd see to it that his people did. It was said Aboriginal kaditja men were relentless in their pursuit of justice, and in Jon's experience that was so. Gerry Worrall, a bastard of a bloke was speared to death by a kaditja man for killing Aborigines, and he too had suffered punishment at the hands of one – Yildilla – out in Paradise Canyon. He knew first hand what they were capable of, so the question was, would it be one of their executioners who would exact revenge or would they opt for bone-pointing? Stan Colley had told him about bone-pointing, said it worked on whites as well as blacks.

Jon was convinced Albert Cooper and Miki Barker's killer would be punished, one way or another. His thoughts shifted to Miki Barker. He'd been a likeable young fella, one of the single stockmen who had joined the mob at Jindalee one muster when they were short staffed. Miki had been about Albert's age and the two of them had palled up and, after the muster, he'd asked to be taken on.

He'd liked Miki instantly, his open, honest face and wry sense of humour had appealed to him, and he'd been popular with the other stockmen. Reliable types were increasingly hard to come by and Miki hadn't been the sort to go out and get drunk on his days off; he'd been a good influence on Albert who'd been hot-headed and

273

the type to get himself into trouble.

But now he had a problem; no one seemed to know where Miki had come from and Jon worried about letting his family know of his death.

A couple of weeks passed and still the atmosphere at Jindalee and at the Aboriginal camp was tense. Further, Ben Saxby had been in touch to say he was no longer interested in buying Jindalee, that all the business with the blackfella killings was a blight he could do without, and that he'd put in an offer on Wanndarah instead. Jon wasn't sure whether to be relieved or not, but the fact of the matter was he had too much on his mind to worry about it.

Back at the homestead Shirley was taciturn and uncommunicative. She cooked the meals expected of her, looked after the vegetable plot, did the basic housework and that was it; the rest of the time she spent either in her room or out riding in the bush on one of the quieter stock horses.

Shirley's new-found interest in riding surprised Jon. Ruby had taught her to ride soon after she'd come to live with them but she'd never really taken to it. She'd ridden out with the others when Ruby, Jamie, David, Tom and Daisy had gone to one of the pools for a swim and a picnic, and sometimes she'd accompanied Tom when he went out with his sketchbook, but she'd never been a serious rider. It worried him, her going off alone and he'd pointed out the risks, but she wouldn't listen. He'd seen the stubborn, intractable look on her face and knew he was wasting his breath. Perhaps, Jon concluded, losing Albert had changed her attitude; maybe she liked the solitude of riding in the bush as much as he did.

They'd drummed into her the need to say where she was heading and when she'd be back, and usually she did, but Jon suspected that sometimes she said she was going one place and went to another. He was often reduced to keeping his fingers crossed, hoping that nothing serious happened while she was out alone. And then there were the nights she didn't return and Jon wondered who it was she'd shacked up with, whether it was another of the Aborigines or one of the white stockmen from a local station. He suspected the former, and hoped it was the latter but the nearest homestead to Jindalee was Reef Hill and he couldn't see Shirley willingly going back there, not with Todd still living at home.

274

Jon despaired of the tensions at Jindalee following Jamie's death, Val's absence, and the murders of Al and Miki. Since his arrival home he'd eagerly awaited the post, and a letter from Val. He hoped she'd received his, sent before he'd gone walkabout with Yildilla, where he'd written that he loved her, missed her and David, and that he'd put Jindalee on the market. In a more recent letter he'd begged her to return, and had told her all the rest that had happened while he'd been out in the desert with Yildilla. He'd also written that he could no longer deal with everything on his own, that he needed her help with Shirley, her woman's touch, but each day came and went and still she did not return.

Mid November Scally turned up with the supplies they'd ordered, and the post.

Scally flopped down on the nearest chair. 'Y'heard from Val recently? I see there's no letter from the Old Country, reckon it's gone four months since she and David went walkabout.'

Jon opened a couple of beers and passed one across to Scally. 'You know what it's like,' he said, keeping his voice light to conceal his disappointment. He'd really expected a reply even allowing for the vagaries of the postal service in the outback.

Shirley leaned on the kitchen door handle and barged open the flyscreen with her backside while carrying a laden tea tray. She placed it on the table in front of Jon. 'You can be mum,' she said, 'I've got to get the scones out of the oven.'

That's a bit of a shiner,' commented Scally looking at the week-old black eye that had taken on a yellowish hue where the bruising had faded.

'Walked into a cupboard door,' said Shirley.

'Y'should be more careful,' commented Scally.

'I'll remember that next time,' replied Shirley tartly. 'You like butter on your scones, or plain?'

'Butter,' said Scally, 'an' thick enough to leave teeth marks.'

'Good job we keep a couple of dairy cows, couldn't keep up with you and butter otherwise,' observed Jon.

'Y'know me an' butter,' laughed Scally. He watched while Shirley disappeared back into the kitchen. 'So, what really happened?'

'I think she spent the night with Todd,' said Jon.

Scally's eyes widened. 'You don't say! I heard he'd raped her a couple of years back, that that was why she ended up living here, didn't think she could stand the fella.'

'She can't, but she says it was worth it.'

'What you on about?'

'I'm not sure, she wouldn't say more, she thinks she told me too much as it is, but I've a feeling she wanted something from him and was prepared to pay the price.'

The flyscreen banged and Shirley appeared carrying a plateful of buttered pumpkin scones, golden brown and hot from the oven. She placed them on the table and returned to the kitchen without a word and Jon wondered whether she'd overheard them.

'Go on,' said Scally, helping himself to a scone.

'I think she wanted a lock of his hair.'

'Yer what?' said Scally, spluttering out bits of half-eaten scone. 'What the hell for, a locket or summat?'

'Wish it were that simple, wouldn't be surprised if she wanted it for a bone-pointing ceremony. She's been spending time over at the camp with Albert's family and then the other night there was a corroboree – dancing and chanting, you know the sort of thing. I took a ride over but the atmosphere was tense, Shirley was there with Albert's mother, sisters and aunts, but the menfolk were out in the bush someplace secret. Can't say for sure but maybe she needed the hair to make the magic more powerful, you know what these ceremonies are like.'

Scally laughed. 'Y'don't believe all that mumbo-jumbo, do ya?'

'Stan did, he told me on more than one occasion about bone pointing, about how the Aborigines could sing a man to his death.'

'Y'know what Stan was like, he could tell a tall tale if the mood took him, he had a reputation for bein' a bit of a romancer.'

'I don't know so much, Stan was right more often than he was wrong about these things,' said Jon.

'Like the gold at Yaringa Creek! I kept tellin' him he was wasting his time but he wouldn't listen, he always said there was a seam there jus' waitin' to be found. Silly old bugger!'

Jon said nothing, only Val and Alice knew the truth of it, that Stan had found gold, scads of it, the gold that had bought Jindalee and kept the whole shebang running despite the poor returns from the sale of cattle in the drought years.

'So y'reckon they've gone and sung Todd Kennilworth?' murmured Scally between mouthfuls of scone.

'We both know that Todd was behind the murders of my men,

and there's a lot of bad feeling down at the camp; they say white-fella law don't protect blackfellas.'

'They may have a point, you know what Nickson's like when it comes to blacks, he ain't got no time for 'em, unless they're young and pretty, that is,' commented Scally.

Jon scowled. Scally was right, although as far as he could tell Nickson was keeping his nose clean, he hadn't heard any word from the Aboriginal camp about any shenanigans out in the bush as in the old days. 'Best if you don't say anything to anyone, Scal. You know what people are like when it comes to blackfella business.'

'Yeah, well, they're not wrong in my view, just don't understand why y'so friendly with 'em. Them blackfellas tek some under-standin', they don't do 'emselves any favours gettin' drunk and goin' on walkabout when the mood's on 'em, and, as I say, y'know my feelin's on the subject of blacks, but y're a mate so I'll respect yer confidence.'

'Thanks.'

'Will it work?'

'Don't suppose we'll have long to wait. If Todd gets took sick and dies then we'll know there's something in it, won't we?'

'Aye, s'pose yer right,' said Scally tersely.

After Scally left Jon took a fresh mug of tea out to the back veran-dah and sat on the swing seat he'd rigged up for Val. He glanced up to their burial ground and reflected upon the earlier conversa-tion about the effectiveness of bone-pointing. His thoughts towards Merle had been less than charitable after Jamie's death. If thoughts had the power to kill she'd have dropped dead on the spot. Old anger stirred in his breast. Whenever she appeared there'd been trouble of some description and he couldn't for the life of him un-derstand what it was that had attracted him to her. And then he knew he wasn't being honest, it was sheer animal magnetism, it was her dark looks, the auburn hair and green eyes; it was attrac-tion at first sight and nothing whatsoever to do with love. He'd been young and impressionable and she was a good-looking woman, but a woman with a cold heart.

CHAPTER 39

It was late by the time Jon drove into the yard after checking the wells and bores on the east side of the station in the lead up to Christmas. He'd left at first light and had done the rounds knowing it would be a long day even if they were all working efficiently. The majority of the black stockmen were still refusing to work and he knew it was pointless to rail at them, that the best thing was to let them come to their senses in their own time. George, ever reliable, had taken Tom with him and had set off to check the water in the southern quarter where at least one of the windmills needed attention.

As he parked up he noticed Wes's spare ute in the yard next to the picket fence and wondered at the reason for the visit. He got out of the cab, collected his haversack and made his way over to the homestead.

Ruby was in the kitchen organising dinner with Shirley.

'You've got a visitor,' she said.

'Yeah, so I've noticed. 'You'd better make up a spare bed for the night, Wes won't fancy driving home in the dark.'

Shirley smirked and Ruby giggled.

'*He's* in the sitting room having tea and scones, you want the same?' asked Shirley, a smile lighting up her face.

'Wouldn't say no.' Jon shrugged off his jacket and threw his hat onto the peg. As he made his way along the corridor to the sitting room he hesitated, a frown on his brow, sure that he could smell Val's favourite French perfume. He dismissing the notion as fanciful, pushed open the door and stood, stock-still on the threshold, for there, not five paces away, sat Val.

Shock, and then delight at the sight of her, coursed through him.

278

He felt his heart pounding in his chest. She'd come back to him!

She stood, a shy smile on her face. 'Hello, hon, long time no see.'

Jon crossed the floor between them, gathering her to him, crushing her to his chest, kissing her as he did so. 'Too true,' he murmured, suddenly aware of the difference in her, his mind again in turmoil. He gently held her away from him and glanced down at her pregnant belly.

She smiled a slow smile, but he saw the anxiety in her eyes.

'Oh, Val, why didn't you tell me? It's wonderful news for us – another baby.'

'You're pleased?'

'Pleased! Of course I'm pleased, why wouldn't I be pleased? You know how I've always wanted children…lots of children.' He pulled her to him and hugged her tenderly as if she'd break in his arms. 'I love you. I'll always love you, and I've really missed you.'

'I love you too,' she murmured.

He held her away from him again and looked down into her smiling face. 'How many months?' he asked.

'Six.'

'When?'

'Oh, Jon!'

And then he remembered; there hadn't been that many occasions. Jamie's death had come between them, but one occasion was fixed in his mind, a night in early June, when they were both overcome with a passion neither of them understood and which had shocked both of them. It was the first time she'd really responded to his lovemaking after Jamie's death, when he felt she'd wanted him as much as he'd wanted her. But then afterwards she'd withdrawn into herself again as if in some way guilt overwhelmed her for forgetting Jamie for a short while.

Val stepped closer and he could smell the French perfume again as he wrapped his arms around her, blinking back tears. He buried his face in her neck and kissed her. He'd almost forgotten how well they fitted together, how it felt to kiss her neck, face and lips, the shape of her, her breasts, her swollen belly, pressing against him.

'Did you know you were expecting when you and David left for England?'

He felt her shake her head. 'No, hon. I didn't even suspect until we'd been there a couple of weeks or so. It was a bit of a shock.'

'Why didn't you write and tell me?' he murmured in her ear.

She pulled away from him gently, keeping tight hold while searched his face, looking for understanding. 'I wanted to but somehow I just didn't have the words, the baby, everything seemed like a betrayal...of Jamie, and then your letters arrived telling me you'd put Jindalee up for sale, and that you needed me, and I knew where I, where we all belong, despite everything.'

They heard the door open behind them and turned to see Ruby and David standing there, smiles on their faces.

Jon let go of Val and crossed over to his son and hugged him. 'You've grown.'

'Two inches.'

'It's good to have you home, son. I've...we've...really missed you, the both of you, haven't we, Ruby?'

'Too right we have.' She punched David on the arm. 'I've had no one to squabble with.'

Jon glanced across at Val. 'Does David know?'

'Not sure,' she said, 'but I think he's guessed.'

'We've something to tell you both,' said Jon a broad smile on his face as he turned back to Ruby and David.

Ruby chuckled. 'You're having another baby, aren't you?'

'She doesn't miss anything, does she, hon?' said Val, as she hugged her daughter.

'I'm glad you're back, it means we can have a proper Christmas, with everyone together, like we always do,' said Ruby.

'Roast beef and plum duff,' murmured Jon, 'in this heat!'

The next morning Jon and Val walked up to the burial ground together while the day was still cool.

'The flowers look nice,' commented Val.

'Shirley waters them,' said Jon. 'I rigged up a hose pipe with a vacuum pump for her, saves her having to carry buckets of water.'

Val breathed in the scent of the morning air, the distinctive smell of eucalypt and the last of the old-fashioned roses with their delicate perfume. 'I've missed this place, Jon.'

'I know, but we can move if you want to. We don't have to stay here.'

'I know that, Jon. But Jamie will still be dead; we'll still have a huge gap in our lives wherever we live.'

Jon gazed at the granite headstone that Mike Tunstall had cut for them, incised with the details of Jamie's short life.

'Besides, our son is buried here, we belong here, and who'd look out for the Aborigines?'

Jon couldn't argue with that, and in any case he knew his heart wasn't in starting again someplace else. His attachment to the land was as strong as Val's in that regard.

'Changing the subject, Mrs Cadwallader, don't you think we should be arranging an appointment at the clinic for a check-up? And we need to book you in for when the baby comes, we don't want a repeat of what you went through when Ruby was born, do we?'

'Oh, I don't know, if you recall a midwife turned up at the last minute and saved the day.'

'I'm serious, Val, we could go to Perth, organise a room for you at the hospital, as we did when the twins were born. We could go to Perth early, make a holiday of it, see the sights in Perth, have a look around Fremantle, maybe even take a trip across to Rottenest Island if you're feeling up to it. The locals say there are some pretty bays there for swimming. What do you think?'

'If that's what you'd like, Jon.'

'I want you safe when the baby's born, I don't want to leave anything to chance. You're not as young as you were last time.'

Val grinned. 'That's true. I'm classed as an old mother now.'

'You're not old to me.'

'But we are, we're both going grey.'

'True, anyway, when is the baby due?'

'End of February.'

'That's fixed then, we'll aim to go to Perth after Christmas and New Year, sometime in mid January. We can make the journey in easy stages, catch the train from Southern Cross, book into a nice hotel and take in a show. It'll make a change from the bush, do us good. We can take Ruby and David with us too.'

'That would be lovely, and maybe this weekend we could drive into Charlestown, go to the film show and stay at The Grand. It'll give me a chance to catch up on the gossip with Connie and Rachel, no doubt by now the word will be out that we've another on the way. Wes will have told them, and I need to return his ute,' said Val.

'What are we going to do about all the bad feeling down at the camp, Val?'

'Have you spoken to Al's family?'

'Tried to, but whenever I've been down there they've been pretty uncommunicative. Things have been a bit quieter since the corroboree the other week. Seems to me there's a feeling of expectancy in the air.'

'In what sense, hon?'

'I think they are waiting to see what happens to Todd; George says they've sung him.'

Val gave a long, low whistle. 'They really want him dead then?'

'Yeah,' said Jon. 'They really want him dead, right enough.'

Saturday night was film night and the town was full of people who had come in for the monthly showing, to gossip, have a beer in the bar or play two-up over in Les's lean-to.

Val and Jon had a leisurely meal in The Grand and caught up on the local news in the bar over a drink with Ed Scally.

'Seems the word is out that them blacks of yours have pointed the bone at young Todd,' said Scally.

'Who said that?' asked Jon knowing that Scally would have said nothing. Scally wasn't the sort to break a confidence.

Scally shook his head. 'I've no idea but Kit was over at Wes's place laughing about it. According to him his lad thinks it's a huge joke. Sez a piece of high-speed lead would be more effective.'

'He's an idiot saying that; someone might take him up on it,' said Jon, 'and shoot the pair of them.'

'Y'know Kit, he thinks he's pretty invincible, but some are saying that he's a worried man.'

'Why? The Abo threat?'

'Nah, it's over the nickel, Les sez he owes him a packet, sez he owes the bank too. Seems he borrowed to buy Glenshea stock. Lost the lot when it all went belly up and now he's struggling to pay off his debts. If y'ask me it won't be long before Reef Hill's on the market, just like Wanndarah before your buyer put in an offer. How do you feel about yer sale fallin' through, Jon?'

'It was probably for the best, Scal.'

'I've told Jon we should stick it out, that we belong here,' said Val.

'I'm right pleased to hear you say that. I never did think Jon was makin' the right decision puttin' Jindalee up for sale, not that he'd ever listen to me. But there's another plus to all of this.'

'And what's that?' asked Val.

'Alex Bartokas, he's a pretty relieved fella now he's got a buyer for Wanndarah. He told me there'd been little or no interest until Ben Saxby came along, so if Kennilworth does decide to sell it'll take a while unless the price of beef picks up and makes the place a more attractive proposition. Hey up, heard any more about Patrick O'Shea and that Glengarry fella?'

'O'Shea seems to have disappeared, there's not a whisper as to his whereabouts,' said Jon, 'and Glengarry, who knows!'

'I should imagine James Glengarry is back livin' at the family's stately pile in Cheshire,' said Val.

'Cheshire?' queried Scally.

'Yeah, his father owns an estate in England, in Cheshire. No doubt he's plannin' another venture even as we speak.'

'I never took to the fella,' commented Scally.

'Me neither,' said Val. 'Shady character that one, his eyes are too close together.'

Scally laughed. 'I've never heard that one before.'

'Haven't ya, Ed? That's because you're not from Liverpool.'

Scally grinned. 'Too right, I'm not.' He finished the last of his beer and glanced at his watch. 'Another one?' He held up his glass. 'We've time before the film show.'

'Don't mind if I do,' said Jon.

'Coffee for me, if Connie can rustle one up,' said Val.

Scally picked up the two empty glasses. 'Coffee it is.'

Jon watched Scally stroll over to the bar. 'Do you think Kit will sell up, Val?'

'Depends how much he owes. Les will be flexible, not so sure about the bank though.' Val sat back in her seat. 'It's a bad time to sell, the drought and all, he's already sold off half his stock, or so Connie told me.'

Scally placed two beers on the table. 'Connie sez she'll be over directly, Val.'

'Thanks, Ed.'

'And y'know what, looks like there might be somethin' in this singin' business.'

Jon frowned. 'Singing?'

'Y'know, them Aborigines. Connie sez Todd's been taken to hospital in Kal, got a bad kick in the chest from a camel while they were out cullin' them over on their northern boundary. Stove in a rib or two, it did, seems he was lucky not to get a punctured lung.'

Jon whistled long and low. 'Nasty! When did it happen?'

'Sometime yesterday, Connie heard about it on the evening

schedule, last night.'

'So that's who it was all about,' commented Val. 'I got the impression it was one of their stockmen, I didn't realise it was Todd. His mother will be upset about it.'

'Yeah,' agreed Scally, 'them camels can be real mean beggars with a kick like a batterin' ram, and so fast they reckon y'don't see it comin'.'

'I suppose he'll be in hospital for a few days,' said Jon.

'Aye, and then he'll have to tek it easy, no gallivantin' after the sheilas for a week or two.'

'Changin' the subject, will you and your family join us on Boxing Day, as usual?'

'You betcha,' said Scally, a broad grin on his face.

The next morning Jon left Val nattering to Connie while he headed down the street to Wes's garage. He found the mechanic, his head under the bonnet of a ute, replacing a head gasket. 'How you doing, Wes?'

Wes stood up, put his hands on his hips and eased his back. 'Not so good these days, me back's playing up, I'm getting too old for this job.'

Jon smiled. 'I can't see you throwing in the spanner any time soon. What would you do with yourself?'

'Aye, maybe you're right.' Wes took a pat of swarfega and massaged his hands, then wiped off the softened grease and oil with a rag and finished them off on his trousers. 'You heard about Kit's lad? Word is he's in hospital, kicked by one of the camels they've been rounding up over on Reef Hill.'

'Yes, Connie told Scally. She heard about it on the evening schedule.'

'Kit was by the other day, told me that some of your blacks have been bone-pointing, singing his lad, that true?'

'Al's family were pretty upset. They believe there isn't any white fella justice for blackfellas. They say a blackfella steps out of line and they're thrown into the lock-up pretty damned quick but the same rules don't apply to white fellas.'

'Yeah, they're right about that, and it seems to me that blackfellas don't do too good in the lock-up either, kill themselves, they do, can't take being confined.'

'Either they kill themselves or someone kills them,' said Jon.

'You saying the police murder them?'

'Well, let's just say they often end up with a bad beating and then they're left to it, either way more than a few end up dead in custody. You can't blame Aborigines for not looking to us for justice, Wes.'

'Nickson's not that bad. I know he don't expend much energy when it comes to blacks but it don't seem likely he'd beat 'em up. Haven't heard of any deaths in Pilkington lock-up for a while now.'

'What about Sammy White?'

'He was drunk, wasn't he?'

'Yeah and left on his back on the cell floor; they say he drowned in his own vomit.'

'You can't blame Nickson for that, Jon.'

'Maybe not, but Nickson's not exactly the best around here. George gave him the spent cartridge cases they'd found at the scene of Al and Miki's murders, distinctive they were, crimps in the metal that were identifiable and Nickson ignored it, said it wasn't evidence, that he couldn't go checking every rifle in the area without more proof.'

'That so?'

'Yeah, and I found similar cartridge cases over in the breakaways when someone shot my horse from under me. I think that was Todd too. Those cases had distinctive crimps and were the same calibre as those used to kill Al and Miki. If you ask me it wouldn't take much to check his rifle.'

'Did you report it?'

'No, not at the time, although as I just said, George gave Nickson the spent cases they'd found near where my men were shot, but Nickson didn't want to know.'

'So that's why those Abos have sung Todd.'

'Yeah.'

'And you think that is why he's in hospital?'

'No…I didn't say that, Wes. I'd call it coincidence; we've had similar injuries at Jindalee over the years. You know how dangerous camels are, especially when they're fully grown and wily. Years of avoiding the round-ups and musters gives them the edge and makes them dangerous, that's why we often shoot them instead of trying to yard them.'

'By the way, it's nice to see Val's back. When's the baby due?'

'End of February, she says.'

'It'll be good for you to have a little 'un to care for. I know it won't replace Jamie but it'll give you both a new focus, take your mind off your tragedy.'

'Yeah, you're right. Came as a bit of a shock though. I didn't know she was pregnant.'

'Yeah, you've both been in a crook place these last few months.'

'When the baby is baptised will you be its godfather, Wes?'

'Oh, I dunno, I'm not exactly the religious type and I'm not Catholic like you and Val.'

'Catholic in name only, we're not regular church goers, neither of us. I'd really like you to be godfather. You've been a good mate over the years and I know you'll look out for it. What do you say?'

'I'd be honoured, Jon. I'd be honoured.'

CHAPTER 40

Two mornings on the run Jon spotted Shirley crossing the yard to the homestead at the crack of dawn. On the second morning he investigated and found the horse she'd been riding lathered up. He rubbed the animal down, fed it, returned to the house and knocked on Shirley's bedroom door.

'Yes,' she called.

He opened the bedroom door and stood on the threshold. The first thing he noticed was that she'd changed her clothes from the britches he'd just seen her wearing. 'Where have you been?'

'Nowhere.'

'Don't lie to me, Shirley, you were out again all last night. I saw you coming back.'

She shrugged.

'Have you been down to the camp? Have you been staying with Al's mother?'

'No.'

'A fella? Because if you have it's not exactly wise, you know how people around here feel about white girls going with backfellas.'

'I've not been at the camp.'

'So, where have you been?'

She didn't answer.

'I'd rather you didn't go out riding at night, anything could happen. The horse could stumble; you could be thrown and hurt. You know none of us go anywhere without telling someone where we are going – it's too dangerous.'

Shirley shrugged again, her gaze fixed on the horizon.

'You hear me?' He had difficulty keeping the irritation out of his voice. 'And in future you look after your horse, you don't leave it lathered up and without water.'

'I won't do it again,' she snapped.

'Good, now you'd better get to the kitchen and help Val with breakfast.'

After breakfast Jon, George and a couple of stockmen set out to do a round of the traps they'd not checked the day before for camels and brumbies. So far during the drought they'd caught dozens of the animals.

As they drove to the first of the windmills Jon reflected on the effects of releasing camels into the bush to fend for themselves. Over the years they'd become a plague, thriving in the semi-arid outback. Mostly they only spotted them in the distance but in a dry spell they became a real menace, destroying fences as they came onto the station to water at the wells and bores. But not only did they damage the fences, they concertinaed the tanks when they leaned into them to drink, allowing gallons of the precious water to pour out onto the ground. And a camel could drink a prodigious amount in one go leaving none for the cattle. One or two camels wouldn't have mattered but the mobs sometimes ran into tens and it wasn't unknown for a mob to contain a hundred animals or more.

Since they'd bought Jindalee they'd built cattle yards adjacent to wells and watering troughs. When the gate to the yard was kept closed animals could only get water through a trap which allowed the animals in to water but then kept them corralled. Usually they used this method to muster cattle for sale, especially in the early days when they were short of stockmen for a full-blown muster, but in the dry spells they used them to trap camels and brumbies.

When they arrived at the first windmill they found a few cattle, including a cleanskin bull that had escaped earlier musters, three camels and a couple of brumbies.

'What do you want us to do with 'em?' asked George. 'Shoot 'em?'

Jon leaned on the rail looking at the emaciated brumbies. They'd shot dozens of them during the course of the year. Sometimes they cut out the best for fattening up and breaking in to replace older stock horses but the rest they shot and left the carcasses to rot out in the bush. 'Yeah, shoot them and let the tagged cattle go. Brian

Harris will be over later today to pick up the camels from here and over at David's Bore and he says he'll be back tomorrow to pick up the scrub bulls we've collected.'

'Meatworks?' asked George.

'Yeah, They're only good for meat extract I should think; they're pretty ropey looking.'

'You'd think the Government would do somethin' about the camel problem. Charlie saw a mob of 'em out near Lake Desolation last week, said there were sixty animals if there was one.'

'Aye, and the brumbies, they're a real problem too, nothing surer,' admitted Jon.

'And we ain't even mentioned the ruddy kangaroos,' added George. 'Pity we can't shoot 'em like we did a few years back.'

'That's government for you,' said Jon. 'Now let's cut out the tagged cattle and release them or we'll be here all day.'

It was late by the time Jon and the stockmen arrived back at the homestead, to the news that Shirley was missing.

'When?' asked Jon.

'Don't know for sure, some time this afternoon, I think,' said Val. 'She went to her room about midday with a headache and when I looked in on her later she wasn't in her room. Seems she's not down at the camp either. I checked.'

'She taken one of the utes?'

'No, they're all in the yard.'

'I bet she's taken one of the horses, like last night and the night before.'

Val glanced at him. 'You didn't say.'

'Yeah, well, I've spotted her coming home at dawn twice now. She's meeting someone, probably one of the blokes from the camp. Seems she prefers the company of blackfellas to white.'

'I'm worried about her, Jon. She's still very young.'

'But she's got an old head on her. She'll be back in the morning, you'll see,' said Jon.

The following morning while Val tuned in to the early morning schedule on the office radio Jon sat at the kitchen table with a mug of coffee, watching Shirley busying herself clearing away the breakfast things. He caught Shirley's eye. 'This staying out all night won't do. Didn't you say you wouldn't do it again?'

Shirley scowled and didn't bother to answer.

'If you keep staying out all night I'll have no—'

'There's been an accident over on Reef Hill, it seems Todd's been shot.' said Val, entering the kitchen.

'Shot?' said Jon. 'When?'

'About an hour or so ago as far as anyone can tell; it seems he was crossin' the yard to the dunny and someone shot him.'

'Will he survive?'

'He's dead, whoever did it shot him in the head. He was dead when he hit the ground.'

Jon gave a long, low whistle. 'Bloody hell! Who shot him?'

'No one knows, Ned Ackroyd has taken charge, Nancy and Kit are in a hell of a state apparently. Nickson's on his way out there to investigate.'

'Who's dead?' asked Ruby, as she helped herself to more coffee.

'Todd,' said Val. 'I wonder who did it?'

'Could have been anyone,' said Ruby, 'he's plenty of enemies.'

'No one deserves that,' said Val. 'He had a nicer side.'

'Oh yeah,' sneered Shirley.

'Yes,' said Val, 'he did. He came to see me after Jamie was killed, said how sorry he was to hear of Jamie's death.'

'Maybe he was just being nosey,' said Ruby.

'I don't think so, he seemed pretty genuine.'

'Ruby's right, he'll have wanted something, even if it was just to nose around and see your grief,' said Shirley.

'You shouldn't speak ill of the dead, Shirley, and by the way, where have you been since yesterday afternoon?' asked Val.

'The camp,' said Shirley as she started to do the washing up. 'I was visiting Al's mum, she's still upset about Al's murder.'

'Well, if you are plannin' to go off to see someone we'd appreciate you tellin' us before you go, especially if you are intendin' to stay out all night,' said Val gently.

'You'll get yourself a reputation,' said Ruby.

'I already have,' said Shirley, a rueful smile on her face.

'Don't you care?' asked Ruby.

'Bit late now,' said Shirley. 'Anyway, why should I care? No one else does, in any case what's wrong with white girls going out with blackfellas?'

Jon caught the almost imperceptible frown on Val's brow and noticed a jauntiness in Shirley's bearing. Had she found a new fella? – is that where she'd been? – and if so which one? Jon shook his head in exasperation. There was going to be trouble, there was nothing surer.

'Will you be back down the yards again today, hon?' asked Val.

'Yeah, Brian Harris said he'll call early to pick up the scrub bulls we've sorted out, and then we'll move on to Willy-Willy Flats' Windmill and Jeb's Bore and start over clearing the traps there.' Jon looked at her and smiled. 'How are you feeling today?'

'All right, a bit of backache, the odd twinge, nothin' to worry about.'

'I'll call you when we get to Gimlet Spring, about midday.'

'I'll be fine.'

Jon smiled. 'Just worried about you. If you need me I can be back in two shakes.'

Val patted her belly. 'I'm not due for a few weeks yet, so don't go gettin' panicky on me and I've got Ruby, she'll look after me.'

Jon picked up his rifle and a box of cartridges.

'Pick out a good camel for killin',' said Val. 'they make better eatin' than skinny cows.'

'What about a brumbie?'

'No, the last one was as tough as old cow hide and there was no meat on it, besides you like camel, don't you? – cooks up fine and tastes good.'

He couldn't argue with that, camel often tasted better than prime beef. 'Pity the cattle aren't in such good shape,' said Jon ruefully, 'and it's costing a packet keeping our best on agistment.'

'Yes, but you'll have some prime heifers and young cows to re-stock with once the drought breaks.'

Val was right, They'd moved their best breeding animals south, and they'd reduced their stock holding by a third. He flopped on his hat and kissed Val on the cheek. 'I won't be late, we'll be back in time for tea.'

As soon as Jon arrived at Gimlet Spring he connected the portable transceiver to the truck battery and threw the aerial over the nearest suitable tree and called Jindalee.

Val answered immediately. 'Jon! Thank God you called!'

'What's wrong? The baby?'

'No, no, I'm fine, but you need to go to Pilkington.'

'Why? What's happened, Val?'

'Charlie. Nickson says Charlie's the one who shot Todd. He picked him up just after you left and has taken him to the lock-up in Pilkington.'

'That's ridiculous.'

'The word's out that Charlie's to blame; it's all to do with the singin' and the bone pointin'. There's bedlam down at the camp, the women are wailin' like there's been a death.'

'Charlie hasn't been off the station.'

'Nickson says he's got a witness.'

'Bring him to the radio; let me have a word with him.'

'I told you, Jon, he left ages ago, they'll be back at the lock-up by now. You need to get there as soon as you can. You know what those places are like.'

No sooner had Jon disconnected the transceiver than he called George over, explained the situation then set off for Pilkington, taking the direct route across the gibber plain and through the salt-bush and spinifex that lay beyond the creek. Even so the journey took a couple of hours of rough driving. In Pilkington he parked up in front of the police station and stepped into the office, his eyes blinking as he entered the gloomy building.

Nickson stood up from behind his desk, hitching up his britches as he did so. 'Afternoon, Jon.'

Jon ignored the greeting and Constable Curran hovering in the background. 'Val tells me you've arrested one of my men, Charlie Cooper, that so?'

'Just brought him in for questioning, seems your man has been where he shouldn't have. He's got a few questions to answer about Todd Kennilworth's death.'

'Charlie hasn't been off Jindalee property since before Todd was killed. He hasn't shot anyone.'

'That's not what Ned Ackroyd says, Kit says his head stockman saw Charlie early this morning on a horse heading back towards Jindalee pretty damned fast. Ned says he recognised Charlie's check shirt and that old hat he always wears.'

'It wasn't Charlie.'

'You got proof of that?'

'His family will vouch for him, and George, my overseer.'

'Abos!' The scorn in Nickson's voice grated.

'Yes, and not only that, Charlie was working with me at the homestead from first light, before we heard the call go out on the schedule about Todd's death, my men will back me on that.'

'Seems to me there's been a fair bit of animosity between you and the Kennilworths for a while now,' said Nickson.

'Just, what are you getting at?' said Jon.

'Well, you've accused the Kennilworths of tampering with your fences.'

'Yeah, I have, someone's been cutting them and it isn't my men, and it's not camels trampling them either.'

'Well, it won't be a Kennilworth. Only a lunatic would break down boundary fences in a drought. The Kennilworths certainly wouldn't want Jindalee cattle taking their water, now would they?'

Nickson had a point, but everyone knew Todd was a foot short of a yard, thick he was and vindictive with it. Todd wouldn't have cared tuppence that there was a drought, he didn't like station work anyway, it was common knowledge that Todd was itching to leave and get a job someplace else, although what job that might be Jon couldn't think. And everyone knew that Kit had had no control over Todd for a while.

'What is Charlie supposed to have shot Todd with?' demanded Jon. 'He doesn't have a gun.'

'You sure about that?'

'Sure as I can be. And we both know Todd has made more than a few enemies over the years. It could have been anyone who holds a grudge.'

'What! Someone prepared to sit and wait for Todd to appear and then shoot him as he crossed to the dunny…at the crack of dawn?'

'Where was the shooter situated? Have you picked up any spent cartridge cases?'

'No, why?'

'To compare the crimping – you know different guns can leave different marks on the cases.'

'No, can't be sure where the fella was holed up.'

'Have you looked?'

'The bush is a pretty big place to look.'

'Yeah, but there will only be a limited number of places with a good sight-line.'

'I see you think of everything,' said Nickson, his tone chilly.

'No, I just want Charlie out of the lock-up. He didn't do it, and I don't think you've enough evidence to prove he did.'

'Yeah, well, he stays here until I've finished my investigations, I don't want him going off on one of them walkabouts like they do when there's trouble.'

'Okay if I have a word with him?'

'I s'pose, supervised mind,' growled Nickson.

'Where's Charlie?' asked Val when Jon drew into the yard after dark.

'Nickson's keeping him in the lock-up while he does his investigations. He thinks Charlie did it and he doesn't want him to abscond. I told him Charlie wouldn't do that but he wouldn't have it. You know what Nickson's like.'

'What are we goin' to do about it?'

'I don't know, but it wouldn't hurt to have a word with Bindi. She's had a lot of experience with these situations.'

'Will you write?'

'No, I'll drive into Charlestown tomorrow and call her from Connie's phone.'

'Did you get to speak to Charlie?'

'Yes, but only with Nickson present. Charlie says he's been nowhere near Reef Hill Station, says he's glad Todd's dead, but he didn't kill him. He's still angry that Nickson did damn all when Al and Miki were killed. He's a bitter man.'

'Can you blame him?'

'No,' admitted Jon. He frowned. 'Charlie says he hasn't got a rifle and Nickson says Todd was killed by a single bullet.' He turned his full attention to Val. 'Good God! Do you think it was Shirley?'

'No,' said Val, a frown creasing her brow even as he spoke, 'she wouldn't...would she?'

'You sure? She's been going out at night and coming back at dawn. And she was out last night when Todd was shot.'

'She hasn't got a rifle, Jon. She's never even used one.'

'She has,' said Jon, 'and she's got a damn good eye. Remember that time when Harry and Ruby had a bet over who was the best shot and they lined up all those tin cans on the far fence? Well, Shirley had a go then and so did Noel, Graham Eastman and Bertie Grey as well as our boys. They all did a hell of a lot of shooting that week until they got bored – remember?' Jon suddenly recalled what Nickson had said about Charlie's shirt. 'Has Shirley got a check shirt?'

'Yes, we all have.'

Jon got up.

'Where are you goin', hon?'

'To check the gun cabinet in the boot room.'

'Oh, Jon, surely not,' she said, hurrying to follow.

Jon retrieved the key and unlocked the gun cabinet. As soon as he opened it he saw one of his rifles had been carelessly replaced. He took it, pulled back the bolt and sniffed. 'Where's Shirley?' he asked, a grim look on his face.

'In her room, I think. She said she has a headache,' said Val.

'I'll give her headache,' muttered Jon. 'I think we need to find out what's been going on, don't you? Call her, will you? Tell her we want to see her in the kitchen, now.'

Still holding the rifle, Jon returned to the kitchen, laid it on the table, sat down and waited.

Val returned with Shirley and indicated a chair.

Shirley glanced from Jon to Val, to the rifle and then back to Jon again, and sat down.

'We want to know exactly what you've been up to. What have you been doing with my rifle?' asked Jon. 'And don't tell me you haven't had it because I can tell it's been used.'

Shirley sat staring down into her lap, refusing to answer.

'Did you shoot Todd?' asked Val.

Shirley shook her head.

'You know Constable Nickson has taken Charlie into custody? He thinks Charlie shot him,' said Jon.

'Val said,' whispered Shirley. She looked up then. 'Charlie didn't do it. They'll have to let him go.'

'Isn't always that simple,' said Jon.

'They didn't arrest Todd when Al and Miki were shot.'

'You can't go arresting people without good reason,' said Jon conscious of the irony of the situation.

'Todd killed Al,' she said, her tone clipped, 'and Miki, he shot him too.'

'We might believe that, but Todd said he didn't and his father and Ned Ackroyd say Todd was with them when they were shot.'

'Which means he has an alibi,' added Val.

'Mister Kennilworth and Ned Ackroyd are lying bastards,' yelled Shirley. 'And what about those bullet casings George and Charlie found? George says they were proof. But Todd just laughed in my face and said "So what?" when I accused him. He said—'

'When did he say that?' asked Val.

'When I went to see him.'

'You went to Reef Hill!' said Jon.

'Yeah,' her tone defiant.

'Why, for God's sake? You hate the man,' said Val.

'I wanted some hair.'

'Hair…what do you mean, "hair"?'

'Al's mother said they needed some hair to sing him.'

Jon threw his hands up in despair. 'And you stayed the night, didn't you?'

'What are you sayin', Jon?' asked Val.

'While you were away she didn't come home one night. I caught her creeping in at dawn with a black eye and a split lip.'

'Did he rape you again?' asked Val.

'No.'

'So how—'

'I wanted the hair, didn't I? It was the only way to get what I wanted, and then he hit me, after, when I accused him of killing Al and Miki, that's when he said…' She started to sob. 'That's when…he…said…Al was vermin and deserved it, sleeping with a white woman even if she was a slut like me.'

Val handed over a handkerchief and Shirley blew her nose and mopped up her tears. 'The hair didn't work,' she added miserably.

Jon stared at her open-mouthed. 'So you…so you—'

Val shook her head at Jon, raised a finger to her lips. 'Shirley, have you told anyone else about this?'

'No.'

'What about Al's mother? Did she ask how you got Todd's hair?'

'No.'

'Then I don't want you to say anythin' to anyone about this, not about the hair or this mornin's shooting. You understand?'

Shirley nodded.

'You don't tell anyone anythin' unless we say it's all right, you understand?' reiterated Val.

Shirley gulped back more tears. 'Will they hang me?'

'No one is goin' to hang anyone. Now, I think perhaps an early night will do you good.'

'What about the rifle?'

'Don't you worry about the rifle, Jon and I will look after that.'

Shirley hesitated for a moment or two, she glanced at Jon, then at Val and left the room.

Jon expelled a long sigh. 'What the hell are we going to do about this? Do we tell Nickson what we know?'

296

'No,' said Val.

'Shirley killed Todd in cold blood. It was premeditated, Val. We can't go taking the law into our own hands like this.'

Val gave Jon a long, cold look. 'That's ripe comin' from you.'

'What do you mean?'

'You didn't report Jimmi when he speared Gerry Worrall and killed him back in '48, did you?'

'That was different.'

'No it wasn't, it was exactly the same. The law had no intention of bringing Todd to justice, you know that; he got away with all sorts over the years, rape, attempted murder, and murder. I know it and you know it. We're not goin' to say anythin',' said Val. 'And we're going to get Charlie out of the lock-up and then Nickson will have another unsolved case on his hands. It certainly isn't the first, and knowin' Nickson, it won't be the last.'

'You're right.'

'I know I'm right. You told me that Gerry Worrall wasn't questioned about the killin' of Buni and Wally back in '48 either and now the same thing has happened over Al and Miki. And you know as well as I do that there have been other Aborigines who have died over the years and no one has been brought to justice, unless it's been another Aborigine. It seems to me that Gerry Worrall's death and now Todd's falls into the category of rough justice.'

'Yeah, maybe, except the law wouldn't agree.'

'Well, I can live with it, and I know you can. So the next thing is Charlie. What are we goin' to do about Charlie?'

'I'll have another go at Nickson in the morning. If he won't listen to reason and charges Charlie with Todd's murder we'll get Bindi over. She'll get the charge dropped.'

The next morning Jon drove back to Pilkington police station.

'Is Nickson about?' asked Jon when he saw Reg Curran.

'No, he's out on police business,' said Reg.

'Okay if I have a word with Charlie?'

Reg hesitated. 'You'd better wait 'til Ben gets back.'

'I'm not taking no for an answer. You haven't charged him with murder, have you?'

'No.'

'Well then.' When Reg didn't answer Jon added. 'I'll fly in a lawyer if I have to, I have the money.'

Reg eyed him some more and Jon knew he'd won.

'I'd better warn you, Charlie had a bit of an accident last night.'

'Accident!' said Jon.

'Yeah, he slipped and bashed his head.'

'On what?' asked Jon.

'On the edge of the cot,' said Reg, refusing to look Jon in the eye this time.

'Let me see him,' snarled Jon.

Reg grabbed the keys and crossed over to the door leading to the lock-up. 'If he says different, don't believe him, you know black-fellas.'

Charlie lay on his cot and Jon saw that one of his eyes was swollen and closed, he had a bad gash on his brow and extensive bruising on one side of his face. As Jon entered the cell Charlie tried to roll onto his side but the effort made him gasp and he clutched his ribs as he eased himself upright.

'Ya had a bad fall, didn't ya, Charlie?' said Reg closing the cell door behind him. 'Y'need to take more care, don't ya, mate?'

'He didn't fall,' said Jon. 'Open the door; I'm fetching a doctor for him.'

'He don't need a doctor,' said Reg. 'He'll be right as rain before you know it.'

Jon ignored him. 'I'll be back soon, Charlie.' He turned to Reg, 'And you'd better see to it that he doesn't "fall" again while I'm gone, you understand?'

It was the clinic nurse who examined Charlie, taped up his ribs and stitched the cut on his brow. Soon after she'd left Nickson arrived and Jon gave it to him straight. Charlie was to be released without further charge. He, Jon, would vouch for him and so would George who could prove that Charlie hadn't left the camp the night of the shooting.

'You can't take the word of an Abo,' said Nickson.

'And what about the state of him?' asked Jon. 'If I fly my lawyer in and she takes one look at Charlie you'll be for the high jump and the nurse will back me up. She says the damage wasn't done by a fall.'

'He fell,' snarled Nickson.

'And,' said Jon, 'if you don't release him I'll bring my mob over

298

from Jindalee and we'll hold a vigil outside the lock-up until you do. It'll be a pretty big mob of us and I can't promise they won't sing you if they get fed up with waiting for justice.'

'I don't believe all that rubbish,' said Nickson.

'Neither did Todd and the word is that he was sung.'

'He was shot,' said Nickson.

'Dead's dead,' said Jon. 'You want to take the risk?'

'I haven't finished questioning him.'

'Have you any evidence?'

Nickson didn't answer.

'If you get evidence you can come and pick him up again. I'll see he stays in the camp – he won't be going anywhere.'

Nickson scowled, picked up the set of keys and unlocked the cell door.

Jon drove back to Jindalee with a battered and beaten Charlie sitting next to him in the passenger seat.

'When we get back, you're to take it easy, Charlie, let those ribs heal and I'd appreciate it if you didn't go walkabout. I gave my word to Nickson you'd stay around in case some new evidence comes to light.'

'I didn't kill Todd.'

'I know you didn't, but, like I said, you need to stick around for a while, all right?'

'Okay, boss, reckon I'm too crook to go walkabout anyway.' He thumbed in the direction of the bush. 'Not in a drought.'

As Jon drove he looked about him, at the parched land. Six years of drought they'd suffered early in the last decade, then they'd had two years of near average rainfall and now more drought. Were they looking at another long spell without rain? They'd had damn all rainfall in the past two years; even Alice admitted it was bad, and when it did rain it was light and disappeared into the dry earth without a trace. They'd already reduced their stock holding and were still finding it hard to supply their animals with water. A couple of wells had dried up altogether and they'd had to move their animals to paddocks with water, and ship in fodder, but it was only a stop-gap measure.

'Can you sing me up some rain, Charlie?' asked Jon.

Charlie grinned. 'Yeah...for you and me both.'

CHAPTER 41

The whole of January had been dry. As they entered February Jon checked the barometer twice daily, watching for falling pressure that would, hopefully, herald rain, but it stayed stubbornly high. February was usually good for rain. When a cyclone blew through they'd often have too much and the creek would run a banker, sometimes overflowing, taking with it fencing and washing away the trees along the creek's edge, but he couldn't see it happening any time soon.

Val, heavily pregnant, was finding the heat oppressive and their planned trip to Perth was put on hold and plans made for a local midwife to attend when the baby was due. It's my fourth, Val had said, and there's only the one, a singleton, it'll be an easy birth and I'd rather be here than in Perth when the time comes. Jon hadn't been happy but Val was intractable on the subject and in the end he'd stopped arguing and encouraged her to sit on the swing seat so she could put her feet up and read while catching what little breeze there was. Meanwhile Ruby and Shirley took on the responsibility for the domestic side of station life, baking the bread, preparing meals for family and visitors and helping out with anything else that needed doing at the homestead.

Jon felt on edge, he couldn't quite put his finger on what was causing his disquiet – worry about the lack of rain, the impending birth of his child, worry about Shirley, or the surliness of the Aboriginal stockmen harangued by the troublemaker, Sid Barton, with his talk of Aboriginal rights.

'What's the matter, hon?' asked Val at breakfast as he paced about.

'Just unsettled, feels like something's about to happen, or maybe something I should have done, I dunno, I feel uneasy, like I did before Yildilla came and we went off on walkabout.'

'Why don't you take a ride over to Jarrahlong? It's a while since you last saw Alice and Alistair, and the break will do you good, a change of scenery and all that. You could stay a couple of nights.'

'I can't do that, not leave you here.'

'Yes you can, I'll be fine; the baby's not due until the end of the month, in any case if you don't go now it could be ages till you get another opportunity, especially once the baby arrives.'

'No, I need to be here, Val.'

'Well, go and do somethin' outside, watchin' you pace about like a caged dingo is wearin' me out.'

'I suppose I could replace the broken axle on the truck.'

'Anythin', just go, it'll give you somethin' else to think about.'

An hour later, when Jon had the truck on blocks and was lathered in axle grease Val interrupted him.

'Jon, we've just had a call over the radio from the police in Pilkington—'

'What now?' said Jon unable to keep the irritation out of his voice. 'Has Nickson dug up some proof against Charlie?'

'No, nothin' like that, it seems a woman prospector went off alone and hasn't returned to the camp.'

'Which camp?'

'The one over beyond Pilkington, near The Crags, he said. Apparently there is a mob of them, retired people mainly, who've camped out there hopin' to make their fortune with a big find. They've been fossickin' along the dried-up creek, and this bloke's wife decided to go off on her own after an argument, then, when she didn't return the others went lookin' for her but she was nowhere to be found. They followed her tracks as far as they could but lost them, they think she may have got confused by a survey line one of the minin' companies cut through the bush searchin' for nickel and the like. She may have followed one believin' it to be a graded road.'

'Bloody hell!' muttered Jon. 'Don't these people have any sense?'

'Seems not,' said Val, 'and, as Nickson says, anyone goin' out in temperatures of over a hundred degrees is just askin' for trouble.'

'When did she go missing?'

'Yesterday, and she only had a single canister of water with her.'

'Idiot! Does he want trackers?'

'No, he's got his own Aboriginal trackers, what he wants is us to help by carryin' out an aerial search, asked if we'd fly the Cessna over the area.'

'What about Sam Johnson? He's closer.'

'Nickson says their Cessna is up in Darwin undergoin' its annual maintenance check.'

'What about Harry?'

'Harry's in the Northern Territory, remember? – that big job he was tellin' us about when we spoke on the parrot schedule.'

'Oh yeah, I forgotten about that. Have you told Ruby she's needed?'

'No. Shirley says she's gone off with Tom, over to Breakaway Ridge, he's been paintin' over that way and Ruby said she'd go along with him; help him carry his canvases, said she needed a change of scene.'

'I'll send George to fetch them back and while we're waiting for Ruby I'll fuel up. You'd better contact Nickson and tell him we'll be there as soon as we can.'

By the time George returned with Ruby the Cessna was ready to go. Soon Ruby had the throttle full out and they were bowling down the runway. As always Jon's stomach looped the loop. He never did like flying spotter and was invariably sick, but someone had to do the job.

When he opened his eyes Ruby was dangling a sick bag in front of his nose. 'I packed extra.'

Jon grabbed the sick bag, opened it and concentrated hard on not vomiting as the Cessna gained height.

'Once we reach Pilkington we'll need directions, Mum said it wasn't clear where exactly we're to search,' shouted Ruby above the engine noise.

Jon didn't bother to answer; he just kept his eyes fixed on the horizon, glad that they hadn't started the search proper, wanting the time to get his stomach used to the feel of the plane. Not for the first time he knew he'd never make a pilot. He found flying to England bad enough, all the landing and taking off that the journey entailed, even flying in one of Qantas's Boeing 707s.

All too soon the landing strip at Pilkington came into view and Jon saw a ute parked up near the hangar; Nickson's offsider, Curran, no doubt, waiting to give them instructions.

As soon as they landed Reg Curran gave them an update. Their Aboriginal tracker had lost the missing woman's trail. Their best guess was that she'd been heading east from The Crags beyond the gibber plain to a spot where an earlier fossicker had found a few good shows, but the area was covered in scrubby mulga and not easy to search on foot. Nickson and a mob of volunteers from Pilkington were out there already, as was David Kenton and stockmen from Harrison Station, the closest station to where the prospectors were camping. Mr Bates was, according to Reg Curran, beside himself and neither use nor ornament in the search. What they wanted was for Jon and Ruby to conduct a grid search paying special attention to any seismic lines they came across on the off chance Mrs Bates was attempting to walk back to civilisation, thinking the track she was on was leading to town.

Ruby opened out a map of the area and planned the search. 'We'll start at the camp and make our way east from The Crags, to the point her husband said she was heading, and then grid the land from there, all right?'

'Yeah,' said Jon, 'let's get it over with.'

Ruby turned to Curran. 'Was she wearing anything distinctive? A bright colour maybe?'

Curran shook his head. 'I dunno, nobody said.'

'Pity no one thought to ask,' said Ruby. She folded the map. 'We're not going to have long today, maybe three hours, four at the most.' She saw the frown on Curran's brow. 'The light goes, can't spot anyone in poor light.'

'Yeah, of course. Oh, and before I forget there're drums of aviation fuel on Harrison Station at the Gritstone crossroads. David Kenton says to use it if you need to; Mr Bates says he will cover the cost.'

'Thanks,' said Ruby. 'Ready, Jon-Jon?'

'Would you rather fly spotter, Reg?' asked Jon. 'I don't mind keeping an eye on things here if you prefer.'

'Nah, I'm co-ordinating the search, can't leave my post,' said Reg, 'besides, I'm no good. I'd just bring up m'breakfast.'

Jon knew the feeling as he climbed into the passenger seat, ignoring the grin on Ruby's face.

'It's all right for you,' mumbled Jon, sucking on a boiled sweet, 'you've got the flying to concentrate on, takes your mind off a jittery belly.'

'If you say so,' said Ruby as she checked the instruments, then she powered up the engine and soon they were airborne, travelling in a north-easterly direction towards The Crags and the prospectors' camp.

As they flew towards the search area Jon concentrated on the landscape before and below them, a landscape of red earth dotted with acacia – the ever-present mulga – and the ribbons of lighter soil, the dried out creek beds with larger mulga and mallee along the banks, their roots benefiting from the moister soil deep underground.

In the far distance were The Crags, a red sandstone cliff that seemed to grow out of the earth, the lower half skirted in scree, rock that had fractured, splintered and eroded over the millennia. In the foreground, and dotted up the lower slopes, was the greyish-green vegetation that seemed to thrive in the harsh conditions.

Ruby followed the line of the old droving road out towards the tableland. 'Reg said the prospectors' camp's to the north so keep your eyes peeled,' she said.

Jon muttered his assent and looked out as they headed in an easterly direction, The Crags dead ahead.

As they flew, dust swirled in the distance, willy-willies, the sand picked up by the twisting currents of air. Down below was the remains of an abandoned homestead constructed of the local stone with a roof of timber and corrugated iron, now broken and the timber partially consumed by white ants, lying littered around the semi-collapsed walls of the homestead. Jon couldn't imagine anyone thinking it a suitable location for a homestead, the nearest creek was some distance away and the territory was harsh in the extreme. And I thought Jindalee was a tough place to live, he mused as Ruby flew on and higher.

'Can you see that camp yet?' asked Ruby. 'It must be around here somewhere.'

'There,' yelled Jon, 'over there, to your left, about half a mile.'

Then they spotted water, deep blue reflecting the sky, a lagoon in an old open-cut mine, the sides smooth, the landscape around it barren and forbidding. The feral goats that lived in the bleak landscape fled at the sound of the engine and then, further on, the remains of a homemade poppet-head of another mine, also long abandoned, came into view.

'No wonder they've chosen this area for fossicking,' said Jon, 'no doubt they're hoping to find what others missed.' And as he scanned the landscape below he wondered what the Dreaming was in the area. He was certain there was Aboriginal Dreaming attached to the place, there was the unusual rock formation and the likelihood of permanent water in the vicinity. He'd put money on it. But now part of it was destroyed and as Curly had once said to him: you can't sing the footprint of the ancestor if the land has gone. Had the Dreaming been destroyed when they'd mined the site that was now abandoned and filled with water? He supposed it would be hard to discover the truth of it, there'd be very few Aborigines left who'd know.

'We'll begin the search proper now,' called Ruby over the sound of the engine. 'I'll start the grid.'

Below them they spotted vehicles, the drivers carefully picking their way along the edge of a breakaway, following an old trail through the rocky terrain.

'Yell if you see anything out of the ordinary,' called Ruby looking out of her side window even as Jon looked out of his.

They flew the classic search grid, eyes peeled as they covered the ground, looking for signs of the female prospector.

'Pity she isn't wearing something bright,' said Jon. 'She's not going to stand out against the saltbush, blue bush and spinifex if she's wearing khaki or some other drab colour.'

'Worse still if she's taken shelter in the mulga,' said Ruby. 'You know, I've a horrible feeling we're not going to find her.'

'What makes you think that?'

'Just a gut feeling. Maybe she's already dead.'

'Unlikely,' said Jon. 'She should be able to last three days or so if she's sensible.'

'What if she's had a heart attack?'

'I take your point,' yelled Jon.

They slipped into silence, concentrating on the ground, flying as low as the landscape allowed. The minutes slipped into a couple of hours and still they'd found no sign of her and it seemed those on the ground hadn't either. No one waved a "thumbs up" sign and the woman was still missing as they prepared to abandon the search for the day and return to Pilkington.

An hour later as Ruby brought the plane into land she indicated Nickson waiting below. 'You have a word with him and I'll get the old girl refuelled.'

Jon climbed down from the cockpit and walked over to Nickson and Curran. 'No sign of her then?'

Nickson shook his head. 'I've had my boys out all day and

they've found nothing, the trail disappeared early on, seems she headed onto higher ground, more difficult to track, as you know.'

'She did go off alone, didn't she?'

'What do you mean, Jon?'

'What I say, did she go off of her own free will?' Ruby's theory that the woman may have had a heart attack had led him on to another tack, one he couldn't ignore.

'Are you suggesting she might have met with an accident?' asked Curran.

'They say these things come in threes,' said Jon, drily, 'my two stockmen, Todd Kennilworth and now this woman is missing. Are you sure there wasn't a bad argument and things got out of hand?'

'Nah,' said Nickson, 'the poor old fella's beside himself.'

Jon hesitated briefly. 'Just a thought, there and again she might be dead from natural causes, heart attack maybe, these things happen.'

'Well, aren't you the positive one,' said Curran with a sneer. 'I suppose you'll be going home then?'

'No, Ruby and I will be back out tomorrow. Mrs Bates needs to be found for everyone's peace of mind.'

'Let's just hope that the cyclone out in the Indian Ocean swings to the north, if it doesn't then she'll be in even more trouble,' said Nickson.

'You think it might swing south?' queried Jon.

'There's no telling. Reports are mixed, it's a waiting game.'

'What's a waiting game?' asked Ruby as she joined them.

'The cyclone sitting out in the Indian Ocean,' said Nickson.

'Yeah,' she said, 'fingers crossed it stays on track, if it doesn't then—'

'Then we've got problems,' Jon finished, 'although, God knows, we could do with the rain. I'd be grateful if you'd let Val know our plans on the evening schedule, Ben.'

'No worries,' said Nickson, 'will do.'

Like Charlestown, Pilkington had only one hotel left from the old gold-rush days, the rest having fallen into decline and then into disrepair and cannibalised for newer buildings or just left to rot and crumble, the timber consumed by white ants, the termites that thrived in the outback.

The Commercial, whilst of the same era as The Grand, was of a different, less exotic construction. It was single storey with a wide bull-nosed verandah roof that ran along both frontages of the hotel, it being situated on a corner plot at a crossroads. The main entrance with its double doors was on the corner and two further entrances were located half way along each elevation. The poles supporting the verandah roof were painted the same dull green colour as the corrugated-iron verandah roof and were simple posts with no fancy ironwork to leaven the look. Above the verandah was a façade of turreted plastered limestone that contrasted with the ironstone block work of the main building, lightening the look of the place. Maintenance had been reduced to the bare minimum over the years, paintwork was peeling and the double doors had dirty, cracked glass, testimony to the duration of the neglect.

'What's the food like?' asked Ruby.

'Passable, so long as you're not too fussy.'

'That bad?'

'Yeah, that bad,' agreed Jon.

The dining room was an L-shaped room behind the bar and when Jon and Ruby arrived for the evening meal there were only two other people present, both middle-aged men. One was a buyer from a local meatworks and the other a prospector who lived at the hotel when he wasn't out fossicking for gold.

Dinner was a choice between roast mutton or roast mutton so they both chose roast mutton and then stared at the unappetizing greasy meat with its mound of boiled potatoes and carrots despite the hot weather. Pudding was Spotted Dick with custard, the whole sticky enough to cling to the ribs and as heavy as it looked. Coffee was the one redeeming feature, strong and hot and over a second cup they discussed the search as strengthening winds battered the building.

Jon indicated the wind rattling the shutters. 'Will you be able to fly in this?'

Ruby nodded. 'So long as it doesn't get any worse.'

'Did you check the barometer in the porch?'

'Yes, it's still dropping, it's not looking good.'

'Maybe the cyclone will swing north, it does more often than not, but, hopefully, we'll at least get the tail end of it. As I said yesterday, we could do with the rain. It's been hot and dry for too long.'

'The latest is that it's tracking south along the coast. It might continue down towards Perth and miss us altogether,' said Ruby.

Jon frowned. He was torn between wanting safe flying conditions and needing the rain that the cyclone would bring. 'Fingers crossed we get the tail end,' he said.

'Do you think she's dead?'

'Who?'

'The woman prospector,' said Ruby.

'It's a possibility; she will be if we don't find her.'

'Constable Nickson says you think the two of them had an argument that got out of hand.'

'No, I don't really believe that, but I did raise it as a possibility.'

'You're still annoyed with him, aren't you, for not bothering to investigate the deaths of Miki and Albert?'

Jon nodded. 'But I do think she might be dead, it's a logical explanation, especially as no one has found any trace of her.'

'Maybe, but there and again she could just be lost, didn't pay attention to the route she was taking, you know what these inexperienced amateur prospectors are like.'

The following morning the wind continued to gust and the barometer to drop. Over breakfast the conversation centred on the cyclone and the latest weather reports on the radio and everyone present agreed that it would swing north. Only once every twenty years or so they'd get a bad blow and Dick Benton, the proprietor of the hotel, was convinced it wasn't shaping up to do any damage.

'It'll blow a few cobwebs away, maybe lift a few sheets of iron, drop a few points of rain, and that'll be that,' said Dick.

'Well,' said Jon, 'I hope it dumps a fair few on the way through, it's been one hell of a dry spell, we could do with a break.'

At the airfield Jon sat in the passenger seat as Ruby prepared to take off. 'No risking our lives if the wind worsens, all right, Ruby? I don't want to be caught out in the eye of a cyclone just because some stupid prospector can't keep track of where she should be.'

As they flew out to the search site they saw trucks below them travelling in the same direction.

They resumed the search grid but after a couple of hours they'd found nothing. Ruby flew to the refuelling site and while she refilled the tanks Jon stretched his legs and made a note of the wind speed and direction. He couldn't be sure but it seemed to him the gusts were stronger and carried the smell of rain.

Once back in the cockpit, Ruby turned to Jon. 'We're not going to find her; at least we're not going to find her alive.'

'Oh, you never know, stranger things have happened.'

Ruby rolled down the graded road she had used to land the aircraft, increasing speed and soon they were airborne again.

Flying became increasingly difficult as the afternoon progressed, the light aircraft was buffeted about and in the end Jon told Ruby, enough was enough.

She checked her watch. 'I suppose it is about time we called it a day,' she said. She adjusted the controls and flew back toward the prospectors' camp where a group of people were gathered.

'Odd,' said Jon. 'They've packed up early.'

'Maybe they've found her.'

Ruby flew low, circling the campsite and indicated that they were heading back to Pilkington. On the ground, Nickson acknowledged the signal and soon they were flying in the face of strong wind and heavy rain that lifted and jolted the plane despite Ruby's best efforts to keep on a straight flight path.

At Pilkington the landing was bumpy to say the least, the ground slick with water. Ruby managed to get the plane down and then she taxied over towards the hangar.

'Can't leave her out in this,' she yelled above the noise. 'Hop out and open up the hangar doors, will you Jon-Jon.'

The wind almost whipped the cockpit door out of his hand as he made to do as asked. On the pan, he leaned into the wind and rain and pushed his way over to the hangar doors wondering how he was going to get them open. But get them open he did, chocking them to stop the wind slamming them back into the plane as Ruby taxied it into the safety of the hangar.

They were drenched by the time they got back to the Commercial Hotel, and the wind was battering the building, rattling the corrugated-iron roof, and slamming debris against the walls.

'Let's hope Jindalee is getting some of this rain,' shouted Jon above the roar of the wind, 'we could certainly do with some.'

That evening Jon spoke to Val on the evening schedule.

'How's everything there?' he asked.

'Fine, hon. The wind's strengthenin' but nothing to worry about, and there's rain with it, but that's all to the good, you should hear the sound of it on the galvanised iron, it's beaut.'

Jon grinned to himself as he imagined Val listening to the drum roll of heavy rain. 'And how are you? You all right? Baby all right?'

She laughed. 'We're just fine. Any news of that woman prospector?'

'It's not good; they found a body late this afternoon. Seems she may have had a heart attack but they won't know for sure until they've done an autopsy, but that's what it's looking like.'

'Oh, that's sad, her poor husband.'

Jon didn't comment. It was sad, but the stupid woman had brought it on herself going off like that in stinking hot temperatures, and at her age! Some people had no sense.

'So you'll be home tomorrow.'

'Yes, we'll fly just as soon as the wind drops; the general view is that we're catching the tail end of the cyclone and it'll move north overnight.'

'Well, you take care, and look after Ruby for me.'

'Yeah, will do and I'll call you on the morning schedule just before we leave, all right?'

'Righto, hon.'

That night Jon and Ruby ate more mutton followed by a sponge pudding and the talk in the dining room was about the woman prospector and the idiocy of people unused to the harshness of life in the bush. Bored with the conversation that seemed to go round in circles, the two of them left the others to it and retired to their beds.

CHAPTER 42

During the night the rain hammering on the roof kept Jon awake and come morning they were experiencing a full-blown cyclone. Local stations were reporting anything from 220 points of rain to 830 points depending on the location of the station, and Val, when he finally got to speak to her, told him that the creek that had been running a banker had overflowed sometime during the early hours and that the garden and the yard were now flooded.

'What's the situation now, Val?'

'Still rainin', George and some of the others have moved the ute, the trucks and stores to higher ground.'

'Thank goodness for that.'

'I can't see how you're goin' to be able to get home today. The landin' strip's a lake and if the creek is anythin' to go by then it'll be the same all the way along the road to Pilkington.'

'You haven't been doing anything daft, have you, Val?'

'Like what?'

'I dunno, rescuing stuff.'

'No,' she laughed, 'I can barely waddle about as it is.'

'You still feeling all right?'

'Yeah, you know what it's like; the last three weeks are always a bit grim especially in the heat.'

'But are you all right?'

'Yeah, just the odd twinge and…'

'Val?'

Jon twiddled with the dials, picking up static.

'Val?…Val?' he shouted into the microphone. 'Bloody hell,' he muttered, guessing the water had washed away the mast he'd rigged up for the aerial. Now what did he do?

He found Ruby in the lounge. 'Your mum says the creek has overflowed and it seems it's washed away the aerial. I was in the middle of talking to her and the line went dead. Everywhere is flooded, the garden, the yard and the airstrip. I can't wait for it to dry out; I need to get back home.'

'Why? Mum'll be fine, there are plenty of people around to look out for her.'

'I don't know, just a feeling. Anyway, I think you should stay here until the cyclone passes. I'll hire a truck and drive home, is that okay with you?'

'I suppose,' said Ruby. 'I could always come with you and then pick up the Cessna later.'

'I'd rather you stayed,' said Jon. 'When I get back I'll do a recce, it might not be too bad, you might be able to land after all.'

'Better I wait, then,' said Ruby.

'Yeah, you might have to pick up your mother and bring her into the clinic if the baby decides to come early.'

'It's not exactly likely to, is it?' said Ruby.

'You arrived early.'

Ruby grinned at him. 'Mum always says I'll be early for my own funeral.' The smile left her face as she realised what she'd said. 'Sorry Jon-Jon, I didn't think.'

'No worries, and you are right, your mother has said that in the past, but I still think I should get home. I'd rather be there with her, you understand?'

Ruby nodded.

The last time Jon had driven through a cyclone he'd been out in the goldfields south of Leonora eighteen years back. Then the conditions had been as bad, he'd ended up at Boobook Mine checking up that the Cafferty brothers were all right and had found Matt Cafferty with the top half of his head scythed off by a piece of tin sheeting and his twin, Luke, still down Boobook Mine unaware of the tragedy that had unfolded above him.

Jon changed down through the gears in the Holden, the only vehicle available for hire at short notice. It was a beat-up old ute and the clutch felt stiff. Jon prayed it would hold out and not let him down as he edged forward to the first of the creeks on the route home, but it was soon clear that it was impassable, the water was too deep and still rising.

312

Jon considered his options and decided on the claypan route, sure that he could skirt the water there in the hope that the graded road further along was passable. As expected the claypans that had been dry for years were full to overflowing and the graded road beyond it was under water. Twice he had to dig his way out and he was glad he'd anticipated the need to borrow a winch to haul the vehicle free.

Once round the claypans he made his way west again through thick bush, the branches lashing and battering the vehicle as he pressed through the tangle, praying that he didn't puncture a tyre. After almost an hour of hard driving he rejoined the road he'd left at the swollen creek ten miles back, and headed once again towards Jindalee. Would the next creek be as bad? Would he have to detour through the sandhills, and if he did would the Holden cope? – the Toyota Land Cruiser back at the station would, but he wasn't confident the old Holden had the capacity.

Forty-five miles from home the road was again washed out and the route was a couple of feet deep in red silt. He stepped out of the cab into torrential rain and peered through the downpour. Now what?

It was already late, he'd only covered a bare fifty miles and the evening was drawing in, he had no choice but to sleep in the ute and wait for the morning but first he needed to get to higher ground, well away from any widow-makers that might blow down in the storm and crush the cab.

At first light he set off again, leaving the silted-up road for the mulga scrub. Once off the road Jon knew he'd have to keep the speed up despite the obstacle course through the mulga and over sandy ground in order to avoid sinking. Bogging in claypan was bad enough but sinking axle deep in sand was another matter altogether, and he didn't have any sand mats with him, nor would there be any suitable trees to hitch a winch to.

The roller-coaster ride was gut churning but his prayers were answered and eventually he rejoined the road again further along the dirt track. Twice more Jon had to deviate when he came across washaways where torrential rain had scrubbed out the road, dragging fencing with it, and still the rain came down, although at least the wind was dropping. Perhaps the eye of the storm had passed through, he hoped so because there was still one more creek to navigate before he reached Jindalee.

Despite himself he clock-watched, wishing the time away, wishing he were at Jindalee, when he saw the station Toyota ahead, pushing a bow wave of water ahead of it as it ploughed through the knee-deep water swamping the track, and close behind it was the station truck.

Jon stopped and waited for them to approach. Where were they going in these conditions? His heart leapt in his chest, was someone injured? Had Val gone into labour?

George pulled up the Toyota and jumped out of the cab even as Jon did the same.

'Where you going, George?'

'Pilkington, to get the midwife.'

'Val, is she all right?'

'Yeah, she's fine. May's with her, she sez it's just the early stages, sez it might be a false alarm but May reckons we need to fetch the midwife, just in case.'

'I tried to call on the morning schedule but I lost the connection.'

'Yeah, the creek's in flood; it's swept away the fencin', includin' the mast. We had a helluva job to rig the aerial up again.'

'Did you get through to Pilkington?'

'Yeah, y'missus did, told 'em the situation and said I'd be comin' out to get the midwife.'

'What about the airstrip? Can Ruby land if she flies in?'

George shook his head, 'No chance, boss. It's under several inches of water. It'll be a while before it dries out.'

Jon hesitated unsure of what to do for the best.

'Look, boss, why don't y'let Charlie drive y'back; I wouldn't risk crossin' the creek in that.' George nodded towards the Holden. 'Then Charlie can come back with Tom and the two of 'em can folla me in case I git bogged. That way Tom can drive the Holden back to the garage in Pilkington. What do you reckon?'

George's suggestion made sense. 'You'll need to go around the road up beyond Widdi Creek, the road is knee deep in silt there, for about a quarter of a mile as far as I could tell, and then you'll need to skirt the claypans as the creek up there is also running a banker.'

George walked over to the driver's side of the truck as Jon climbed into the passenger seat. 'You're to take the boss back to the station, Charlie, and then you and Tom folla me t'Pilkington. Okay, mate?'

Charlie grinned. 'We'll have caught up with ya by the time y'git to Widdi Creek, jus' see if we don't.'

'Y'reckon?' said George.

Charlie started the engine and had turned the truck round before George got back to the Toyota. 'George sez the little 'un's in a hurry.'

'Yeah,' said Jon, 'can't wait to get here.'

'Takes all sorts,' said Charlie, 'maybe this un will like the bush better than them lads of yours, it bein' in such a hurry, an all.'

'Aye', said Jon, 'maybe you're right.'

Jon lapsed into silence, shocked by Charlie's slip of the tongue. Being reminded of Jamie's death came hardest when he was least expecting it.

Charlie gave up on conversation and drove, crossing yet another swollen creek with water lapping over the running-boards. Half an hour later he pulled into the yard, dropped Jon at the homestead, and drove on over to the barn to find Tom. Soon the two of them were heading back to Pilkington just as Jon let himself into the house.

CHAPTER 43

Jon yanked open the kitchen door and without bothering to kick off his boots yelled 'Val?' at the top of his voice.

'In here, hon,' she called back.

The sitting room! Why wasn't she in bed? He pushed open the door and saw Val standing next to the French windows leading on to the verandah. She had both her hands on her lower back and was stretching herself.

'Are you all right?'

'I'm fine, didn't George tell you? – it's just the early stages.'

'Yes, he did, but these things don't always go to plan.'

'And I've got May. May's had two of her own and she's been keepin' me company, there's nothing to worry about. I'm fine, really I am. How's Ruby?'

'Ruby's all right, she's got a room in the Commercial Hotel. And as soon as she can she'll fly back.'

Jon joined her on the verandah. 'It's a bit of a mess, isn't it?'

They both looked down at the water flowing across the garden carrying branches, small bushes, fencing posts and wire, oil drums and other station paraphernalia that hadn't been saved from the flood.

'We've had over 500 points since yesterday morning. But I think the water level has started to drop now. Have you had anythin' to eat?'

'Not since breakfast yesterday.'

'You must be starvin', Shirley'll rustle up somethin' for you.'

'And tea, I could murder for a cup of tea. Where's May?'

'I've asked her to get things ready for me, just in case.'

'Just in case it's not a false alarm?' said Jon.

'It's always best to be prepared, hon.'

While they waited for the midwife to arrive they sat on the verandah where it was cooler, Val pacing when the contraction built.
Every now and again Jon rubbed her lower back but he couldn't
conceal his anxiety about the impending birth.

'Stop worryin',' Val said when she saw Jon's frown and the tension in his body. 'It's goin' to be all right, I know it is and it's not
as if it's our first, hon.' When Jon didn't reply she continued, 'You
never told me about what happened in that cave with Yildilla, the
cuttin' stuff you mentioned.'

She was right, he'd avoided talking about that, still not sure in his
mind what it had all been about. 'And you never told me what you
and David did in England while you were there.'

'That's easy answered. I enrolled David as a temporary pupil in
Duane's school and took a short course at the Tech. I just needed
to get out of the house, nice as our Evelyn's company is.'

'You went to college! Well I'll be damned! What did you study,
for God's sake, shorthand?'

'Book keepin', decided that seein' as how I'm the one who does
the station books I'd better learn the right way to do it, save on our
accountancy bills. And then for leisure I took David along to
Kathy's Dance School and we learned ballroom.'

'You went dancing!' said Jon his eyebrows halfway to this hair-
line. 'Dancing! What sort of dancing.'

'Everythin', hon: foxtrot, quickstep, waltz, rumba, samba, cha-
cha, tango, you name it and we gave it a go. It was fun.'

'Can't see there being much opportunity for tangoing out here,'
said Jon.

'Anyway, that's what we were doin'. At least we weren't gettin'
ourselves scarred for life like someone I know.' Val looked at him
with a quizzical eye. 'I'd like to know. It's not like you to agree to
somethin' like that. You hate tattoos and what you've ended up
with looks far worse.'

'I didn't know he'd done it until after,' said Jon.

'You didn't? How come?'

'I think I was drugged. Yildilla threw leaves on the fire and
smoke filled the chamber, it was kind of aromatic, made me feel
sort of woozy, as if I was out of myself...like you get when you've

317

a bad fever.'

'So he drugged you and then cut you, that it?'

'Yes, I suppose that's what happened, but first I saw everywhere like it used to be.'

'I don't follow you.' Val stretched herself and turned away from him so he could massage her back again.

'Australia in the Dreaming, before people, when there was only Perentie Man.'

'That totem of Curly's you told me about?' She gasped as another spasm rippled over her.

'Yeah, the monitor lizard. Well, it was travelling over the land, transforming it from a vast nothingness, creating hills, rivers, clay-pans, everything, and then I saw it like a wild Eden. It was beaut, Val, a paradise, not like it is now, dry and arid.'

'Or swamped,' Val quipped, nodding towards the deluge lapping against the verandah.

Jon grinned. 'No, but it was weird. I just belonged as if I were part of the landscape, the whole. And distance was meaningless. In the blink of an eye, or so it seemed, I was in the ranges and then in the next on a gibber plain. One moment I was high, like a wedge-tail looking down, and then the next on the ground like a bilby see-ing each individual sand particle and each blade of spinifex. It was really peculiar but exhilarating at the same time. And dead people, Val, people I once knew were there including Curly and Stan, and they said Jamie's spirit was back in the land again, waiting.'

'Waitin' for what?' asked Val, her voice suddenly tense.

'To be born again.'

'You don't believe that, do you?'

'I don't know. At the time it seemed to make sense. You know, like that reincarnation belief the Buddhists have.'

'Yeah, well, Catholics don't believe in reincarnation.'

'I know, but it seems Aborigines do, or sort of do.' Jon caught the look on Val's face. 'Are you all right?'

'Yes, I'd just forgotten how a contraction takes your breath away. It'll pass.' She leaned against a ladder-backed chair Jon had brought for her until the spasm eased. 'I still don't see why Yildilla drugged you, if that's what he did.'

'Maybe he wanted to show me what they see, maybe he wanted to show me the outback in a new way.'

'Even though you'd decided to leave, had already put Jindalee on the market?'

'Perhaps that's why.'

'You mean the old bastard doesn't want you to go? Easier ways than that,' said Val dryly. 'He could've just said, and then there's this scarrin' business. What was that all about?'

'Making me an honorary tribal member, I think. The marks are similar to his.'

'Bit extreme, isn't it?' said Val, biting her lip against the pain. 'Has it made a difference?'

'To what?' asked Jon, rubbing her back again.

'To how you think about this place, the Aborigines.'

'I suppose it has, but not in a way I can put into words, at least not right now.' Jon looked at his wife and then at his watch. 'The midwife should be here by now. If she doesn't hurry up I'll be delivering this one like I did Ruby.'

Val chuckled. 'At least you'll know what you're doin' this time.'

'True,' said Jon. 'And Ruby turned out all right, didn't she?'

'Yeah, she did and so did our two boys. You might say we're what you'd call blessed, despite everythin',' said Val as Jon mopped sweat off her brow.

It was gone midnight before George arrived back with the midwife. Never before had Jon been so relieved to see someone. In the hours he'd been sitting at Val's side, holding her hand and encouraging her when the contractions kicked in, he'd relived the night Ruby was born, and the fear he had felt when he thought he was going to lose Val and the baby. Then there'd been no back-up. He'd seen lambs and calves born but never a baby and he'd been terrified of the whole process and of Val's distress. Since then there'd been the twins, but they had been born in hospital and he hadn't been present, they'd been presented to him afterwards, all freshly washed and bathed and he'd occasionally asked himself whether that, in part, was the reason he hadn't been as close to his boys as he was to Ruby. Had helping her into the world created a bond between them that hadn't happened with his boys?

By the time the midwife was organised, Val was well on the way to giving birth. In the bedroom all was quiet and calm. Outside the wind still rattled across the roof but its strength was waning and the receding storm was, in a strange way, a comfort for them both.

'Right, off you go,' ordered the midwife, a middle-aged woman who had, in her own words, delivered more babies than Jon had

had hot dinners. 'This is no place for a man.'

Jon hesitated. He really didn't want to leave Val alone, even though Nurse Cottrell looked capable enough. They'd both been through a lot over the last year, and over all the years they'd been together. It seemed wrong to abandon her when she was on the point of giving birth to their child, as he had when the twins were born.

The midwife saw the hesitation. 'Out,' she ordered, 'you can see mother and child later.'

The contractions faded and Val sensed the tension in the room. 'Jon stays,' she said, the tone brooking no argument.

'But—'

'No buts, I want my husband with me,' she patted the chair at the side of the bed and smiled at him.

Nurse Cottrell harrumphed and muttered under her breath as Jon took the seat and Val's hand. 'It'll be fine this time, hon,' she said.

The birth was relatively easy and the midwife oversaw everything, and May was there, fetching and carrying to Nurse Cottrell's orders: clean towels, more hot water and, during a lull in the proceedings, a stiff whisky for Jon.

When the sweat started on Val's brow, Jon wiped it away with a cool flannel, when she needed someone to push against she pushed against him and when the pain was at its worst she swore at him as she had when Ruby was born and it was then he knew it wouldn't be too long. Outside the dawn was breaking, the sky awash in muted peach streaked with turquoise and very soon afterwards their daughter took her first breath.

'Is she all right?' asked Val when Jon told her they had a daughter.

'She's absolutely perfect,' said Jon.

Nurse Cottrell scowled at him and proceeded to check over the baby. 'Baby is fine,' she announced just as their daughter let out a long wail.

'She's got a good set of lungs,' commented Val.

'Yes,' agreed Jon, 'just like Ruby.'

The nurse handed over the baby to Val. 'What are you going to call her?'

'I don't know, we haven't decided on a name for her, have we, hon?'

Jon looked down at his new daughter. They'd not even discussed names, not wanting to tempt providence. He gazed at his daughter lying against Val's breast and noted her colouring. Ruby had been born with a shock of dark red hair that had deepened to auburn over the years, but this one was blonde, like her mother and Jon was sure she was going to be equally beautiful.

Later, after the midwife had retired for some rest, Jon sat with Val in their bedroom gazing down at the baby girl in the cot at the side of the bed.

Val stroked her daughter's cheek. 'What're we goin' to call her?'

Jon too gazed at his new daughter. What were they going to call her? They'd been avoiding the name thing, both too afraid that something would go wrong at the last minute, but now she was here and already they'd been asked twice what name they were going to give her.

'Do you think she will love this land?' asked Val.

Jon gave the question some thought. 'Time will tell.'

'Is there anyone you'd like to name her after?'

Jon recalled the names of his mother, grandmother and sister and knew none of those names would fit his child. He wanted a strong name for her, one that she'd like and, if possible, a name with meaning. 'No, can't think of anyone, what about you?'

Val laughed. 'You mean after my mother or sister? No thank you, not that I don't like the names Beryl and Evelyn, but I don't think they'd suit our daughter.'

'What names do you like?'

'Well, I quite like Vivien.'

'Vivien is all right, we could call her Viv.'

Val frowned. 'How about Jess?'

'Jessica?'

'No, just Jess.'

Jon looked down into the cot and looked at the tiny child, wide-eyed, looking up at him, watching his every move. 'Jess?' he said and she blinked. He glanced at Val. 'What does the name mean?'

'Haven't a clue, I just looked at her and she seemed to look like a Jess.'

'Jess Cadwallader,' murmured Jon to himself. 'Jess,' he said to the child – 'Jess of Jindalee.' Her eyes never left his face as he returned her gaze. 'You know what, I like the name. It's a strong name. I think it will suit her very well.'

'Jess it is then,' said Val.

CHAPTER 44

The christening party was arranged for the second weekend in April, the middle of the school holidays, following the baptism in the church at Pilkington by the Reverend Bartholomew Gates.

In the lead up to the party, Jon and George went out into the bush to look for a good killer, a prime bullock for roasting. They soon found a suitable animal which they felled with a well-aimed bullet. Back at the homestead the carcass was butchered and handed over to Yang-dhow to roast on the specially prepared spit over a pit of bone-dry mulga wood.

Shirley, with May's help, organised the benches and trestle tables and with the preparation of the rest of the food. Meanwhile, Jon rolled the area they used as a cricket pitch after having smoothed out the bumps and hollows caused by the flood. Then he collected together the bats, stumps, bails, ball and scoreboard ready for the afternoon's entertainment. Alice and Alistair, who were staying over for a few days, kept an eye on Jess and generally oversaw proceedings, while Val greeted their guests who had driven in from Charlestown, Pilkington and from the local stations. Those who had travelled some distance had come equipped to stay overnight; others dossed down in the stockmen's quarters, settled themselves in the dongas or camped out close to the homestead.

By the time everyone had arrived the cricket pitch was set up and benches and tables arranged under the shade trees next to the bar where Ruby and David were handing out beers and soft drinks.

Jon and Val greeted people as they drifted in and directed them to the bar and the trestle tables laden with food prepared by Yang-dhow, May and Shirley. Later, they sat back for a moment with beers, looking at the crowd who had turned up for the social event of the season. Jon had never really stopped to think about the younger generation but there was quite a mob of them: the Henderson's two – Joe and Amy; the Kenton's lads – Nick and Daniel; and George's two – Tom and Daisy; as well as Ruby and David; all happily chatting with each other despite the range in age. Mind, thought Jon, Ruby, Amy and Daisy, while younger than most of the others, were good-looking, and handsome young lasses were in short supply. Jon took in the rest of the group. There were the Karundah youths he'd taken in – Graham Eastman and Bertie Grey; and Harry Hammond who'd flown in specially, saying he wouldn't miss the party for anything; and of course, Shirley, another good-looking girl – a baker's dozen of them if he included Gabriel Kennilworth, who, he could see, was deep in conversation with Ruby.

Val had insisted on inviting the Kennilworths even though Jon hadn't been keen. He'd thought it unlikely they'd accept and he'd been right, Kit and Nancy had declined but Gabe had turned up and Jon grudgingly agreed it had been the decent thing to do.

'See,' said Val, handing Jon another beer, 'Gabriel's havin' a good time.'

Gabriel and Ruby had been joined by the Kenton lads and Harry. Harry had clearly said something funny because they were all laughing as if they'd been close friends all their lives. Only Shirley kept her distance, chatting to Daisy and Amy while the other lads gravitated towards the most dynamic girl at the party – Ruby.

'She reminds me of you at that age,' said Jon.

'Who does?' asked Val.

'Ruby. Alistair is right; she does take after you.'

'Well, she's always been outgoin', and straight, calls a spade a spade which doesn't always go down well with some, but her heart's in the right place.'

'Too right,' said Jon a smile on his face.

'Anyway, we can't stand here chattin', ignorin' our guests, hon. Are you goin' to organise the cricket?'

As the cricket match commenced those not in a team sat in the shade and enjoyed the spectacle, listening to the sound of leather on willow as the teams clocked up runs under a cloudless sky on a gloriously warm autumn day.

Jon didn't last the fast pace of Tom's bowling and before he knew it he heard the familiar yell "Howzat!" as the ball demolished his stumps. He grinned as he tucked his bat under his arm, clean bowled and out for a duck, and walked towards the shade trees as

323

Daniel Kenton strolled out to the crease.

Jon stopped to pick up a beer and had a brief chat with Charlie, George and Alistair – who were discussing the merits of Brahman cattle over Herefords – before joining Connie Andersen and Wes Chapman.

'I see you couldn't hold your own against young Tom,' said Wes as Jon sat down on the spare seat next to him. 'He's a fine fast bowler, has anyone suggested he could make a career out of it?'

'He's not interested,' said Jon, 'he prefers wielding a paintbrush to a cricket bat, not that George approves. George would rather he learnt station management. He says painting isn't a living for an Aborigine.'

'Is he any good?' asked Connie.

'Station management or painting?'

'Painting.'

'Well, I think so,' said Jon. 'You know the painting in our sitting room of the billabong over near Breakaway Ridge? Well, he painted it.'

'Tom did that!' said Connie. 'I thought it was one of Alistair's.'

'No, but one of Alistair's is there too, the one of the picnic at Sandy Spit. Alistair's work is good, but even Alistair agrees that Tom's painting is more distinctive and he's still learning and developing his style. According to Alistair, Graham Sutton, his agent, takes everything Tom paints and wants more. Graham says he's sold Tom's paintings overseas too, hinted that one of them is currently hanging on the wall of a most prestigious establishment in London.'

Wes whistled long and low. 'You don't say!'

'Aye,' said Jon. 'Alistair was a tad miffed at first, but he isn't the envious type, and underneath it all he's tickled pink that Tom is doing so well, after all, he was the one who first encouraged Tom to give it a go, gave him paints and canvases back when Tom was still a nipper.'

'What about Ruby, can she paint?' asked Connie.

Jon laughed. 'She's not bad with a broad brush and a tin of creosote. Head her in the direction of the shed and tell her to get on with it and she's happy enough, but that's about it.'

Wes chuckled. 'You'll have trouble with that one. I've never met such a character in one so young and I've met a few that aren't backward in coming forward, Alice, Val and Connie here—'

'Thank you for that, Wes.'

'You're welcome, Con, anyway, as I was saying, that Ruby's in a league of her own. Seems to me nothing is beyond her if she sets her mind to it and she's a natural batswoman too, not afraid to hit the ball for six.'

Jon reflected for a moment, watching his adopted daughter as she played in the outfield position.

'What does Ruby think of my god-daughter?' asked Wes.

'Loves her to bits, tells Val off if she thinks she's not looking after her right.'

'You see what I mean!'

'Pity your sister couldn't come,' said Connie.

'Yeah,' said Jon, 'she's too busy with her ballroom-dancing business.'

'And what about Val's family?'

'We invited them but they weren't overkeen on making the trip, too long a flight, they said, and they think this is frontier country and dangerous.'

'They're not far wrong on that though, are they?' said Connie dryly, 'especially in the light of recent events.'

'No, I daresay they aren't,' said Jon not wishing to dwell on the recent murders, 'but that aside Val doesn't exactly get on with her mother, not a lot of love lost between them. Evelyn's nice enough and Val and David stayed with her and Bob back last winter and spring when they went walkabout. Val writes to them two or three times a year but that's about all it runs to for the most part.'

'Family's important,' said Connie, 'especially when you don't have one; mine are all dead and long gone.'

'Sorry to hear it, Con. We're well blessed for family; we've got Alice and Alistair, you, Wes, Scally and his mob. What more could a fella want than good friends who are closer than family?'

Jon's thoughts shifted to Stan Colley. When Stan was alive he'd been closer to Stan than anyone else in the months after he'd absconded from Karundah. It was Stan who'd taken him under his wing, just as Alice had done; without the two of them steering him in the right direction God knows how he'd have turned out.

'Yeah, and don't forget your old mate, Stan,' said Wes as if he'd read Jon's mind. 'He really liked you, did Stan. He looked forward to your visits, they meant a lot to him.'

Jon was touched by Wes's words; it was good to hear someone else say Stan was as fond of him as he had been of the old fella. But then there was another old fella, Yildilla, whose life seemed to

325

cross his own periodically and whose behaviour had had such a profound impact on his life. Even as he thought of the Aborigine he was conscious of the scarring deep in his thigh, that still pulled when he walked, giving him a permanent limp.

If he was honest he didn't know what to make of Yildilla and their relationship. It was complicated and complex. Somehow, his life was bound up with Yildilla's and their recent journey together deep into the Nullarbor had changed things. Yildilla had shown him things he'd never seen or fully understood before, about the importance of the land they lived in, the Dreaming and the plight of the dispossessed Aborigines.

'Howzat!' came Tom's call across the cricket ground as Joe was clean bowled just as he had been. A ripple of applause came from those seated around the pitch as Joe walked off, high colour in his cheeks as he handed over the bat to Gabe Kennilworth.

'I'm surprised to see him here,' said Wes.

'Who?' asked Connie.

'Gabriel Kennilworth,' said Wes.

'Val insisted on inviting the Kennilworths,' said Jon. 'She said it was about time we started mending fences.'

Wes chuckled. 'That's a good 'un.'

'What do you mean, Wes?' asked Connie.

'Didn't Jon tell you? The Kennilworths were forever cutting the fence between Reef Hill and Jindalee. Kit blamed it on the camels, or Abos, but it wasn't, was it, Jon?'

'No.'

'Still surprised you invited them though,' said Wes.

'As I said, it was Val, she said we should forgive and forget. She pointed out that they've lost a son, just as we have, and Kit always did favour the younger lad; they say Kit's a broken man now Todd is dead and gone.'

'That's true,' agreed Connie, 'Kit seems to have aged since Todd was killed, it's really knocked the stuffing out of him, but Gabe is nice enough, there's no side to him, and now Todd's no longer around perhaps he'll make something of himself. There's talk that he's persuaded Kit to buy in better breeding stock like you've done, Jon, and it seems Kit isn't arguing about it. Mind you, Gabe won't have much money to play with; Kit invested a lot in Glen-shea Holdings...we all did.'

'And lost a small fortune,' said Wes.

'I didn't know you'd bought shares, Wes.'

'Aye, well I did despite your warning, Jon, but not so many as I might have done, but enough to make my eyes water,' said Wes. 'I should have had more sense.'

'You ever hear anything from the McGhees?' asked Connie.

Jon shook his head. 'Merle is back in Liverpool working in the hospital there, and Pete's marriage went west. Daphne's old man said he wasn't having his daughter messing about with a shyster like Pete and sent him packing with a financial sweetener. I think Daphne would have overlooked Pete's shenanigans but the money was more important to him. You'd like Daphne, Connie, she's a down-to-earth type and nice with it, a bit like Val, but not in Val's league, if you get my drift.'

'So they're not living the high life on our savings?'

'No, but I should think Patrick O'Shea is. He certainly took Pete and Merle to the cleaners along with everyone else, but I'm not sure about James Glengarry, seems he's now back living on the family estate in Cheshire.'

'Bastards!' muttered Connie under her breath.

'And Connie and me are sitting on a wad of worthless shares,' added Wes.

'One day they might be worth something. I'd hang on to them if I were you, you never know, another mining company might find a more efficient way of extracting the nickel from the ore.'

'I won't hold my breath,' muttered Connie. 'What's the score?' she asked, changing the subject.

'Fifty-four for six,' said Jon, glancing across at the scoreboard that Noel Boswell was busy updating.

Jon hauled himself out of the chair. 'I'd better go, Val said I was to circulate and talk to people, make them welcome. You'll both stay over, won't you? We've organised beds for you.'

'Wouldn't miss any of it for the world,' said Connie. 'Haven't enjoyed myself so much since that cricket match a few of you or-ganised two years back.'

'What? The Charlestown/Pilkington match?' said Jon. 'It was a disaster. Charlestown could barely muster a team.'

'I know,' said Connie. 'You even sent me in to bat, you were that short of players but Charlestown won't have a scratch team next time around.' She indicated the pitch. 'Not with this lot to pick from. I think we should organise a return match. What do you say?'

'The same thought has crossed my mind. Have a word with Mike

Tunstall and Les Harper, Connie. They'll be up for it and Wes here will umpire for us, won't you, Wes?'

'Again!…I s'pose so, if I must.'

'There you go,' said Jon, 'and you can count me in too.' He grinned. 'I'm sure you'll do an excellent job, Connie.' He raised an empty glass to them both. 'I'll see you later.'

He left them yarning about the cricket match and crossed over to Charlie, George and Alistair. 'Who's going to win then?' he asked.

'Ty's team,' said Alistair, 'he's got Harry Hammond with Tom as his runner, never seen a bloke as handy with a bat as Harry.'

'I'm glad you and your mob joined us,' said Jon, nodding in the direction of Charlie's family sitting in a group over by the fence. Charlie glanced at the small mob of Aborigines yattering over in the shade.

'They got everything they need? Tucker? Soft drinks?' asked Jon.

'They's fine,' said Charlie, 'a pity the rest of 'em didn't take ya up on y'offer.'

'That's all right, just so long as they know they're welcome, you never know, they might come by later.'

'Yeah,' said Charlie, 'don't reckon they're much into this cricket game. Alistair's explained it but it still don't make a lotta sense to me.'

'You just swing the bat as hard as you can and belt the ball to kingdom come,' said George, 'that's all there is to it. Oh, and you have to run about a bit in-between whackin' the ball.'

Val joined them, smiling a greeting to the others. 'Yang-dhow says the beef is ready when we are, he says it's a pretty fine animal and will make good eating.'

Jon glanced at the scoreboard. 'Tell him we've just three left to bat and then we'll be right over.' He glanced towards the horizon, at the sun sinking in the west. 'I think that's what you call pretty fair timing, don't you?'

When Jon turned back to the last of the match, Gabe was standing next to him, his cricketing gloves tucked under his arm.

George grunted a greeting to Gabe before following Charlie across to his mob for a natter.

'Thanks for inviting me, Jon. Haven't had a game of cricket in years, had to put saddle soap on the gloves to soften them up.'

'That's all right, Gabriel, I'm glad you were able to come over.'

'About the fences—'

'Now's not the time, Gabe.'

'About the fences, Jon. There won't be any more trouble, you've my word on it. And if you need access to the creek for your cattle, drought or no drought, just let me know, we can sort something out.'

Jon looked at Gabe and studied him properly for the first time and saw the open look on his face, the deep brown eyes returning his look without wavering. 'What about your dad?'

'Dad's not himself any more. He took Todd's death hard. He thinks you shot him.'

'Me?'

'Yeah...or that you got one of your stockmen to do it.'

'Why does he think it was me?'

'Revenge for what Todd did to you.'

Jon kept his thoughts to himself not liking the direction the conversation was going, and wishing Val had kept out of it all instead of trying to mend things. 'You don't kill a bloke for breaking down fences,' said Jon carefully, keeping his face neutral.

'I'm not talking about fences.' Gabe slipped his hand in his pocket and took out a spent cartridge case and held it out to Jon. 'Recognise it?'

Jon looked at the cartridge case that was identical to those he'd shown to Constable Nickson, the distinctive markings clearly visible. A shiver rippled down his spine and he wondered what was coming next.

'Here,' said Gabe, handing it over, 'it's from Todd's rifle. Dad wouldn't have it but, between you and me, there was something not quite right about our Todd, that's why Dad kept him close, Dad reckoned he could control him better that way...and Todd was useful to him. Dad might think it, but Todd'd do it...you get my drift?'

'Are you saying everything Todd did was your dad's idea?'

'No, there was plenty Todd did off his own bat.'

'Such as?'

'Your dog, for one.'

Dog! – what was Gabe talking about?...and then he remembered. 'Todd shot—'

'Your dog, yeah, he did, 'cos he knew how much you thought of it.'

'He shot Blue!'

'Yeah.'

Jon clenched his fists as he recalled finding his dog in the bush, shot through the heart. At the time he'd blamed George and even though George denied it he hadn't really believed him. 'Did Todd tell your dad what he'd done...that he'd shot my dog?'

'Yeah, Todd thought it was funny, and he was the one who shot your horse from under you.'

'He shot me too. I've still got the crease in my skull, very nearly killed me, he did,' said Jon pleased to have his suspicions finally confirmed. No wonder the Kennilworths believed he was the one responsible for Todd's death. 'Did he shoot my stockmen?'

'Yeah, I reckon so,' said Gabe.

Jon said nothing for a minute or so while Gabe stood next to him, waiting, as he absorbed the information.

'I didn't kill Todd,' said Jon finally, 'and Charlie didn't either, though, God knows, Charlie had good reason...better reason than a dead dog, a dead horse and a few dead cattle.'

'I know you didn't and Charlie neither, but there're more than a few with good reason to hold a grudge against our Todd. But it just so happens I'm an early riser, never have been one for sleeping in after four o'clock.' Gabe looked Jon in the eye. 'This nasty business, what say we draw a line under it?'

Jon inclined his head.

'Good, now I'd better get back to the party otherwise your Ruby will be calling me a miserable so-and-so.' Gabe nodded a farewell and left Jon standing, watching as he walked back to Ruby and the others.

Gabe knew! Gabe had seen Shirley, he knew who it was who'd shot Todd and yet he'd said nothing to Nickson and he could have done. And on top of that he'd handed him evidence, evidence that it was Todd who had tried to kill him in the breakaways, and was the one responsible for murdering Albert and Miki. Nickson must have shown Kit, Todd and Gabe the spent cartridge cases George had given him.

Val joined him. 'What was that all about?'

Jon shook his head in disbelief still struggling to come to terms with what Gabe had just told him. 'I'll tell you later, Val, but one thing is for sure, you were right to invite the Kennilworths.'

'I was?'

'Yeah, I was wrong, and that Gabe, he's a decent fella.'

'I know, and you know what? Jess likes him.'

'She does?'

'Yeah, he asked to see her and you should have seen the smile she gave him.'

'Wind,' said Jon.

'That's what I thought at first, but it wasn't and you know who else Jess likes?'

'No, tell me.'

'Noel, she's really taken a shine to him, gurgles with pure delight whenever she sees him and he's equally smitten.'

'So that's why you insisted she have two godfathers.'

'Yes, Wes, Noel and Connie will always be there for her, no matter what.'

More Aborigines drifted in from the camp as the meal got underway. Yang-dhow carved large slices of beef and handed loaded plates to Ruby, Amy and Daisy who passed them round along with hunks of bread and baked potatoes.

'Pretty fine piece of beef you've got there,' called Les Harper as he tucked into a sizeable slice.

'There's more where that came from, if you're still peckish,' said Jon.

After the meal came dancing to the music of an ad hoc band made up from guitar, accordion and violin players. All the young people danced the night away while their parents and older neighbours looked on, remembering their youth and, long after dark, when the old ones had retired for the night, Jon, Val, George and May watched the younger crowd sitting around the campfire, laughing and talking, their faces rosy in the flickering light as the flames consumed the mulga wood stumps.

'It's been a pretty fine corroboree,' said George, 'but I'm 'bout ready for me bed. Comin' May?'

After the two had left, Jon and Val sat quietly, enjoying the last of the evening, gazing at the crowd round the fire, whitefellas and blackfellas on a balmy night, replete with food and tired out from cricket, dancing, laughing and yarning about God knows what.

Jon leaned back in his seat. It was many years since he'd spent such an enjoyable evening. He'd sat around campfires often enough with family or with stockmen when out on musters, and there'd been picnics at Sandy Spit, but seeing a mob of youngsters in their teens and twenties enjoying themselves was something he and Val had never enjoyed at that age and neither, tragically, would Jamie. But despite the sadness he'd always feel whenever he remembered his elder twin he, nevertheless, thought how wonderful it was to be young in the 1970s, when it seemed to him that life for everyone was about as good as it was going to get.

He glanced at Val. 'It's a bonza life, isn't it? It's good to see youngsters enjoying themselves without a care in the world.'

'I wouldn't quite go that far; some of them have worries, must have, but I know what you mean. Tonight they're all foot-loose and fancy-free.'

'True,' agreed Jon, 'let's just hope they make the most of it while they can. Life can be tough enough and they'll need the good times to see them through the bad.'

'That's a bit deep, isn't it?'

'Well, we both know the truth of that, don't we?'

'You're right,' said Val in a quiet voice and Jon knew they were both thinking of Jamie who was no more.

'I'm sorry I wasn't there for you, Val.'

'Neither of us was there for the other.'

'I know, but I should have been.'

'Why? Because your mother died? And Curly and Stan? You think seein' death a few times makes it easier to cope with when it's your own child?'

'No, it's not like that...'

'Because you're a fella?'

'No, Val, it's...it's...'

'I know,' said Val, putting a hand on his arm. 'Nothin' prepares you, does it? And it's the wrong order, parents shouldn't outlive their children.'

Jon looked at her and leaned across and kissed her on the cheek. 'I'm sorry, Val. I just wish we could go back to before.'

'But we can't.'

'I know, I know, so we move on and we never forget.'

'That's right, hon, we never forget.'

CHAPTER 45

Most of the guests had left by mid-morning, with only a few of them staying over for lunch.

'It was a fine party,' said Connie, raising a glass in Jon and Val's direction. 'Whose idea was it to hold a cricket match?'

'Jon's,' said Val, 'whenever he's stumped for entertainment then—'

'Out come the stumps,' interrupted Ruby. 'We all had to learn to play cricket when we were kids. We've got the lingo: bouncers, googlies, hat-tricks and yorkers and we had to learn all the positions on a pitch. Jamie got to play first slip mostly 'cos he was quick when the batsman snicked the ball; and I always drew the short straw, deep square leg because Jamie said it was the only fit place to plant a girl as there was less chance of me losing the match for them there. David, the jammy so-and-so, always gets the best position, silly mid-on, because he rarely drops a ball even when it comes at him straight and low.'

Alistair looked at Jon with renewed interest. 'All these years and I didn't realise you were such an aficionado of the game, Jon!'

Harry grinned. 'Jon used to rope us all in…and the stockmen, not that they were keen, but Al Cooper was good with a bat and Tom is a brilliant fast-bowler, and his dad isn't half bad either, if you can get him on the pitch.'

'The only thing we've never done is wear whites,' said Val. 'Red dust and whites don't go.'

'I suppose you were the prime mover in trying to reintroduce the Charlestown/Pilkington "Ashes" match?' said Alistair.

'Yeah,' said Jon, 'along with Mike Tunstall and Les Harper, it seemed like a good idea at the time. It filled a gap in the social calendar, trouble was the turnout wasn't as high as we'd hoped – we should have advertised it better – and then three of our best players weren't available; Harry was in the army and George and Tom were at a family do in Queensland. The Pilkington team thrashed us. It wasn't what you'd call an unbridled success but the return match will be better planned. Connie's taking charge, aren't you, Connie?'

'Yes, I am. How's about I put your name down, Alistair?'

'No fear, with me on the team you'd lose. What about you, Wes? Do you play?' asked Alistair.

'Umpire,' said Wes, 'Jon roped me in, made me learn the rules.'

'Ty, Harry and Tom are the best batsmen we have,' said David, 'they regularly hit the ball for six.'

'And Ruby, she's pretty good with a bat,' said Wes.

'So why cricket?' asked Connie.

'I dunno,' said Jon. 'I suppose it suits the climate better than football. Imagine playing soccer in this sort of heat.'

'You've got a point,' agreed Alice.

'And most people can catch a ball and wield a bat so it's something we can all have a go at and I wanted a game everyone could join in with. None of us knew much about cricket at the start. I never watched a match in Liverpool, it was all football then but O'Leary, at the orphanage, was keen, we'd occasionally have a game there, not that we were any good.'

'And you're not exactly short of space for a cricket pitch, are you?' said Connie, an impish look in her eyes.

'No, we've got a fair few acres to choose from,' agreed Jon. 'How are the sales of your pictures going, Alistair?' he asked, changing the subject.

'Very well, thank you, and Tom is selling all he can paint. Did you know he's a talented artist, Connie?'

'No, I didn't, not until Jon told me yesterday and showed me the painting of Breakaway Ridge.'

Jon left them all nattering and wandered over to the verandah to enjoy a beer and some peace and quiet. It was occasions such as these that made him appreciate how lucky he'd been in life. And with hindsight even the bad years, those he'd spent at Karundah, had ultimately helped to mould him into the person he now was.

He scrutinised his oldest friends, Alice, Wes and Connie who, from the early days, back when he'd first run away from Karundah, had, in their separate ways, accepted him, and it was through them that he'd learnt to be a better person. For the most part he'd earned their respect, but it was their generosity that had allowed him to develop his better self. Without their support and acceptance he wouldn't have become the man he was; and then there were the others in his life who were no more: Curly and Stan, one in his teens when he died and the other in his seventies, and yet both had been instrumental in his development, they were people he'd come to love and would never forget.

'Penny for them,' said Alice, a knowing look on her face as she joined him on the verandah, a generous tot of bourbon in her glass.

'I'm a lucky bugger, aren't I?'

She smiled.

'What did you think, Alice, when I first arrived at Jarrahlong?'

'You mean when you first scuttled into the wanderrie grass like a goanna looking for cover?'

Jon looked at her wide-eyed. 'You saw me?'

'Aye, I was looking out of the parlour window waiting on Ed Scally's arrival.'

'You never said.'

'You never asked.' Her eyes glinted as she squinted against the light. 'You were just about done in, never seen such a mucky pup, your clothes were covered in red dust and you looked half starved.'

'Why didn't you tell Scally I'd stowed away on his truck?'

'Ed? What good would it have done? You'd have been back at that orphanage as fast as he could have taken you.' She chuckled. 'It took you a while to come out of hiding. I reckoned the smell of beef frying would draw you out, but it didn't.'

Jon recalled the aroma drifting across the yard, the feel of his stomach squelching with hunger, and retching up bile from fear and anticipation. 'I reasoned you'd be more amenable with a full stomach.'

Alice laughed. 'You hated me back then, didn't you?'

Jon nodded. 'I thought you were a hard woman, that you'd send me back once we'd got your sheep to better pasture, but you didn't; mind, you did make me work for my tucker.'

'Everyone has to earn their keep at Jarrahlong.'

'Everyone?'

Alice looked at him. 'As you once said: "It was their land first", I reckon I owe them a free meal now and then. And while you're on

335

your feet I'll have another snifter of that whiskey.'

Jon hauled himself out of the easy chair and fetched a double measure of her favourite bourbon, reflecting, as he did so, on the woman he was closest to other than Val and Ruby. He'd had no inkling that Alice had seen him leaving Scally's truck and had watched him sidling over to the stockmen's quarters, and had then waited patiently for him to hammer on her door and ask for work. Had they all guessed? Had Wes realised he was a runaway? Scally certainly had, he'd recognised him straight off and so had Stan. So why hadn't any of them given him away? 'Why?' he mumbled half to himself.

'Because you were in need of a break,' said Alice, 'and then when Stan took to you like he did I knew you were a keeper. Stan was a good judge of character.'

'You didn't stop me leaving Jarrahlong, though, did you?'

'What good would it have done? You'd have left anyway and besides you needed to find your sister...and you came back. The place had got under your skin. It does that to some people.'

Jon laughed. 'Stan said something similar, Alice. He said: "It grabs them by the balls and it never lets them go".'

'Stan said that!' said Alice.

Jon nodded. 'Yes, he did.'

A gentle smile illuminated Alice's face. 'Aye, that was Stan for you. You ever talk to him about Karundah?'

'A bit.'

Alice took a sip of bourbon. 'You had more than your fair share of floggings, didn't you? Your back looked as if you'd been whipped with razor wire...the scarring; I'd never seen anything like it. Was that the worst of it?'

Jon glanced across at Alice. She had never asked about his time at Karundah apart from the one comment as she and Belle had dressed his saddle-sores on his second day at Jarrahlong. He'd thought at the time she didn't care.

'No, Alice, it wasn't.'

She looked up and caught his eye. 'You know, I thought you'd tell me in your own good time, but you never did.'

'You could have asked,' he said, remembering her earlier response and smiled. 'It wasn't a good place, Alice, and bad things still happen there, but not like in the early days. There are men of God in that place who are pure evil. I've come to the conclusion that some use the Church for their own sick ends; it's a good place

336

to hide perverted predilections from the world and the good ones are in no position to stop it.' He remembered the horror of finding Father William's body hanging from a cross-beam in the laundry the morning he and Freddie Fitzpatrick had been sent to fetch fresh linen for the refectory. Father William had been a good man, kind and gentle, a priest who never abused his position, or little boys, like some of them did.

'Why didn't you tell someone?'

Jon laughed bitterly, surprised at the anger still there just below the surface, an anger he thought was long gone. 'O'Leary? The man was a wrong 'un, a sadistic bastard who got his pleasure from flogging boys and he never missed an opportunity.'

'Was he the one who flogged you?'

Jon nodded.

'Why?'

'The last time?'

'Yes, the time I saw your back in that terrible state.'

'For thrashing Father O'Brien.'

Alice watched his face, a questioning look in her eyes.

'He'd buggered Stephen Hicks for years, and then he picked on a new lad; he was straight off the boat and scared witless. He was only a nipper, eight, and skinny; he had rabbit eyes and O'Brien picked him out for "special favours", left the lad traumatised and bleeding, someone had to stop him. And it wasn't just the rape, Alice, it was nothing short of slave labour the way we were made to build the bloody place, the dormitories, O'Leary's church, quarrying the rock and building with it. Boys died, their spirits crushed along with their bodies. You saw the light go out of their eyes in less than a week at Karundah. Only the strongest came through more or less unscathed, and even they carry the scars if you dig deep enough.'

'I didn't know it was that bad,' said Alice.

That bad! thought Jon. How on earth did a body begin to tell others of the atrocities that had been carried out at Karundah? Of boys who'd been flogged to within an inch of their lives for trying to run away from the place; of the fifteen-year-old lad who'd had his head plunged into a bucket of liquid lime for a throw-away remark about O'Leary; or of the little boys sodomised by the Christian Brothers, who were anything but Christian, and who left kiddies weeping on filthy, urine-soaked mattresses. And, worse than anything else, the lack of human love and compassion, boys so traumatised that

337

learning to love and trust again became a protracted process, and in some cases probably never happened. Grown men permanently emotionally scarred, unable to love or accept love. And how many had failed marriages behind them – men who hadn't been lucky enough to have a Val, or an Alice in their lives?

'I was fortunate, I had you and Stan. It was you two who helped me to live again, and to trust.'

'We did?' said Alice, the surprise clear in her face.

'Yes, you, Stan and Val.'

'And what about Yildilla? Where does he fit in all of this?'

Alice's question pulled him up short and he remembered her earlier acerbic comment that Yildilla wasn't a blood relative. Had what happened under the Nullarbor changed that? Did Yildilla now regard him as such? Then there were his words: "You one of us now". 'I'm not sure, Alice, but something happened out there in the outback. I think I've been accepted by him, sort of.'

'What are you two yarning about?' asked Val as she joined them on the verandah.

'Oh, this and that,' said Alice, 'about the old days.'

Val looked at Jon and then at Alice. 'You putting the world to rights then?'

'Something like that,' said Jon.

'Well, you need to come and say goodbye, the others are about to leave,' she said.

'And we should be going too,' said Alice, 'wouldn't want to out-stay our welcome.'

'You couldn't do that, Alice, you're family.'

'We still need to be going,' said Alice. 'Alistair will want to get back to his painting; his agent will be expecting more canvases when we're next over in Perth.'

CHAPTER 46

Jon and Val were sitting on the verandah taking afternoon tea with their children after their guests had left.

'You and Alice looked very serious earlier, what were you talkin' about?' asked Val as she rocked the cradle where Jess lay.

'Alice was asking about my time at Karundah.'

'You never told her about it?'

'No, not until today, it's not easy to talk about.'

'No,' said Val quietly.

He hadn't told Alice about his experience in the cave under the Nullarbor with Yildilla but he could imagine her reaction when he did. She'd be bemused by the whole thing, especially the cicatrices, and he wasn't sure she'd appreciate the significance of it all. Truth be told he barely did himself.

'Who's that?' asked David, squinting into the sun that would soon sink below the hill where Jamie had been laid to rest.

They all looked in the direction of the burial ground and there, backlit by the dying sun, was a figure silhouetted against the sky, a thin figure standing on one foot, the other tucked behind the knee of the leg upon which he balanced, leaning against his staff.

'Yildilla,' said Jon softly. 'It's Yildilla.'

'What does he want?' murmured Val, shading her eyes against the light.

Ruby got to her feet and bent over the bassinet where Jess lay happily entertaining herself, pudgy hands reaching for her feet as she kicked her legs in the air. 'He wants to see Jess,' she said as she picked up the baby.

'How do you know?' asked Val.

Ruby shrugged and gathered her sister to her chest. 'Come on,' she said to no one in particular.

Jon glanced at Val and then at Ruby. Yildilla had spoken to Ruby as he did to him sometimes – telepathically, his wishes transferred directly, as he had when Jon had heard his command: *You bin come with me.*

Ruby turned back to them. 'Are you lot just going to sit there?'

David got to his feet first and hovered, waiting for Jon and Val to make a move, anxiety clear on his face. 'Will he hurt her?'

'Don't be daft,' snapped Ruby. 'Come on you lot.'

Jon stood and helped Val to her feet. 'We don't have to go.'

'Of course we must,' said Val. 'It'd be rude not to.'

They made their way up the slope, with Jess gurgling contentedly in Ruby's arms.

Jon's mind was in turmoil, his mouth dry. What was Yildilla playing at? What was the old fella thinking, wanting to see the baby, a white baby and a girl to boot! Had the initiation ceremony in the cave deep under the Nullarbor anything to do with it? Did Yildilla believe he had a claim on the child?

'Are you all right, hon? – you look pale.'

'Yes,' Jon said, his voice tight, his eyes fixed on Ruby's back as she walked ahead of them, carrying Jess.

Finally, they reached the burial ground and skirted the wrought-iron fence until they stood before Yildilla.

Jon took in the Aborigine's lean torso, the chest marked with cicatrices, marks that mirrored his own – marks Yildilla had made when he was drugged by the narcotic smoke in the tribal cave under the Nullarbor. The old fella's impassive face was deeply lined, his brown eyes sunken under hooded lids, his eyebrows and hair pepper and salt with age. But Jon knew the old man was strong even though he was as thin as a lath; Jon knew he could travel for miles across the outback without tiring. He looked Yildilla in the eyes and, not for the first time, speculated about his age, eighty, older? Then he realised it didn't matter. And, as he looked, Yildilla acknowledged him, just a slight tilt of the head, but a greeting nevertheless.

Ruby addressed Yildilla in his own language and Yildilla replied. Jon wondered what words were being exchanged as he listened to the suprisingly deep voice that came from such a wire-thin body.

The conversation continued and Jon heard the baby's name mentioned twice.

When Ruby held out the child to Yildilla, Jon made to step forward, but Val stopped him. 'She's safe, Jon.'

340

'How do you know?' he murmured still unable to trust the old man despite all that had happened between them.

'I just know, and Ruby will look after her.'

The old kaditja man pulled away the cotton sheet covering the baby, exposing her tiny body to the last of the sun. He ran a gnarled finger over her brow and down her chest to her navel, muttering as he did so, and then once again he caressed her brow.

'What's he saying, Ruby?' asked Jon.

She half turned to him, smiling. 'He says Jess belongs to this land, that she came from it, and that she will return to it one day, and he gave her an Aboriginal name.'

'What name?'

'It's a lovely name, Jon-Jon, you and Mum will wish you'd thought of it.'

'What name?' he demanded, still fearful for his child.

'Jinda...Jindalee.'

Yildilla watched impassively as Ruby spoke.

Val glanced at Jon and then Yildilla before acknowledging Yildilla's gesture with a small bow. 'It's a lovely name, Yildilla, thank you,' she said, her voice steady and clear.

'He hasn't given Ruby and me Aboriginal names,' complained David.

'I've got one,' said Ruby, 'he calls me Jeeljarup.'

Jon remembered the Aboriginal name Yildilla had given him deep under the Nullabor – Yallambee. Now, it seemed, both his daughters had been accepted by the ancient people, as he had been.

David scowled. 'That's not fair; why have you two got names and not me?'

'Because you don't love this land, you can't wait to leave and Yildilla knows that.'

'That's not true,' said David, 'and Jess is too young to love anything, she's just a baby.'

'But she will,' said Ruby, 'Yildilla says her destiny and mine lie here, beyond the mulga line.'

Yildilla looked directly into Ruby's eyes one last time as she held Jess and murmured something only she could hear. Yildilla turned to Jon and nodded briefly, a farewell, Jon guessed and then the old fella took his staff, spun on his heels and set off towards the desert from where he had come.

'What was that all about?' murmured Val, taking Jess back from Ruby.

'Acceptance, I think,' said Jon remembering all that had happened under the Nullarbor and afterwards at the corroboree when he'd been given a tjuringa, the tjuringa he'd since kept safe in the strong box in their study.

'He's a strange man.'

'This is a strange land, Val.'

'It is,' interrupted Ruby, 'but I love it.'

'It's not a place for the faint-hearted,' said Val.

Jon smiled and stroked the baby's cheek.

'Do you think Yildilla is right? Do you think Jess will love this land like Ruby does and as you do?' mused Val.

'I think so,' said Jon quietly.

'Yes, she will,' affirmed Ruby, 'and more to the point Yildilla knows she will.'

As they made their way back to the homestead Jon remembered the time Yildilla, the old kaditja man, had sent his half-caste granddaughter, Bindi Henderson, to rescue him from Paradise Canyon after he'd speared him through the thigh – Aboriginal retribution for a crime against their culture. On their long journey home Jon recalled one occasion when they'd been far out in the desert, sitting under an immense Aboriginal sky, eating Aboriginal food and watching sunlight playing over a land that had been inhabited by Yildilla, Bindi and Curly's ancestors for millennia; the the sense of belonging then had been overwhelming and heartfelt and now he'd had the same sensation once again as he'd stood on the hill top before Yildilla, the old man seemingly accepting their daughters as his own.

The outback was a strange land, right enough, but it was his land, and Val's, and he knew instinctively, as Yildilla had done, that it would be as true for Jess, Jindalee he'd called her, as it was for Ruby.

Val slipped an arm through his. 'What're you thinkin', hon?'

'Just that we have the best of it, out here, don't we?'

'Yes,' she said, 'and we must never doubt it.'

Jon turned to her and smiled. 'No, we won't, not ever again.'

* * * * *

342

ACKNOWLEDGEMENTS

This novel has taken far longer to complete than expected. Truth be told, it was almost ready for publication two and a half years ago but I had to undergo extensive surgery for secondary cancer in my lungs and liver which left me without the necessary energy or enthusiasm needed to complete the editing process until now.

There are a number of people to whom I am indepted for reading through the manuscript, they are: my sister, Kate Dring, who died recently following a tragic accident; my brother, Sam, who has always been supportive of my writing; Alison Jones who also generously offered to read through the manuscript; Margaret Joy and Kathy Boladeras, both published authors whose advice and support has been invaluable; Rick Brejaart who adapted a photograph taken on Kathy and Malcolm Boladeras's cattle station in Western Australia for the cover image; Michael Greaney for creating and maintaining my website and finally, but not least, Brian Whittaker, a fellow writer from our MA creative writing course at John Moores University, Liverpool, who has been there at the end of an email with encouragement when I needed it most, when the process of revising and editing seemed overwhelming.

Profound thanks also to Tony for looking after me following surgery over the years and who has always been there to ferry me to and from hospital appointments. Further, he has always been on hand to sort out computer problems and glitches and has rescued my manuscript on more than one occasion. Thanks also to Bolingbroke Writers and all my other friends – you know who you are – for your continued support and encouragement.

My thanks also to those of you who have waited patiently for book three of the *"Outback Trilogy"* to be published. I hope that you have enjoyed reading it. If you have then I should be grateful if you would recommend the book to your friends and, if you have the time, a short review on Amazon (or Booktopia, Barnes and Noble, GoodReads etc.) would be appreciated. It really does make a difference.

Finally, I have not given up writing despite ongoing medical treatment. I have several ideas for future novels and intend to start writing one very soon.

Website: www.sejenkins.com

The Kookaburra Bird, published in 2011.

The Kookaburra Bird.

S. E. Jenkins

In 1946 Jon Cadwallader escapes from a Western Australian orphanage following a traumatic death. He returns to England to find the little sister he left behind in Liverpool, but much has changed and an unexpected setback ultimately affects his life in ways he does not foresee. He returns to Australia without his sister, but his new beginning is complicated and riven by lies, deception and death. Then, when he least expects it, a stroke of good fortune provides him with an opportunity that has the power to transform his life forever and confirms in him a growing conviction: Australia belongs to him as much as he belongs to Australia.

* * *

A Place Like Jarrahlong, published in 2012

A Place Like Jarrahlong

S. E. Jenkins

Jon Cadwallader has inherited a rich gold mine but wants to pre-serve the land and the Dreaming from a gold rush. Chips Carpenter's quest for a lost gold reef threatens Jon's plan and jeopardizes a hidden canyon sacred to the Aborigines forcing him to make a re-turn journey to a place that holds terrible memories for him. Jon's life is further complicated by his friendship with Val, a fellow Pom, and Greg, Alice Macarthur's resentful nephew.

A spell in the goldfields provides the cover Jon needs for his new wealth and his future finally looks assured. But, soon afterwards, news from home turns his world upside down and the fallout from a political decision made by the British and Australian Govern-ments affects him, and others, setting in motion a chain of events that ultimately requires him to re-evaluate his feelings towards those closest to him.

* * *